All My Firsts

The Blue Ridge University Series

Book One

by Krista Swanson

First published in 2023 by MoDaMa Publishing

ISBN: 979-8-9876062-0-9 (Paperback)
        979-8-9876062-1-6 (eBook)

Chapter art photo by: Maddie Swanson

Cover designed by: Niki Ellis Design

Edited by: Chloe Cran

To my better half,
You make me melt, too.

Trigger Warnings

This book contains themes that some may find triggering such as violence, sexual assault, and rape. If these topics bother you, this book may not be for you.

Prologue

This damn conversation. To say I'd been dreading it would be an understatement. It had been hanging over my head for weeks, and I couldn't avoid it anymore. I knew he'd fight me on my decision; most likely he would feign ignorance about the original arrangement. Begging wouldn't work with him. Nothing worked with him. I would just have to . . . do it.

I had just gotten back from the park, where I'd been sitting in my car, people watching. I did that a lot. Sometimes it was to find people I wanted to be like, people who appeared carefree and were living what seemed to be their best life. Other times, I yearned to see people like me, trapped, so I wouldn't feel so alone and isolated. That day, I was doing it to take my mind off of what I needed to tell Max. While I made the call to him, I was watching a happy couple eating ice cream together. Oh, the irony.

Max wasn't happy about having to leave work, but he promised to meet me at the house.

As I waited for him by the pool, I was hoping to avoid the eyes and ears of my mom, who was inside. It was our typical location to hang out anyway, far enough away from the main house, affording plenty of privacy. Max never wanted our time together to be under the scrutiny of either of my parents. Even though he had started working for my dad, it hadn't helped their relationship any. Everything was a façade with all of us, and we were always walking on eggshells around one another.

The sweat was dripping down my back as I sat in the lounge chair, the early May sun scorching us already. I didn't have a suit on because I never felt comfortable going in the pool when Max was around. Instead I saved my swims for late at night when I knew I'd be alone. Daydreaming in this pool, wishing my life could be different, was a favorite pastime of mine. The visions of me heading off to college, escaping the home that had become more of a prison, and starting over. And that was the plan I had conceived. Took me three years to do it, but the time had come.

I just needed to make sure Max didn't fuck it up.

I heard the footfalls of his approach but chose not to turn my head to see him coming. With my nose still in my book, I pretended not to hear him until he announced himself. It was what I always did.

"Lanie," he barked.

And even though I expected it, I still jumped. I closed my book to find him glaring down at me. His crossed arms were further proof he was annoyed with having to do this.

"What is so fucking important I had to leave the office?

Why couldn't we talk about this over the phone or tonight?" The edge in his voice made me nervous, but if we stayed outside by the pool and didn't go into the cover of the pool house, I should be OK.

"I talked to my father, Max. Didn't he tell you it was OK to come over?" I whispered. The bravado I felt before he arrived was dwindling, but I needed to maintain some of it. I needed to do this.

"Yes, but that still doesn't answer my fucking question. I've got shit to do, Lanie, and not just for *your* dad, but my dad, too." His eyes avoided mine whenever he spoke about anything related to "work" and the expectations his father put on him while he was employed by my father.

My father was a congressman in Texas, had been for the past fifteen years. He was well liked in our state and quite successful. However, a few years ago, the Marcello family contacted my father for some favors, one being to help Max with a political career. He'd been working in my father's office ever since.

At the same time, Max and I conveniently started dating. I was only sixteen at the time. Max was already eighteen. His parents wanted him to work while taking online classes for college, preferring him to advance politically as quickly as he could.

"Um, well, I'm sorry, but this couldn't wait until to-night." I straightened myself on the chair, hoping to remain strong. "We need to have the talk about me going to college. Max, it was part of the deal; everyone said yes, that I was going to whatever school I wanted to once I graduated high school. You can't keep me from going." I tried to make my voice as forceful as possible, but that was a first for me. I had never stood up to him before. Not once in the two years since we had been thrown together by our parents.

He put his hands in his pockets and looked off into the distance. If he wasn't such an asshole, I might have enjoyed some of my time with him. He was handsome, and on occasion we had a happy moment. But his demons got in the way too often and made him ugly in ways that were indescribable.

Like at that moment.

His silence was bone chilling and starting to scare me. I saw the dark clouds shadow his eyes, as if his soul was being taken over by some outside force. He took off his suit jacket, taking care to fold it and place it on the chair next to me. Then he walked two measured steps to bring himself up against my chair, his long leg lifting over so he could straddle the bottom half. I found myself scrambling to the top of the lounger to put as much distance between him and me as I could, fearing what his next move might be.

"I love the fear in your eyes when you have no idea what I'm going to do," he snarled. His hand reached out, close to my feet, and grabbed the book I'd been reading. He flipped through the pages a bit, laughing while doing so. "These stupid books you read—why do you bother? If you go away to school, you won't have time to read these, ya know." As soon as he said that, he tossed it over his shoulder, directly into the pool.

His eyes never left mine as he did it, studying me for my reaction.

"Hmph," he let out. He seemed to be a bit upset about my nonreaction, but I'd trained myself over the years, learning the hard way. "Are things so bad here you can't wait to get away? I thought we came to an agreement and things have been better?" As he said this, his hand made its way to my foot, pulling my one leg toward him. He probably thought he was caressing me as his fingers dug into my calf, not letting go. The bruises would be there by the next day. He tilted his head at me, as if waiting for me to give him an answer.

"Well, um, things . . . were better, I guess. But we still argue a lot." My voice had gone weak, as quiet as a mouse.

And then he slammed my leg against the chair.

"That's because you don't do what I need you to do! I always have to force myself on you, Lanie! What guy wants to force his girlfriend to have sex with him?" He shot up and pushed me so hard the entire chair slid back, scraping against the cement. It stopped when it hit the bush behind me. He started pacing. "Fuck! Do you really think I want to be forcing you to do those things?"

I wouldn't voice my answer to that question. No answer was needed.

Cowering against the back of the chair, I was hoping this would be over soon. I knew I should have just sent the "yes" to the college without having this conversation. What was he going to do, physically stop my parents from taking me?

He started raking his hands through his hair, the frenzy in full effect. I had to brace myself for what was coming next.

And as if right on cue, he stalked toward me. The rage in his eyes made my stomach curl, and I knew what he probably wanted to do but couldn't out here in the open. But he still came at me, his hand coming right for my face. My cheeks were in his grip, his mouth centimeters from mine as the verbal assault continued.

"I don't want you going to school," he spat between clenched teeth, "because I don't want anyone looking at or touching what is *mine*. You are mine, Lanie. Do you understand me?" The spit coming from his mouth as he snarled his words was settling in the corners of his mouth, making me want to gag. The tears forming in his eyes were real, and his emotions were real, but for all the wrong reasons. "I will go crazy if you aren't here. Don't you get that?"

I tried shrugging my face out of his hand; he had never before gone for my face. He was always careful about making sure there was no visible evidence.

But not this time.

"Max, you're hurting my face." I tried to speak with my mouth still squeezed tight, hoping he would come to his senses. I didn't want to wind up in the pool house today.

"Hey, guys, everything OK?" The voice that came from behind the bushes startled Max enough for him to release me. I tried to stand from the chair, knocking it on its side before I could get completely up.

"Hey, Karl, what's up? What are you doing here?" Max tried to play it cool, but there was an edge to his voice. His annoyance that Karl interrupted us was obvious.

"Your dad sent me here for some paperwork," Karl said, his eyes bouncing between us, "and Lanie's mom told me you were both by the pool." His wary eyes moved to me when he said that. Karl may have been Max's friend, but there were signs of that friendship breaking down. "Lanie, you OK?"

"She's fucking fine, Karl." Max was angry, but Karl didn't let it bother him.

"Well, why are you even here? Shouldn't you be at work?" Karl was looking back and forth between Max and me again, trying to make sense of what he heard and saw.

I decided to take advantage of what might be my only shot left.

"I asked Max to come. I needed to talk to him about me

going to college. My decision is due tonight, and I wanted to talk it over with him before I sent that off." The look I shot Karl resembled an SOS, and I hoped he was able to read it.

"Oh, that's awesome, Lanie. Where will you be headed in the fall?" Karl reacted with a keen eye on me as he asked.

And just like that, Karl became my savior.

There was no way Max could, or would, react the way he truly wanted to after that. He wouldn't risk showing his true colors in front of someone else, especially Karl. Our conversation continued, mostly between me and Karl. Max remained stoic, quiet.

Angry.

"I could use a ride back to your house, Max," Karl said, turning toward him as we started on the path to the house. "I already got what your dad needed, and he's waiting on me. I was up the road at Brianne's, and I walked. So, are ya heading back to work now?"

Tiny goosebumps spread across my body, and the hairs on my arms stood on end. Would Max be leaving with Karl? Was Karl doing this *for* me? I knew there would be no way to know for sure, but it wouldn't matter. As long as Max was leaving, I didn't care. I avoided any eye contact with Max and stepped around him to follow Karl on the path that led to the house.

"My mom needed me to help her with some things soon anyway, so that's great timing." I hoped my inward delight wasn't evident in my voice. Knowing Max was right behind me, I knew things could change at any moment. And like I had anticipated, once we got to the foyer, he grabbed my hand and pulled me to him.

"Hey, Karl, give me a sec. I'll meet you at my car."

Karl gave me a wary look, as if he didn't know if he

should head out the front door, but he did.

"Lanie," Max whispered. His softer side always came out after he calmed down. "Are you really helping your mom with something right now?" As he asked this, his fingers stroked what must have been marks on my face left there by him. "Ya know I'm sorry, baby. I didn't mean to do this. I just get so angry thinking about you leaving." The apologies always came right after. It was such a set pattern with him. He leaned in closer, as if he was going to kiss me.

"I think she's actually coming now." I turned my face away, pretending to look for her. I knew she wasn't coming, but it was enough of a distraction to stop the onslaught of the kiss. Max backed away a bit, the breath I had been holding escaping with a hiss. "And I can get out of helping her. I can tell her I have too much homework or something." Max was so removed from my life he had no idea that I had no relationship with my mother anymore—at least not one that a normal eighteen-year-old girl usually had. These past few years had somehow created a wall between her and I. She stayed distant, never wanting to intervene or get involved at all.

Reaching up, I touched my face, wondering how bad it looked. I knew he was only concerned about appearances. But Max watched and winced, calm Max still present.

The front door pushed open, and we both turned to see Karl pop his head in.

"Hey, sorry to interrupt," Karl said, but he was looking directly at me, "but your dad called, wondering where I am. We should get going, Max."

Max nodded his head at Karl, then looked at me. "I'm sorry again. Go take care of the college thing. It was decided long ago that was the plan. I have no right to change that."

I nodded, surprised he was still being compliant. Yeah, the apologies always came, but they didn't always last this long. It seemed as though he walked in slow motion toward the door, taking forever to close it. The moment he did, I ran to lock it and took off up the stairs for my bedroom.

My laptop was open to the site before the two of them pulled out of my driveway. As I saw the taillights turning onto the road, my finger was pushing "Accept."

I did it.

I was getting out of here. And away from him. He had no idea I planned on ending us right before I left for school.

And this was the escape clause none of them had anticipated.

Chapter 1

It had been so long since I'd been truly happy, I didn't remember if this was how it felt. When I left home to come to school, I had this vision of what my life should be like. Parties, friends, classes. But that was not in the cards for me. Not because it wasn't there for the taking. Rather, I realized I wasn't ready nor interested in those things yet. Instead, I was sticking to what I knew: solitude. But what made it even better was the absence of Max. That allowed me to finally feel, for the first time in years, possibly happy.

The bench I had chosen to sit on was under a beautiful tree with a wide canopy, its leaves the size of my palm. They rustled in the breeze and filtered the sunshine overhead. I sat here so I could people watch, just like at home. It helped get me out of my own head.

I caught sight of a couple as they walked along a path up ahead. They seemed to be the epitome of "happy" as she clung to him and he smiled down at her. Her arms wrapped around his torso. Her smile was vibrant as she laughed at something he said. Her arms were bare; she was wearing a tank top. Her arms free of marks, free to be bare.

He stopped walking, pulled her closer, and put his arm around her neck while placing a kiss on top of her head. It was sweet, almost sickeningly sweet. I would put money on them being a new couple, considering we were only a few weeks into the fall semester. New-relationship bliss was a thing; I'd watched it happen countless times. I'd be curious to observe this couple again in a month to see if the honeymoon phase had worn off.

I was interrupted by a raucous group of guys who looked like athletes walking together. Even *they* looked happy, fist bumping and pushing each other as they passed right in front of me.

Was everyone happy?

Pulling my attention from the gaggle of jocks, not wanting to get distracted, I saw another couple. These two were not as outwardly affectionate yet seemed content with one another, almost in a long-term way. She was sitting on a ledge, her feet reaching the bench her apparent boyfriend was lounging against. His hand was rubbing slow circles on her ankle as she seemed to be busy on her phone with something of importance. Their comfort level with each other struck me as I watched her pick a piece of leaf out of his hair.

Her hair was piled on top of her head in a messy bun, a common style for a day so hot. My own hair was piled high, and I was still not used to being able to wear it up and off my neck so often.

Eventually, another couple approached and they were all engaged in conversation and laughing. I watched from afar, the longing inside nagging at me. They were unaware of how unassumingly perfect they were and how it had the potential to destroy others.

"Lanie, what are you doing?" I jumped as a body plopped down next to me on the bench. "Thought it was you when I walked out of the union, but I wasn't expecting to see you sitting here. Want some company? I have a few minutes before I need to go to class." Becca talked in run-on sentences all the time. I thought she must have an oxygen tank hidden in her backpack.

"I'm just hanging out here, waiting for my next class." My response was short; we didn't talk to each other much. Completely my fault.

She looked around, enjoying the view as much as I was. "I didn't hear you leave the room this morning—you're quiet. I hope I'm as quiet as you are, but something tells me I'm not, so I'm sorry ahead of time for all the times I'll wake you up. I guess you had an early class."

Her eyes found a guy who was walking toward us. She looked him up and down as she flipped her hair over her shoulder while smiling. Confidence was not something Becca lacked; the guy smiled right back at her.

"I can see why you chose to sit here. The view is divine. I might have to join you more often. Well, anyway, I need to get going; my class is clear across the other side of campus. Maybe I'll see you in the cafeteria for lunch? See ya later, Lanie."

I assumed she was already used to my silence, and she was on her way before I had a chance to say anything back.

But I wasn't going to respond, and she knew that.

It was then I noticed another couple walking down the path toward me. The guy looked familiar, and I was pretty sure he lived on my floor. The girl was hanging all over him, but he seemed disinterested, since no part of his body was intentionally touching hers. Yet her hands were trying to make themselves known to all the parts of him. He didn't seem to be mad, definitely wasn't being mean, simply disinterested. His body language was loud and clear; she was just not capable nor willing enough to read it. He was gorgeous, so I was sure she was infatuated with him. And she was stunning, so I was confused as to why he would not be returning the attention.

They were a compelling duo to watch.

He turned his head toward her, said something that made her stop walking, and she looked dejected. He turned around, waved goodbye, and she moved on.

I wasn't sure I could figure this one out, even after all the years I'd been doing it.

And that was when I got caught.

He was looking directly at me.

I realized it too late. I'd been staring at him for seconds longer than was natural. I tore my gaze from his, embarrassed, the heat already surging up from my neck onto my cheeks. When I'm people watching, this sometimes happens. Of course, people will catch me watching them.

But this time was different.

His look was different.

Plus, we lived on the same floor. I was going to see him again, and this made it more uncomfortable.

It was hard to keep my eyes on my lap, the temptation to look back up strong. But my fear of him still being there was stronger. I waited for what I felt had to be a reasonable amount of time for him to be on his way. I raised my eyes only to find him there, frozen in place, staring at me. His deep blue gaze was peering into my soul, penetrating me in a way nothing else ever had; it was as if he saw something familiar, and it scared the hell out of me.

Did he know me?

Did he know Max?

My hands were shaking as I put my tea down on the bench next to me, afraid I might spill it. I was nervous, unsure of how a simple look from a person I didn't even know could put me on edge.

I decided to sneak yet another peek, praying he had turned away or miraculously disappeared.

He had not.

This stranger had been staring at me for minutes, his intense look unnerving. I should have been afraid; I should have been nervous. Yet I felt as though I didn't need to be. Simpler things had sent me into panic attacks before. I wasn't sure why he wasn't.

My interest was piqued.

However, I had no interest in winning this staring contest. I decided to move along and packed up my things.

And as I stood to walk away, I realized I had chills running down my spine, though they had nothing to do with the weather. It was a balmy eighty-five degrees . . .

No, the chills were all him.

Chapter 2

*M*ax used to tell me to smile more, which was ironic because he was the reason I never did. Now that I was away from him, I tried to make a conscious effort to smile because I realized I'd become accustomed to not doing it.

Becca smiled all the time, maybe too much. Some of her smiles should have counted for me. I usually stayed in bed, turned toward the wall, when she was in the room with me. We hadn't hung out together, even though we'd been here for a month. I hadn't given her much of a chance; I came here not wanting many, if any, connections.

But she was making it hard. I'll give her credit—she was persistent and asked me every time she was doing something if I'd like to join her.

I never joined her yesterday for lunch, but I'd decided if she asked again, I'd say yes. She was determined, and it was going to be a long year if I didn't do anything with her ever.

I could do this.

I could hang out with her and at the same time remain guarded about my life, stay a closed book.

She had been flitting around the room, getting dressed and doing her makeup. I'd been trying to stay occupied by reading when there was a knock at our door.

"One sec!" Becca tripped over a pile of her shoes in her excitement to get there. After righting herself and checking her reflection in the mirror, she approached the door.

I, on the other hand, got a bit nervous knowing we might have other people in our room. I sat up in bed, and she took notice.

"Lanie, I thought you were asleep. I think this must be Ty and Logan stopping by. We're going to get some food. Do you want to come?" She said this as she opened the door and the guys poured in. One sat on Becca's bed, which made me nervous. I retreated closer to my headboard as nonchalantly as I could, but the other guy noticed. He chose to sit in my desk chair, and I breathed a small sigh of relief, though I still wrapped my arms around my bent knees, as if they could protect my whole body from these "intruders."

I had been prepared to say yes to Becca, but now, with the guys here in my presence, I wasn't sure the words would leave my lips.

"Hey, guys, Lanie's going to come with, I think, but she needs a sec to get ready. Can we meet you in your room in a few?"

"Sure, but don't take long. We are staaaarving!" The one on my chair said this while he looked at me—no idea which one he was. They both got up and headed out the door. Becca leaned up against the back of the closed door with such anticipation in her eyes.

"So, what do you say? Want to come with us? I mean, you have to eat anyway, so you may as well do it with us. I know we haven't talked much yet, but I'd really like to get to know you, Lanie. I don't want us to just be roommates; I want us to be friends. But we can do it at your pace. I won't push. If you don't want to come, I'll tell the guys you changed your mind, and I can bring something back for you."

She seemed genuine at that moment; it was going to be hard to say no. And I had decided to say yes to her.

I had no experience in the last three years being friends with anyone. With everything I'd been dealing with at home with Max, it wasn't worth having friends. It would've involved too many lies, coupled with my trust issues.

But her eyes seemed sincere, and it felt like I could trust her. At least enough to get a meal. All I had to do was open my mouth and say it.

"Yeah, sure."

The clap of her hands was earsplitting, her smile wide across her face. She reined it in after seeing my reaction, trying to be more nonchalant. But Becca was an open book by design, and there was no hiding her delight in my decision. I, on the other hand, grudgingly walked out the door, dressed in my jeans, hoodie, and Chuck Taylors, looking the complete opposite of her. I had grown very accustomed to not drawing any attention to myself.

As we walked down the hall, I assumed to get the guys, a tall, looming figure headed toward us. A handsome guy with piercing blue eyes and shoulder-length wavy, dark hair that I recognized from the day before.

I started to panic a bit.

"Hey, Xander, what's up?"

"Hi, Becca."

He was talking to Becca but looking directly at me.

I wanted to look away. I had to look away.

But I couldn't.

It was as if I was mesmerized, in some sort of trance. His eyes held something in them I felt I should recognize, but I couldn't put my finger on it.

I was able to break the connection. But only because I walked right into the back of Becca, who had stopped at a dorm room and started knocking. I snapped my attention to *Xander* to see if he had seen my blunder. A deep dimple appeared on his cheek while his eyes crinkled around the edges, giving me my answer.

Twice already I had embarrassed myself in front of this beautiful stranger who didn't feel like a stranger at all.

But why did I even care?

"Hey, guys, Lanie's coming with us. You ready to go?" Becca was talking into an open door while I leaned against the wall in the hallway. I stood there with my arms crossed, hood still up, eyes down, waiting on everyone to start walking. I saw three other sets of shoes in my field of vision and decided to look up. Becca had started up ahead with the lankier of the guys. But the bulkier of the two was waiting on me. He was eyeing me up like I was a three-headed monster that might eat him for dinner.

"What's your problem? What are you looking at?" I was a lot nastier than I needed to be. I wasn't deep in the friends department, and that surely wouldn't help. But it wasn't part of my plan, making friends.

"Sorry, just trying to figure out why you're finally emerging from your cocoon tonight of all nights. Is it a full moon or something? Are you going to change into some blood-sucking monster I need to be afraid of?"

I knew he was joking, but it still pissed me off. I skirted around him and started walking down the hall. I wanted to catch up to Becca and the other guy, who I heard her say was Ty. So, this winner I was with must have been Logan. And I hoped he wasn't as much of a douchebag as his name and comments dictated.

He ran and caught up to me.

"Hey, I'm sorry. I didn't mean anything by that. I was only joking. I know Becca said you've been having some trouble getting used to being here at Blue Ridge, and I'm sure that didn't help. Can we start again?"

He pulled at my shoulder to stop me.

And that was not the best thing to do.

I yanked myself out of reach at his unsolicited touch as if he had struck me with a hot poker, and it didn't go unnoticed. He jumped back, startled by my response.

"Whoa, Lanie, it's OK," he said as he backed away with his hands up to show he meant no harm. "I didn't mean to touch you. It's OK."

I cowered against the wall but tried to stay calm. I didn't need my first excursion out of the room with other people to end up in a panic attack, but I was struggling. I took a few deep breaths and felt myself coming down from the edge; it was the first time I'd been able to do this in the presence of another person, especially a stranger.

"We good now?" he asked.

I nodded.

"OK, let's go catch up with Becca and Ty," Logan said.

"I'll be right there. Have them hold the elevator, OK?" I mustered up as much strength as I could to speak normally so Logan would give me a few moments alone to gather myself.

The walls around me seemed blurry. They were closing in on me as I leaned back against them. I was finding it hard to breathe, my breaths erratic, my chest pounding.

I pushed my hands down to my knees and forced myself to breathe with measured breaths. Closing my eyes, I started counting to myself, hoping it would help.

As I settled down, I could feel someone watching me and looked down the hall. A set of deep blue eyes were boring into mine, acknowledging, all knowing. He was leaning up against the doorjamb of his room, arms crossed. While he looked at me, that same thing was there in his eyes that I recognized from before but couldn't pinpoint.

I should have felt embarrassed by what he saw, but for some reason I didn't. Instead, I felt a sense of calm come over me. I think he sensed that as he nodded and went back inside his room.

I stood there for a moment after he disappeared through his door, dumbfounded. Why was I not shaking? Running from him? I tabled my unusual reaction for later thought and continued on my way down the hall.

I finally made it to the elevator lobby, all three of them looking at me as if I might break. I got on the elevator without speaking, and we went to the first floor in an awkward silence. They walked ahead of me to the cafeteria while I trailed behind. It made me wonder if I should have stayed in my room.

There was a reason I didn't do people; I wasn't good at it anymore.

There was a time when I was one of the most popular people back at home. Before Max, I had a large group of friends, both guys and girls. We hung out every weekend, at a different house each week. I even had guys interested in me as a girlfriend, but it never made it to that level before Max came into the picture. Once Max and I were "together," I wasn't allowed to hang out with my friends anymore because they were, according to him, "too immature" for us to associate with. And he wasn't the kind of guy who had a large group he hung out with. Karl was his only friend, and only recently had I felt a connection to him. And Karl had a new girlfriend every week, so I couldn't even connect with any of the girls he brought around, they were gone so fast.

And there I was, with three new people, and I still had no one to talk to.

I made my way to the salad bar and made a simple one, not sure I had an appetite anymore. Becca and I met up in line, and we looked for a table together.

"Glad you came with us, Lanie. I've been wanting to hang out with you," Becca said with some hesitation. I'm sure Logan told her what happened between us. She was really trying, but she was probably regretting asking me to come. But I decided to try this with her, so I would. We walked around, finally finding a table for the four of us, and I decided I'd put some effort into conversing during dinner. Maybe even take my hood down.

The guys found their way to us, and we all settled in with our food.

"So, Lanie, where are you from?" Ty asked.

I should have been prepared for this; a barrage of questions for the newcomer to the group was bound to happen. How was I going to avoid answering all of these? I was going to come across as a real bitch if I didn't give them something. Taking my time chewing the mouthful of chicken, I looked at Ty as he was waiting for me to respond.

"I'm from Texas," I started, "but I don't really like to talk about what I left behind, if that's OK with you guys. Very happy to be here and not there, if you get what I mean." I looked around, hoping some eye contact would appease them for a while rather than any more facts from my past.

It seemed to be working. I got some nods and looks of sympathy, all working in my favor.

"I completely get that," Logan said in agreement while stuffing his mouth with his last fajita. He was a big guy, football player big, tall, blonde hair, blue eyes, very good-looking. It appeared he would need at least two more meals like the one he just finished to maintain the massive muscles protruding through his clothes. "I loved coming here and getting away from some crazy shit going on at home. It's nice to have a clean start sometimes."

Maybe Logan understood about wanting to get away and disappear. I opened up the slightest bit and made a connection; that felt good. I smiled softly at him, then looked away, down at my tray. He was sitting next to me, and I saw the slow approach of his hand toward mine, felt the soft touch to my fingers. I was tempted to pull my hand away but knew that would make a scene at the table, so I kept it still and in place.

"You don't have to tell us anything you don't want to. No worries, Lanie." He pulled his hand away and went back to eating what was left on his tray, which wasn't much. I had done it. I let him, another guy, touch me, and I didn't freak out. I motioned my tray toward him to see if he wanted to finish any of my food.

"Are you sure?" he questioned. "You barely ate anything."

"Go ahead, I'm not hungry." He dug into the rest of my salad while Ty and Becca laughed at his insatiable appetite.

Becca smiled at me from across the table, almost as if to say she was happy for me.

Happy I was here.

Happy I was talking.

Happy I just was.

And there it was again. The idea of being happy. It might only take the smallest thing.

It was such a small thing that had just happened—a tiny, insignificant thing to most people. But to me it was monumental.

And how sad was it that I was the happiest I had been in over three years with three people I had just met who knew nothing about me? I survived a panic attack and was eating a meal with three almost strangers.

But for the first time since I came to school, I felt like I belonged.

Chapter 3

"Lanie, you would look sooo cute in this sundress of mine. Why don't you wear this tonight? Why can't you wear anything other than jeans?"

Becca was on my case as we were getting ready. I was beginning to second-guess my decision to go out with her and the guys. We were going bowling. Who really needs to wear a dress to go bowling anyway? Jeans make much more sense, and she had no idea she was never getting me in a dress.

"Nope, I'm good in my jeans. Sorry, Becca. But I'll compromise; I'll let you do my makeup, how 'bout that?" I looked over at her and loved the smile that put on her face.

In the past couple of weeks, I'd been able to coexist with other humans as a person should. I think the distance between me and Max was allowing me to feel more comfortable with people. Becca was being so patient and encouraging, getting me to hang out with her and some of the other girls on the floor some nights. And it had become a nightly ritual for us and Ty and Logan to eat dinner together, the four of us becoming an unlikely foursome.

"Can I do your hair, too? You would look so good with some curls. You have such beautiful blonde hair, but you always wear it straight. Let me curl it for you tonight!" Becca pleaded.

"Makeup only, take it or leave it." She gave me a pouty face, but I knew she was kidding. As far as we had come, she knew not to push or I'd go right back into my shell. I sat in her desk chair so she could start on my makeup, and that was when I felt my phone start to light up.

"Is that your phone getting all those texts? My God, who is that? Seems like it must be something important. Do you need a minute?" Becca stopped thinking I was going to look at my phone, but I knew who it was and I had no intention of looking at the messages.

Right before I left for school, I blindsided Max. I told him I didn't want us to be together anymore. I told him I never wanted to see him again and got in the car with my parents and drove off.

Needless to say, he had not stopped texting me. He called as well; I didn't answer. Dealing with his incessant messages was getting tiring, yet I thought blocking him would make it worse. That would be like poking the bear.

"No, I'm good. It's nothing. But remember, keep me looking natural, nothing too crazy. I don't like a lot of color on my face."

"Don't worry, Lanie. I know you don't need much makeup; you're naturally beautiful. I don't even think you realize how pretty you are, even as you walk around in your jeans and hoodies. Most guys on this campus are checking you out all the time, at least while I'm with you."

I stared up at her in disbelief as she said this to me because I knew she was wrong.

I was mousy, boring, and nothing to look at. It was the exact reason I stayed covered up.

I'd spent years being told how grotesque I was. Max would tell me daily, forcing me to cover up my "hideous body." The constant reminders were enough to ingrain it in my mind.

Becca, on the other hand, was stunning, with her raven curls hanging down her back and her deep green eyes. I paled in comparison when I stood next to her, my light hair and light eyes fading into the background.

"I know you don't want too much eye makeup, but one time pleeaase let me do a smokey eye on you. Your blue eyes will pop out of your head if I do, and they'll look amazing!"

She continued to work in a companionable silence until there was a knock on our door. I was sure it was the guys, and that excited Becca. She made it no secret she was starting to have feelings for Ty, and I was pretty sure he felt the same about her.

I, on the other hand, still got uncomfortable when they were in our room. I tried to appear as though I was adjusting to it, and I think I was starting to. But I wasn't quite there yet. I was fine when we were out in public, but close proximity still set the anxiety in motion. However, tonight I would have to make it work until we were ready to go.

"Hey, girls. Don't you both look amazing?" Ty said with a huge smile.

But he was looking at Becca as he spoke upon entering

the room. Logan followed, a couple six-packs of beer in his hands, a can already cracked open.

It appeared we were pregaming before our big night of bowling. He put the beers in our fridge and then sprawled himself all over my bed, making himself comfortable.

"Oh my God, this bed is amazing. Lanie, is this yours?"

"Yes, that's Lanie's bed," Becca said. "She spends sooo much time in it—not surprised it's super comfy. Her pillows are amazing. She looks like she melts into it every time she lies down. But we're getting her out tonight! So, let's get this party started!"

Becca started streaming music onto her speaker, and the sudden club atmosphere had me frozen in place. I watched as Ty grabbed Becca and they started dancing wildly throughout the room. Logan turned his attention toward me, making me self-conscious. He was still lying on my bed, drinking his beer, the curiosity evident in his eyes.

"Do you want one?" he asked while studying me. "And by the way, you look real pretty tonight."

My palms had started sweating, and my breaths were short and choppy. It felt as though the air stopped moving in the room. I knew I had to look as if I didn't belong here, because that was how I felt.

I didn't know if I could do it.

I didn't know *how* to do it anymore. My anxiety was rising as the temperature in the room went up as well. Logan could see it on my face.

He got up from the bed and stalked toward me, keeping eye contact with me the whole time. His approach made my pulse quicken, and I knew he could see the change in me. He leaned down, but not too close, and whispered, "Are you OK, Lanie? You don't look so good."

"I'm just really hot. I, uh, need to use the bathroom. Tell them I'll be in the elevator lobby when you guys are ready to go, OK?" He nodded, and I sprinted out of the room and down the hall.

Our nightly trips for dinner together had become our thing, but for some reason this felt different.

Suddenly, this felt kind of like a date.

I was racing down the hall, not paying attention, and crashed into something. Rather, someone. I made everything drop from their hands, including a tray of food and a pile of books.

"Oh my God, I'm so sorry. I didn't mean to do that. I'm so, so sorry." My voice cracked with my words. My eyes were facing the ground, working hard to avoid eye contact with whomever I had crashed into. I was on the edge of a possible breakdown because I knew I needed to stop and help with the mess I created, but I wasn't sure I could.

Using my hair as a curtain, I tried to hide the tears that had welled up and were threatening to cascade down my cheeks any second.

"Lanie." The voice was deep but soothing. Of course, I should have recognized it, but because I was flustered, I didn't.

I heard his voice again, his deep, soothing voice.

"Lanie, look at me."

I stopped.

Tilting my head up from my crouched position on the ground, I looked into the deep blue eyes of Xander as the first tear escaped my eye.

"Lanie, it's OK. Stand up, please."

I used the back of my hand to wipe it away, hoping he hadn't noticed. I didn't need him to know I was already crying.

"No, I want to get all of this back on the tray for you." I went back to the scattered items on the floor, gathering them back to the tray. "I'm sorry I did this. It was careless of me to not see you coming. I'm so sorry. Thank God all the food is wrapped up. It's all still good, so . . ."

"Lanie," he interrupted calmly, "please stand up." I had to look at him to understand why he was being nice at a time like this. "You're shaking, and I need you to calm down. Come into my room until you do."

He saw the panicked look come over my face.

"It's a safe space, I promise. I'll leave my door open, but it'll be out of view of anyone else and you can have some privacy."

My head snapped up to look around, and I only then realized there were other people in the hall. They weren't necessarily paying attention to us, but if I made more of a scene, they were bound to.

I looked up at Xander, and his eyes were warm and full of what looked like empathy. As I stood, I tried to pick up as many of the things as I could.

But as I did, I wound up dropping most of it again.

And I was close to my breaking point.

I involuntarily let out a small whimper before more tears started escaping down my cheeks.

Xander reached down and grabbed me by the arms with firm hands and pulled me to standing, bringing me close to him, closer than I had been to any man other than Max in years. It was so sudden I didn't have time to pull away.

I was shaking, but I didn't think it was from fear.

And I had a realization. Strangely, rather than being consumed by fear and anxiety, a tranquil feeling overcame me. It was like a veil of comfort just from his touch. I looked at him with confusion, my eyes wide, wondering how this could be happening.

This should not be happening.

People don't make me feel comfortable; they make me nervous and scared.

But he was different, and I'd known that for a while. I still didn't know why, and I wanted to find out.

"Come on, Lanie, let's get you in my room for a minute." He was guiding me and I was letting him, like I was his puppet, completely under his control.

And I felt safe, like he said.

He sat me in his desk chair while he went back out to the hall to get the rest of the mess I made. He placed his food tray and books on his desk and turned to look at me—study me, actually—but didn't say anything. Yet it wasn't uncomfortable.

How was this any different from what I felt the need to escape in my room? But I was calming down in Xander's room, actually enjoying being here.

Again, it didn't make any sense.

"Thank you." It was all I could get out. I was confused as to what I was feeling. Yet, at the same time, I couldn't take my eyes off of his.

I felt compelled to keep looking, and he wasn't looking away.

"Well, I'm glad you didn't say you're sorry again, and you're welcome."

He chuckled as he said this, pulling up another chair. He sat across from me, at eye level, but not so close we were touching. For the first time in forever, I wanted to scoot forward. I wanted our knees to touch, to see if that calming feeling would exist with as simple a touch as that.

Or would there be something else as well?

I think I wanted that, too.

Although I had calmed, a new sensation I hadn't felt in a long time started deep in my belly. A fluttering feeling that made me self-conscious, as if Xander could see inside me and read the building emotions even I didn't understand. This immediate attraction I felt was perplexing, even troubling. There was no sound reason I should want this stranger to touch me, yet I yearned for it. I wasn't sure if I was attracted to him or if I was simply content to be in the same room with a guy I wasn't afraid of.

"I'm glad you seem to be calming down. And see, the food is all good." He motioned to his meal on the desk. I smiled, about to respond when a gorgeous, busty brunette came stomping into the room.

"Well, Xander, who is this? I thought *we* had plans together?"

Xander's face turned toward her, a look of annoyance now covering it. He made no motion to move from his chair. She stood by the door with her hands on her hips, looking more bothered as each second of silence passed between them until I started to get up from my chair to go.

Xander put his hand on my leg to stop me.

And there it was again.

That feeling I had been craving, the sense of calm. But this time it was infused with an added bolt of electricity.

And I think he felt it too, because when my gaze jerked toward his hand, it lingered.

He looked at his hand on my leg in bewilderment. His hand remained, though, and then our eyes connected again. He seemed just as surprised by what was happening between us as I was.

I saw something in his eyes, a message I couldn't quite decipher.

And then that voice again.

"You have got to be kidding me. It's like I'm watching a fucking Hallmark movie with the two of you, Xander, and I'm supposed to be the one here with you right now. What the fuck? Who the fuck is she? She looks like some lowly freshman."

Xander's hand retreated from my leg once he remembered we weren't alone in the room.

He started responding to her but never took his eyes off mine. That did a little something to my heart.

"Mia, why don't you head to the lounge? That's where we're going to study anyway. Get set up and I'll meet you there in five. Lanie and I are almost done here."

Mia didn't enjoy being dismissed like that. I also don't think she enjoyed being called out on the fact their "date" together was a study session. Xander very handily put her in her place, and I appreciated that about him. He did it without being condescending. She left as quickly as she arrived, and Xander and I once again found ourselves alone.

"Lanie, I'm sorry about her. She can be, um, dramatic."

"That's one way to describe her."

Once again, there was silence.

Still, not awkward. We looked at each other and it was as if we were still communicating somehow, our eyes speaking to each other.

But it gave me a moment to realize that I knew nothing about this guy. In the five minutes I'd been in his room, another girl had come crashing in. I needed to be careful. Careful with who I brought into my life.

Careful with my heart.

And then I heard my drunk friends coming down the hallway. I knew my time here was drawing to a close. I stood up and started moving toward the door to leave, and Xander followed me.

"So, are you helping Mia with a class, or do you tutor?" Against my better judgment, I kept the conversation going rather than just thanking him and leaving. Even though I knew I needed to leave, should leave, I had a strong desire not to leave his room. There was a pull like I was a magnet and he was steel. But the voices in the hall were getting louder and closer.

"I tutor some people for credit for my one professor. I help him out, and he helps me out. He sends some of his students my way, so I don't have much of a choice who I get." His eyes shifted the slightest bit when he spoke, making it seem like it wasn't the whole story. "It helps pay for college."

"That sounds like a great arrangement. Good for you. Thanks again for being understanding about my clumsiness. And if you haven't heard them already, those are my friends coming down the hall." I stopped talking once I realized I'd been rambling. My palms were getting sweaty as I looked toward the open door. My gaze returned to Xander, an unreadable look on his face. That added to my unease, the sudden shift making me want to leave, yet the oncoming group was not who I wanted to be with. "We're going bowling," I told him, hoping to change the mood back to what it was. "I'm not sure what I've gotten myself into tonight; hopefully I can handle this."

My words put a huge smile on his face. I hadn't seen him smile like that before, and it was quite a sight. His deep dimple on one cheek softened the sharp angles of his model-like jaw, and his eyes crinkled.

"What are you smiling at?" I asked with genuine bewilderment.

There was a subtle shake to his head before he started talking.

"You just sounded so . . . calm, happy, and—I don't want to offend you by saying this because we don't even really know each other yet, but—*normal,* when you were talking. You were on the brink of a breakdown a few minutes ago, and you sound normal right now. That makes me happy for you, that's all. It made me smile."

He was still grinning, but not quite as hard, more cautious now, I guess nervous I might be upset by his comment. Apparently, my nerves went unnoticed. Either that or he was being nice by ignoring them.

"Can I ask you something?" He held his phone out to me. "Can you put your number in my phone? With the night you've already had, and you heading out with drunk friends, I'd feel better if you could text me if you needed someone."

I was starting to think this couldn't be real. College guys aren't supposed to be this perfect. I was waiting for the other shoe to drop with him. I wasn't sure at first, but I took his phone and entered my number. The next thing I knew, a text pinged, and he smiled at the sound.

"Thank you," I said shyly. "I, uh, um, thanks for everything." I knew I should have said more, so much more. But I was back to being short on words. His small smile and the dip of his chin told me he understood and that it was enough.

That I was enough.

He guided me out of his room with his hand on my

lower back. I stiffened slightly as goosebumps erupted on my skin. A small smile formed on my lips, and I knew he saw it. That encouraged him to rub my back with his fingers before removing his hand as we entered the hall. My emotions were all over the place as we walked side by side. My brain was yelling at me to move away, that I was too close to a stranger. Yet my heart contradicted everything I knew I should be doing. I forced my eyes to look forward. But they wanted to peek left, to see his profile. I could *feel* him, his imposing height looming over me as our steps fell into rhythm, our silence still comfortable.

Our silence was interrupted by the rambunctious behavior of my friends waiting for me. All of their heads turned as we rounded the corner together.

Xander continued to the study lounge and said goodbye as he went in. As soon as he left, I felt his absence. Did that mean . . . I missed him?

How is it possible to immediately miss someone you didn't even know?

When I turned to look at my awaiting friends, they stared at me with wide eyes and had their mouths agape.

And they had fallen silent.

But not for long.

"Lanie, why were you with Xander James?"

"Were you in his room?"

"He's a man-whore, Lanie. Did you know that?"

"Lanie, you can do better than him."

I was stunned into further silence by their barrage of questions and statements. All three of them obviously had their predetermined opinions about Xander, and I guessed they weren't good. As I looked at them, I think they realized they might lose me if they continued with the way they were going. I knew Becca had recognized the concern on my face, as I saw her elbow Ty in his side.

"Sorry, Lanie. We don't mean anything by any of that; we just weren't expecting to see you with him, that's all. He doesn't usually hang with freshman girls. He has the upper girls in and out of his room all the time, so it was a surprise to see you with him."

Logan was staring at me with a look of concern at this point, and I needed to diffuse all of this, immediately.

"Hey, guys, aren't we going bowling? Is that still the plan? Because it seems like we've been standing in this elevator lobby a lot longer than necessary. Can we get going, please?"

"Come on, Lanie's right." Logan was chuckling as he pressed the button to call for the elevator. "Let's get this show on the road. Besides, my buzz will wear off soon if we don't get going, and I only snuck a few beers in my pockets."

Becca came and put her arm around me and whispered in my ear, "You'll tell me later what went on with you and that hottie though, right?"

She had a twinkle in her eye when she looked at me through her curls, slurring her words a bit. I was hoping she was drunk enough she would forget to ask me about this later. Because it seemed like Xander had a reputation, one I should be wary of. One that should keep me away from him.

We all moved on downstairs to our waiting Uber and me on to my first night out with friends in years.

I only hoped I wouldn't wind up regretting this.

Any of this.

Chapter 4

Max stole many "firsts" from me in my life.

He took my first kiss from me, and many other firsts from my body.

He took every other first from me I could think of.

Last night, I felt like I stole some of them back. Well, I guess I couldn't actually get them back, but it felt good to do some of them on my terms.

I lay in bed. The sun had just come up, and I was wide awake because I couldn't stop thinking about my night. The giddy feeling in my stomach from my thoughts made me think it could have been a dream, but it happened. It really happened, and it was my life.

I had actual friends, and I couldn't be happier.

I looked over at Becca as quiet snores escaped from her; she was likely to be asleep for many more hours. I was thankful to have been placed in a room with such a patient person. I had no plans to make any connections or friendships when I came here, but she had started breaking through my tough exterior, and I was grateful.

The bowling alley had been packed. Loud music blasted from speakers while everyone bowled, dancing in between games. I started slow, Becca and the guys giving me time and space to adjust to the party atmosphere. When we first walked in, I wasn't sure I would make it, my eyes wide at the size of the group already there. But we found a spot along the side wall that afforded me what felt like safety. Before long, sweat from dancing dripped off my temples. I even had a few beers.

I had a blast.

So my night out was a small victory, a "first," while here at school.

The other part of my night was Xander. Since going out went well, there was no need for me to text him an SOS. But once I was home, he texted me.

Xander:

> Just checking in to see if everything is ok since I didn't hear from u hoping that means u had a good night

Before going to bed, I responded:

Me:

> I did have a good night thx

That was it. Simple, but it made me smile.

Yesterday with Xander, I felt as if I was being touched

for the first time by a guy. They were simple touches on my arms, legs, or back, nothing serious. Yet they felt more intimate than any sex I was ever forced to have with Max.

But I didn't know him. There were so many things that could go wrong if I let Xander into my life. I could actually fall for him. Or Max could find out about him. And then there were the ideas that Becca and the guys put in my head.

Ugh, how quickly I had shifted my mood. I'd gone from elated about my night to paranoid about trusting my gut about Xander. But I came here intending to stay isolated, to keep to myself, and I'd already broken my rule about that. I needed to stay the course and stick to my original plan to get my education and avoid going back to Texas at all costs.

I had constant reminders of why I didn't want to go back home. All the texts I get from Max were the complete opposite of the one from Xander. There were plenty of those last night as well, yet I chose not to look at them.

I hovered my finger over my phone, afraid of what it would show me.

Max:

Why are you not answering my calls

You might think we aren't together, but think again

Lanie, I've been calling you all week you need to answer me

When I text you bitch you answer me. When I call you, you answer me

You're probably whoring around aren't you

This is unacceptable behavior from you, answer the fucking phone the next time I call or I'm on a plane

That last text had my blood running cold. Would he really do that?

Me:

> Max, we are broken up I'm sorry if you're not willing to ac-
> cept that but we are not together anymore I'm not going to
> respond to your texts or calls

Shit, I hoped that would shut him up. I couldn't have him coming here—never even had that thought crossed my mind. I needed to keep him in San Antonio at all costs. The thought of him here, in my safe space, sent chills straight to my bones.

I felt my phone buzz, which was crazy, because it was super early back in Texas.

Max:

> Fuck, I'm sorry, I'm sorry I get like that
>
> You know I don't mean it when I get like that
>
> I get so crazy thinking about what you could be doing, who could be talking to you, touching you
>
> I'll do better I just miss you can you call me it will help
>
> I can't live without you, you have to know that

He always did this, made excuses for his behavior, thinking his apologies made up for the wrongs.

An apology doesn't make bruises go away.

Flowers don't give me back my virginity.

I wasn't sure I could lie in this bed much longer, since sleep continued to evade me due to my own thoughts. I needed to forget about him.

I decided to go for a run, hoping that would help. I tiptoed across the room to change my clothes, grabbed my sneakers and earbuds, and headed out the door. It was a beautiful morning, and the campus I lived on afforded me a view of mountaintops veiled in mist and clouds that took your breath away. It was an alluring backdrop that kept my mind off my own troubles as I pounded the pavement.

More than thirty minutes into my run, I was circling the pond on the outskirts of campus and heard footsteps behind me in between songs on my playlist. My nervous nature kicked in and I veered off my trail, deciding to stop at the nearest bench so I could look at my nearby companion. As I sat, I turned my head, my timid eyes peeking behind me. A familiar face was smiling down on me.

"Morning, Lanie! You're up early after a night out."

Xander, in all his sweaty hotness, was approaching me in his shorts and a tank that was showing off biceps I hadn't known were there.

They were most definitely there, and I think he caught me looking at them.

There was also a tattoo on one of them, though I couldn't make it out. But it did a fine job of highlighting the definition of said muscle. The shirt was loose enough to show the hint of another tattoo on his chest, but I couldn't see the whole thing. It only added to his allure and sexiness.

Oh my God. The fluttery feeling in my stomach—you know, that feeling when an elevator makes a sudden drop. Well, I had that. Just from seeing him in front of me.

"I didn't know you ran," he said. By then, he was standing next to the bench I had sought refuge on.

"Um, yeah, I did at home, but this is the first run I've gone on since getting to Blue Ridge University."

Silence again. I should have been able to say more than that, more than one-sentence answers, but I shut down and got too nervous. He seemed to understand, and I didn't feel silly or embarrassed. Rather, he carried the conversation for me.

"Well, you picked the best route to run here at BRU. This is my favorite spot. Sometimes you can see the otter in the pond if you time it right, too. I, um, I didn't make you nervous coming up behind you, did I?"

His face was genuine, and I was immediately second-guessing my doubts from this morning in bed. I felt such a strong desire to trust this guy, but it wasn't in my nature to trust someone I barely know. Why was I?

My face and body language must have given away my answer. I pulled my legs up under my arms, and his response was immediate.

"Oh shit, Lanie, I'm sorry. I didn't mean to scare you. I saw it was you, and I got excited and sped up to not miss you. I didn't know which way you were going to go up ahead and I wanted to catch you, is all." By this point, he was sitting on the bench near me, but not too close. He was always very conscious of my fears, it seemed.

"It's OK, really. It's something I have to get over. It's me, not you."

Typically, I would look away, but with him, I couldn't. I was staring straight into his eyes, unable to break the connection.

That magnetic pull I felt around him was back, and I immediately started to relax. I had such a strong desire for him to come closer and touch me, do anything so I could feel that feeling again.

"Well, at least it doesn't look like I'm going to send you into another panic attack." He said this with a kind smile, and I could do nothing but return it. At this, he leaned back on the bench, as if we were going to be sitting here for a while together, and took out his phone. His tank inched up and revealed a portion of stomach that was as ripped as his biceps. It also exposed that little line of hair that disappeared below the band of his shorts, and a tiny gasp escaped my mouth. I became self-conscious and had to turn my head away from him.

"Ya know, when I got this text from you last night, I was glad to hear it went well and you didn't need me. Did you guys have fun?"

I got caught off guard that he was still talking to me. These unfamiliar feelings teemed through my body, deep in my core, creating a warmth that spread. The newness of this was unnerving, sending shivers from head to toe. I was sure I was blushing; thank God my face was still red from running. I took a breath and focused.

"Yeah, we, uh, actually had a great time. I even had a few beers when we got there." Xander couldn't understand the magnitude of this for me.

"Do you not normally drink? You say that like it was your first time."

And even though his comment could have been hurtful, he was not the least bit condescending, just perceptive.

"I didn't drink the last few years I was in Texas. Lots to that backstory there. And the other night was my first chance to actually do it here. I haven't been very social since I've gotten to school. Not for lack of Becca trying, but I was resisting. I'm trying to let her break me in slowly now, though. I'm doing OK, but as you saw, I still have my moments. Thank you again, by the way. You were really nice to me."

I felt myself blushing a bit at the confessions I divulged. I had to look away, still embarrassed about my blunders from the other day.

At the same time, I blushed from his simple touch to my leg, a touch that vibrated through my body like a tuning fork.

And I wanted him to touch me again at that moment.

I stared out over the pond, trying to take my mind off the memory, hoping he mistook my shaking and goosebumps for nerves rather than desire. I was confused by these feelings, these emotions. I didn't know him.

"Well, I'm glad I could help, and don't we all have things back at home we would like to leave there, right?" He looked out over the pond contemplatively after saying that. "So, if you're still looking to try to get out more, maybe I could help."

I looked over, very hopeful at this point, but at the same time nervous he might ask me out. I didn't want a boyfriend, but for some reason, I welcomed his interest in me.

"I like to have room parties sometimes, and I'm going to have one in a few days. Was thinking you, Logan, Becca, and Ty would like to come. I can't invite everyone on the floor, and most freshmen don't get an invite, but I'd thought I'd ask you since you don't get out much." He said this with a wink, but all I could focus on was the fact that he paired me off with Logan when he was talking.

Did he think Logan and I were together?

"That's awesome. Thanks for thinking of us. I'll definitely be there, and I'm sure Becca will, too. I'll let the guys know. They might have something going on; I'm not sure."

I sat back on the bench, feeling our time here was nearing an end but not wanting it to. He started fiddling with his earbuds.

I looked over at him and he was staring at me, which should have made me uncomfortable, but of course, with him, it didn't. I challenged his stare, hoping to keep him here longer. His dark waves were falling over his eyes a bit, and he ran his hand through them to move them out of his face.

And that may have been the single most sexy thing I had ever seen.

Oh man, I had it bad, yet he thought I was interested in someone else.

"Sure, Lanie. You not running anymore?"

"No, I'm pretty comfy right here, and I'm really liking this view. I've been out running for over half an hour anyway, early morning for me. I'm going to hang here for a bit." God, why do I always ramble around him?

He smiled as he got up from the bench and shuffled backward as he spoke again. "I'm sure I'll see you later, on our floor."

He then decided to lift his shirt to use it as a towel for his sweaty forehead, giving me a full-frontal view of his torso.

And oh my God.

The view provided by this move included the tight, muscled V that receded into his shorts. It left me wanting to see more, hoping for more. I only had seconds to recover before he pulled his hands back down from his face, his eyes finding mine immediately.

"Bye, Lanie." He waved and gave me an earth-shattering smile that exposed his equally appealing dimple.

He was on his way down the path around the pond. My heart was still pounding from the display I witnessed as I continued to watch him until he was out of sight. Any healthy girl would; he was gorgeous when running.

I should have felt happy or content knowing I'd see him at the party in a few days, yet all I felt was a sense of foreboding. This insecure feeling I had because of what he thought about me and Logan didn't sit right, and I needed to fix it.

But I didn't know how.

I didn't even understand why I cared.

Chapter 5

Some of my best memories from my childhood were from when my mother would take me to the library for story time. I loved choosing the little piece of carpet we'd sit on from the pile. All the kids would rush over, trying to find their favorite one from the mountain in the corner of the children's section. Mine was a blue shag piece because I loved running my fingers through the fibers while I listened to the stories being read. My mom would disappear to the adult section, choosing her books for the week while I sat with the neighborhood kids. We anxiously waited for the librarian to select and read whatever author she featured that week. Afterward, my mom would help me pick my own books for the week.

When we got home, I would run up to my room and plop on my beanbag chair and spend hours looking at my books. I thought I could read, but I couldn't yet. My mom would read the books to me before bed, and I would try to remember the words and say them out loud the next day. I pored over them all week and couldn't wait to go back again the following week for story time.

This time in my life instilled my lasting love for reading. I loved the idea of a library, borrowing something, taking care of something that wasn't yours, and bringing it back for others to then enjoy.

As I was sitting in the university library trying to get some work done, I heard little voices somewhere that kept distracting me, bringing me back to memories of my childhood.

I was enjoying the distraction; I don't think about good memories from my time back in Texas as often as I should. I had fifteen years of life that were amazing before Max came along, fifteen years of memories I needed to hold on to and remember.

As I sat there, I thought back to the condition of the books I took home as a child. Some were in pristine condition, but others were literally falling apart at the binding. I always wondered why people didn't respect the books they borrowed.

But that's exactly what Max did to me. He borrowed me, mistreated me. But unlike the borrowers returning books to the library, he was very careful to hide the damage he had done.

My parents were in the dark about the abuse I was enduring. The only way they would have known was if I had told them. I was always careful with clothing choices and hairstyles, but there was no one as observant as I was. And the threats from Max were a strong deterrent as well.

Abusers are very smart that way; they know exactly what to say to their victims to intimidate them into silence.

They know exactly where on the body to inflict harm so it will not be seen.

They know exactly how far to push before the person goes over the edge.

The ping on my phone broke me from my trance-like thoughts, and my heart sank. I prayed it wasn't another manic text from him. They'd been getting more numerous, and it was starting to concern me.

I took my phone out of my bag and smiled, seeing who it was from.

Becca:

Me and the guys are going for food, you done studying yet

Me:

Almost and I'm starving save me a seat I'll meet you guys there

Perfect timing. I couldn't concentrate anymore. I might as well pack this up and head on out.

"Lanie!" Logan screamed my name from somewhere in the crowd. I looked around and saw him running to catch up to me. "You headed to the cafeteria?"

"I am. Did you get the text from Becca, too?" We fell into a stride together, his steps slower than mine due to his long legs.

"Yeah, good thing, too. I'm starving. But when am I not, right?" His smile was wide as he looked down at me. Logan and I had become closer. We had an unspoken connection. He must have had some traumatic past haunting him as well, because he just seemed to get it. The other night, Becca had been getting on my case about not going to the football games. To be exact, she wanted me to go to the tailgate parties. But I wasn't ready to be in crowds that large. Logan shut Becca down. He told her to leave me alone and that I would go when I was ready.

It had been a long time since I had someone on my side, and it felt kind of nice. I wasn't expecting it to be some huge, brooding ex-football player.

Looking at my phone as we continued walking into the cafeteria, I wasn't watching where I was going. I was trying to see if Becca had mentioned where she was sitting so Logan and I would know where to go. The scrape of the metal chair legs on the tile floor as we approached should have been a sure sign. I didn't see the person who was pushing from their seat right in front of me. He stood up, and we collided. His hands were immediately on my arms to steady me, and before I raised my eyes, I knew who it had to be.

It was Xander.

I was making a habit of doing this.

"Oh my God, Xander, I'm so sorry."

"Hey, Lanie, you OK?"

"Yeah, I should probably look where I'm going more, huh?"

"You could be more careful getting up, dude." Logan's tone made both Xander and me snap our heads in his direction. His eyes were glued to Xander's hands, which were still on my arms, while Logan's own hands were fisted at his sides. He stepped toward me protectively, coming closer as if to take me in his arms.

I glanced at Xander as I shrugged out of his hold, not wanting this to escalate. His eyes moved from Logan to me and back again. This was my first time seeing this side of Xander; he was angry. I saw the slow swallow in his throat, the measured breaths as he tried to maintain control.

But then he looked at me again. Me, while I was wringing my hands together with nervous energy because I had caused this. I backed away from them, and they took notice.

Xander spoke up next, trying to defuse the situation. "Yeah, so it's Logan, right? You're right, man. Sorry, Lanie. I should be more careful." He glanced at Logan briefly, but his eyes came right back to mine. I heard the sincerity in his voice. "I'm actually glad we ran into one another, Lanie." He smiled at his pun. "I wanted to let you know about the party I'm throwing next week, the one we talked about." This time, he looked right at Logan.

Logan's response was to expel his pent-up breath. Loudly. I elbowed him in the ribs. Hard.

Christ, they were like children. And I really had no idea what was going on between the two of them.

"So, anyway," Xander continued, "I'm having people over on Wednesday. I hope that works for you." He hesitated as he forced his hands into his pockets, his eyes darting around as if he didn't know how to continue. He then turned his attention toward Logan. "And I guess if you two are together, that means you're invited, too."

"Wait, what?!" I yelped. As soon as I did, I noticed the wince on Logan's face. But he squared up quickly and spoke first.

"Nah, we aren't together. She's got this sick ex

from home she's still dealing with. She's not ready for a boyfriend."

That one sentence from him said and did so many things. I felt dizzy at the notion that people knew about Max.

"Logan, how do you know about that? I haven't told anyone. Becca barely knows." The words were a whisper between the three of us. I never intended to allow that part of my life to reach me here.

"I guess I just listen well." Logan wanted his words to hold weight with me; I saw that in his face once he said it. I couldn't answer him. I couldn't do anything. All I did was shift my eyes from his stare, but I was unsure where to look. My eyes landed on Xander.

His look told me that Logan's words did hold weight with him.

It was as if all his questions about me were answered in that one sentence from Logan. Like he could put the final piece of the puzzle known as Lanie together. But I wasn't that much of an open book; he may have thought he'd solved the mystery of me, but there was no way he knew it all.

Because no one knew it all. No one but me.

"Well, I'm sure Logan won't go talking about anything you don't want him to. Am I right, Logan?" Xander's words held a bit of a threat toward Logan, and this needed to be diffused. I didn't need a pissing match between two guys over me when I had no intention of being with either of them. I looked over at Logan, his shoulders a bit deflated as he realized he'd overstepped with this one.

"He wouldn't do that, no worries. We'll see ya later, Xander." I grabbed Logan by the sleeve and pulled him away from Xander.

Logan and I continued on our way in silence, awkward

silence. As we got further into the room, I saw Becca waving feverishly for us to come to the table she had.

"Becca's over there," I murmured.

"Yeah, um, OK," Logan stammered. "I'll be there in a sec." He took off in the opposite direction, seemingly to get food. I turned around and forced myself to not look back. Becca was staring me down as I approached the table. I knew she saw the three of us talking. I also knew she would have questions.

"Xander's having a room party on Wednesday, and we're all invited. And yes, that's it." She gave me a look, knowing there was more. But she also knew when it came to me, I would shut down on the turn of a pin, so she didn't push.

"OK, then. Well, I'm glad you finally made it." Her knowing look told me she understood the talk she witnessed was something we would eventually have to discuss, although I would avoid doing that at all costs. "I'll come with you to get your food. I have something to tell you, and I don't want to do it around Ty."

I would have been scared of those words if she didn't have the darndest wide smile on her face I'd ever seen. "So, I've been nervous to tell you this, and I don't want it to change anything between any of us." And just like that, I, of course, knew where this was going. And I was thankful for the distraction. "But Ty and I are kind of seeing each other."

She stopped and stared, I guess waiting to see my reaction, which of course was elation for her. I had known for the longest time that she liked him.

"Becca, I'm thrilled for the two of you! I knew you both liked each other. It was obvious for, like, forever. So I'm glad you guys are giving it a go. You deserve to be happy."

I leaned in and gave her a hug.

But inside, I had to admit I was worried about how this would possibly affect the four of us. The two of them would pair off, obviously in a much different way than Logan and I would.

After I had gotten some food, we started toward the table where Logan and Ty were already eating. Thankfully, Logan didn't acknowledge me when I sat down. Maybe we could both forget what had happened between him, Xander, and me.

"I'm glad you're not worried, because I think Logan will be." She whispered this in my ear as we were sitting down.

And Logan was.

As soon as we sat, he blasted Becca and Ty with his questions.

"So guys, when you get into your first fight, which you will, where does that leave me and Lanie? What are we supposed to do? We can't take sides in it. How does this affect all of us if you guys break up?"

OMG! Great minds thought alike!

"Logan, how do you even know we're together? We haven't even told you yet!" Becca whined.

"Are you kidding me? Ty's been pining for you for weeks. Once I knew he was finally talking to you, I knew he worked up the nerve to ask you. Took you long enough, dork. I was sick of hearing it every night—Becca this, Becca that. If he wasn't going to ask you out, I was going to ask you for him."

"Shut up, Logan!" Ty yelled as he threw fries at Logan's face. The smile he then had for Becca made it obvious he was kidding. "We're adults, dude. I think we'll be able to handle being friends if things go south. Right, babe?" His question was directed at Becca, who was basically sitting on his lap, and who stuck her tongue down his throat the second he stopped talking.

But Ty pulled back for a minute and looked seriously at Logan. "I think you have something *you* need to take care of yourself, don't you?"

"Nope, don't go there, Ty. It's not happening. I told you it's not, didn't I?" He glared angrily at Ty, the angriest I think we'd ever seen him. Even angrier than he was at Xander. At that, Logan pushed his chair back with a screech and abruptly stood up, grabbed his food tray, and started toward the garbage.

"I'm done, guys. I'm heading back to the room. See ya later."

He left us all with our mouths wide open. Ty and Becca gave each other a knowing look as Logan stormed off.

"Ignore him, guys," I said. "I'm happy for the two of you. I'm sure you're both adult enough to handle anything that happens down the road between you, and we can all still be friends."

They gave each other giddy smiles and kissed again as I spoke. I was happy I had elevated the atmosphere, but it didn't eliminate my own fears about our group. But, hey, who were we to stop their attempt at love? They had every right to be happy, regardless of our need for us to be friends afterward. It was selfish on our part.

Life goes on. It would be our new normal.

Ty and Becca became one of those cute new couples I'd always enjoyed watching from my bench.

Except this time, I had an up-front view of the action.

They were cute to watch, like the couples I viewed from my bench. I couldn't tell where their limbs ended or began; they were constantly wrapped around one another. They didn't get much schoolwork done from what I could see, and Logan and I were getting locked out of our respective rooms often.

Plus, I still hadn't seen Logan since his outburst in the cafeteria the other day. Between the incident with Xander and him storming off that day, there seemed to be a few things he could be mad at me for. He and I had just started getting closer, and now days had gone by without a word. Not seeing much of my new friends was causing feelings of abandonment to creep up inside of me. I couldn't help it.

I knew I needed to confront him. But confrontation was something I tried to avoid, surely due to some form of PTSD from Max. My inability to confront the issues in my life was a major concern, one I knew I needed to work on. But as far as problems went, this one with Logan was small. With that in mind, I decided I needed to do this; I could confront this problem in my life. I could go talk to Logan.

I started for his room.

However, my anxiety rose as I approached his room, all the potential outcomes running rampant in my brain. Would he get angry and yell at me for coming to him? Would we not be friends any longer? Oh my God, how would this affect the whole group? Standing outside his open door, I froze, afraid to make the next move.

But I did peek in and found him alone. My small hand barely made a sound as I knocked on his door, and his head turned my way as I stepped halfway in. He was lying in his bed, looking at his computer, doing work. His large frame barely fit on the small beds provided in the dorms, his feet hanging off the edge.

"Hey, Logan." My hands were sweating at this point.

"Hey, Lanie." He was still quiet as he made eye contact with me, looking almost embarrassed.

"Logan, what's going on? Ever since the cafeteria the other day, you haven't said more than two words to me, and now with Ty and Becca spending every second together, I miss you. Did I do something to make you mad?" My breathing was ragged, but I got the words out.

His head jerked up, and his face softened once I finished.

"Oh my God, Lanie, you didn't do anything. I'm such an ass." He stood up and came toward me with slow steps. "What Ty said the other day in front of you guys fucking pissed me off, and I've been too embarrassed to see you. I didn't even stop to think you'd feel *you* did something. It was absolutely nothing you did at all. It was all Ty." As he spoke, he looked down into my eyes, and I felt a hint of intimacy in the moment. "I could never be mad at you, Lanie. Not in a million years could I be mad at you—always know that."

Shit. I had been right those other times when I thought Logan was flirting with me, but this was more. This was heavy; this came with feelings. It felt as though he was about to make a major declaration when, thankfully, Ty and Becca came bouncing into the room. Logan and I both jerked our heads toward the door.

"Hi, guys! Are we interrupting something?" Becca squealed with excitement.

"No!" I yelled.

"Yes!" Logan screamed at the same time.

I pulled away from Logan, needing the separation to be greater than the room afforded with the four of us in it. I wanted to make a run for it, bound out the door. But the moment was awkward enough already. It would have been made worse by a sudden departure, so I stayed. But my reluctance had to be evident to everyone.

"Hey, Becca, uh, didn't you and Lanie have to do that thing you told me about?" Ty said and made some weird eye motion to her to give her the unsaid message.

"Oh, yeah, Lanie, let's go. I forgot, and we're going to be late." She grabbed my hand and led me out of the room and had her head against mine the second she could. The whisper that wasn't a whisper assaulted my ear. "What was going on in there? Were you and Logan going to hook up? That would be great. The four of us could go out all the time, Lanie!"

"No, Becca, that's not why Ty did that." I was frustrated at this point with Becca constantly trying to push us together. "I'm not interested in being with Logan, and it seems Ty understands that. Maybe Ty can try to talk some sense into him. I'm in no position to be in a relationship with anyone right now, and I thought Logan knew that." I turned around and started back toward our room. My frustration was spilling out. I didn't want to make a scene while rushing down the hall.

At that exact moment, Xander's door opened and a girl, a girl I recognized, was coming out. It was the girl I had seen him with the very first day I saw Xander, the one hanging all over him, the one he sent on her way. She turned back toward the open door and giggled something as she said her goodbyes.

I was frozen in place as my heart sank.

I think I would have been less upset if it were Mia. But this girl was different, one just as beautiful, maybe more stunning, even. And she didn't seem as caustic and insincere as Mia. She seemed nice, normal.

She seemed like a girl I would be happy for Xander to be with.

That made this hurt more for some reason, but it wasn't allowed to hurt.

He wasn't mine.

I had no claim over him, as much as I would like to.

It took a moment for me to realize I was still standing in the hallway, not moving. Becca nudged me from behind, encouraging me to move forward, toward our room. I looked up and saw Xander at the edge of his door. He was looking at me as the girl passed me in the hall.

The look on his face was unreadable, indifferent. I think that hurt even more, though I'm not sure what I was hoping for. Did I want him to rush over and apologize for what I saw? Or did I want him to gloat about the girl who left his room? I didn't want either, to be honest.

I passed him in silence, my eyes on the floor because if I looked at him again, he would see the water building up in them. But why was I almost crying? No idea why this was making me so flustered, so upset. Xander and I were not together; we were not a thing. For all I knew, she was his girlfriend.

Becca guided me to our room and gently closed our door.

She was quiet for a few minutes, knowing that was what I needed. I curled up on my bed, aware we were going to have to talk, but dreading it.

This friendship thing had its perks, but this was not one of them. I liked being a loner in this department, not having to divulge all of my feelings to someone just because they wanted to know what was going on.

And what *was* going on? I was hurting.

It hurt to see him with someone else, and I didn't even understand why. But I felt the pain cut deep, a sweeping pain that went straight to my core and settled there, taking my breath away.

These were not feelings I ever experienced with Max. My emotions with him were limited to fear and loathing.

But the pit-in-the-stomach feeling, this deep pain that consumed me and was brought on by Xander, this seemed to hurt more than all the years of pain I endured with Max. And the difference was, if one of them threw me a lifeline, I would hold on for dear life; the other, I would choose to drown. One thing I did know was when I was near him, I wanted nothing more than to be nearer to him.

And this made no sense. I barely knew Xander. Why would I have such strong feelings for someone I barely knew?

But I did know Becca was getting restless. She was cleaning things in the room; that was my clue.

"Becca." And that was as far as I got before the line of questioning started.

"Lanie, what the fuck? First, I walk in and see what looks like you and Logan about to kiss, and then that look between you and Xander could have lit up an entire city, and right after, another girl left his room! You have a lot of explaining to do, and I feel like I haven't really talked to you for the past day or two! And then you still have this guy at home—which, by the way, you have yet to really tell me much about Max. I mean, I know you told me you ended it with him, but he still texts and calls all the time, so there's a story with him. And didn't I warn you about Xander? I swear there is a new girl in and out of his room every day, so be careful with that one. Now Logan, he's another story. He's infatuated with you, has been since the beginning of the semester. And oh my God, wouldn't that be so much fun? The four of us going out all the time together."

She finally came up for air. She was pacing the room the entire time during her diatribe, flipping her curls behind her back, throwing her hands up in the air, very dramatic. I gave it a moment, not sure she was completely done, before I spoke up.

"OK, that was a lot."

Her head snapped in my direction as she only then realized and remembered who she was dealing with, and she got nervous. Coming over to my bed, she sat down, angling toward my curled-up body. My body was still; not a muscle moved the whole time she spoke.

"I'm sorry, Lanie. I know I can be a lot. But I'm actually very excited for you. You being in a relationship here at school could be good for you. You obviously were in one at home, and maybe that makes you feel comfortable, so I was thinking if you found someone at school you liked, it could give you a level of comfort here as well. Everyone knows long distance doesn't really work."

She really was a sweet girl, and she was looking out for me most of the time. Her thought process wasn't far off, except she had no understanding of what I was trying to escape from at home with Max.

I'd made a conscious decision not to discuss him, but sometimes I wanted to blurt it out to someone and get it all off my chest.

This would be the perfect time to tell her everything about him, to have a confidante, but I just didn't know if

I was ready. They were such dark secrets; I wasn't ready for her to look at me differently, and I knew she would.

She was still sitting on the edge of the bed, waiting for me to say something. I moved farther in toward the wall, motioning for her to join me. She let out a giggle and lay down next to me.

"Oh my God, this bed is heaven. I feel like I'm sinking into feathers." She settled and looked into my eyes now that we were face to face.

"Becca, I don't feel that way about Logan. I know you wish I did, but I don't." I noticed there was no disappointment in her face, only acknowledgment.

"OK, I won't push you with him, but there was definitely something between you and Xander in the hall. What was that about?" She paused, biting her thumb in anticipation. When I didn't answer, she went on. "I've seen you two talk a couple times over the past few weeks. He doesn't talk to many people on the floor like he talks to you. Are you interested in him?"

I didn't answer her—I couldn't. But I think my answer came in the form of my silence.

"Oh my God, Lanie!" she shrieked. "You like him, don't you? Well, what are you going to do about it?"

"I don't know if I like him, Becca. I feel something; I'm just not sure what it is yet. He makes me feel, I don't know, like I can do more, or be more *me*. And that was only from that little bit of time I talked to him the night we went bowling." I was struggling with words to describe how I felt. I think that was because I had no idea how I felt. "And you saw the girl who came out of his room. He obviously is hooking up like you guys said. Plus, even though I ended it with Max, I'm still dealing with him. It's all so complicated, but I'm working on it. I want to talk to you about all of it, I do, but I'm not ready yet. I promise I will when I am, OK?"

Becca nodded as I said this.

"I don't care one bit about the girl who came out of Xander's room, by the way. I saw the way he looked at you, Lanie. It was like that other girl didn't even exist anymore once he saw you. And Max, well, we all have 'complicated,' so I'll be here whenever you're ready, no worries." She reached over and gave me a squeeze. I felt myself melt into her embrace, comforted by the fact I knew I had someone with me, someone on my side.

"His room party is tomorrow night, isn't it?" I nodded as we pulled away from each other. "Well, we may have to make you look so super sexy that he won't know what hit him when you show up. And as far as Logan goes, I guess Ty is trying to take care of that. It might be tough on him for a while, but we'll make sure things stay normal."

I nodded in agreement. But we both knew it wasn't going to be easy dealing with Logan.

"Let's figure out what you'll be wearing to Xander's party so you can knock his pants off ! I have the cutest dress!" She put her hands up in a pleading position, begging me.

"Nope, not gonna happen. I'm sticking with my jeans, but I will let you pick out whatever top you wanna put me in."

And then there was a knock at our door. Becca went to it, assuming it was Ty, which it always was.

But this time it wasn't; it was Logan.

He poked his head in the door as Becca held it partially closed, easily looking around the room over her head. He eventually found what he was looking for when his eyes landed on me. His once stiff body relaxed somewhat, but the tension in his eyes remained.

"Lanie, can we talk? Alone?" He pushed the door open all the way as he said this, coming fully into the room. Becca took the hint.

"Uh, I need to talk to Ty anyway. You OK with this, Lanie?" she asked.

I nodded, and Becca took off down the hall. Logan took a couple steps into the room but then stopped, looking like he wasn't sure he should move any further. Neither of us spoke for a couple of minutes, the silence lingering for an awkward amount of time.

"Logan, what did you want to talk about?" I finally had to urge him on, which gave him the courage, it seemed, to find a seat at my desk. He sat there, fidgeting with his hands, looking around the room.

"Yeah, OK, I know, uh . . ." he stammered. "Here's the thing. There are a couple things I need to apologize for. I'm just trying to figure out where to begin." He had resorted to biting a cuticle in between his words to me, he was so nervous. "The other day in the cafeteria, when we saw Xander, I was a dick." He jumped to standing and paced around the room. I brought myself to the end of my bed, legs hanging over the edge and about to get up when he plopped down next to me. "So, I went to him. Xander."

"You did?" I was shocked. "Why?"

"Well, first, I didn't like that I acted like that, to him, in front of you. So I wanted to apologize for being a dick to him. And I want to apologize to you for acting like that in front of you. I know he's your friend, and I was, I'm . . . well, I just shouldn't have done that. It's a part of me I've been trying to work on, to change."

He turned to face me on the bed, but we were far

enough apart that I was still comfortable. I only then real-ized I was alone in a room with a guy, on a bed. I was a bit nervous, holding the panic in place. I think he saw it on my face. But he continued.

"Yeah, I'm also sorry for what I said to him about you. It wasn't my place to tell Xander anything about your personal life. That was fucked up of me, and I'm sorry. I wanted him to know that I shouldn't have done that and that he needs to keep his mouth shut."

Wow. I was impressed. Not many eighteen-year-old guys would take it upon themselves to initiate a conversa-tion like that.

"I don't know if you can forgive me, but I would like us to still be friends. These last few days have been hard on me, too." He looked sad, his head facing the ground as he spoke. His one hand inched toward me, but I could tell he was unsure if he should touch me. He knew me well, I would give him that.

"Yeah, Logan, we're still friends, don't worry. And thanks for coming to me. I think it's more about us need-ing each other right now, with Becca and Ty ditching us all the time." Talking about them as a couple didn't seem to help the conversation. His open mouth snapped shut, and he clammed up.

"So, how are things with you and Xander now?" I asked, more curious about Xander than anything. Also, trying to change the subject.

"Believe or not, he's a cool guy. I misjudged him. He wasn't a dick about anything when I went to him. I mean, there's no way he could take me." He pulled his shirt up and over his arms as he said this; his smug smile as he showed off his biceps lightened the mood. "But, yeah, he's a nicer guy than I thought. He doesn't give off that vibe at first, but I like him."

I nodded. Nice guy. Yeah, I'm sure Xander *was* a nice guy. But to how many girls? And did I want to be one of those girls?

And Logan and Xander both were under the impression I wasn't interested in a relationship.

But I wasn't, right?

I felt the buzz in my back pocket as I was leaving class. I didn't want to look because chances were high it was him. My decent day would be ruined if I read his messages. But the buzzing against my backside was incessant, forcing me to reluctantly reach for my phone.

Max:

> Lanie, answer your fucking phone
>
> Last chance before I make your life a living hell
>
> Keep your eyes out today

Me:

> Max, I just got out of class, you sent those all in the span of twenty minutes you have to give me more time to answer
>
> can I call you in 5

This was getting harder and harder to handle. Obviously, the talk I had with him before coming to school did no good. He was still acting as if nothing had changed, like we were still together. And what the hell? The last message scared the shit out of me. I'd avoided talking to him on the phone up to this point, only texted. I'd told him I'd call but never did, avoiding the confrontation as much as possible. Maybe one call would end this for good.

Smoothie in hand, I decided I would head to the pond to make the call, since it would likely be the most private spot. However, as soon as I walked out of the cafe, I immediately had a pit in my stomach. It was the exact feeling I got whenever Max was anywhere near me.

I felt him.

Near.

I stopped walking and slowly made my way to the closest bench. Putting on my sunglasses, I hoped they blocked my eyes as they ping-ponged from person to person, trying to catch anything that seemed off.

I thought I had prepared for this, but my shaking hands told a different story.

I was starting to hyperventilate.

"You don't need to say anything. Just sit there and listen, Lanie." Karl had sat down and started talking before I could even react. "Max wants a full report from me every day I'm here, and I'll have to give it to him." I heard something in his voice I wasn't expecting, so I chanced looking at him. The sympathy was evident in his eyes as he kept talking. "You won't see me again, but I'll be here. So as long as you behave and I don't see anything I shouldn't, everything'll be fine."

Why the hell would Max send Karl to watch me?

"I don't . . ."

"Listen, it's better if you don't ask questions. The less you know, the better. Trust me. He's expecting to hear from you. Give him a call. Maybe it'll make things better; maybe he'll call me home." He leaned forward on his knees and blew out a breath as if frustrated with our conversation. With his head hanging low, he turned his eyes toward me before speaking again. "Don't get me wrong, I'll have to do whatever he tells me to do, but I won't like it one bit. So please, Lanie, please just listen to him."

My eyes went wide in horror at his words.

"But Karl, I ended things with him before I left. We aren't together anymore." My voice cracked, the tears barely held back.

"You have no idea who he or his family is, do you?" Karl asked me, his head tilted toward mine.

All I could do was shake my head. My words weren't coming out.

"Well, that's not for me to say. Just know you're taking a risk any time you don't do what he asks of you. I shouldn't even be telling you that, but I like you, Lanie, always have. Be careful, OK?"

At that, he got up and walked away.

I knew my life with that monster was fucked up, but this took it to a whole new level. I was frozen in place, afraid to move, afraid of being followed. My body was shaking from the cryptic words Karl offered about Max and his family. I had known from the beginning that our "relationship" was a farce, our parents integral players. But this had my head spinning with more questions than answers. Knowing I couldn't just sit here, I forced myself to get up.

My walk to the pond was spent building up the nerve

to actually make the call. Karl's visit had shaken me to my core, and every step I took I felt as if he was going to appear.

Plus, Max wasn't the easiest person to talk to. And considering the last time we spoke was my apparent failed attempt to end our relationship, I had no idea what to expect. Now I had Karl telling me I should listen to everything Max told me to do.

I needed to walk a bit around the pond to get away from a few students enjoying the day. Finally, I had some privacy. But my hands were shaking so much I felt like I couldn't even press the buttons on my phone.

But I did. And it started ringing.

I knew he answered because it stopped ringing. But there was silence on the line. And that scared me.

"Hello? Max? Are you there?" My voice was weak, shaking, not the voice of the strong Lanie I became in the past few weeks. It angered me that he had this much control from so many miles away.

"It's about time, Lanie." And then there was more silence. He was trying to control the conversation with his silence, and it was working. I was getting nervous and scared.

"I'm sorry, Max. I've been, uh, really busy getting settled here. Starting classes and getting my work done, learning the layout of the campus, getting to know my roommate." Shit, this was not going well.

"Lanie, shut up."

More silence. And I was shaking, my phone about to come out of my hand.

His words were biting through the phone lines.

I felt the slap on my face, the one I knew he wanted to give me.

I knew I was rambling; his silence did that to me.

I needed to learn to stay silent like he did. That would be better, saying nothing, but I hadn't gotten there yet.

There was not going to be a nice side of Max during this call.

"I'm assuming you were paid a visit today. Karl will be keeping tabs on you. As long as you stay in line, you won't know he's there."

He paused, and I stopped breathing, waiting for him to continue.

My heart was beating out of my chest, and I thought for sure it could be visible through my shirt. I looked around again, this time feeling as though there were eyes on me. Was Karl watching me now?

"There is absolutely no fucking reason you could not pick up the phone and call me. There is absolutely no fucking reason you should not be texting me every night and every morning. I thought the original agreement if you went to school was that you went to class and the rest of the time was spent in your room—that was it. No social life while you're there," Max seethed.

"But before I left, I told you . . ."

"Shut the fuck up, Lanie," Max screamed. "You told me what? That we were over? You don't get a say in that, remember? It has nothing to do with you, or has your stupid little brain forgotten that already? Karl will make sure you stay in line, that you don't do anything stupid. We can't have a repeat of that shit you pulled last year."

Last year. When I thought going to my guidance counselor and reporting his behavior to someone of authority would be the smart thing to do. It didn't turn out the way I'd expected. Instead of the typical response one would expect, the counselor called Max's father directly. Not the police, not my parents—Max's father. That was the first sign I was dealing with a situation out of my hands. One I had no control over.

Until college arrived. My escape clause.

Max was still yelling through the phone. The rest of what he spewed in my ear was so vulgar I started to shut down. It was the only way I'd survived over the years; I had to shut it out, not listen, not hear what he was calling me or telling me he was going to do the next time he saw me. I didn't know how my brain did it. It allowed my head to go someplace else, to escape during the worst of what he said and did. But it didn't change that the abuse was still happening. And even over the phone, it didn't feel any different.

But while my brain shut Max down, it did start thinking of more recent events. Flooding my thoughts were my times with Becca and the guys and how they'd made me feel like I belonged. Our night bowling, our meals together, our hang-out times in the dorm. I had friends again, and I'd started having normal experiences most college kids expected to have. Then there was Xander. There may not have been much between us, but it showed me I could feel comfortable around another guy. I never would have thought that possible after Max. These thoughts were giving me a newfound strength, something I'd never felt before.

I felt . . . hope.

"Lanie, are you listening to me? What the fuck? Are you still there?"

I guess my zoned-out session was longer than normal. But something had changed in me.

Something big.

"Yeah, Max, I'm still here. And I'm listening, but I don't think you're remembering our last conversation before I left for college correctly. I remember it a lot differently than you do." My first mistake was pausing in the conversation. Over the years, I should have learned from him to continue to spew my thoughts.

"What the fuck are you talking about? Whatever the fuck I said was just to make you shut up. I hate it when you cry; you're such a pansy ass."

In my head, I could see the sneer that would be on his face as he spoke.

"Well, if you think back, our conversation went something like this. I said I wanted to go to college, and when you put up a fight, I said I would go to my father. You didn't want me doing that, since you were just getting started with your new job with him—you know, your new image and all. How is the campaign going, by the way? I know your end game is to kick my dad out of the way and take his place eventually, but whatever. He'll probably thank you for it when you do it." I heard Max huffing and puffing on the other end of the line, but I gave him no chance to interject. I had finally learned from him. "So it's unlike last year, when you prevented me from doing what I needed to do then. And I still have no idea how you pulled that one off. How the hell did you have my guidance counselor in your back pocket anyway? A school counselor gets a plea for help about abuse and calls the abuser? That's some sick shit. But I'm done, Max." I was pacing back and forth at this point, wearing a path in front of the bench. "I'm done listening to your every demand. *We are over!* And there's nothing you can do about it!"

And I hung up.

I hated him.

I hated that he had so much control over my life from

over thirteen hundred miles away.

I hated that I allowed him to have that control.

I hated that my whole body responded so strongly to him from so far away.

As I stood there, in front the bench, I felt stuck and frozen in place. My chest felt tight as the first tears sprung loose. Before long, my shirt was wet from crying as I struggled for each breath, my lungs burning.

The pain hurt every muscle, every cell. The sobs racked through my body, but this time, I was alone, truly alone.

No one was going to hit me, or beat me, or berate me for just being me.

And I felt a shift inside.

The tears were still streaming down my face, but I realized something . . .

I.

Was.

Furious.

How dare he have someone follow me?

How dare he tell me I can't have friends?

Finally, I let out a blood-curdling scream.

The birds that were settled on the pond flew away in a rush due to the sudden noise. All the critters in the nearby woods quieted, thinking there was a danger present.

And I guess to them, there was a present danger.

I can only imagine what I looked like, my hair a tangled mess, my eyes red and swollen, and my face blotchy and wet with tears. But since letting out that scream, I had started feeling better. I'd never done that before, and maybe I needed to; the release of emotion felt good, really good.

And I started to think I could do this.

I felt the bindings that tied him to me loosening, and

with a little work, I could wiggle myself a bit freer.

I looked around, took inventory of my surroundings, and realized I was still alone. Feeling shaky, I slumped against the bench to figure out my next step. I looked out to the pond and lo and behold glimpsed the rumored otter that made this place his home.

He seemed to look right at me.

"Hey, dude, what's up?" His little snout peeked over a log on the far edge of the water. "You're probably thinking I'm some lunatic, but I promise I'm not." I laughed out loud to myself, and him, I guess. "You were my witness. You saw me make the biggest change in me I've ever made, little guy. My life's a mess, ya know. I'm doing the best I can, but I think I've decided I have it in me to fight. How will I fight? I don't quite know yet, but I'll figure it out. Baby steps, right, little guy?"

He was still looking at me, as if he was waiting to see if I was done talking to him. In the next moment, his head dipped under leaving a ring of ripples in the water. I couldn't find him again.

But it felt good to say something out loud, to talk about it, even if it was only to an otter. Sooner or later, I would bring myself to tell Becca, and I knew I would feel better for it. Until then, this would have to do.

I realized how late in the day it already was, and I hadn't even eaten yet. Odd that I even felt like eating.

Before I started walking back toward the main part of campus, I texted Becca to see if she wanted to get lunch. She answered immediately, saying she was eating with Ty. I was happy to have company after what I'd gone through, which was another change for me.

Becca texted to say she had grabbed me a sandwich and

a water so I could just find them at their table, which was even better. Once I got there, I looked around and found them canoodling at a corner table.

The walk back allowed my heart rate to settle, but my physical appearance was not something I could address right now. I had pulled my hair into a low ponytail, but I could feel the puffiness of my eyes. No way to fix that. I hoped they were too interested in each other to take notice of my disheveled presentation.

Unfortunately, as soon as I sat down, Logan took the seat across from me.

"Hey, Lanie, what's up with your face? It's all blotchy. Are you having an allergic reaction to something?" As soon as he said that, the others looked at me with inquisitive eyes, and all three of them were waiting for an explanation.

"I'm fine, really. Nothing to see." I tried to hide my face by eating my sandwich and moving my hair to block as much of my eyes as possible. Becca leaned over, close to my ear.

"Lanie, are you OK? Seriously, I need to know that you're OK right now, because you're kind of scaring me."

I knew I was going to have to tell them something.

"I had a blowup fight with Max. I finally told him it was really over," I said, exasperated. "We had a bad fight on the phone, and I was crying. That's all this is. I'm OK, really." I looked at them as I spoke, knowing eye contact helped.

I think they bought that as enough of the truth. It wasn't a complete lie either, just not the whole truth.

I started picking at my sandwich again, hoping they would leave well enough alone, and I think they took the hint. The table was quiet for a few minutes, but then normal conversation started up between the three of them.

"So, is everyone still planning on going to the party in

Xander's room tonight?" Ty asked. "I know I can't wait. It'll be cool to hang out with some guys Logan and I will eventually be rushing with."

I had almost forgotten tonight was the party that Xander had promised me. It seemed so long ago that he made those plans.

"You guys are going to rush Xander's frat?" Becca asked both of the guys.

I didn't know Xander was even in a frat. I wouldn't have thought that. This was a complete shock to me. I'm not sure why. He had the look, I guess, but he didn't come across as the type.

"Yeah, we went to a Greek rush event the other night and had a chance to talk to him and a bunch of the brothers. They're all really cool. We obviously misjudged Xander." Ty's eyes connected with mine, almost in apology. "So, yeah, we're looking forward to hanging out tonight."

This wasn't helping the knot in my stomach at all. I had kind of forgotten about tonight, what with all the craziness of my day. Becca recognized the look on my face, and I knew she was setting herself up for disappointment. She was really looking forward to us going.

"Lanie, you almost done eating?" She gave me a look like she wanted to talk, but I was OK with getting out of here. We said our goodbyes to the guys and left together.

Once we were outside, she hooked her arm through mine and leaned into me.

"I'm not going to push; I know better. I can see it on your face." Her head was now on my shoulder as she paused. "But know that I'm here if you want to talk more about what happened with Max. Also, I can tell you're thinking about bailing tonight; I see it in your body language. I want you to rethink that. I think you'll regret it if you don't go. Remember that Xander really put this together mainly for you."

At that, she stopped us from walking and turned me to look at her.

"I know you feel something for him, and 'guydar' says he feels something for you, too."

"I don't have feelings for . . ."

But Becca cut me off. "OK, you're not sure how you feel about Xander, but I think he likes you. I would hate for you to miss out on an opportunity to see where it could go. But I know your limits, and I'm nervous you've reached them, so I won't push you, I promise. And I won't even ask to dress you for the party if you decide to go."

She smiled at me, grabbed my arm again, and started walking us back to our dorm. All the while, on the inside, I was thinking how lucky I was to have been given such a gift in her. Especially today of all days. I truly believed there was no other person on this campus I could have been placed with who could have "gotten me" any better than she did.

I squeezed her arm as we walked, knowing I had a true confidante by my side.

ecca left me alone for the rest of the afternoon. I think she hoped that would help me feel more like myself and I would decide to go to Xander's. I'm sure I looked like I was reverting back to my old ways, the behaviors I was more prone to at the beginning of the semester. I curled up in bed, facing the wall, not talking.

But as I lay there, I continued to think about what happened by the pond. I knew I wasn't the same person I was back in Texas, not even who I was at the beginning of the semester.

I needed to get up and do this for her tonight.

And to be honest, it wasn't just for her. I wanted to go. "Becca?"

She was flitting around in her closet, trying to look busy. But the moment I said her name, her head popped over her dresser. The apprehensive look on her face made my stomach drop. She was afraid to say the wrong thing and receive the wrong outcome. This wasn't fair to her, and I felt a pang of sadness at the fact that I'd put her through this so early in our friendship.

"I'm sorry I'm such a pain in the ass, and you're right—I promised you and Xander I'd be there tonight. I shouldn't give Max that much power, the ability to ruin my whole day and night, right? So, get your wardrobe skills ready, and maybe even your makeup skills, too!"

The squeal that emerged from that girl's mouth was enough to sound an alarm.

"Oh my God, Lanie, I'm so happy and excited! And you're right—he does not have the right to do that from so far away! Screw him and that Texan horse he rode in on!"

She came tearing around with a handful of tops she must have already decided on when she was hoping this would be my decision. I didn't see much material hanging from the hangers, but I gave her carte blanche to dress me above the waist. At least I knew my legs would be covered.

As I watched her gathering all of her makeup to get started, I realized this was another first I had stolen back from him.

I had a best friend, a real, true best friend.

And he couldn't take her away from me.

Becca looked amazing, her raven curls rolling down her back. She highlighted her bright green eyes with the right brown eyeshadow, her long eyelashes curling almost up above her brows. She wore a short skirt with a red silky tank and tall, knee-high boots.

She was a knockout.

I, on the other hand, paled in comparison next to her, with my platinum white blonde hair and blue eyes so light at times I thought they held no color. My hair was so straight I could never get it to hold a curl, but somehow Becca performed hair magic tonight and I had curls. Not the same gorgeous mane as on her head, but waves nonetheless.

She was good to me with my makeup, kept it simple. I had my jeans on, didn't budge with that, and I still had my Chucks on my feet. "No one will even see them in the dark room" was my argument. The silky black top she chose was definitely not one I would have picked, but it looked good, I guess. It was low cut and accentuated my chest, considering it barely covered my bra. And Becca made me wear her sheer, lacy, black thing that barely counted as a bra as it was. So yeah, I was barely covered.

"You look hot, Lanie. Xander is going to go crazy when he sees you. That bra does all the right things to your tits."

I rolled my eyes, not telling her about the cluster of butterflies that had taken up residence in my stomach. My nerves were suddenly on edge.

"I think you're gonna give Ty a heart attack going into the party looking the way you do. You're going to have every guy in that room clamoring for your attention. I hope he can handle that."

Becca smiled widely at that. "Good. He needs to know what he has. Make him keep working for me." I liked her attitude. It was good to see her assert herself in the relationship. "But he knows deep inside I'm leaving with him at the end of the night, so it's all good. Let's go—let's get drunk tonight!"

She looked at me, walked over, and put her hands on my shoulders. "Hey, I know today was a hard one, and I'm really proud of you for rallying, so if you need to leave, say the word and we're out of there, OK?"

"Becca, what did I do to deserve you? And all the crap I put you through, the drama. Who needs that? I'm going to try, really try, to leave it all behind and be an easier person to be friends with." I reached out and hugged her tight. "Thank you. Thank you for being you."

"You don't need to thank me for being a friend, Lanie. That's what friends do for each other. If it were reversed, I know you'd do the same for me. And never change who you are for anyone, you hear me? You're going through shit, we all do, and I'm here for you to help you get through it. I'm glad I can be." She pushed me away from her and looked at me with stern eyes. "Now, we have to stop because I worked way too hard on both of our faces to have us start blubbering, so let's go!" She grabbed my hand, and we started off down the hall toward Xander's room.

The moment we stepped foot out of our door, we heard the beat of the bass coming from his room. We both got excited, and our feet were racing down the hall to Xander's room. We pushed the door open, and it was lit up with LED lights blinking to the beat of the music.

It was like we were in a club, the atmosphere electric!

Xander saw us immediately, his head snapping our way the moment we walked in. It was as if he'd been waiting for us to come through the door. We walked around the room saying our hellos. Well, I walked—Becca bounced. I was trying to act casual, not look his way. But I couldn't help but sneak a peek every once in a while. And each time

I did, his eyes were on me. His eyes traveled the length of my body, his appreciation apparent. And I didn't expect to appreciate him doing that. Those butterflies in my stomach were doing a dance, and the sweat had started on the back of my neck because of it.

Becca was being her typical social self. And I was the tagalong, pretending to care and listen as I stood by her side. Yeah, progress was made, but this was a whole new level. There had to be almost twenty people crammed into the tiny room, which left little space to maneuver. We were basically shoulder to shoulder. We were talking to two girls, Ashley and Lena, who lived at the opposite end of the hall. They were actually really nice, and I thought I could be friends with them if I wasn't so socially awkward.

But then more eye contact was made.

He started to make his way over to us.

"Hi, Lanie. Hi, Becca. I'm glad you made it. Are your guys coming, too?"

Becca's head snapped toward mine. She pushed her elbow into my side as she screamed to Xander over the music. "Xander! I think you've got some misinformation there, dude! Come see me if you want some clarification!"

He looked at Becca with interested eyes as the two of us found our way to the bucket of drinks. I reached in and pulled out two cold seltzers, handing one to Becca.

"I told you he thought Logan and I were together. It doesn't matter. I shouldn't be pursuing anyone right now. I just got here, just ended a really bad relationship. It's not the right time." Becca was rubbing off on me. I was starting to ramble more and more lately. I cracked open the cold drink and took a long chug. All the while, Becca was staring at me. In disbelief.

"Who said anything about you having to be in a relationship? You know you can just hook up with a guy, right? He's fucking hot. Like, really fucking hot. Most girls would give their left tit to even have him talk to them, let alone look at them the way he looks at you." Her eyes darted back and forth, as if she was checking to make sure no one could hear her. Which was hilarious in a packed room with deafening music. "Just fuck him."

My drink sprayed all over her shirt as I choked and spit.

"Becca!" I whisper-yelled at her. "I am not going to just have sex with him!"

"Why not? We're in college, in the prime of our life. Now's the time to do it. If you don't want to be in a relationship, just use that body of his, but fucking do it. Because, shit, you can't let that go to waste." Her eyes trailed toward Xander as she spoke, obviously enjoying the view. And I couldn't disagree with her there.

He was hot. Really fucking hot.

But I was not at a point in my life where I could use someone for personal pleasure. I didn't know if I could ever do that.

"If that's how you feel, why are you in a relationship with Ty?" It was an honest question.

"I want to be in a relationship. I don't want the occasional fuck right now. I want it all the time, plus I want the cuddles that come with being a couple. But I know you think you don't want that right now, so that's all I'm saying."

Then I saw him walking toward us again. I nervously grabbed Becca's hand to make sure she wouldn't abandon me.

"Lanie," he said as he sidled up next to us. "I'm really glad you made it." He was giving me a huge smile, one that put his dimple on full display.

It made my knees weak.

"Yeah, I made it." I smiled back at Xander, a real smile like he gave me.

But his eyes held contact with mine for a moment longer than was natural. Someone should have looked away by now. But then another girl came up and grabbed his arm, pulling him away. He hesitated but gave in and walked away with her.

Talk about mixed messages. Hoping Becca had seen that, I turned to her, noticing an incredulous look on her face.

"Don't worry, I saw that, and no, you're not seeing things. He did stare at you, he did make it seem like it was just the two of you for a brief moment, even with that girl all over him, but then bam, he up and left. And all to say the same damn thing he already said to us? I think I need to go have a talk with him, Lanie. Set him straight."

"No!" I screamed. So loud people around us turned and looked. I grabbed a hold of her arm, pulling her back as she started toward him. "No," I continued, a bit quieter. "Don't, it's OK. He's talking to all those girls now. Don't make a scene." That was the last thing I wanted after the day I'd had.

"I got you, girl. All I need to do is quietly let him know that you and Logan are definitely not an item and you're on the market. Trust me."

She stalked toward him on a mission, and I didn't want to watch.

But it was like watching a car wreck: I had to.

She discreetly grabbed a hold of him and talked in his ear as best she could to keep it private. I had no idea exactly what she was saying, but I knew the moment he was told the news.

His eyes jerked toward me and had a different look about them. From across the room, I saw a look of want, a look of understanding, and a look of apology all wrapped up in one.

Becca gave him a triumphant smile and came back my way. I couldn't look over there anymore. I was mortified at this point. She grabbed me and twirled me around to the music.

"You can thank me later! And shit, he smells fantastic! Let's go dance!"

She grabbed my hand and led me to the middle of the room where others were already grinding and moving to the music. We found ourselves grinding up against new friends from the floor, now no longer strangers. By my third drink, the alcohol removed any remaining inhibitions I had, my body responding to years of pent-up frustration as I bounced from every guy and girl in the corner Becca and I were in. My eyes kept seeking Xander out, connecting, lingering. But he kept his distance. I was working up the nerve to ask him to come dance with us. He kept watching me dance and would smile. But then his attention would go back to the barely dressed girls that were hanging all over him.

I wasn't enjoying this game we were playing with each other.

That was when Ty and Logan sauntered through the door. They went straight to Xander, who pointed me and Becca out. All three heads pivoted in our direction before the guys began their trek toward us through the crowd. It took some time, as they stopped to say hello to other frat brothers along the way. They made this tiny dorm room feel enormous with how long their journey to us took.

Becca grabbed Ty immediately and started grinding up against him. "Finally, Ty. Where the hell have you guys been all night? I want to dance with you!"

That left Xander, Logan, and me. It was only slightly awkward.

"Hey, Lanie, I'm soooo glad you made it tonight. How 'bout a drink after the day you had?" Logan slurred.

Shit, that was not what I needed him saying.

And right on cue . . .

"What happened today, Lanie? You OK?" Xander's eyes pinched together, and I heard the worry in his voice.

"I'm fine, really."

"She's fine, Xaannderr. We got her. We're her crewww, and I'm her guy. I've got Lanie covered, dontcha worry."

Oh my God, I couldn't believe he said that. And Logan was already drunk. I didn't know where he and Ty were before they came here, but he was swaying as he stood in front of us.

Xander picked up on it, too, anger pouring from his eyes. The two of them may have been on better terms the other day, but Logan had done a fine job of destroying that in one sentence. And with Logan's words, I was sure Xander wasn't going to believe what Becca told him. This entire night was on track to be an utter failure.

"Well, that's good news, Logan, that you're her *crew* and her *guy*. Hope you're sober enough to take good care of her." Xander glared at me before returning to the posse waiting on him.

My anger toward Logan was about to boil over as I stormed away in search of Becca. His attempts to follow me, as he stumbled around the room on my tail, enraged me more. Finally finding her in a dark corner with Ty, I pushed through the growing crowd and pulled her away by the arm. The look on my face held a clear message.

"What's wrong?" she asked with as much panic in her voice as was on my face.

"You will never believe what Logan just did!" Her face fell as I told her, and she tried to calm me down. We looked over toward the guys, Ty trying to hold Logan up he so was drunk. "This night is not going the way I wanted it to."

"Don't worry—let's go dance. Forget about Logan. Let him do his thing; ignore him tonight. Xander will see he means nothing to you. He was really excited when I told him, Lanie. Just stay away from Logan and keep making those googly eyes at Xander that you always do." She made it sound easy, like it was just going to happen. She and I both moved back over to the people we were dancing with earlier, trying to steer clear of Logan.

But she eventually ditched me for Ty, and it felt like too much work. Xander was mad, and I didn't want to be around Logan for another minute. The only option at this point was to leave. My bed was calling me. It was destined to be a bad night from the beginning of the day anyway. I should have read the signs from the start.

But in the next moment, Logan was standing by my side. He reached over and put a heavy arm over my shoulder, using me to hold himself up. "Hey, Lanie, where didja dis'pear to? I was looking for you."

If it was possible, he sounded even more intoxicated. I should have left when I could have. I looked around for Becca or Ty, hoping they would come help me, but they were nowhere to be found. Then I saw a small couch in the corner.

"Logan, let's get you over there. I think you need to sit down for a bit. How much have you had to drink already?" As I tried to move his large frame, his lumbering steps made him crash into party goers on the way. I could smell the booze on him. It smelled like hard liquor, and a lot of it. I pushed him onto the sofa once we got through the crowd.

"Whatcha mean, Lanie? I'm good. I wanna dance with you. I've been waiting for this night all week, waiting to be wi' you. Come on, let's dance."

He tried to get up from the loveseat by pulling on me.

I felt it happening but couldn't stop it.

He pulled on my arms to stand up, but he was so big and heavy; I couldn't move away, and I felt myself going down.

I tried to pry my arms from his iron grip, but there was no way that was happening, and the next thing I knew, I was pulled down onto his body, splayed across his lap.

To any outsider, it easily could have looked like I was intentionally on top of him on the couch.

He moved quickly, pulling me toward him once I was there.

His arms were around me instantly, making me wonder if he hadn't orchestrated this.

I was flustered, and I didn't react right away. But when I did, I put my hands on his chest and pushed myself up, our eyes connecting. The look there told me he wanted to be exactly where we were.

I felt trapped.

I needed to get off him right then.

"Logan, let go of me please." My voice was quiet but stern. I started to try to get up, pushing against his chest harder, but he wouldn't let go of me. We were in a dark corner of the room and the music was loud. No one could hear me.

"Lanie, let's sit here . . . togever . . . fer a while. I like you on top of me. You feel soooo good, just how I knew you'd feel." He said this into my ear, the way *he* would have, the hot breath mixing with the alcohol. He started moving his hands over the backs of my thighs, and they were moving up toward my ass.

I started panicking.

All my senses went into overdrive. In the past, I would have lain here passively, let Max do what he wanted.

But this wasn't the past, and this wasn't Max.

I couldn't let someone else do this to me.

I wouldn't. I found new strength.

And I started fighting back.

I pushed as hard as I could with both hands, trying to gain leverage, but his hard chest wasn't giving an inch. His large hands were roving over my body, trying to keep me still, to keep me from moving. Both his arms wrapped around me, holding me tight up against him, and my labored breaths seemed loud in my own head. I wanted to move my knees, my legs, but they were pinned by his, our limbs an entangled web.

I wasn't getting anywhere, his large frame too strong for my small body.

I started feeling the hopelessness settle in.

Then I realized I was screaming and crying. The next phase for me was to shut down because I knew I wasn't going to be able to fight him off.

"What the fuck are you doing, Logan? You sick motherfucker!"

I felt myself being lifted off Logan by strong arms while Logan's body was being dragged away from me. There were so many bodies, arms, and fists flailing, it was hard to distinguish who was doing what. I knew it was all happening fast, but it felt like it was in slow motion.

I was pushed aside, I don't know by whom, and wound up on the floor. I felt a new set of arms wrap around me and knew immediately it was Becca. She was saying soothing words in my ear, but I couldn't discern what they were. Everything was a blur. I continued to see punches being thrown, then Logan being dragged out of the room.

"What happened, Lanie? Are you OK?" Becca was looking me straight in the face now, concern in her eyes.

I was getting kind of tired of people having to look at me with concern in their eyes.

We were sitting on the small couch together, and I was trying to catch my breath. The tears were still coming, and I was trying to form into words what had happened when Xander walked over, his hand covered in blood.

"Lanie," Xander's voice boomed. It was full of concern but tinged with anger. "I need to know you're OK after what I saw him doing to you." His hands shook as he stood there, the fury rolling off him. "He was assaulting you, and fuck, you couldn't get away. I saw it happening from across the room and got to you as soon as I could." Becca's eyes grew larger and larger the more she heard what Xander had to say. She couldn't understand the words coming from his mouth.

"Logan was attacking you, Lanie? Oh my God, that can't be. Are you sure? Why would he do that? He likes you."

I stiffened in her arms. She backed away, obviously feeling the change in me.

She didn't believe us?

"Becca, why don't you go with Ty and take care of Logan? He's a mess anyway. I'm shutting down the party.

I'll take care of Lanie."

She looked at me, then at Xander, and shook her head, not sure what to make of this situation. She stood up and walked away.

I think that broke me more than I was expecting it to, new tears forming. Xander looked at me but stepped into the center of the room.

"That's it, guys. Party's over, nothing to see, everyone out!" he yelled at the top of his lungs.

I startled at the anger in his voice. Everyone who was still in the room scampered about and was gone in a matter of seconds. I guessed they heard something in his voice as well.

I watched him as he locked the door after the last person was ushered out. He kept his hands on the back of the door, his back to me, for much longer than he should have. I felt as if I could see the anger emanating from his body as he stood there, calming himself, physically shaking it away.

Was he mad at me?

Did he think I brought this on myself?

He continued to grasp the knob, his knuckles turning white. Eventually, his hands were gripping his hair, his fingers nervously running through it. It appeared as if his hands were trembling. I continued to watch him from the couch, cowered in its corner.

As I waited, I saw the transformation in his body; the anger finally dissipated. I still didn't know if he was mad at me or not. The anger that emanated from him a moment ago, well, it scared me.

And I was starting to feel like I wanted to leave the room.

But then he backed away from the door and slowly turned to face me. What I saw in his face, his eyes, surprised me.

No, it nearly broke me.

There were tears welled up in his eyes, and they started spilling over.

I had to look away, not wanting to fully come to terms with the gravity of what really happened to me again.

How many challenges could one person face in a day? I still hadn't completely come to terms with the fact that Max had someone watching me. That was coupled with the verbal lashing I'd suffered through earlier, and then this.

The strength I thought I gained by standing up to Max had drained, slowly taken with every stroke of Logan's hands on me.

Xander's presence as he approached the couch was that of a warrior who had returned from battle. His muscles still rippled from tension, his towering height imposing as he raised his arms, hands behind his head, almost in defeat.

He seemed to be such a dichotomy, his teary-eyed expression clashing with a surge of hostility that seemed to roll off him. The intensity forced me to look away, yet again.

But then I felt him before I saw him, the couch dipping with his weight. I was curled up in a ball on the other end, my head buried in my knees, which I held tight. I turned my head slightly, one eye peeking above my knee, enabling me to glance his way. His outstretched hand was tentatively approaching, him not sure if he could touch me yet.

I wasn't sure if he could touch me yet.

But then I felt it. His gentle fingers, first on my arm, then up to my shoulder. Trying to affirm that he was here for me. Not pushing, but waiting. I sat there, still, figuring out what my next move should be.

Lifting my head, I looked at him full on only to see his red-rimmed eyes rivaling the look of mine. My cheek was resting on my knees, new tears cascading down. His touch didn't waver, rubbing consistent circles against my shoulder.

And I didn't want to respond to his touch right now, not after what happened.

But it was impossible, inevitable.

His touch ignited a fire inside of me, a spark that went straight to my heart. He seemed to know exactly what I needed.

I let go of the restraint I was holding on to.

It snapped and seemed to allow me to feel something again for someone else. That feeling deep inside that had been forced into hiding, forbidden to be presented to the world for years. The bonds were being shed, one by one, simply by his touch. I felt myself pulling away from those bonds, trying to stay away.

Our eyes met again, the connection unmistakable, strong.

And I launched myself into his arms.

And he caught me.

He wrapped his arms around me with such strength, holding on in a way that made me feel safe.

Everything unleashed from inside of me. The utter devastation that this happened again, with someone else, was hitting me.

His hands were stroking my head, his fingers running through my hair. Xander wasn't trying to stop me from crying. He knew I needed this and let me get it out. Moving me from the couch to his lap, he kept me in his arms. I dropped my head to his shoulder, my arms holding him as if my life depended on it.

And at that moment, I think it did.

The torrent of emotion rushing from me caused my body to shake and shudder as he held on.

Eventually, my tears ran out. I was still hiccupping from the massive cry, having trouble breathing, calming down. He took a hold of my face, his fingers guiding me to look at him.

The pain I saw in his face, pain for me, was startling.

He wasn't mad.

He was devastated and broken along with me.

"I know these tears aren't just about tonight. Your soul is damaged. I see it and recognize it, Lanie. You can talk to me. I'm here for you. We're the same, you and me. And you may not feel ready to talk, I get that, but when you are, I'm here."

His thumbs were rubbing the tender skin under my eyes, attempting to keep it dry, to no avail. But then I saw something in his deep, blue eyes.

I saw recognition, understanding. And I saw his pain.

Chapter 8

$\mathcal{I}$ don't know how long we sat there, silent, him holding me. He continued to rub my back, maybe to let me know he was still there. I felt like it could also be to keep me awake, to encourage me to talk.

And I wanted to. I was trying to work up the nerve. But I felt if I started, it was all going to come bubbling out, and I needed to be sure I was ready for someone to know all of my darkness.

I didn't want Xander to see the real me, the one on the inside. The real me might scare him away. But the silence was hurting. I needed sounds, words, something. I somehow found my voice, though it was hoarse from all the crying. I pushed myself out of his arms and turned toward him, surprised at what I saw.

"Why do *you* look sad, Xander?"

He sat up a little straighter before answering me, seeming to be looking for the right words.

"I'm sad for what that piece of shit put you through tonight, claiming to be your friend. No friend would do that." But he no longer looked sad. His hands rolled into fists at the mention of Logan. He took a minute to calm himself down before he could continue.

He looked at me, then bent his head over his knees, trying to gather his words as he stared at the floor.

"My shit happened a long time ago, Lanie, but I'm in a good place now. I don't know, maybe you hearing about it could help you realize there's hope." He stood and paced a bit. "If I'm going to tell these stories tonight, though, I need another beer." He chuckled as he said this. I was glad to hear the laugh, happy he returned from that angry place. "Are you thirsty for anything?"

"Do you have any water?"

He nodded as he went to his fridge. He came back with our drinks and settled on the couch again.

He pulled my legs up onto his lap, getting me comfortable, while I was lying on the couch facing him. He pulled my sneakers off and started rubbing my feet. This seemed intimate for two people who didn't know each other well.

He settled in and popped open his beer, taking a long draw on it. Looking over, he appeared ready to start his tale.

"Not too many people have been told this. As a matter of fact . . ." He took pause, lost in his own thoughts for a moment. "I don't think I've told it to anyone. The only people who know about it are the ones who lived it. So, yeah, you're kind of special."

I got the feeling he was saying this to make me feel more comfortable. Regardless, it worked, and I laid my head back and looked at this beautiful creature, amazed at how he was capable of calming me.

He was leaning back on the couch, which looked ridiculously small with his six-foot-three-inch frame hanging off it. His legs were basically on the floor they were so long, his head leaning on the back cushion, his eyes staring up at the ceiling. His one hand held his beer while the other lazily rubbed my foot. I could get a good look at his profile from this angle, and it was that of a model's. The angles of his cheekbones and jawline would be sought after by many professional companies for sure. His dark hair, a tad long, just below his ears, gave him the allure I'm sure most of the girls were attracted to.

I guess myself included.

And that scared me for so many reasons.

Xander turned his head and looked at me. I don't think he intended his look to elicit what it did, but the heat of his stare would have brought me to my knees if I were standing. And that was exactly why I was scared. I felt as though I couldn't trust my own feelings.

I was just attacked. And hysterical.

Yet a simple look from him was making my breathing hitch. It made no sense. Thankfully, he started talking again.

"Lanie, when I first saw you earlier this semester, I saw a darkness behind your eyes that I recognized. I knew you were living through something I was very familiar with. Then, when I would see you struggling with your emotions in crowds, and you trying to deal with handling your new friendships, I knew there was a connection. I've wanted to reach out to help you. I know how it can feel—near impossible to come up from the depths of that despair you've been feeling. I know because I was there, but I survived it. Not only did I survive, but I'm thriving. It's not easy. I won't lie and say it is, but it gets easier."

He stopped at this point, seeming to need a moment to gather his thoughts. During his pause, I thought about what he said.

That was where I felt I was, at the bottom, with no one to help me up.

"There's something else I won't lie to you about, especially considering what I learned about Logan tonight and what he did to you. I'll admit, I did think you were together. I thought the four of you were a neat little package."

None of that surprised me. Considering the circumstances of the past week between him and Logan, I was surprised when Xander accepted his apology. Now this.

"Wanting to help you is only part of it. I'm attracted to you, like, big time." A big smile spread when he said this, his dimple deep. "And I feel like we have a connection beyond our, I don't know, past shit we've both gone through. But I also know with the demons you're fighting, you're in no position to be in a relationship, let alone start a new one." He paused for a moment. "I didn't need Logan to tell me about your ex. It was evident you had a past, but knowing it's due to a crazy ex, well. Let's just say it's info that's good to have. But I wanted to be honest with you about how I feel. I felt you deserved that."

My heart was racing. I didn't know how to respond. I wanted to do something, say something. He deserved it after that. And I thought I had feelings for him as well. I knew I was past denying that.

The silence was lasting too long, even for us.

"You don't have to say anything." His eyes focused on me while he spoke. "I can see the wheels spinning in your head. It's OK. You've had a rough night. I wanted you to know, that's . . ."

"Xander," I interrupted him, "I'm glad you told me that." I turned and pressed my head into the couch cushion, too shy to look at him, knowing what I was about to declare. My beet-red face on full display, even in profile, I spoke into the couch as I continued. "I have feelings for you, too. But it scares me, because you're right—it's not the right time. If you only knew what was going on in my life, you'd understand."

His hand moved up to rub my calf, to reassure me. "It's OK. I'm more than OK with us being friends. Let's start there."

It wasn't what I really wanted.

But what I really wanted couldn't happen. There were too many dark secrets, ones I wasn't willing to share yet. And the one who caused them, he would not go away without a fight, it seemed. Neither he nor the friend of his watching me.

"But I'd still like to tell you, if you're up for it. I think it could help," he offered.

"Yeah, as long as you're willing to share it, I want to hear it. And yeah, I want us to be friends. I'd love that, too." I smiled at him, a genuine smile, and he smiled back.

It was such a simple moment, but one that held such gravity.

Because there was now trust between us, something I've never truly had with another person, ever. Our pasts, our secrets.

And I think he felt it, too.

He took a few moments, seeming to prepare himself, or maybe to allow me to prepare myself, I wasn't sure. I could sense his hesitation, him deciding if continuing was a good idea. But eventually, the words started coming.

"I'm going to start with the end of my story for you so you'll understand that I'm OK." Another pause, our eyes connecting, his hand reaching out and finding mine, our fingers entwined. I had to look at our hands, the moment suddenly very intense. "My dad's in jail, so I need you to understand everything I'm going to tell you resulted in him being punished the right way, OK?"

My breath hitched the moment he said this, and I wasn't sure I wanted him to continue. I yanked my hand from his and pulled my legs under my chin. I felt myself curling inward, my body beginning to tremble.

"Lanie, look at me. I'm right here, and I'm safe. Everything happened years ago. We made it through, and I'm OK." He reached out for me, trying to pry my hands from their iron grip on my legs. "How about the abridged version, not everything?"

He allowed me a minute. We both just sat there, his hands on mine, frozen. Eventually, I relented, allowing him to bring me to his lap again. He held me close, holding my head to his shoulder. "I'm right here. I'm OK, and so are you. You hear me, right?"

I nodded. "I hear you," I whispered in his ear. "But I don't want to even imagine your father doing unimaginable things to you. At least the monster in my life is not someone related to me. I couldn't imagine if it were. I'm sorry."

I looked up. I needed to see him. He looked determined, not wavering in his resolve to continue if I was ready.

"Hey, no apologies, and I really just need to know you're OK with me telling you more."

It was a simple touch of his fingers to my chin, lifting

my face to see for himself how I was. But it felt as though his whole body had touched mine, the warmth in his one fingertip spreading throughout me. Nothing was abrupt or harsh with him, so unlike what I was used to. He continued to gently tip my face up toward his, waiting.

"I'm good. I want you to tell me. I want to know how you got through this." My eyes pleaded with his, and he saw something that told him I was OK. I felt a strong desire to hear this, a compulsion to know his story, how he survived.

I heard the change in his breathing, felt it even up against his chest. He was nervous. He took another swig of beer and cleared his throat.

"One of the things that probably made it a bit easier for me was I had my older brother during all of it. We were both going through it together. My dad was abusing both of us, including my mom. Thankfully, if there is anything to be thankful about, all he did was hit us, ya know, no other type of abuse. He kept it strictly to beating us up and fucking with our heads." He smirked a bit after saying this, acknowledging the irony of his comment.

"I don't know how long it had been going on with my mom before it started with us, but he started beating on me and Bryce, that's my brother, when I was six and he was ten. Before that, things seemed kind of normal. He was never the kind of dad who hugged a lot or anything. He did yell, but he didn't hit before that. It was little things at first. He would slap me or Bryce across the face if we talked back to him or Mom, but then he would apologize. Our mom, she would try to keep us safe from him the best she could, but there was nowhere she could go. There was no money unless we stayed with him. I guess, looking back, she should've taken us to a shelter with her, but I think it's better how things worked out in the end."

His words paused, but his hand did not. The circles Xander rubbed on my back made me feel so comfortable with him that I mindlessly found myself doing the same on his stomach. But I think it was helping him in some way, too. He let out a soft sigh before continuing.

"As you can imagine, the beatings got worse as we got older and bigger. It was as if he had to keep proving he could always beat us, no matter how much we grew up. Bryce and I would hear our parents fighting at night, and then he'd beat up our mom. Eventually, it got to be too much. By the time I was thirteen and Bryce was seventeen, we were pretty big guys already. We had already had several trips to the ER because of him, all of them blamed on fights between brothers. But then we decided we'd had enough."

Xander paused with his story again, although this time he seemed to have to gather the strength to continue. My hand stilled on his stomach as he sat there, while his hand moved up to my head, fingers running through my hair. He pulled my head closer to his, and I could feel his lips putting a gentle kiss on the top. He took a deep, cleansing breath before continuing.

"We knew that if we didn't fight back against him, and soon, one of us would not survive him. The cops were at our house all the time, got called by the neighbors, but my mom was always too afraid to press charges. We decided we would have to come up with a way to do it without her. We learned my brother, as a seventeen-year-old, had some rights now, so we hoped we could file the charges against him ourselves the next time we had to. Like clockwork, the following day, the beatings started. He started with me, but I was OK with that. Better me than my mom."

I could feel the anxiety building in him, the muscles under my cheek tensing up and his legs tapping on the floor.

"Xander," I whispered, interrupting his story. "This seems like it's too hard for *you* right now. You don't have to keep doing this." Hearing what he went through as a child was horrific. I wasn't sure if I wanted to hear the whole story anymore.

I tried to stop them, but the tears welled up and spilled over, streaming onto his arm.

"Shit, don't cry. See, you're not ready to hear this. I don't want to make you upset." He twisted me to face him, looking torn as to what to do.

"Xander, your story is sad. It deserves tears. I'm OK, really."

He lifted my chin before he said, "Just remember, there's a happy ending. My dad's in jail."

He rubbed my bottom lip with his thumb, and his other fingers traced under my eyes, wiping away the wetness. I tried to give him a small smile, my attempt at letting him know I was OK. But it may have come across more as an invitation as his thumb went back to my lip.

Such an intimate moment brought on by the pain we both had in our lives. But then we settled back into our spots on the couch.

"The story is almost done." He paused, then started talking again. "That last night, Bryce made as much noise as possible in the house. We needed to make sure the neighbors called the police. We knew our mother never would. He started throwing things at our dad, which we never did before, and it took him off guard. This time, we really fought back. The two of us ganged up on him, and if the police didn't break it up, I think we actually would have done some real damage to him.

"In the end, I had a broken arm and nose, and Bryce broke his hand. He told the cops he wanted to press charges against my father for assault. They weren't sure it was possible, but they had come to our house so many times hoping to take him in, so they just went ahead and did it. I'm not sure if it was legal or not, but we got the ball rolling. Once he was in police custody, it gave my mother enough courage to do something about it. She finally pressed charges herself.

"We found out later, through lots of therapy together, the reason she never followed through was because he threatened to kill one of us if she ever did." He let out a relieved sigh, obviously happy to be done telling his tale.

"So, there you have it: the abbreviated version of my fucked-up childhood and family. My mom is one of my best friends now. And my brother, who is now a cop, is my best friend. It's ironic he became an officer. We had so many run-ins with them over the years, especially me. But I guess he found himself on the right side of the law in the end. And we got through it, Lanie. Not easily, but we got through it."

He sat upright and pulled me to look at him with a smile on his face. "I don't expect you to tell me anything about what you're going through, but please know, when you're ready, I'm here."

We sat that way, each studying the other's face, searching for what emotions we were feeling. I knew he was trying to discern if I was ready. Ready to divulge all of my deepest, darkest secrets.

"I'm sorry you had to deal with that as a kid. That must have been terrible." I leaned into him, putting my head on his shoulder, unable to take the intensity of his gaze any longer.

Yet I had never felt more comfortable with another man in my entire life. This felt perfect. Even after the awful story he had told me, I never wanted to leave this spot, safe in his arms.

It was as if all the storms raging inside of me were calmed and stilled by his touch.

"But we made it," he said. "We had each other, and we made it. That's the point of my story." He leaned in closer, his mouth next to my ear as he spoke.

Feeling his breath close to me sent shivers through my body and stilled my breathing. I knew he saw the effect he continued to have on me.

Whispering, he said, "I want to be here for you, Lanie."

His words stirred my hair as he spoke, the meaning of them, however, going straight to my heart.

"I want to hold your hand when you stand tall to face this, and I'll be there to catch you if you fall."

Chapter 9

"His name is Max. And I was sixteen and he was eighteen when we were, um, introduced."

I blurted out the beginning of my story to Xander but then sat there, silent, for a long time, twisting a thread on my jeans. Contemplating how much I was willing to share had me stalling. He would look at me differently, because I was . . .

I was dirty.

Max made me dirty.

But I'd been desperate for this for so long, for someone I could tell. Desperate to get it out of me. And I didn't think a better person to tell would ever come along. I needed to summon the courage to continue.

Xander felt my struggle.

"Lanie, this is your story, your timeline. Don't feel

that you have to tell me tonight, or ever." He spoke these words into my hair as held me in his arms. I felt the tears welling up again, the burning knot in my throat telling me they would spill over soon.

Why was crying felt so strongly in the throat? The knot I felt there made it hard to swallow my own spit. It was as if my throat was closing and all the saliva was being drawn into my tear ducts to be expelled from my body in another place. I was having such trouble breathing, I had to sit up. Gravity made the tears fall, and Xander saw them.

"Hey, I don't want this to make you go through a whole thing again." He was rubbing my face as the hiccups started, as I tried to hold in the sobs. Tired of needing to be consoled by everyone all the time, I turned my face away from him.

"Xander." My voice wasn't strong, but I continued. "As tired as I am of crying, I'm more tired of these secrets being bottled up inside of me. I've been alone with this for too long." As I finished talking, I pulled out of his reach, to the other end of the couch.

He was too much of a distraction.

The hint of dejection faded quickly once he realized I was settling in and getting ready to talk.

"Ya know," I started with a meek voice, "I missed my prom, homecoming dances, football games, and bonfires, all because of him. All because he wouldn't go with me or wouldn't let me go without him. So many 'firsts and onlys' I will never get back because of him." My fingers resorted to fiddling with the loose thread on my jeans. Anything to not look him in the eye. But I knew I needed to keep going.

"I think if that was the worst of it, I wouldn't be this damaged girl sitting here, but you probably already know that isn't where my story ends. And unlike you, I can't give you the ending, because I don't know it yet." I looked at him after saying that. I needed strength at that moment, and I was hoping he could provide it.

He reached out for me to come to him, to sit with him in his arms. I only shook my head.

"Let me finish first."

And then silence.

"The abridged version, that's what we're doing tonight, right?" I asked. His slow nod was full of encouragement. "So, he took a lot of other things away from me I can't ever get back . . ." I felt the knot return to my throat, but I was determined to finish this without crying. "He, uh, would tell me what I could and couldn't wear. He was controlling. But in the beginning, he would do it in a way that made it seem like he cared, like I looked prettier in the things he told me to wear."

I looked at Xander, his expression calm. But when I looked at his hands, I could see them in fists, him trying to control his anger. I understood. I was angry, too.

"Of course, it got worse. He would hit me, especially if I tried to stand up to him about anything." I paused. "But then he would try to make it up to me. He would apologize, buy me gifts, and in the beginning, I actually believed him. To some extent, I still do. He's damaged, and I know there is a part of him that doesn't want to be doing what he does to me." I couldn't look at Xander, worried he might think me weak for believing that. "By this time, he was working for my dad, in my dad's office, so he felt really important. My dad is a congressman back in Texas. Max's attitude about things kept getting worse, and how he treated me along with it." There was so much more to tell; I knew I was beating around the bush. I kept wringing my hands together in my lap until I jolted off the couch, Xander taken by surprise in the quiet room. I started pacing, needing to move.

"Fuck! I just need to say it. I need to get this off my chest, Xander, but it's hard. It's like once I say it, it's so real." I turned to look at him. He was sitting on the edge of the couch, hands together between his knees, eagerly awaiting my next words.

Yet I believed he already knew them.

"Max . . . raped me. Repeatedly. It started the first night we were together."

There. I said it. I said the words. They hurt, but they didn't break me. My dark secret was out, and I was still breathing, still standing, the earth still spinning. Looking at Xander, though, I knew what I would see.

But I didn't see it. I didn't see the sympathy I was expecting. Instead, there was a small smile on his beautiful face as he stood up and took measured steps toward me. His hands came up to my shoulders, holding me at arm's length, his head dipping down so our faces were level and our eyes could stay connected.

"Lanie, I'm proud of you."

I had divulged my scariest, darkest secret. Yet, rather than filling my life with more sorrys and back rubs, he gave me encouragement and the idea I could do this.

"Thank you." I smiled back at him, the relief of the moment settling in. He guided me back to the couch, pulling me toward him, and I willingly fell into his arms. We sat like that for a few silent moments, exhaustion setting in. But then I felt him getting restless, movement in his body beneath me.

We weren't done.

"So, I guess it's safe to say your parents don't know

much of what has gone on between the two of you?"

My head snapped up, fear and shame slamming into my chest.

The tremble started slowly, but it built, and I knew he felt it as his hold on me increased, trying to keep me from slipping away completely. My breaths were shallow already, but then were barely there.

I felt the blackness coming for me, ready to soothe me in its veil.

"Hey, Lanie, stay with me. It's OK." His hands grabbed my face, my neck, holding me up. "Make sure to breathe. Take even breaths and stay with me. Look at me."

I found his eyes, those beautiful blue eyes, staring into my soul. He was trying to read my mind, and he was digging deep, learning more of my dark secrets, the skeletons in my closet. But I didn't want him to know them all, not yet.

I wasn't ready.

He wasn't ready.

"Not yet, Xander. I can't tell you more, not yet." I curled into a ball, my breaths coming too fast, the sweat dripping down my back, between my breasts. I felt the room starting to spin, my mind starting to go blank.

And that I was ready for, ready to give in to its darkness and let it take me away like it always did.

Then suddenly I was cold, his touch gone fast. I wasn't expecting to miss it, to want it back. But then I felt him put a cold water bottle up against the back of my neck, my head.

"Here, take a drink." He came back to sit with me, his arms around me, comforting me. I took a big gulp of water before settling back against him. The drumming of his heart was all I felt as my head rested upon his chest. The sound was a comfort in the silence of the room. "Take your time, or be done, whatever is best."

How quickly it changed with that one question about my parents. My strength sapped, gone.

We sat this way for a long time, him holding me. As if he was holding me together so I wouldn't fall apart.

And I felt if I had told him all my secrets, I would fall apart. I was barely being held together by a thread, my story the thread keeping it whole as much as it could.

I never thought I would ever tell my story to anyone.

There I was in the arms of someone I felt could handle hearing the whole sordid tale.

Someone who could survive it with me.

Just not yet.

"I'm not ready to say more about my past. But, I don't know, maybe I can tell you a little about what's going on with him now."

Xander stilled slightly under me, seemingly not sure if he should move or not. Maybe in anticipation of what I was going to say next.

I couldn't believe I was going to do this, reveal another part of my darkness to someone. Of course, a part of me was terrified of the outcome, the possibility that Xander wouldn't want to deal with someone with so many issues, so much darkness surrounding them. But there was also a part of me that was eager, longing, even, to finally release the locked-up demons, the storms constantly battering my soul.

I turned my head slightly and found his profile. His eyes were patient. His body was a contradiction though, full of tension. I hoped I wasn't making a grave mistake, and he read my hesitation. His hand came to my cheek, soft, caressing.

"Lanie, only when you're ready, and only what you

want to tell me. But I won't lie, I already hate him." The tension continued to roll through his muscles, which were coiled tight as he held me. I could feel him trying to relax, our bodies clinging to each other.

But his declaration soared through my veins and gave me strength.

He was on my side; I had a confidante.

"Max continues to bother me here, harasses me with calls and texts." I held out my phone. Easier for him to read them himself. He scrolled through all the texts I'd been getting over the past month. "Even though I tried to end things with him before I came to school, it's only been getting worse. He threatens to come here, but then this week, he sent someone he works with, a friend, to follow me."

Xander was speechless at first.

"Wait, what did you say?" The slow pivot of his head as he turned toward me displayed the disbelief in his eyes. It was as if he was waiting for me to change my story, as if it couldn't be possible. "You're serious, aren't you?" His eyes remained on me, waiting, hoping. When I only continued to look deep into his stare, I could see his body finally give in to acceptance.

"Holy shit, Lanie, this is insane. How are you dealing with this while taking your classes and doing your work? And now this shit with Logan?" He shook his head in disbelief. "You're strong, Lanie, so fucking strong." He handed me my phone as if he didn't want to see any more of what Max had to say to me on it.

"You've told Becca about all of this, right?" he asked.

I looked at him and gave a slight shake of my head.

Xander's eyes widened. "She doesn't know?"

"You're the first person I've told. Ever," I proclaimed.

And that statement broke me.

Emotions I didn't know were in me needed to come out. I was unraveling.

Again.

Xander immediately grabbed a hold of me as the sobs racked through my body.

Again.

I was holding on to him for dear life.

Again.

I felt like I wouldn't survive this. It was the third time today my body and soul were deceiving me, and I couldn't control the heaving howls coming out of me. Could someone die from crying too much? I felt like I could. I felt like my body was about to give out.

"I . . . can't . . . do . . . this . . . any . . . more . . ."

I could barely talk, hyperventilating as I was trying. But there was a shift in the air, the atmosphere surrounding us. His hands found my shoulders as he steadied me, his fingers trailing down my arms, him pulling my hands up to his chest.

"Lanie, you don't have to do this alone anymore. That's what I'm trying to tell you." He was holding me close now, trying to hold me up, my body a dead weight in his arms. "Hey, I've got an idea." He sat me on the couch and reached out for my phone. "What do you think about blocking his number? It would make it so much easier for you to not have to hear from him." He saw the panic set in.

"I don't know, he would get so mad . . ." I shifted my eyes to the floor, shame consuming me as I tried to stifle my sobs.

"But he's not here. I'll help you make this break from him final. You've been walking alone through this nightmare for too long, and that's over now. I'm here with you, and

I won't let anything bad happen to you ever again." He reached out, his hand on my chin, lifting my face. "Do you hear me? Not ever again."

I wasn't sure if I could trust or believe his words, but I desperately wanted to. I needed to. I needed to have something, someone, to believe in, and I wanted it to be Xander.

For so long, I had no one. My parents acted as if they had no idea what was going on between Max and me, but I had my doubts. There was little chance they didn't know something was wrong with our relationship. There were too many signs. What teenager doesn't have any friends or doesn't do any of the events related to high school? I had to wear long-sleeve shirts in the heat of Texas, all while using obscene amounts of concealer to cover up the evidence. Some friends tried to stick it out with me in the beginning. But when I never returned calls or went out on the weekends, they gave up. And I didn't blame them.

I had no one.

But coming to Blue Ridge University had changed that. I had people here supporting me. Yes, I wanted one of them to be Xander.

"OK, I'll do it. I'll block his number." I tried to pull it up, but my hands were shaking. "Xander, could you . . .?

"Give me your phone." He took it, found Max's number, and it was blocked before I could let out another strained sob.

I knew what I expected my reaction to be: the sink into the oblivion of panic coursing through my body. But instead, I felt . . . lighter. As if my body were lifted a bit. I felt relief.

As Xander handed me my phone, he noticed the look on my face. I knew he wasn't comprehending what I was feeling. Regardless of any shared traumas we might have had, he had no idea what I really went through. I was only hoping that his action wasn't going to come back to haunt me.

"And I agree, we need to be friends for now. You have too much going on. But I'm here for you." He looked toward the window behind us. "And look at that, we've practically made it the entire night. It's almost sunrise," he said. There was a tinge of sadness in his voice.

"Wait, what? Are you kidding me? I've never stayed up all night before! And I've never seen a sunrise either!" I was full of excitement as I got up and ran to the window to lift the blinds. The night sky had lightened at the horizon, the dark navy hues mixing with some deep indigo. "Thank you."

He came to my side by the window, wondering what I was thanking him for.

"You've given me some firsts tonight, some new ones *he* can't take from me. It's nice to feel like I'm living again, like I can still have some new experiences he won't ruin, so thank you."

I went back to looking out the window, not wanting to miss a moment of the sun coming over the mountains in the distance and the glorious colors it was producing. There was not a cloud in the sky to hinder the gift being given. Xander reached out and held my hand as the sun came up, his fingers threading through mine. The warmth from his touch flooded my body. I felt the need to focus on the view outside the window, but he was such a distraction.

"Is this OK, Lanie?" He looked at me intently with concern in his eyes, then peered down at our entwined hands. My stomach fluttered with the idea that someone was asking me for permission just to hold my hand.

"Yes," I said, almost too quickly, "it's more than OK." I felt the heat rising from my chest to my cheeks, and I moved my gaze back to the window.

The sun was rising slowly, but at the same time it seemed to be over instantly. I was in awe of the oranges, pinks, and reds the sky was now painted with.

"My God, isn't it beautiful, Xander?"

He didn't respond right away. "It is."

I looked at him. But he wasn't looking out the window; he was looking at me.

He started leaning in toward me, and I felt myself leaning toward him. My hand burned in his as his grip on me tightened. With his other hand, he brought our faces together so they were touching, cheek to cheek. I felt his head shift slightly as he brought his lips close to mine, tentative.

I stopped breathing.

His lips touched the outer corner of mine lightly. It could barely be called a kiss, but it was perfect.

It was the perfect end to a perfect night we had spent together.

Our first night together.

Chapter 10

I stood outside the door to my room, afraid to go inside. To be honest, seeing Becca after my night with Xander was the last thing I wanted. I'd prefer to forget that part of last night with her and Logan even happened.

But Xander convinced me I needed to have this talk with her sooner rather than later, and he was right. She needed to realize what Logan did was wrong regardless of her relationship with Ty and him. I pushed the door open and went inside, ready to deal with whatever waited on the other side.

"Oh my God, Lanie, thank God you're back. I'm so sorry. I didn't think you were going to come back. You don't hate me, right? I thought you hated me and that you were going to move out. I'm so sorry—I can't believe I said that to you last night. I was such a bitch. I know I was wrong.

Can you forgive me? Please forgive me. I don't know what came over me." She was pacing the room as the words continued to spill from her mouth. "I think I was just being selfish, nervous about how it might affect me and Ty, but that's ridiculous, and I see that now. And I was so wrong, and I'm so sorry. Please, please forgive me?" She looked like she hadn't slept all night and had been crying.

"Becca, that's all I needed to hear, that you're sorry. Thank you for that."

She ran and tackled me onto my bed with a bear hug. She was bawling her eyes out at this point, and I didn't think I could cry anymore, but my body found a way.

"Becca, it's OK. We're good, really."

"Lanie, are you really OK? I mean, after what happened, how could you be? Where were you all night?"

She finally started letting me up so we could both sit and start breathing again. Recognition lit up her face as her mouth formed a small O and she suppressed a giggle.

"Wait, you didn't, did you? I mean, he fought for your honor and shit, so he obviously cares about you, Lanie. I knew it. Didn't I tell you that?" Her eyes got huge as she wiped away more of her tears.

"We had a special night, but he knows I'm not ready for a relationship. We're in the friend zone. But it was . . . it was a good night. I'll leave it at that." I couldn't wipe the smile from my face.

"I'm sure that 'friend zone' is temporary. He'll find a way to fix that. But I'm happy for you, whatever you want."

The pause in our talk revealed the elephant in the room. I knew I needed to ask her, but I was too afraid to hear the answer. Afraid it would change things between us.

"How's Logan?"

"Um, well, he's pretty messed up. Xander beat him up pretty good. But he obviously deserved it. By the time we got him back to his room, he had sobered up enough to realize what he had done and was a basket case. It took a long time to get him to calm down. He almost went back to Xander's room looking for you. He's hoping to have a chance to talk to you today, if you're willing." Becca had hope in her eyes.

I didn't answer her right away. I couldn't. I wasn't only upset about what Logan had done to me. But I had also lost a friend in him. I knew I wouldn't be able to see Logan for quite some time, and I was nervous about how Becca would take that.

Funny, we all thought it would be her and Ty breaking up our foursome.

"I'm not sure I'm up for that today. I'll need some time before I can see him. I have a lot going on in my life from home that would explain why I can't, and I wish I was ready to talk about it, but I'm just not, not yet. It's too much, it's all too much, and it overwhelms me a lot of the time. And what happened with Logan actually made everything worse, believe it or not. I know you see it. You're observant when it comes to me and how I handle things, or more how I can't handle things." The look on her face told me exactly what I thought. "I'll have answers for you, I promise. I'm not there yet. I hope you understand."

She reached over and gave me a hug. We both leaned back against the bed, getting cozy together under a blanket. She grabbed for her laptop, and I knew what was coming next.

"No explanations needed. I'll tell Ty and Logan they'll have to wait and keep their distance for a while until you're ready, no worries. I've got your back, Lanie, I promise." She smiled while moving her finger across the finger pad on the computer. "So what will it be? *Vampire Diaries* or *New Girl?*"

"I think I'm in a Damon mood."

She smiled even wider. "Great choice."

Me:

Can you meet me for lunch around 1

Xander:

I'll see you then

A couple days had passed since Xander's party, and we had only seen each other in passing. It wasn't like me to be the one to reach out, but bottom line, I missed him. I enjoyed the level of comfort and calm I felt in his presence. And even if the line had been drawn for us to be friends, friends still spent time together.

I finished up my work and headed to the cafeteria to meet up with him.

He was easy to pick out of a crowd. Even though he was sitting at a table, I found him immediately. He was doing work with a friend when I walked up.

"Lanie, hey." His dimple was deep as he stood up to greet me. "Blake, this is Lanie. Lanie, Blake. He's a frat brother and also a lineman on the football team." The guy stood, and my hand disappeared in his as he shook it. He towered over Xander, who was well over six feet tall himself.

"Hi, Lanie. I've been hearing a lot about you from this bozo here. Not sure what you see in him." He gave Xander a shove, then started gathering his books from the table. Interesting to learn that Xander was talking about me to his friends. That was information I wasn't expecting to hear. "Thanks for the help, Xan. Later. Nice to meet you, Lanie."

I offered a small wave as he walked off, and then I turned toward Xander. "Do you help everyone with their work?"

"He needs my help to stay on the team. He's not officially one of mine, but I do it since he's a brother."

I was starting to think Xander was literally too good to be true.

"I'm assuming you're getting your standard salad with chicken?" Xander gave me an elbow to the rib.

"OK, I'll switch it up today. What do you recommend?" We were in the cafe today, which had lots of different food stations.

"I think you should join me by the stir-fry station. They customize it with anything you want in your bowl. It's amazing!" The exuberance in his voice made me excited to try the new food, so I followed him to the line. While we were waiting, my phone started lighting up with text messages.

"Aren't you going to see who those are from?" He looked at me curiously.

"Well, we both know who they aren't from, which is kind of nice." I was hoping my appreciative smile was conveying the thanks I needed to give him for blocking Max's number. "I'll take a look once we sit down." The only other people I got texts from were Becca or the guys. But since the party, the guys were keeping their distance, so my guess was Becca.

"Do you want to go sit with your fraternity brothers? I think that's them waving you over." I pointed my chin in their direction.

"Nah, we haven't seen each other. I'd like to sit with you if that's OK."

My stomach felt like it had butterflies in it all of a sudden. I wanted nothing more than some alone time with him, but I played it off as nonchalantly as I could.

"Sure, that's good." The blush on my cheeks betrayed me, though, hoping he didn't see it.

Again, beyond "friend zone."

But again, I didn't mind.

I felt as though I should mind. I knew I was getting myself in too deep with him way too quick. But he clouded my judgment.

He found a small table in a corner by the windows, and we sat down. Suddenly, a package of Ring Dings landed on my tray.

"How did you know these were my favorite?"

"I pay attention to things that are important," he said with a wink.

The fluttering feeling in my stomach told me this was a special moment, one to pay attention to. I tried to hide my smile and the crimson that was surging up my chest and across my cheeks, but he saw it. The smile on his face matched mine yet held something else in it. I couldn't put my finger on it, but it seemed to be a promise of more to come.

Unfortunately, the moment was short lived because my phone began to ping continuously again.

"Ugh, I never checked my messages." I pulled my phone from my back pocket and was met with a name on my screen I wasn't expecting. Xander noticed the drop in my mood.

"Hey, everything OK?" I could hear the apprehension in his voice, knowing he thought Max found a way.

"Um, yeah, I guess. They're all from my dad. We don't really talk too much, just a check-in once in a while, so it's odd for ten messages to come in the past half . . ." And then my words were caught in my throat.

I knew time couldn't really stand still. It's not a physical possibility in the realm of science. However, in that moment, I swore the earth stopped rotating, the clouds stopped gliding by, the students stopped eating with their food mid-way to their mouths, and my lungs stopped working, all at once.

Then, like a meteor crashing to the earth, it all started up again, but not everything was able to catch up to the lost time. My lungs were trying to work, yet I couldn't catch my breath. And during that stalled time, Xander, in slow motion, came to my side and had me in his arms before the panic attack even started. Somehow, he managed to get us out of the public eye and down a hall of the cafeteria. My body was trembling as he found a chair in a dark corner and put me in it.

"Lanie, what is it? What's going on?" He was hunched over me, trying to make eye contact while staying discreet. But I was like a zombie, and I couldn't form words through the tremble in my mouth, my lips.

I handed him my phone, which shook in my hand, hoping he would take the hint. Look for himself.

"It's locked. I need your password, baby. What's your password?" My panic was spreading to him, his words a little louder than they needed to be. My glazed eyes stared up at him, and I was unsure if I could even remember my code, my brain a frazzled mess. He reached out for my finger to use the pad and finally got it open.

And he read them.

And he froze.

I didn't need to look at him to know. I could feel the anger radiating off him. He knew.

"I'm gonna go get our things. I'll be right back." He tried to keep the edge out of his voice as he rushed off, leaving me in the chair. But I didn't care. I wanted to be alone. I wanted to disappear.

I wanted this all to stop.

Xander was back quickly, our bags in his hands. He threw them on the floor and got on his knees in front of me, his hands gripping my thighs.

"Lanie, look at me. You're OK. You're doing OK." My head snapped up when he said that.

"I'm not OK, Xander, and I'm not going to be OK! You don't know what this means." My voice was cracking. I wanted to be strong, stronger than I was. But this was the worst thing that could have been happening.

"He's coming. Max is coming. He's coming here!" I screamed as I pushed Xander away from me and jumped to my feet. I started pacing in the little bit of peace he had carved for us tucked away in this alcove. "You have no idea what that means for me! What he could do to me, will do to me. And it's all because . . ." I paused, because I almost didn't want to say my next words. But I was angry. "It's all because we blocked him. He's coming because we blocked him."

I fell back into the chair, defeated. Because nothing I seemed to do ever worked with Max. He always haunted me; he always showed up.

I didn't want to look at Xander, afraid of what I might

see. He was most likely ready to ditch this crazy situation, or at the very least he was mad at me. The tightness in my chest was increasing, like a cinder block had landed on me. My breathing became labored, and I knew what was happening. The attack would hit me from all sides, and I wouldn't be able to stop it.

"Lanie, put your head between your legs and close your mouth. Breath through your nose only." His words were firm but kind as he guided my head lower. He sat on the floor next to me. "That's it—breathe very slowly. Slow, measured breaths." His hand was on my back as he spoke next to my ear.

I felt my breathing leveling off, which had never happened so quickly before. I pushed up a bit, my elbows on my knees. He pulled his water from his bag and offered me a sip.

"How's that? Better?" he asked, his voice void of his normal confidence.

I nodded while looking at him. His brows pinched together as if he were in pain, and his eyes were glassy. I still had so many feelings reeling within me, but I didn't expect my heart to hurt seeing him that way.

"Lanie, I'm . . ." His voice broke as he tried to talk, forcing him to stop. He bent his head, resting it on my knee. "I'm so sorry. I did this; I made this happen." My fingers went to his head, rubbing and working through his hair.

The whiplash of emotions, my anger so easily shifting to concern, was not something I was used to. I had to believe it was due to the fact that I never cared enough with Max. I never cared enough to give up on the anger and the hate—I held on to it. But not with Xander. I wanted to be mad. It was his idea to block Max's number, so I could easily blame him. But he wouldn't have done it if I hadn't agreed to it.

"I'm not blaming you, Xander. There's no one to blame here but Max. It was a mutual decision to block his number." He lifted his head from my leg. "I should have done it a long time ago, and I needed you to encourage me to do it. This would have happened regardless."

He looked at me, giving a sharp nod while his hand reached up, stroking my cheek with his knuckles. While gathering our things, he looked around apprehensively.

"Do you think you should call your dad and get some more information? Try to figure out when he's coming?"

"Yeah, I can just text him." I stood up with him, ready to head back to our dorm, not sure what my next step really was. My face must have let on that I was a ball of confusion, because Xander dropped everything and came to me.

"Hey," he said softly, "we'll figure this out. I told you that you won't have to do it alone anymore." His hands cradled my face as he spoke. And it was comforting to know I would have him by my side during this. But I had just realized my new reality.

Xander, and everyone here at school, was going to bear witness to my nightmare.

Somehow, we made it back to Xander's room. On the way, I texted my dad and learned that Max was still in Texas but had put in for that coming Friday off.

He would be here by the weekend.

Xander went on the hunt for Becca, thinking she needed to know what was going on. He was in the process of devising a plan and wanted to talk to the both of us about it. But then I heard some yelling. Xander came storming back into the room with Becca following him. He looked pissed, while Becca looked concerned, maybe even a bit nervous. Her eyes found me on the couch, and I saw she was afraid to say what she wanted to.

"Lanie," Becca started, "Xander told me what's going on with Max, but there's some other stuff going on, too." She looked anxiously over at Xander, wringing her hands together. Xander's stance showed his anger, hands on his hips. He refused to look at her, his back turned to both of us. That was not a good sign.

"Xander doesn't want me to even tell you, and he might be right, but . . ."

"Then why even start, Becca? Hasn't she been through enough already, especially from him?" Xander turned toward us, yelling, throwing his hands up in the air. "Why would you feel the need, after what I told you is going on with this shithead of hers from home? Why would you even feel the need to press this about Logan right now? He doesn't deserve her time at all after what he did, and especially not now with this other shit she's got going on!" He was furious, yelling at her to the point that she was on the brink of tears.

"I'm sorry—you're right. He's not the priority here. I need to keep that in perspective." She was working hard to keep it together. I was still sitting on the couch, watching all of this play out in front of me. It was as if they had both forgotten I was in the room.

She finally looked my way. "Logan is drunk again, and we keep trying to get him to understand he needs to be sober to do this, to apologize. Ty and I have talked about taking him home for a few days, getting him out of here. They're both from the same town, so I could go with them and stay with Ty."

She was looking at me as though I could break.

I wasn't sure I wouldn't.

"We're going to do that, OK, Lanie? Get him out of here for a few days, maybe talk some sense into him. We'll leave tomorrow, probably stay there through the weekend, be back Sunday night."

I just nodded. She looked at Xander next, who nodded at her as well. And then she walked out of the room.

Xander was still pacing, the anger rolling off him. He finally forced himself to stop moving as he bent over, hands on his knees. The deep breaths he was taking were calming him, and he lifted his eyes to find mine.

"I'm sorry I blew up at her, but she needs to understand that you're my priority. I couldn't give two shits about Logan."

Again, I just nodded. I was kind of stunned by everything that happened. Xander came over to me on the couch.

I sat up straighter before I spoke to Xander. I'd had a few moments since Becca left to digest what she said. And I realized I felt bad for her, being caught in the middle.

"I think she was wrong, but I also think she's struggling to find a balance in her life right now. Her relationship with Ty is new, and now this drama going on between her best friend and his best friend . . . well, I think she's nervous it could pull them apart. Cut her some slack if you can. She really does mean well when it comes to me, and I'm sure Logan can be very convincing when he wants to be."

"You're much more understanding than I am." Xander still looked upset, refusing to make eye contact, but I knew his anger was misplaced.

"It's someone else you're really mad at, right?"

He jumped up from the couch, and I could see the muscles in his jaw twitching. He balled his fists as if in preparation.

"You can't fight him." I walked to his side, wondering if being close would help. But it didn't seem to do any good. "I won't have you getting hurt or worse, in trouble, over me. We need to have a plan in place so we're prepared for anything that could happen when it comes to him."

I knew this time was going to come, that I was going to have to deal with Max here. I plopped onto the couch, almost in defeat, not sure what to do next. Xander came and sat next to me, leaning back in thought. I knew he was thinking about what to do, how to help me, and that was what scared me. I mean, I won't lie, I never thought I would have support when dealing with Max, and it felt kind of good that I did. But at the same time, my stomach was in knots as I thought about how wrong it could go for us, for Xander. It was giving me mixed emotions. Max was ruthless, and I was petrified Xander would wind up getting hurt because of me.

"Well, I think I do have a plan. It's not a great one, but at least it's something."

I looked over at him and his eyes were pinched together in worry, and that was exactly what I didn't want. I hated that I'd brought this upon him. His life only weeks ago was much simpler, calmer, without the likes of me or Max trampling through it. I started to say as much when he stopped me.

"I know what you're thinking, and you're wrong. I want to be doing exactly what I'm doing. I want you here, and I wouldn't want to be anywhere else. Don't have that look of guilt on your face, like you wish you didn't put me here. You're an open book. Fate brought us together for a reason,

Lanie, and I am pretty sure this is the start of it."

Xander's plan was very basic.

"I want you in my room. He won't know to come here. But you'll have to stay here the whole time. And since Becca won't be here this weekend, your room will be empty, so that's good." He was pacing as he was talking. His nervous energy surrounded him, yet he was confident at the same time. Now that he had a plan, his mood had definitely shifted. "I'll get us a bunch of food and snacks, and we'll hang out and watch movies all weekend. It'll be fun!"

His attempt at keeping this lighthearted was sweet. But as hard as I tried, I couldn't match his enthusiasm.

"How do you feel about it?" Xander asked, looking hopeful. He calmed even more, now sitting on the other end of the couch.

"I guess OK. Maybe we could talk to some of our friends on the floor, some people we trust, and tell them what's going on. Do you think they would lie for me? That way I could go out a bit on this side of the hall, at least a little."

"Maybe, and I think it's still OK to go out today. Your dad said he's still at work, so I don't think we would need to shut it down until tomorrow. And here's the thing too: once he comes here, everyone's going to know what you're dealing with at home, you realize that, don't you? I don't expect him to keep it together while he's here, do you?"

"Yeah, I know. I'm not happy about the secret I've been trying to keep being shown to everyone here. But I don't have a choice anymore, do I? Why not clue people in ahead of time? If it could help me and they're going to learn about him anyway if he shows up, what's the difference?" I couldn't believe I was suggesting this, but it made sense, and it seemed like Xander agreed.

"Let me worry about that stuff. For now, go get some of your things from your room. You won't be going in there for a few days. And clue Becca in on our plan before they leave. I guess it is a good thing they're leaving."

He held me in his arms for a moment before holding my face and looking into my eyes.

"We've got this, Lanie." And he kissed my forehead.

Becca wasn't there when I went into our room, so I put a bag of essentials together. I made my way back to Xander's room and knocked. When he opened the door, I couldn't see him, but I heard his laugh.

"Are you moving in for the month? What the hell did you grab?"

Did he not know what was required to be a woman? And I was a no-nonsense girl. He had no idea what would be coming in here if he had Becca moving in for a few days. He took a few things from my hands, and I dropped the rest in a corner of his room.

"So, where am I going to pee this whole weekend? We didn't think about that, did we?" I stood with my hands on my hips, hoping for a logical resolution.

"I'm coming up with a plan. Don't worry your pretty little head—I'll have it all covered. I promise. How about we head out to do something this afternoon, though, before we get stuck in this room for a while. I have something real quick to run out and do, but then let's go for a walk. Sound good?"

We seemed like we were exiting the "friend zone" quickly; these were very close to relationship-status activities. But we were going to be spending the next three to four days together, nonstop; by default, that took us out of that zone.

And that made me very nervous.

But also excited.

I found the remote and settled in with an old episode of *New Girl* to watch while I waited for Xander to return. It wasn't long before he was back with his arms full of bags of what looked like groceries.

"I thought if we're going to be in here for a few days, we need lots of snacks to help with our binge-watching of TV and movies." He had a huge grin on, and it appeared as though he was sincerely looking forward to our prison term in his room. He started unpacking the hordes of snack foods and drinks onto the shelves by his fridge.

"Grab your sweatshirt. You might need it on our walk." He grabbed his backpack and my hand and walked us out the door.

We walked toward the pond, which put a smile on my face. It had quickly become one of my favorite places on campus. I loved the serenity it offered, plus the views of the mountains in the distance. Once we got there, Xander started taking some snacks out of his backpack.

"You packed us a picnic?" I asked with such surprise in my voice he had to stop and look at me.

"Have you never gone on a picnic, Lanie?"

I shook my head.

"Well, then I guess I've given you another first, haven't I?"

I couldn't put into words the emotions that were swirling around inside of me at that moment. Happy, hopeful, thankful, even optimistic. The problem was, I had no idea what all of them together could mean. No one had ever made me feel this way, and to be feeling these things with the impending doom approaching—well, that was downright witchcraft.

We flapped the blanket in the air together, and it sank to the ground gracefully.

"So, what will it be? Chocolate pudding, potato chips, or a turkey sandwich? I was limited in what I could grab from the cafeteria, but we'll make do with what we've got, right?" He pulled the food out of the bag with precision, placing each item on the blanket in front of us as if presenting a feast. "I don't know about you, but the pudding is looking mighty good!" All I could do was stare at his dimple as he lay back on his side while throwing his head back and laughing about pudding.

"How are you so relaxed right now? This is such a mess we're in, that I've put you right in the middle of, and you're laughing about pudding. I wish I could be more like you, Xander. I wish I could learn to relax and live life more." I was on my back and looking up at the blue sky. It was getting dark already, probably only about thirty minutes before sunset considering how late in the season it was.

"Lanie, c'mere. Come lie closer to me." He pulled me to lie on my side facing him. His hand pushing the hair behind my ear and lingering on my cheek.

"I know you're worried about this weekend, and I'm not taking it lightly, trust me. I am fully prepared to keep you safe if that monster shows up. And I still feel responsible for him even coming. But on the flip side, I'm thankful he's given me the opportunity to spend this time with you. We have this found time together we wouldn't have had."

He stopped for a moment, his hand now moving from my cheek down along my jaw.

"I'm going to take full advantage of this to show you how a real guy should be treating you. You have no idea what being in a relationship really is. So, when you say you've had a boyfriend, I say bullshit. I say no, you haven't. He was nothing but a coward who had no idea what he had in front of him all those years and has lost forever. And I'm hoping to gain what he's lost."

Does swooning still happen in the twenty-first century?

Or while you're lying down?

Because if so, I was swooning right then. My God, those words went right to my soul. If I didn't know better, I would think he had been reading some of my romance novels on my e-reader. I actually got a little embarrassed by his declaration and had to close my eyes and turn my head away. He gently turned my face back toward his.

"Hey, look at me. Don't shut me out, please."

"I'm not, I promise. I've just never had anyone say anything like that to me before and I really don't know how to handle it or respond. You seem too perfect to me, Xander. I'm lying here thinking I don't deserve you; I don't deserve everything you're sacrificing or doing for me. But I'm no less thankful for it. I need you to know that. From the bottom of my heart, thank you."

We lay on the blanket, quiet for a while, both of us staring up at the sky. We were simply enjoying the peace of our surroundings. I think we realized that the next few days might be a bit stressful.

"So, can I ask you a question?" I broke the silence with a shaky voice.

"Sure, what's up?"

"You don't have a, um, girlfriend, right?"

He turned on his side to face me before answering. "I've only been with two girls since coming to BRU, and neither were a serious thing. No, I don't have a girlfriend. Never thought I wanted one." He went back to looking to the sky, avoiding looking at me after saying that.

I never expected him to be a virgin—Lord knows I wasn't. I felt like I still didn't know him. But I did know when I was with him, I felt safe. When he touched me, my skin begged for his touch, ready to ignite. When he held me, I craved for his arms to never leave me, to always catch me like he'd promised.

And I never thought I would feel that way with a guy. Ever.

I felt his movements while lying on the blanket as he shifted and turned to face me. He pulled me to face him, our noses almost touching.

"There are so many good reasons for us to just be friends right now," he said, and he reached out to put some hair behind my ear. "But I think we both know this is headed in a very different direction."

His hand stayed on my face, his eyes never moving from mine.

"I'll let you guide us there, give you time, but I need you to understand that is where I want us to go. Please know, there's no one else for me. No one."

I wasn't expecting him to say these things, yet I wasn't surprised by his words either.

I held his gaze, the moment pivotal. My words were clogged in my throat, the knot the size of an orange, the emotions strong.

Then his fingers were gently gliding down my cheek,

and that electric pulse I usually got from his touch was teeming through my body, hitting in parts that have not been awakened in a long time, or maybe ever. My eyes fluttered closed, and I heard a slight sigh emanate from the back of his throat.

"It already feels like we've left the friend zone." I said it hoping he wasn't going to stop what he was doing. I wasn't sure what I wanted anymore.

"Yeah, I'm having trouble with that. I'm trying, I promise." And that was when he pulled his hand away. "And I won't push you until you're ready for more, but I care about you, Lanie. I care about you more than I've cared about anyone ever before."

I needed to focus on the part where he said he wasn't going to push me, because this was all so overwhelming.

"And I had an ulterior motive in bringing you here today, not knowing that the picnic would also be a first I could give you. I had a plan to give you another first today."

My eyes shot open, almost in a panic, when he said that.

"Come here, Lanie, and relax." He sat us facing each other. "You can see the sun setting behind me, right?"

I looked over his shoulder and realized the colors of the sky were changing to amazing hues of purple, pink, and orange. It was the most marvelous sight I'd ever seen, and I was awestruck.

"You told me the story about how your first kiss was stolen from you." His eyes found mine, and at first my heart stilled. But in the next moment it was beating out of my chest. "I plan on giving it back to you tonight. I hope I do it justice."

I think I stopped breathing.

Xander held my face reverently in his hands, almost as

if I was a cherished piece of treasure he had found. I let out a breath as his fingers moved my hair off my face, behind my ears. His thumb rubbed my bottom lip gently, and my mouth responded by opening slightly, a moan escaping.

Xander responded with something that sounded like no less than a growl from deep within his chest.

I tried hard to keep eye contact, but the feelings were overwhelming. All I wanted to do was close my eyes and revel in them. His one hand reached behind my neck, his fingers threading up through my hair while the other hand remained on my face.

I found my hands on his thighs, gradually moving them up to his stomach, feeling the hard, rippled muscles under his shirt. This time, I heard the moan come from his throat as his eyes closed momentarily, and I knew he felt exactly what I was.

I felt his mouth coming closer to me before I saw it, feeling his warm breath closing in on my face. I opened my eyes to see his dark, stormy blue eyes looking directly into mine with such promise in them.

His soft lips touched mine finally, gently pushing against me at first. Then, with more pressure, his tongue begged for entrance into my mouth. But it was done carefully so as to let me know I was still in control. I answered him with my tongue pushing into him, and the kiss progressed with intensity as his hand pulled my head closer to him, my hands coming up to wrap around his shoulders, his neck, pulling him tighter against me.

My mind was spinning, a whirlwind, lost in the moment. But then out of nowhere, the black veil arrived, towering over me, a shadow of darkness and evil reminding me I was not allowed to feel loved or wanted. My body stilled in

Xander's arms.

"Lanie." His murmurs were a whisper against my mouth. "It's you and me. It's OK." He brought his fingers to my mouth and rubbed his thumb along my bottom lip, my tongue darting out to taste him. "It's just you and me. You're safe."

And I felt it—the tether temporarily snapped. I broke free and was able to be present in that moment.

Xander felt it and pulled me onto his lap, my legs wrapping around his waist. Our bodies were touching, but the focus was on our mouths. His tongue explored my mouth, setting off tiny explosions inside me as his hand worked its way down the side of my face to my neck and eventually to my waist. He pulled me even closer, our bodies aligned, our breaths mingling together as one. My hand twisted in his shirt, trying to get our bodies even closer, to no avail.

The kiss seemed as if it was lasting an eternity, yet it was over too soon.

We started coming up for air, him peppering me with tiny pecks on my lips and around my mouth before pulling back and looking at me with eyes full of passion. The colors of the sky surrounded him like a shroud from behind, as if he were in a watercolor painting.

I didn't think that moment could have been any more perfect than he made it.

I was close to tears when he pulled farther away, but he still had my face in his hands. His mouth was close to mine when he started whispering again.

"I forgot to tell you . . . I also brought your favorite, Ring Dings."

Chapter 11

I was dreaming about our picnic.

And our kiss.

That incredible kiss.

But in my dream, it didn't stop there. In my dream, Xander did other things to me, things that made me break out in a sweat in my sleep. I heard him saying my name in my dream, but it seemed real.

"Lanie, Lanie, you need to wake up! He's here, Lanie. Max is fucking here. Wake up!" I shot up in his bed when I processed what he said, it finally stirring me from my sleep.

"What! How do you know?" I started to climb out of his bed in a panic.

"Just stop and listen."

And that's when I heard it: the loud, obnoxious knocking on a door down the hall. The incessant knocking that didn't seem like it was going to stop, ever.

"It's five thirty in the morning. He probably thought by coming now, he would definitely catch you in your room. Thank God we got you out of there."

We heard other people open their doors and tell him to shut up. It didn't seem to intimidate him, and I knew it wouldn't. On the contrary, it incited him to start screaming my name.

"Lanie, open the fucking door!"

"Hey, Einstein, don't you think that maybe, just maybe, there's no one in that room at the moment? Can you knock it off? We're all trying to sleep."

That sounded like Ryan, the guy who lived directly across from me. My worst nightmare was coming true: my darkest secret was being revealed to my world here. To everyone.

Eventually, we heard his footsteps disappearing down the hall. Xander got a text from someone who lived by the elevator saying the crazy dude left.

I was frozen in place.

Hearing his voice again, knowing he was near, in my space, had the panic racing through my veins. My immediate response was the intense need to curl up into a ball, hide away, disappear.

How could I be so dumb? How could I think he wouldn't come here for me, wouldn't continue to destroy me? It was his life's mission. He would never stop.

Xander came to me and held me, knowing I was breaking.

"I'm here. I won't let anything happen to you. But I'm going to take a walk downstairs, make sure he's gone. Will you be OK for like five minutes?" He pulled back to try to look me in the eyes, but I refused to make eye contact. Pulling away, I stomped over to the couch.

"I'll be fine," I tried to assure him. He waited for a moment, staring at me. "I promise," I said with more emphasis.

But I wasn't OK.

Xander slowly stepped away, unsure if he should leave me, but he unlocked the door and stepped out. I heard the lock click into place as the echo of his footsteps faded down the hall.

I was on high alert waiting for Xander to come back, thinking that while he was gone, Max was waiting somewhere on the floor for him to leave.

I sat in the room, expecting the hard knocking to start at any second.

The yelling of my name to resume.

I curled up in a ball in the far corner of the bed, shaking uncontrollably. The silent tears streamed down my face; I couldn't risk him potentially hearing me.

I already felt the hard slap to my face I knew I would get, the yank to my arm as he dragged me away, the intense push to the ground to force me into a submissive position. I imagined we wouldn't even get farther than his car before he would feel the need to punish me more. The pain he would inflict on me would be unimaginable considering how bad I'd been—ignoring him, not answering his calls.

No one could save me from this. No one.

He was a monster who always won.

I heard someone fumbling at the door with keys. Xander would not have trouble opening his door. It had to be Max.

The door opened.

I stayed completely still with my head facing the wall,

hoping he wouldn't see me tucked in the corner. I heard him coming closer and started to whimper—I couldn't help it. Then I felt his hands on me and started fighting him off, screaming and flailing.

How did he get in the room?

He must have hurt Xander somehow and gotten his key.

Oh my God, he's got me!

I couldn't let this happen. I'd come too far. But what was I going to do?

"Stop, Max, please, stop! I'll listen to you, I promise. Don't hurt me, please!" I started begging him, hoping he would have mercy on me. "We can go to my room. My roommate isn't here. We can . . ."

"Lanie, it's me. It's Xander, Lanie. Stop. Relax! Stop kicking. It's me, babe. It's Xander." He was trying to get a hold of me, but I wouldn't stop.

My irrational brain wouldn't listen to his voice, wouldn't recognize the reality of the situation. He finally got me in a bear hug and lay next to me, talking calmly in my ear.

"It's OK. Shh, shh, I've got you. I'm not *him*. It's me. He's gone. I checked everywhere, and there's no sign of him anywhere. Please calm down, baby. You're OK. I've got you."

I froze.

Oh my God. What was I doing?

I couldn't look at him, but I didn't have to. I finally knew who had me. It registered. I felt the safety of his embrace, smelled the familiarity of his scent. The warmth of his arms broke through the madness in my head.

But the panic wasn't going away. It was right under the surface, ready to break through again at the sound of Max's voice. The only thing that separated Max from me was a six-inch wall and a door. How was Xander possibly going to keep me hidden from him?

Max always got what he wanted.

Yet here I was in Xander's arms, feeling his warm breath move my hair as he spoke.

"Lanie, what did that monster do to you?"

I remained frozen, unmoving in his hold. The chaos in my brain telling me it would do no good to divulge the madness. No one could help; no one could save me from him. I chanced a look at Xander, seeking out his watchful eyes, dreading what I might see.

But I did see it—the change.

His eyes were different, looking at me as if I were broken, in need of saving.

And I was.

But I wasn't ready for him to do it, not yet.

I struggled to find my voice. I needed to know.

"Are you sure he's gone? It's not normal for him to give up like that." My voice was cracking, breaking through my quiet whispers as I tried to keep the small bit of control I had found in place. "I kind of feel it, like it's going to happen. He's going to get me." I finally looked up, fully facing Xander at this point, needing the complete truth.

His eyes searched my face for a moment before his hand came to cradle my cheek, my head instinctively dipping toward his warmth, eyes fluttering shut. It's amazing how a simple touch could offer my soul such comfort. I will never understand this immediate connection to an almost stranger, my need to be near him, my desire to be close.

"I didn't see him anywhere. I will not let him get you." He let the tiniest bit of what sounded like contempt come through in his voice. "I won't let him anywhere near you.

You're safe. I'll keep you safe."

Xander didn't understand there was no such thing as being safe in a world with Max in it.

But he seemed hell-bent on trying.

He held me for what seemed like hours, us both quiet. There weren't any words for what we had witnessed and lived through that morning. I think I spent most of the time trying to stop my body from physically reacting, the tremors and tears eventually subsiding.

Xander was also trying not to respond physically.

I could feel it in him. His body tensed under me, every muscle going hard as I moved around. He was trying to restrain it, I could tell. But his control was waning. He was getting antsy. He was struggling.

Suddenly, he got up, stretching his strained muscles, reaching, causing his shirt to ride up and give me a glimpse of his taut midsection.

And how fucked up is it that my abuser had returned and I was around him for the first time in months, and I was thinking about Xander's body?

In *that* way.

Why does the human mind deceive us?

Or was my heart trying to guide me in that direction? I was so confused; it was all a jumble inside me at that moment, literally making me nauseous.

"I'm going to take another look." He was itching to find Max, I knew. Or maybe he needed to move, to get up. "I'm going to look farther out on campus and get us some food while I'm out there. I think someone should be here with you, though. Who should I get?"

He seemed on edge, rattled, like he was ready for a fight that couldn't happen.

"I don't want anyone here with me, Xander. I just want to be alone. I'll be OK." He didn't look convinced, but he also knew he wouldn't win this argument. "Please be careful. You have no idea who you're dealing with." I looked up, my eyes pleading with him to truly understand what I was trying to tell him, my untold secrets.

"Lanie, he has no idea who he's dealing with in me."

He was back in less than twenty minutes with a full tray of food, but the enraged look on his face concerned me.

"What's wrong?" I knew immediately that he'd seen Max.

"He's literally sitting in the cafeteria with a cap on, in the corner, hiding. He's waiting for you. He's a sick motherfucker. I really wanted to go over and take him out."

He was pacing, hands fisted. I hated seeing this side of Xander and knowing that Max was the one bringing it out in him.

This time, it was me calming him down. I reached out, holding his face, looking him in the eyes. I pulled him closer, beckoning him to grab a hold of me, which he did by putting his hands on my waist.

"Stay with me," I told him.

Our faces were only inches apart, our breaths mingling, and I felt his breathing starting to match mine. I leaned in and touched my lips to his, and he responded by digging his fingers into my hips tightly, holding on to me like a lifeline.

My mouth was by his ear, and I whispered, "I'm glad you came back to me instead. To be here, safe with me, to take care of me. I need you, Xander, in more ways than I can put into words."

And I kissed him again, this time more fervently. He immediately wrapped his arms around my waist as he pushed me against the wall.

I froze, not sure if I could do this, and Xander felt the change in my body.

"I'm sorry, that was too much." He pulled slightly away. "I would never hurt you. Tell me if you want me to stop. Just say the word."

I remained still, not sure of my next move. His body was firmly up against mine, the heat between us evident. The feeling in my lower belly was one I'd never felt before. As it spread and warmed me, I felt my hips push forward, betraying me, feeling good while doing it. My hesitancy was slipping, but I was scared to move forward.

The energy around him transformed, his anger morphing into desire right before my eyes. I was not afraid of him hurting me, only afraid of what he could do to my heart.

I knew my heart wanted this, but my mind was fighting it, with good reason.

"We'll take this at the pace you want. You're safe with me, Lanie."

I nodded into his neck as he held me against the wall, my resolve now melting away as my desire grew stronger with every breath. He felt the change in me, a low groan of approval coming from deep within him.

His hands slowly slid down my body, causing me to

shiver against him. He grabbed the backs of my thighs, lifting me as I wrapped my legs around him, using the wall to support us. I brought my mouth back to his, and he moaned deeply. The hum of it vibrated on my lips.

His fingers trailed down my arms, finding my waist under my shirt. That sent shivers up and down my spine, tiny explosions happening at every spot he touched, making my head spin.

I had no idea this was how it felt. The sheer desire running through my body was enough to topple me to the ground. The fire burning deep in my core fed the need for him to keep going.

Eventually, his fingertips found their way to the band of my bra, rubbing along its edge, trying to ask for permission to go inside. But instead, his hand slid up slowly, tenderly, across the lace of my bra, cupping my breast in his hand, the weight of it heavy.

His thumb ran over the peak, which came alive from the attention, all while sending shock waves to my foundation. The small sounds coming from my mouth should have been embarrassing. Yet they seemed to be a turn-on for Xander, who swallowed the sounds in his mouth the more I made them.

I was rubbing my fingers through his soft, messy hair, about to start lifting up his shirt, when he caught my eyes with his and the storm in them made my breath hitch.

And then I froze.

Something went wrong in my head.

Really, really wrong.

My body went completely still, and Xander gently put me down on the ground. He slowly backed up, putting his hands up as he went.

"Hey, you with me, babe? It's me. You're OK. It's me—it's Xander."

He kept repeating those words over and over again, but it sounded as if I was under water.

And then there was nothing.

The pain in his voice was heartbreaking.

"Lanie, wake up, baby. I'm so sorry. C'mon, Lanie, come back to me." His fingers gently caressed my face, my jawline. I knew I was lying down, but I couldn't tell where. My eyes felt like they were glued shut when I tried to open them. No words would come out of my mouth.

I finally felt like I could move my fingers. I reached out and found his hand, gripping it tightly.

"Lanie." It was a whisper, a reverent whisper. He lifted my hand gently to his mouth, holding it there for long moments. Eventually, my lids were able to crack open, and the light flooded in. Xander cradled my head at his chest, shielding me from the light, from everything. "I'm here." He was shaking. I thought he was crying, and I hated that I'd done this.

"Xander."

"Shh, Lanie."

"No, Xander, I'm sorry. I didn't . . ."

"Lanie." He abruptly sat up, holding my face in his hands, the torment evident in his face. "Stop—never apologize. Never. We won't do anything until you're ready. I'm sorry if I pushed you. I'm sorry."

"How long was I out?" I asked, knowing it probably

wasn't long. It never was.

"A couple minutes, maybe not even. But you scared the shit out of me." He was white as a ghost. Most times when I shut down like that, I was with Max. He never gave a shit. He never even acknowledged it most times; he probably thought I'd fallen asleep. "Should we go to the hospital?" Xander asked.

"No!" My sudden outburst startled him. "I mean, I'm OK. It's happened before. My mind kind of shuts itself down."

A look of devastation overcame him.

"I didn't mean to . . ." Xander started to say.

"That's what I'm trying to tell you. You didn't push me. I thought I *was* ready. I'm just not, I guess."

He pulled me close, his arms a shield around me, a force to be reckoned with. This embrace was an apology as well as a promise.

He whispered in my ear, "We'll wait as long as we need to."

We made it through the evening and the whole night without any visits from Max, which was a welcome change from the night before. We knew we couldn't trust that meant he was gone.

"I'm gonna look on campus. I want to see if he's stalking anywhere in particular for you. Maybe he's looking for you at the library or something. I don't know. It'll make me feel better if I can get a sighting of him and know where he is instead of being taken off guard."

I wasn't sure about this, but I could tell it was something he really needed to do. He was agitated again. He came to me and hugged me close, knowing I was still struggling from last night. I pulled away, trying to let him know I was OK. I just wanted to change the subject.

"Well, I need a shower today. How am I going to get that accomplished?" I didn't want to be out of the room with Xander not here.

"Ashley and Lena both said they'd help with that, and they said you can hang out in their room with them until I get back. Is that OK?" I gave him an unsure look. "One of them will stand guard in the bathroom area and the other will be in the dressing room part of the shower with you, so it'll look like she is the one taking the shower if, God forbid, he forces his way into the ladies' bathroom. We've got it all figured out, Lanie. Don't worry." It actually sounded like a solid plan. Ashley and Lena lived together on the other end of the hall. I'd had lunch with them a few times since Xander's party, so at least I was a bit comfortable with them.

"That sounds like it could work."

He smiled, and I got my stuff together. He opened the door and looked out in the hall. He had texted the girls already, and they were waiting by their door for me.

"The coast is clear. Let's get you into the bathroom," he said. I took off running, trying to get there as fast as I could.

As I passed the girls by their room, they took off running with me, laughing as we ran down the hall. I was glad they could find some levity in the situation, and I was glad we made it unseen. But my heart was pounding.

"Oh my God. Thanks, guys, for helping me with this. It's crazy that I even have to do this." I was a bit embarrassed to have to talk to them about all this shit with Max.

"Oh gosh, Lanie, don't think twice about it. I had a boyfriend from home who was an asshole too—I will say, not to the level of yours, but we all have skeletons, right? Go take your shower. I'll be out here, and Lena will sit on the bench in there with you."

Lena followed me into the showers and gave me a sincere smile. "I hope you can make it all work out. Especially with Xander. He really likes you, Lanie. I've never seen him like this with another girl. I've known him since the first day of freshman year, and every girl I know, including myself, has had a crush on him." She gave me a shrug. "But he's different with you. He's never been so happy, so serious before. So, I hope you guys can make it work."

"Thanks."

That was all I could say. It was weird to hear about how many girls had their eye on Xander, but I understood why. I quickly jumped in the shower and finished my business. Then the three of us got to their room without incident.

I was brushing the knots out of my hair as the girls and I were talking about mindless things: our classes, homework. We were in the middle of sharing some of our professors' names when I heard him.

The loud booming.

The yelling of my name.

The knocking on the doors.

I quickly ran, turned off their TV, and motioned for them to be quiet, to act like they weren't in their room. I noticed their door was already locked. There was nothing more to do other than endure listening to his tirade.

"Lanie! Where the fuck are you? I know you have to be in one of these rooms." His footsteps could be heard getting closer to our room. I cowered in the corner, hands over my ears. Ashley came to my side and put her arms around me. She was trembling as much as I was.

"I've checked this entire campus, and you're nowhere else. Are you in one of these rooms hooking up with some douchebag?" Max screamed through the hall.

Ashley's sharp intake of breath startled me. Her compassionate eyes held my gaze when I turned toward her.

"He'll be gone soon," she whispered in my ear.

But Max wasn't done. He had resorted to knocking on every door he passed. Thankfully, no one was opening up for him. "You fucking someone? I bet that's what you've been doing since you got here, you fucking whore!"

But then we heard another voice coming down the hall.

"Dude, what the fuck is your problem? You've done nothing but harass everyone on this floor all weekend. Haven't you taken the hint Lanie doesn't want to see you?"

It was Xander. I hoped he knew what he was doing. It sounded like he was antagonizing Max.

"Do you fucking know her? Where is she?" Max demanded.

"Yeah, I fucking know her. Everyone on the floor knows her. We all live together. Doesn't mean we're fucking her. Last I heard, she went home with her roommate for the weekend, so you're wasting your time. Why don't you give us all a break and get the fuck out of here? And if you don't, I think my next call will be the cops."

"Are you fucking threatening me? I don't think you want to do that, asshole. Not a move you want to make with me." His venomous voice was something I recognized all too well.

"Well, I just did, and I have a few friends to back me up. Want to have me ask them to escort you out, or will you leave on your own?" Xander threatened.

Lena's eyes shot up at this. Then we heard lots of people yelling in the hall and mutterings and curses being thrown around. Lena went toward the lock as if she was going to open it, and I panicked.

"Please don't!"

"I promise, if anyone is close by, I'll shut it immediately and lock it right up."

She opened it a crack and looked out. She opened it more, pushing her head out for a better look. She snapped her head back in the room, her eyes wide when she turned around.

"Guys, Xander's entire frat is here in the hall," she whispered, "and they have bats and pipes with them!" She quickly pulled the door closed as noises seemed to get closer.

There were still lots of curses being thrown around, and we heard shuffling and what sounded like someone being thrown against a wall, maybe. I continued to sit with my hands over my ears. I couldn't stand hearing any of this going on with Xander out there with him.

Next thing I knew, Xander was throwing the door wide open, looking around the room, running for me as soon as he saw me. He pulled me in for a hug, then pushed me at arm's length to look me over. He was shaking uncontrollably, either out of fear or anger—or both.

"Are you OK?"

I nodded.

He held me close, and I felt his words up against my cheek.

"I will go to the ends of the earth to keep him away from you. I hope you're starting to understand that."

I nodded again.

I was starting to.

Chapter 12

"So, it sounds like we have a lot to tell each other."

Becca and I were in our room together after she and the guys returned. She'd heard some rumblings from people on the floor about the craziness that took place while they were gone. There was no way to avoid telling her about Max any longer. It sounded like there was a story from her weekend as well.

"I heard your asshole boyfriend from home actually did show up here this weekend. I'm sorry I wasn't here to help you with that, but it was good to get Logan away. I don't think it would have been good for them to have met." She gave me a knowing look, understanding Logan was better, but not great.

"It was a challenging weekend, I'll put it that way. We had a lot of help from people on the floor and Xander's frat. We got through it without Max seeing me. So that was good." Becca's face contorted when I paused, and I was sure she didn't grasp the intensity of what had really happened here. "Unfortunately, a lot of people here got to see the shit I have to deal with. He was on full display with the tantrums he pulls when he doesn't get his way, and it's not fun. I'm thankful for the guys being able to scare him off."

I was trying to keep the story to a minimum, not ready to divulge my secrets to her about my relationship with him. I was embarrassed to be in such a situation and not be able to get out of it, even with such distance between us.

"I'm hoping he takes the hint and leaves me alone now, but that's not in his nature. He doesn't give up what he considers 'his' that easily. Ya know, we told him I was at your house for the weekend to make him think I wasn't anywhere on campus."

"That was smart." Becca was sitting on her bed, me on mine. She wasn't making direct eye contact with me, and her words were clipped. All of this was odd behavior for her. It made me think things were still a bit strained between us. I didn't necessarily mind that she seemed distracted. I didn't need her to know much about what happened anyway.

"Lanie, listen, I'm sorry about how all of this is happening. I feel like we have so much going on at the same time around us, so many balls to juggle between Max and Logan. And now you've got Xander to consider, and I have Ty to think about. It's a lot right now." She seemed more nervous about this than I was hoping for. "Logan's OK, but not as good as we'd like. Apparently, he had some issues coming into college. It's not all stemming from you. I don't want you to feel guilty about it. But I guess this is putting him over the edge a bit."

Becca looked really worried now. I moved in to console her, to comfort her the way she had for me so many times. She accepted it immediately, the hug tighter than I expected as I rubbed her back.

"Becca, we'll figure this out. We do have a lot going on, but this is life. Xander is helping me realize I can't go through my life alone, can't face what I'm facing without help. So I'm glad Logan has you and Ty as his support, because he obviously needs it. And you and I have each other, too."

She pulled away, looking at me now, nodding in agreement. Her somber demeanor hadn't changed much, but her smile showed hope that the Becca I knew and loved wasn't far away.

"I like hearing you talk about Xander and what he's doing for you, Lanie. That makes me happy," she said with a wide smile. "I'd love to hear more about the time you spent together this weekend. I honestly don't care about the 'asshole.' You can tell me more about him if you want, but I really just want to hear about you and Xander. Your face lights up when you say his name."

I didn't know how to respond to that. I gave her a shy smile.

"So, I know it's really important for Logan to talk to you. He needs to, so I hope you'll let him do that soon." I think that was what had been weighing on her this whole time. Her eyes implored for a response that would be beneficial for her and Logan.

"I can definitely do that. I think I need that, too. I need to go back to the way things were, or something close to it. Please tell him to come find me when he's ready."

I felt like I was ready. For whatever reason, after facing

Max this weekend and surviving it, I felt stronger. So why not face Logan, too?

Becca let out an audible sigh. It looked as though this was the first time she'd breathed normally since we started sitting together.

"Becca, we will be OK."

Later that day, Becca and I were heading to class, and I knew I was running out of time to ask her what I needed to.

"So, hey, I have a favor. I have nowhere to go for Thanksgiving. I was hoping I might come home with you that weekend."

"Oh my gosh, Lanie, of course you can! My mom'll be psyched to have you with us! But your parents, won't they miss you? Why aren't you going home?" One look at me and she realized the question went too far. "OK, I get it, not now."

My heart broke. I knew I should tell her. I didn't want the pity, the different looks I knew I would get if I told her. But I decided to give her something. She deserved it.

"Thanks, Becca, I appreciate it. My parents don't actually know I'm not coming home, though. I guess I should call and tell them. We're not that close anymore, so I don't think it'll surprise them all that much. But more about that another time, right?"

We grabbed our bags and started down the hall together. "So, how are you and Ty doing? All this talk about problems, I haven't heard any good news. Did you have fun seeing his hometown and meeting his parents?"

She was quiet for a minute before talking, which was unlike her. "We had a good weekend together. I mean, a lot of the time was spent worrying about Logan, but Ty and I had some alone time." And there was that quietness again.

"What are you not telling me, Becca?" I stopped walking, forcing her to stop as well. But she wouldn't look at me, would look everywhere but at me. "Becca, come on, you've been here for me so many times. Let me be here for you." When her eyes met mine, they were filled with unshed tears. We had made it outside our dorm, so I dragged her to a nearby bench. We sat just as she started to crumble.

"They didn't know about me!" She almost yelled it, so much anger coming through.

"What do you mean, Becca? Who didn't know about you?" I wasn't fully grasping what she was upset about.

"Lanie, his family didn't know about me. They had no idea I was his girlfriend. He didn't even introduce me to them that way. As far as they know, I am just a random friend from school, nothing special." Her tears were coming hard and fast as I leaned in and wrapped her in a hug. "He wouldn't even touch me, hold my hand, nothing in front of them. It was like he was embarrassed of me." Sobs racked her body.

"Oh, Becca, I'm sorry he did that to you." I pulled her back so she could look at me. "But there has to be a reasonable explanation. That doesn't make any sense."

"Well, anytime we weren't at his house or with anyone from his family, he was normal. He would hug me, hold my hand, kiss me. All the normal stuff. But the second we stepped in that house, it was as if I had some disease or something. It was weird and it hurt. A lot." She was wiping the tears away, trying to calm down, looking around, not wanting to make a scene.

"Did you talk to him about it, ask him why?"

"I was too nervous to hear his answer." At that, she started crying all over again. "What if he really is embarrassed of me? Or what if he knows they won't like me as his girlfriend?"

"I know you're upset, but do you hear yourself? That's ridiculous. You're beautiful, intelligent, and the sweetest person I know. There's no way any of that could be true." But I could tell she was so upset there would be no getting through to her. "I think the only way to fix this is to talk to Ty. He needs to give you an explanation." She settled again, and I rubbed her hands as I held them. It was heartbreaking seeing her like this.

Was this what she went through with me every time I broke down?

"I know, I know, but I really don't think I want to hear his answer. But you're right, I'll talk to him." She leaned back on the bench and let out a deep breath, as if it was the first time she was breathing in days. "It feels good to tell you. I was alone with all of it the whole weekend. I didn't want to make it about me, ya know, since we were really home for Logan." She took another deep breath while looking up to the sky, seemingly looking for the answer there.

"You see, you were thinking of everyone but yourself. You're such a good person, Becca. They'll see that, and they'll love you!" My encouraging words did little to lift her spirits. Ty's family really did a number on her.

"I guess, but there's so much else going on. And since we got back, everything is back to normal, at least with him. But I can't shake this feeling from the weekend—something isn't right." She promptly stood up, grabbing me with her.

"Come on, let's get to class. Thanks for listening. I feel a lot better. Even knowing you know is helping a lot."

We walked arm in arm on the way to our building. There were so many things upside down in our lives. But I would have to make a point of staying on top of this with her.

"Can we meet for dinner tonight, all of us? That would be my best medicine." She looked at me, hopeful, knowing Logan and I hadn't spoken yet. "I'm hoping Logan will find you by then and we can try to have a meal together. Do you think Xander will be OK joining us?" Becca really wanted all of us to get along.

"I'll ask him." We set a time to meet later to eat and branched off at our buildings, each headed in a different direction. Hopefully Xander would find it in him to, once again, be friends with Logan.

After class, I found my bench near the student union. I hadn't sat on it in quite a while and decided I could use some alone time to think after everything that had happened lately. With my hot tea in hand, I sat under my favorite tree, its leaves a deep orange, many of them on the ground around me.

My first thought was Karl. Was he still here? I hadn't seen or heard from him, but he had said I wouldn't. I had a feeling he was gone because Max made his appearance, but I wasn't sure that boded well for Karl.

I looked around, observing the people milling about, wondering about the couples I was seeing and how many of them had survived the semester so far.

Were there any still together?

How many were brand new?

I looked at their body language and tried to decipher for myself the duration of some of the relationships between the couples that walked on by. And now I could be considered part of one of these couples. What did people see from the outside when Xander and I were together? I knew we were not officially a "couple," but more and more it was feeling that way.

"Hi, Lanie."

The bench shook when his large body plopped down next to mine. Looking over, I became a bit nervous.

"Hi, Logan." We sat there for a few minutes, staring ahead, neither looking at the other. The silence became a bit uncomfortable, but not enough for him to start talking. I felt it wasn't my place to start this conversation, so I let him take the lead.

"I, um, have a lot I need to say to you. I hope it all comes out right." He was wringing his hands together, obviously very nervous. "I am sorry, first and foremost. That's what needs to be said. I am sorry. I never should have touched you the way I did that night. You don't deserve that, and I'll forever be mad at myself for doing that to you."

He was trying to keep eye contact with me, looking up every few words, but it seemed unless he kept his eyes focused on the ground between his feet, he would lose his train of thought.

"I got too drunk that night—many nights, actually. It's not an excuse, but it's a reason for my behavior. I wasn't in control of my actions that night because I had too much to drink. And I've been doing that too much lately, I think to try to forget a few things."

There were unshed tears in his eyes when he looked over again. The faintest hint of a blue bruise remained beneath his left eye, which meant he had a constant reminder every time he looked in a mirror.

I felt he could use a hug, but that wouldn't be a possibility from me for quite some time. Besides, I could tell he wanted to finish with what he had to say.

"I was hoping there would maybe be more than a friendship between us, Lanie, but I know now that isn't in the cards for us. I'm not gonna lie, it hurts, and I still care about you. But I can be satisfied with you being happy. So, if us being friends can make you happy, then that's what I'd like. If we can work back toward that, I want us to be friends." He rubbed his hands along his thighs, the anxiety of the moment reaching a threshold too great for him to withstand much longer.

"Logan, I'm thankful for your apology. I'm more thankful for the sincerity of it. I'm sure we can work toward being friends again, and I'd like that, a lot."

I reached out and put my hand on his leg, knowing I couldn't do much more than that. He put his hand over mine and squeezed it, looking at me as a tear spilled over and slid down his cheek, and he quickly wiped it away with his arm. But he smiled, and I smiled back. This would have to be slow, he knew that, but we were taking the first step.

"Everything good here?" I startled at Xander's appearance over my shoulder, but Logan seemed to expect him to be there.

"Yeah, Xander, everything's good. I think according to Becca, the three of us are supposed to all head over to meet them for dinner now or something." As he stood up, he looked unsure about following through on those plans at the moment. I stood and moved toward Xander.

"I think dinner together should work, don't you, Lanie?" Xander grabbed my hand while talking, a point not missed by Logan, who was now staring at our entwined fingers. It made me feel good but uncomfortable at the same time.

These lines were so blurred.

"Absolutely," I said, a bit too chipper. "Tell them we'll be there in a few, OK?" Logan took off for the cafeteria, hands in his pockets and shoulders slumped a bit, but I was sure he was glad that was over. "So, I guess you were aware this was happening?"

"He came to me about it, actually." Xander's expression was unreadable. "I wanted to punch him the second he showed up at my door, but I heard him out and he sounded sincere. So hopefully he can straighten himself out. You and I both know we all come with baggage, right?" He was handling this much better than I anticipated.

"Yes, Xander, you're right, and thanks for being understanding. I hope things can work out with Logan. But I do want you to be with me while I'm around him for a while." I squeezed his hand, and he squeezed mine back.

"Lanie, I won't let anything bad happen to you ever again." His expression when he said that literally took my breath away. His eyes portrayed a promise I couldn't believe. It sounded like a forever promise.

Not only were the lines blurred—we had raced past them.

Chapter 13

Xander and I were hiding out in his room, doing couples things without letting others see us. We cuddled together in his bed, watching a movie. We both knew we weren't going to see each other for the long holiday weekend starting the next day.

"I'm going home with Becca for Thanksgiving, I forgot to tell you." I murmured my words into his chest. He pushed us both to sitting and gave me an incredulous look. I was confused.

"What's wrong?" I asked him.

"Nothing." It didn't seem like nothing, but he effectively changed the subject. "Have you heard anything from your dad about Max since he left?"

I didn't want to answer his question because it would reveal another secret. So I did my best at deflecting as well.

"Xander, how often do you talk to your mom? Like, do you talk to her every day, or once a week?" But my deflection only led to more questions instead of answers.

"Have you not talked to your dad? It's been almost two weeks." As soon as he said it, he saw the impact his words had on me. I tried to pull away from him in the bed, but he resisted. His hold on me was firm but gentle as he wrapped his arms around me and rolled us onto our sides. He lowered his voice an octave or two when he talked again. "Um, well, my mom and I talk a lot. Usually it's every day if we can. I take it that's not the case with you and your parents?"

All I did was shake my head a bit. I didn't want to talk about this, but Xander wasn't willing to let it go.

"Do they know you're not coming home for Thanksgiving?"

And again, all I did was shake my head. My words wouldn't come. Our faces were close; we were sharing the same pillow. So it was impossible to hide the embarrassment that spread across my cheeks.

"Hey, it's OK. Everyone has their own relationships, doesn't make it right or wrong." His hand stroked my cheek in an attempt to console me as I was starting to fidget, my distress showing. "What can I do? How can I help?"

I knew what I needed to do, but I didn't want to. But maybe with Xander's help, it wouldn't be so . . . terrible.

"Well, I do know that I need to call my parents to tell them I'm not coming home this weekend." I sat up, and my arms instinctively wrapped around my knees. It was my protective stance, and Xander recognized it.

"I could help you, be there for you." He moved toward me, his hands starting to reach out but retreating. He picked up on the intensity of the moment and my fragile state. We sat across from one another for a quiet moment.

I finally spoke up. "OK." He looked relieved. "I'd like if you'd be there with me when I call my dad."

Xander let out an audible breath and smiled. "I can do that."

I wasn't used to having someone with me, on my side, all the time. I was still skeptical and not completely ready to trust Xander with all of my darkness. But I was slowly letting him in. He was proving to be someone who I could depend on.

It was too late to call that night. We made a plan to call my dad the next day during a break he and I both had between classes. Xander seemed content with that plan as he scooped me up in his arms and resumed watching the movie. Drifting off to sleep, I felt at ease. Our bodies were so close I could smell his familiar woodsy scent, most likely from his soap.

My body and soul felt protected as my dreams took over. Dreams, not nightmares.

Me:

Can we meet in your room to make the call in like 10

Xander:

Sure see you then

Before my knuckles hit the door, it flew open. Xander pulled me inside his room, closing the door with a kick of his foot. He had me in an embrace before either of us said hello.

He felt the tension in my body. Every part he was touching on me was tight and tense, including my lips.

"OK, now is probably not the right time for this, so let's get this call over with, Lanie."

I pulled from his arms and walked to his couch. I'd never been more thankful for Xander's roommate never showing up this year. He was lucky enough to have a single but in a double room. It gave him plenty of space to have parties. But it also gave us privacy. I turned toward him once we both sat.

"I don't know what to say to them. It's been so long."

Xander's look softened, and he rubbed the back of his knuckles along my cheek.

"Lanie, I don't think you have to have anything prepared to say to them. They're your parents, and regardless of what you think has been going on with them, I'm pretty sure they still love you. Why don't you let the conversation happen naturally? Maybe just ask them what they're doing for Thanksgiving as you tell them about you."

"OK, I can do that." I opened my phone and dialed my dad's number, putting it on speaker so Xander could hear the whole conversation. My dad picked up after one ring.

"Elaina? Is that you?" My dad's voice was strained, nervous sounding.

Xander looked at me with strange eyes and mouthed, *"Elaina?"*

"Yeah, Dad, it's me. Hi, how are ya?"

"Oh my God, Elaina, I'm glad you finally called us. I'm so glad you're OK. You are OK, right?" my dad asked.

Wow, I was not expecting him to sound like this.

"Yeah, Dad, I'm OK. I, um, was calling to find out what you and Mom were doing for Thanksgiving and to, uh, tell you I'm not coming home." I shrugged my shoulders at Xander, hoping this sounded natural. He nodded, encouraging me, so I guess it sounded good.

"Lanie, your mom and I left Texas about six weeks ago. We've been staying in DC. I'm guessing you didn't get my messages. There's so much going on that I should catch you up on, but not now." He stopped talking, and I heard noises through the phone, like he was moving items on his desk. "Most importantly, I need to let you know about the account I have set up for you. I'm going to give you the account numbers over the phone now so there's no trail for anyone to trace, OK? I've put aside enough money to keep you safe. You don't ever have to go back to Texas," my father said.

My eyes were bulging and tearing up at the same time.
My dad knew.
He knew the whole time.
He knew what was happening to me.
I started shaking as the silent tears spilled over my lower lids.

"Daddy . . ." I couldn't say anything more than that. My voice cracked, and I started sobbing.

"Lanie . . . I'm so sorry, honey . . . I . . . never . . . I . . . just so you know, your mom never really knew about any of this. Please don't blame her or be mad. She's only really finding out now, and she's a mess. The doctor gave her some meds to help, but, well . . . Listen, we really shouldn't even be talking this long or about it on the phone. We'll need to figure out some other way. But Lanie, honey, please believe me when I say I would never, ever have let him do those things to you if it was not a matter of life or death."

I couldn't hear any more of this. I was going to be sick. I took the phone off speaker mode and was about to disconnect the call when Xander grabbed the phone.

"Mr. Montgomery, this is Lanie's boyfriend. My name is Xander James. I know about her end of it—well, most of it. I'm keeping her safe here, sir. And so you know, that guy from home who came here, he . . ."

I walked away while Xander told my dad the story of Max's visit. But I did hear my father screaming something from across the room.

"She's, uh, I think in a bit of shock at the moment," Xander said to my dad. "Why don't you give me any information you need to provide so we can end this call?" Xander got some paper and wrote down a bunch of numbers and a phone number. "Yes, sir. I'll take care of her. Thanks. OK, goodbye."

I was numb. I didn't feel anything. I wasn't even crying anymore. Maybe I was going into shock. But would I be aware of going into shock if I was going into shock?

"Lanie, look at me." Xander pulled me toward him, forcing me to look at him. All I wanted to do was curl up in bed, maybe with my e-reader or with my music playlist.

"Xander, I can't do this. I don't want to do this." I tried to shake out of his grasp, push him off of me. *"Stop! Don't touch me!"*

He let go of me as if I were on fire. I retreated to the corner of the couch, pulled my knees up to my chest, and curled into a ball. He kept his distance for a little while. Eventually he worked his way closer to me so our knees were touching. I couldn't move any farther away, tucked into the corner as much as I could be. I felt his hand on my leg, the slightest touch, tentative.

I hated that I was doing this to him.

But I couldn't help it. I didn't want to do this anymore. I was done.

"Lanie, please don't shut me out." It was a whisper. A calm voice for the storm inside my head, but it was barely breaking through. Bringing my hands up to my face and covering my eyes, I was hoping it would all just go away. "I know you feel like your world is crashing around you and you have nowhere to turn, but you have me. I'll always be here for you to turn to."

"Xander, I can't do this," I cried with such desperation in my voice, my hands flailing from my face. "Don't you see me right now? I'm a useless shell of a person, used, abused, with nothing left for you. You should get out now while you can." I started to jerk my body away from him, but knew I had to say more. "You know I haven't told you everything. Well, the parts I haven't told you are so bad, they're dark and disgusting. There's a part of my relationship with Max that is so twisted and wrong that I can't even come to terms with it myself." My eyes looked to the ceiling, my self-loathing taking over.

He was quiet after I said that, probably contemplating what I'd said. Maybe even starting to realize the truth in it.

"Lanie, what are you talking about?" He tried to turn me toward him, but I shrugged out of his hold and refused.

Finding my voice, I realized I was furious at the news from the call. "To find out my father knows, that he knew the whole time about Max abusing me, it makes it worse! How could he?!"

Xander kept his distance for a moment, I'm sure wondering if my outburst was over. Eventually, he approached me and looked me in the eye.

"We see things very differently, Lanie. What I see right now is someone who received probably some of the worst news they could have gotten, and what are you doing? You're keeping it together. I see a woman who has gotten strong because of and in spite of all the shit she's been through. You aren't freaking out or punching things like I would be. You're calmly processing it. You're allowing your mind the time it needs to adjust to this fucked up situation you're now in. Babe, you're not a useless person. You are the most amazing human I've ever known."

He had my hands in his, and the warmth I craved from him wormed its way through my veins, up my arms.

"Lanie, please look at me." I didn't feel ready yet, but my eyes betrayed me and listened to my heart instead of my brain. I looked into those deep blue eyes and became lost in them. "With you is exactly where I belong. Remember, I told you I would be here to catch you."

There were no words for this man. I continued to look into his eyes, nodding my head, acknowledging that I'd heard him as best I could.

"I really wish I never made that phone call to him. That was information we didn't need, Xander. What good has that done? It's only shattered me more." We'd moved back to the couch, sitting together. His arms were around my shoulders, and I fell into the crook of his neck, my head nestled perfectly into the spot under his chin as if it were made for me.

"Babe, I don't agree. You might not like knowing your dad knew, but look at it this way. He was trying to help you. He wasn't standing by doing absolutely nothing. There is this account he has for you, and you didn't hear him at the end, but they're leaving the country. I think this is a lot bigger than you even realize. Do you really know who the Marcellos are?" I sat up immediately when he said this.

"Where are they going? What do you mean they're leaving the country? He's a congressman. He can't just up and leave, can he?" I immediately grabbed for my laptop and started plugging my dad's name into the search bar. Tons of news articles popped up about his early retirement from his political position.

"Oh my God, Xander, he quit. That was his life. They forced him out somehow. How does an oil exec force my dad out of office?" I looked over at him with fear in my eyes. "Where is that account number?" He handed it to me, and I started plugging it in. "Did he give you a username and a password?" My voice was choppy with nerves, unsure of what would pop up on the screen.

"Yeah, here," Xander said as he pointed to more information on the paper.

Xander was looking over my shoulder as the account was brought up on the screen. "Holy shit, Lanie, that's insane." There was over half a million dollars in an account without a name attached to it set up for me.

"I really don't know what all of this means exactly. I'm even more confused than ever. Why now? Why didn't he help me before now?" I wanted to believe my father was doing the right thing, that he genuinely was a good father. But he let too many bad things happen to me already.

All of a sudden, there was a sharp knock on Xander's door.

"Lanie, are you in there?" It was Becca.

"Xander, I can't see Becca right now. Look at me. I'm

a mess. What am I going to do?"

Xander went to the door.

"Hey, Becca, what's up?" Xander asked while holding the door so she couldn't see me.

"Have you seen Lanie? I wanted to know if she could be ready to leave a bit earlier. Heard traffic is getting bad."

Xander looked my way, his eyes telling me he thought I should talk to her. I moved toward the door, wiping my eyes as I went.

"How do I look?" I mouthed to him before letting her see me.

"You look beautiful, as always," he whispered as he let the door fall open.

Becca came in like a ball of energy, obviously excited about the long weekend ahead. She froze, though, when she saw my face.

I obviously did not look beautiful. I turned my betrayed eyes toward Xander, and he just shrugged.

"Lanie, what's wrong?" Becca asked, concerned.

All I could do was look back and forth between the two people in my life who I trusted most. But at that moment, I had no words for her. Xander saw me struggling and came to my rescue.

"Becca, Lanie just got some crazy news from her parents. Her dad quit his job and they're moving overseas. They did all of this without telling her, and she's really upset right now." Wow, he was quick. And none of it was even a lie. "She can be ready soon. Give her a few minutes, OK?"

"Sure, I'm still packing up some things. I'll be in our room. How 'bout we leave in an hour, OK?"

I nodded as she hugged me before leaving the room. Once the door clicked into place, I spun on my heels toward Xander.

"Xander, that was perfect! I won't have to lie to her now. Thank you." Pulling him into my arms, I couldn't help but be flooded with mixed emotions about our relationship, with the thought that it shouldn't even be happening. Who would willingly walk into such a fucked-up situation? But when I looked at him, the determination on his face calmed my fears. He seemed committed, decisive in his actions. I needed to stop questioning him.

His look also held something else I was getting used to seeing: desire.

But then he pulled away, his hands cradling my cheeks. He stared into my eyes, the intensity palpable. He seemed like he was about to kiss me, but hesitated.

"I don't want you to pull away. I want you to kiss me," I almost begged.

He was looking at me with uncertainty in his eyes. The stress of our current situation, coupled with what happened last time, was enough for him to doubt this could happen.

I didn't blame him.

But I felt like I could do it.

I knew I could.

I needed to.

Before my next breath, his lips crashed into mine, stealing my air, giving me his.

Our worlds were colliding, becoming one, out of our control.

I felt if he pulled away from me, I wouldn't be able to breathe, to stand.

Our lips were still exploring one another, tongues tasting and delving deep. My hands were roving over the ripples of muscles on his back, reaching around to feel the deep V dipping below the waist of his jeans. I dragged my fingers along his stomach, feeling the ridges as I moved up toward his chest. I loved feeling the bumps spread across the flesh, thrilled I elicited this response in him from my touch. His hands had stilled on my ass during this, holding on, pulling me toward him, grinding into me.

I could feel him, his need.

His mouth left mine and moved on to my neck, licking the saltiness behind my ear, moving onto my shoulder. I shuddered with a fervor to match his.

I grabbed the length of his hair at the back of his head as he kissed down my neck, his hand still holding on to my ass. The moan that escaped my mouth betrayed me. I was trying to stay in control because I knew this shouldn't go much further.

But I didn't want to be the one to stop this, this amazing feeling that was consuming my soul. I had never felt such an intensity with another person, such power in our emotions.

It was overwhelming.

It was thrilling.

It was breathtaking.

It was scary, but so worth it.

But . . .

"I think . . ." It came out barely as a whisper into my ear.

I didn't feel the darkness. It wasn't coming this time. I could do it.

"Xander, I'm good. I'm here."

"It feels amazing, Lanie, but I don't think you're ready for more." Yet as he was saying the words, my body and my hips pushed up against his. He peered at me, the heat in his eyes very clear.

We were about to lose control of ourselves.

"Lanie," he whispered, "you're leaving soon. I don't want to start something that we can't finish. Properly." The tiny kisses on my neck became less and less, and his fingers were no longer digging into my waist with the same intensity.

I looked at him with regret in my eyes, and he saw it. He brought his mouth to my lips and kissed me with so much devotion that his message could not be mistaken.

"Besides, I think we still need to discuss that 'friendship zone' thing, don't we?" He softly chuckled into my mouth as he said this, lightening the mood to exactly where we needed it to be. "Don't get me wrong, you're my best friend. But I need to get out of the 'friend zone' soon. Can we agree on that at least?" He held my face close while looking at me, eye to eye, nose to nose.

"Yes, we can agree on that." I smiled against his lips, his arms going around my waist, mine going around his neck. "I'm still nervous, but I know this is where I want to be, right here with you." His smile was infectious. I knew my life's goal would be to make him smile like that every day.

"We'll take it slow. Especially with what happened with Max and now your parents, I don't think anyone else needs to know what's going on between us." He leaned down and placed a simple kiss on my mouth, his soft lips lingering dangerously long. "We'll keep it between us for now. I think that's best, too, especially until we figure out all this shit with Max."

Reality check: we still had that to deal with.

He walked to his dresser and started packing his bag. We all had to be out by that evening, which meant he was leaving soon, too.

"I guess I should go finish packing, too," I said.

"Wait, don't go yet. Give me one sec." He threw a few more things in a duffle and came back to the couch. "I wanted to ask you something." He hesitated, which was unlike him. "So, your parents won't be around for Christmas either, right?" I nodded, not sure where he was going with this. "Are you going to ask Becca if you can go home with her then, too?" His voice sounded upset when he asked.

"Yeah, I guess so. I don't have anyone else to ask."

There was a prolonged silence between us as he studied my face. But he looked away before saying his next words.

"You could come home with me." And then I understood—he wanted me to come home with him for Thanksgiving as well.

This friend boundary was forever gone.

"That would be a very big step for us. And how do you know your mom would be OK with that?"

"Are you kidding me?" he shrieked. "First of all, she would love you. Second, she would be thrilled to have another girl in the house and not be surrounded by Bryce and me and our grossness all the time. His room is empty because he doesn't live at home anymore, so there's even a room for you. Lanie, it's perfect. We would spend Christmas together. Think of all the firsts I could give you."

His eyes were screaming with excitement while he kept the rest of his face in check. He was working hard to not get too happy before I gave him an answer. How could I say no to him? More importantly, I didn't want to say no. He stayed a few feet from me, hesitant, waiting for my response.

But this was a huge step. Spending a whole month together, in the same house, was a far cry from just stepping out of the friend zone. This was long-term relationship zone. I knew my hesitation to answer him was making him upset and nervous at the same time, but I wasn't sure if this was the right thing to do. But to be honest, where else would I really want to be? I feared if I went home with Becca instead, I would spend the month missing Xander anyway; I missed him here at school if I didn't see him for a few hours.

Oh my God, this was crazy.

"Xander, I would love to spend Christmas with you." He ran toward me, picked me up, and spun me around in circles until I was dizzy and laughing out loud. "You're very good at keeping your promises, ya know."

"What promise is that, babe?" he said while smiling hard as he put me down on the ground. I would never tire of seeing that deep dimple.

"You're showing me what a real boyfriend is like. And you're good at it."

"Lanie, this is only the beginning, babe." His hands were on my face again, looking in my eyes. "Give me time. I'm going to sweep you off your feet in more ways than one."

Chapter 14

"Lanie, turn that up. I love that song!"

We were driving back to school after our weekend home for Thanksgiving, sitting in a ton of traffic on the interstate. We were making the best of it by blasting our music and singing our hearts out. The people in all the cars around us were staring at us, but we didn't care. It was helping pass the time, and we were having fun.

These past few days had done wonderful things for my and Becca's friendship. It had become strained by the stressful situations we had all endured the past weeks. But with no schoolwork, no guys, and good food, all we did was focus on us and just being goofy friends. And she helped me forget about all the crap going on with my parents.

"I've missed hanging out with the guys, Becca. I hope we can start doing that again."

She looked over at me with a huge grin on her face. "Lanie, that made my day, girl! I want that, too! Will Xander be OK with that, though? I know he's not Logan's biggest fan, and I don't blame him one bit." The traffic finally started moving again.

"No, he's not, but I think he'll be understanding enough about the fact that I want to hang out with my friends. Do you think the five of us could maybe do more things together?" I snuck a look at her to see her reaction, wondering if she thought that could work. Even though Xander and I were keeping us a "secret," Becca wasn't dumb. She knew there was something between us even before I did.

"Maybe. We could give it a shot and see. I wonder if those two can be in each other's presence."

I didn't miss her eye roll before I responded. "Ya know, we did all eat together a couple weeks ago." The reminder didn't do much to change her mind.

"Yeah and look how well that went. Logan sat in the corner pouting while Xander spent the entire time clinging to you and puffing out his chest." She wasn't wrong, but I had faith that they'd both moved on a bit since then.

A little while later, we finally pulled into the lot behind our dorm. I couldn't wait to get upstairs to see if Xander was back.

I missed him.

A lot.

I didn't expect to have those feelings. Missing someone was not a part of my history. Rather, any time spent apart was welcomed and cherished. If Max was gone for a weekend with his dad for something, I felt like I could . . . breathe.

Complete opposite this go-round. Every time I got a text, instead of the dread I would normally feel, I was excited, hoping it was from Xander. I felt lost without him, counting the minutes until our return. Well, in my head, anyway. I enjoyed my time with Becca and didn't want her to feel I was not appreciative of her hospitality.

But I couldn't wait to get back to school.

After lugging my bag off the elevator, I rounded the corner, hoping to see his door open, but it wasn't. I hid my disappointment from Becca since we were still trying to be somewhat quiet about the status of us. Becca and I continued to our room and commenced unpacking.

"Ty and Logan are going to come by. Is that OK?"

"Sure, I'd love to see them." And I meant it. It was amazing to feel so positive about things. This was new for me. "We need to eat. Let's go get dinner, just like old times." I smiled as I hung up clothes in my closet.

"Sounds perfect, Lanie. I'll text Ty."

The guys were in our room in a matter of minutes, whining as usual about how hungry they were.

"Your clothes will still be here after we eat, ya know. Can't we go eat now? Come on, guys, I'm wasting away to nothin' here." Ty was complaining, but Logan was kind of quiet, sitting at my desk and fiddling with my phone charger. We'd only seen each other a handful of times since the night of the party in Xander's room. I could sense his discomfort.

"Come on, Becca. He's right. And I'm pretty hungry too. We were in the car forever."

"See, Lanie knows what she's talking about." Ty came over and wrapped his arm around my shoulder as we started down the hall toward the elevators. "Thanks, Lanie. And I mean thanks for going to dinner with us and including Logan. It means a lot to him. He needs it."

I nodded up at him as I hugged him around his waist,

happy to have our group somewhat back together. Becca walked with Logan, trying to get him to loosen up. As we hiked across campus to the cafeteria, I sent Xander a quick note telling him to meet us there if he got back any time soon.

We found a table for the four of us pretty easily. The campus wasn't too crowded yet. I resorted to a basic salad; I overate all weekend long with Becca's mom's cooking for the holiday. The guys came back to the table with mounds of food spilling from their trays, which meant we would be here for a while.

"So, how was everyone's Thanksgiving? Did you two have fun being together at Becca's house?" Logan spoke up first, breaking the ice between us. After that, the conversation flowed between us, and it felt almost normal. I smiled softly to myself, hopeful this was a sign of good things to come.

"I can't believe you didn't come to a single football game this year, Lanie. But at least we have this last hurrah before the ragers are done for the semester." Becca was pouting but also very drunk. And I think I was, too.

The five of us went to Mid Street for the biggest day party of the season other than the football tailgates. Every year, the week after Thanksgiving, and before finals got started, a huge outdoor tailgate was held by all of the fraternities. They called it the "BRU Blackout."

I was happy when Xander suggested we all go together. When he got back from Thanksgiving break, we had a talk. The agreement was, he would hang out with the guys, but

Logan only got one chance. If he messed it up, that was it. And I agreed.

We were at Xander's frat house on the party strip, hanging out in the yard where all the houses kind of connected. Most of the frats had a house here, so on party days it became one huge tailgate party with thousands of college kids.

"I know. What will we do until the spring? This is amazing. I'm glad I came today!" I wasn't too happy with myself for consistently saying no to her about coming to the games. I went to one of the biggest football schools in the country, and I had bailed on going to any of the games.

"Oh my God, Lanie, I'm so glad you finally came. Isn't this amazing? And the scenery isn't bad either!" I saw her checking out her fair share of cute guys, even though she came with her boyfriend. Ty and Logan were in the house somewhere with Xander, I think getting to know some more of the brothers. I gave her a look of caution, looking toward the house to make sure Ty wasn't nearby.

"Ugh, don't worry about Ty. With how our weekend went at his parents' house, let him think I might be straying. I don't know, maybe I will." As she was staring at another hot one, she bumped into someone and almost landed on her ass.

"OK, Becca, why don't we go inside for a bit? See if there's somewhere you can sit for a while." I started leading her toward the stairs when Ty miraculously appeared at our side. "Ty, she needs to go in for a while. She's had too much."

"No, I haven't! I'm fine, and I wanna to stay right here where all the cute guys are checking out my ass!" She struggled to stand while Ty guided her toward the steps.

"It's OK, Bec. There are plenty of other guys in the

house who will check you out, too. Let's go in." Ty was being great with her. I was impressed he wasn't jealous. "Lanie, come on in, too. Xander's still inside. I'll take care of Becca."

We found ourselves in a room that was elbow to elbow and had nowhere to go. Ty moved straight to the kitchen and immediately found Logan and Xander. He said something to Xander, who then pointed up the stairs.

"Hey, beautiful, where have you been?" Xander made his way over, and his words were only for me. They gave me chills as he whispered them in my ear. His one arm snaked around my waist as he artfully played it off as though he were trying to get by me. We were working hard to still keep whatever we were a secret, though I knew he wanted everyone to know. But in true Xander form, he was honoring my wishes.

"I was outside with Becca, but she's had one too many, so Ty brought her upstairs."

He looked at me as if to say, "Not what I meant," but the moment passed.

"I wish we could go upstairs." His now mischievous look was also full of want and need, something I was starting to see more and more on his face.

"Um, well . . . I don't think that would be a good idea." Again, not the answer he was looking for. "I don't want anyone talking; plus Logan's here." That was definitely not the response he wanted from me at all. He walked away, obviously mad.

I caught up to him, grabbing him by the arm. He spun around to face me, the hurt all over his face.

"Lanie, when are we all going to stop walking on egg-shells around him? He's a big boy. I'm sure he can handle it." But as he was saying this, he saw my face, and he changed his tone immediately. "I'm sorry. I know you're not ready, and we made this decision together. But I hope he's not what's keeping us from being where I want us to be. Please tell me we're doing this for you."

I shuddered at the thought of him thinking that. I grabbed his hand and tried to pull him away from the crowd, anywhere we could be alone for a minute. As I was dragging him through the house, frantically looking for a quiet spot, he guided me outside. We found ourselves in a quiet corner of the yard, away from prying eyes.

"Xander, I'm sorry I've made you feel that way. I . . ."

"Lanie, stop. I'm sorry. I don't want you to feel pressured to do anything before you're ready."

I was still holding his hands and I pulled him closer to me, wrapping his hands around my waist. He latched on and held me close, our faces almost touching.

"Xander, it's not for anyone else but me that I'm doing this. I would love to let the whole world know we are what we are, but I'm scared. I'm scared because *wanting* to be with another person feels foreign to me. I've never actually been in a healthy relationship. I'm trying to adjust to these feelings of actually being happy. But now I'm scared you won't wait for me."

At that, his face fell, and I didn't know how to read him. Did I hit a nerve? Was he getting tired of this charade? Did he think I was playing games with him? His face wasn't giving away any clues to how he was really feeling—just a stoic expression remained.

"I don't know how to do this, Xander. But I'm trying to figure it out, to learn, because trust me, I don't want to lose the best thing that's ever happened to me." I was nervous this was it, that he was going to walk away from me. Too tired of all the shit he put up with being in my life. I started sweating, my hands wringing together as I pulled back from him. He finally looked up at me, ready to respond.

"There you guys are. Come on—stop hiding out in a corner trying to cover up that you're hooking up! Let's go. It's a party!"

How was Becca even standing? She grabbed a hold of both of us, Ty and Logan behind her, both shrugging as if they couldn't keep her away. Xander and I struggled against her, but she was not having that.

"This is Lanie's first time here all semester. We need to make this epic!" Xander gave me a forlorn look, which did not offer me any encouragement. We left our peaceful corner in the hands of our drunken friend.

"OK, OK, Becca, we're coming, relax." I was not in the mood to be here anymore, surrounded by partying kids. They all seemed oblivious to the strain my heart was feeling. All five of us reentered the crazy zone, me hoping I could maybe slip out unnoticed.

"Becca, we need one more minute. Then I promise I'll give Lanie back to you." Xander grabbed my hand and dragged us back the way we had come, faster than our original retreat. I was even more hesitant than before to hear what he had to say.

His hands were still holding mine, but I wanted them back. I didn't feel like I could handle this without bracing myself against something.

"You know you're an open book, right?" His question ended with a smirk on his face, a small laugh escaping his lips. This did not coincide with the Xander I was expecting to have in front of me. "Lanie, stop. I see it all over your face. I'm not mad at you. Please know I'm in this for the long haul." He moved his hands up to cradle my face as my first tear slipped out and I tried to look away. His thumb made quick work of making it disappear and kept me looking his way.

"I know you're not ready, or don't think you're ready. That's OK. I'm not going anywhere. If I've made you feel that way, I'm sorry, and I'll work harder to make sure you always understand that."

His eyes conveyed a sorrow I knew I put there. This was making me feel a whole different kind of sad.

"Xander, you've done nothing wrong. It's all in my head, the insecurities, the fear . . ."

"Lanie." He put his fingers gently over my lips. "Stop with the explanations. We're good, very good. Let's move on. I don't want to put you in a position where you have to always tell me all the things you're struggling with. I understand, and it's OK."

I heard the empathy in his voice.

"Besides, Becca reminded me today is another first for you, and we've spent too much time over here. Although I don't mind being in a secluded corner with you, there are other things I'd rather do than talk."

My eyes scanned the yard, making sure we weren't garnering too much attention. Everyone was too far gone to be paying us any mind. I leaned in on my tippy toes. Xander immediately realized what my action meant and took over the moment, grabbing my face with more urgency.

Our lips collided, and all my fears melted away. I was fascinated by his uncanny ability to do this. His hand had a hold of my neck and jaw, his thumb grazing my cheek as our mouths devoured one another. My hands found the hem of his shirt and began lifting it up, completely ignoring the fact that we were in public. His hand was on mine instantly.

"I can't believe I'm going to stop you, but I don't want you to regret anything we do out here with eyes on us." He whispered this in my ear as he was grinding his body up against mine, such a contradiction. Dropping my head to his chest, I willed myself to pull away. "But hey, we can always go back to my room after the party and finish where we left off."

I looked up at him with wanton eyes as I reluctantly pulled myself even further away. "Why do I question 'us' so much? You make me feel so good, yet I'm constantly putting the brakes on us becoming *us.*"

"That's where you're wrong. We're already 'us,' Lanie. You aren't ready for the outside world to invade it, but we're already there. That's what I've been trying to tell you. Your pace, babe, your pace." He leaned in and kissed my forehead.

"Get a room, you two!" We both jerked our heads toward the voice and realized a couple of his frat brothers were watching us intently. Xander put his arm around me as we started back toward Becca and the guys.

We failed today. We failed miserably.

"I'm working on it, guys. Give us time. She'll be mine, so make sure you steer clear."

And once again, he was a master.

"Why did you let me drink that much, Lanie? This is awful. And on a Sunday no less. Why do they have to do Blackout on a Sunday?" Becca had just returned from her third visit to the bathroom, I'm assuming ridding her body of the excess alcohol she enjoyed yesterday. "Please don't let me do that again anytime soon." She plopped on her bed in total despair.

"Hey, there was no way I was going to stop anything you were doing yesterday. But I'll definitely remind you of this morning next time." I was getting my bag ready to head out to class. "Am I to assume you aren't going to class today?" I said this with a sarcastic chuckle.

"I'm not moving from this bed unless I have to spew the contents of my stomach again." She rolled over to look at me as I was starting toward the door. "Lane, FYI, you and Xander are doing a terrible job of keeping whatever you're calling what you guys are a secret."

She laughed when I gave her a quizzical look. "And no, it has nothing to do with the time you both spent in the corner or the hot kiss most of us witnessed. It has everything to do with the way you look at each other," Becca said with a soft chuckle.

My face, I was sure, displayed my surprise.

"I wish Ty looked at me like that. Then I would know how he really felt," Becca whispered, her voice tinged with sadness.

I paused on my way out, looking at her again but now with concern all over my face.

"Don't you worry about me; I have that all under control. He saw me yesterday, and he knows I'm not going to put up with much more of his shit. Maybe I'm going to take up with one of the several guys I could have gone home with."

Her face was all confidence, but I knew something else was behind her shield. "Lanie, I know you're struggling with stuff, but don't lose him. You may not see what others see. I just wanted to let you know."

I was rendered silent. I stood there longer than I should have, now probably late to class. There was a lot to digest in those few sentences Becca delivered.

"OK, so we aren't fooling anyone." I chuckled. "But that's not what concerns me most about what you just said." I trained my eyes on her, knowing she wasn't feeling well enough for a full-blown heart-to-heart. "Are you and Ty alright?"

She sat up a bit, seemingly ready to talk, but then sat back against her pillow with a loud sigh. "We're fine, Lanie. Don't worry about us. I've got it all under control." She looked over, saw my stare still on her, and conceded a bit. "We'll talk, I promise, just not now. I need more sleep." She rolled over, no longer facing me, before continuing, her voice muffled in her pillow. "I mean it. Don't worry about me. I'm fine, really. Normal boy-girl crap, that's all it is."

I rushed to her bedside and leaned in to kiss her head. "I'm here, like you always are for me. I'll be back soon."

On my way to the elevator, I met up with the culprit in Becca's life, plus his roommate. "Hey, guys. How are you both feeling today?" We all had class at the same time, so we usually met up to walk together these days.

"Does that mean Becca is a mess?" Ty had a look of concern on his face.

"She's no worse than either of you have been." I looked at Logan and realized he was very quiet. "You feel OK today, Logan?"

He turned toward me with a small smile. "I'm fine. I didn't drink yesterday. First time at a party that I didn't." He seemed proud of himself. "Looks like it was a good thing. Becca needed me to help her out most of the day. Lightweight." He laughed while Ty still looked concerned. We were stepping outside the dorm when he turned to me.

"Should I go back upstairs? Does she need someone?"

That was the Ty I knew, the one who cared for Becca apparently as much as Xander did for me. But there was obviously something going on that didn't sit right with Becca.

"I think she's fine, Ty. Nothing more sleep won't fix."

He didn't look convinced. "I think I'll head to her anyway, in case she gets worse."

And he was off. I was sure Becca would appreciate his attention, and hopefully she'd open up to him.

That left Logan and me to continue walking to class together.

Alone.

This was the first time he and I had been alone since that fateful night. But it felt OK. I wasn't scared of Logan anymore. Rather, I was sad for him and everything he'd been dealing with in his own life. I looked his way, and he wouldn't make eye contact with me, appearing nervous. I could only assume he was not sure how this would go between the two of us.

"Come on. We better get going or we'll be later than we already are," I said as I looked over my shoulder at him.

His steps fell in line with mine, and we walked in companionable silence for a while. It was a beautiful late fall day. Most of the leaves were now off the trees since it was December.

"So, Logan, are you looking forward to an over-a-month-long break from school?" He didn't answer right away; rather, he was looking out at the mountains ahead.

Thinking.

"I should be, right? But not really. It only means I'll be back at home, and that's not a place I really want to be right now." He snuck a quick peek at me as we continued to walk. His face revealed how much he was truly hurting.

"I'm sorry, Logan. I wish going home was a happy thing for you. But if there's anything I can empathize with you on, it's that."

"Oh shit, Lanie, I'm sorry. I'm such an ass. Here I am complaining about my shit, and you've got much more going on with you at home." He stopped walking to say this, making me stop with him. "I know Xander's helping you out with that asshole, and I'm glad. I really am. Xander's good for you, Lanie. As hard as it is for me to admit that, he is."

"Thanks, Logan, that means a lot." My sadness for him was replaced with a sense of peace at the fact that he and I would be OK.

And that was one problem checked off the list.

Chapter 15

"Lanie, I'm really happy you're coming home with me for the holidays." Xander reached over and squeezed my thigh as he was driving.

There was a sparkle in his eye and joy in his voice as he rattled off story after animated story of Christmases in his family.

"I have so many things planned for us to do. Living close to DC means we can go see the Capitol tree, museums, and there are Christmas markets. Have you ever ice skated outside? I'm thinking that's not possible in Texas." He was laughing when he said this and was vibrating with excitement.

It sparked memories from my childhood, wonderful memories of holidays spent with my parents and grandparents in Texas. It was nice to have the occasional fond memory pop up from my time back home; too much of my mind was filled with the darkness of the more recent years.

"Well, you're right there—no snow in Texas, at least where I lived. I'm excited to have this time with you, too." But then I hesitated as I looked out the window. "I'm a little nervous to meet your family, though. What have you told them about us? I mean, do we even have a label for what we are yet?"

I think he only then realized how nervous I was. I'd been trying to hide it.

"Well, first of all, my mother is going to love you. And you know Bryce doesn't live there anymore, so we probably won't see him until tomorrow. I won't lie, my mom does think we're a couple, but to be honest, Lanie, so do I. And I was hoping you did, too."

His eyes lingered on me longer than they should have, considering he was driving. "I know we aren't saying anything at school yet, but I was looking forward to being able to be with you this month. No hiding. I want that badly. I think I need it." His fingers dug into my thigh with an urgency I wasn't expecting but didn't mind. I grabbed his hand and squeezed it back. I brought it up to my mouth, kissing the back of it, before responding to him.

"Xander, it sounds wonderful to be able to spend the next month not worrying about anyone or anything. And I'm sorry if I made you feel anything less to me than you really are. You're everything, my everything." I looked out the window before saying my next words, unsure of how he would receive them. "I guess the labels don't do it for me. Calling *him* my boyfriend has ruined that label for me, I think."

He seemed to accept that explanation, his head nodding in understanding. I leaned over and kissed the corner of his mouth. The groan that escaped from his throat told me he'd like more than that simple gesture. But it looked like we were leaving the interstate, meaning we were almost to his house.

I was a ball of nerves as he grabbed our bags from the back of his Jeep. He threw them over his shoulder, grabbed my hand, and led me through the door.

"Mom! We're here!"

I heard thudding footsteps coming down a staircase I couldn't see, and a petite, beautiful woman rounded the banister at the end of the entrance hall. Xander definitely didn't get his height from her. I was slightly above average in height at five foot seven, and I towered over her. She had long, straight raven hair. But it was her striking blue eyes that had me staring; they were an exact replica of Xander's.

"Oh my God, Alex, I've missed you so much!" Xander picked her up and hugged her while swinging her around several times. "Put me down. I'm going to be sick. I'm too old for that." She pushed him away but still had him in her hold. "Look at you, still handsome as ever. I like the hair, kiddo."

She then turned toward me with warmth in those striking eyes. "Lanie, I'm glad to have you here. It's nice to meet you." She reached out and wrapped me in her arms. For a tiny thing, she had a strong grip. Then she whispered in my ear, "I'm happy for you both to have each other, and I can't wait to get to know you."

She pulled away, holding on to my arms and looking at me, almost studying me. But it wasn't uncomfortable. I welcomed it. Her warm smile was wide as she rubbed my arms and nodded, almost in approval.

"Now, you two go ahead and put your things upstairs.

I'm turning a blind eye to the sleeping arrangements." She snickered as she walked to the back of the house to what I could only guess was the kitchen.

I looked at Xander with wide eyes. "OK, what just happened?"

"I told you she was going to love you."

"Alex?" I looked at him with skepticism all over my face. "Who have I been kissing these past few weeks?"

"I don't know, Elaina. Who have you been kissing?" He pushed a finger into my ribs and turned toward the stairs. I followed him, still full of questions.

"Where did Xander come from?"

"My full name is Alexander. On the football team in high school, they shortened it to Xander, and it stuck. Mom doesn't like it. She still calls me Alex." We got upstairs, and he turned to look at me with a wicked grin on his face. "Well, now we have a decision to make. Which room do you sleep in? Mine or Bryce's?"

"Was she serious?"

"I really don't know. I've never brought a girl home before, but I don't think she would have said that if she didn't mean it."

I started to get a little nervous. I mean, Xander and I slept in his bed the weekend Max came, but it was out of necessity. This was different. I mean, Xander and I hadn't done anything more than kiss and grope each other.

He saw my face. "OK, too much, too soon. I don't disagree. Let's set you up in the spare but keep our options open. How does that sound?"

He lifted my chin and put his mouth on mine. I shivered at his touch, and he immediately dropped all the bags. He pulled me into his arms while walking me backward into the room toward his bed. Then his hands were all over me, from my head to my neck and down my back. They eventually rested on the tops of my thighs, right under my ass, ready to pull me up toward him.

I immediately wanted nothing more than to be in any bed with him.

"Is this OK, Lanie?"

Such a different person.

Thinking of me and me only.

I looked up at him, nodding my approval, his smile signaling his desire. The mood shifted; a craving had to be met.

My hands twisted in the long hair on his neck, pulling him closer. I needed him closer. I needed that electric pulse I felt every time he touched me. I needed it all over my body. I felt the backs of my knees hit the edge of the bed, and he gently laid me down. His arms, bent at the elbow, caging my face, surrounded me as he lowered his body onto mine. I felt the heaviness of his body, him supporting most of his weight with a knee between my legs.

And then it hit.

The panic.

The anxiety.

The terror.

This was the first time he had been on top of me, his body over me, his weight pushing on me, making me feel as if I couldn't get up.

I felt trapped.

At first, I froze, my mouth stilled on his. His hands stopped moving as he sensed the shift in our atmosphere, neither of us able to breathe any longer.

It only took seconds, but it felt like time stood still.

But I took control the best I could to try to play it off.

His mom was right downstairs. I didn't want to have a panic attack within minutes of arriving at his house.

"Hey," I said, gently pushing him away. "We just got here. I would hate for your mom to walk in on us." Xander searched my face for any sign of distress. I didn't know how good or bad I was doing.

He supported his weight above me, his arms surrounding my head, as he studied my face intently. I held his gaze as best I could, but he knew me. He slowly moved over to the side, turning us to face each other. "You're not telling me everything right now, are you, Lanie?"

I turned my face away, ashamed. I was tired of being incapable of a normal relationship. Tired of not being able to be intimate. He reached out to turn my face to him, but I hauled myself up to the top of the bed and covered my face with my hands.

"Lanie, it's OK." His hands sought mine, trying to pull my arms apart, but I resisted. Instead, he resorted to sitting up against the wall next to me, his legs leaning against mine, his shoulders slouched in defeat. We sat this way for a while, the silence getting louder and louder between us. It was deafening.

I don't know why I suddenly felt ready, but I did.

I felt ready to let him in.

"He was always on top of me, forcing himself on me, not letting me up, ever." I still had my face hidden, these confessions too laden with shame to look up. Xander didn't move, I think afraid if he did, I might stop.

"Most times, when he was raping me, his hands would be around my throat, choking me out to keep me quiet, keep me from screaming. There were times I thought he would kill me, his hold was so tight, and there were times

I wished he had." I snuck a peek only to see him staring straight ahead, his eyes distant but appearing to gather tears. His hands were balanced on his bent knees as he twisted them together.

I was nervous this was going to change everything. Change us forever.

"Ya know, that first night, when Max and I were introduced, it started then. We were in my parents' pool house, and he attacked me, ripped my panties off, groped me, invaded my body with his hands. He didn't have 'sex' with me that first time, but he did other things, things that scared me and messed with my head. My first kiss was only minutes before, and here he was touching himself while he was touching me, all over my body, ripping my dress off."

I paused, gathering myself. This was harder than I expected. I'd never spoken these words to anyone. But now that I'd started, I felt like it all needed to come out.

"I haven't worn another dress since that night." I finally looked up and turned my head to find Xander's gaze upon mine, his face unreadable. "I refused to make it easy for him ever again."

"Alex? Lanie?" Xander's mom was fast approaching his room, and he raced to the door so she wouldn't interrupt us, knowing this moment was too important.

Xander ran into the hall to intercept her before she made it to us, closing the door behind him. All I could hear were quiet mumblings before he came back in, the door clicking back into place.

"She's going to call us when dinner is ready." That was all he said as he returned to his spot next to me on the bed, but this time, he reached out and grabbed for my hand. I relinquished, allowing him to hold it in his, enjoying the support it offered.

The interruption seemed to kill the moment, and I wasn't sure how much more I wanted to divulge. I absent-mindedly started rubbing his hand with my thumb, my mind stuck between wanting to tell him everything and wanting to protect myself from what really happened.

"Do you want to tell me any more?" Xander's voice was calm.

"I honestly don't know." I looked up at him, thinking I could decide once I saw the look on his face.

"Is there a lot more to tell?" It seemed as though he was afraid to ask this one, afraid to know the answer.

I didn't know how to answer that question. Of course there was more to tell, but I didn't really want to tell it.

This was enough for now. All I could do was nod.

He pulled me closer, my head resting on his shoulder. I relaxed against his body, not thinking I could fully relax after what we had just been through, but thankful for it at the same time.

"Thank you for trusting me with your story. I know that had to be really hard, and I need you to know I'm here for you in any way you need me to be. If it's to hold you, I'm here. If it's to listen, I'm here. If it's to just sit in the same room with you, I'm here." His lips brushed against my forehead once he finished as I reached around and gripped him tighter. I felt his warmth wrapping me up like a blanket, soothing me with every beat of his heart I felt against his chest. He reached his hand around to grip my chin, pulling my face up to see his.

"I'll always be here for you. I'll always catch you."

Xander managed to drag me from the bottom, dig me up from the depths of my despair, and bring us both back to the surface. He was magically able to turn a tragic moment of gloom into one of growth in our relationship.

He rubbed my lip with his thumb, and my eyes closed as I relished the feeling. I was surprised he could easily bring me back to a moment of desire after my collapse.

"Alex! Lanie! Time for dinner!"

"Oh my God, you have got to be kidding me. She has the worst timing!" Xander slammed his back against the wall we were leaning against in frustration.

"Xander, I think she knows exactly what she's doing. Unfortunately, she has no clue she isn't interrupting what she thought she was." My sadness came through, and Xander came to me immediately.

"Hey, no worries. That's what's great about all of this. We have this whole break together. We don't have to rush with anything. Let's take our time. Your pace, right?" He leaned in and rested a soft kiss on the outside of my mouth.

"I don't think I deserve you, Xander."

"No, you've got it backward. It's me who needs to work at deserving you, and I'm going to spend every day doing that."

"Let's get going. We're gonna meet my mom and Bryce at the farm stand in town, pick our tree today." We bundled up, me especially since I wasn't used to this northern winter weather. As we headed to the car, my phone pinged with a message from Becca.

Xander continued to be concerned that Max would find a way to get in touch with me, his eyes on my phone as I read the message.

"It's Becca just checking in. Don't worry." We continued out the door to his Jeep while I read her text. "She's not too happy with Ty, apparently. I guess I'll get an earful when we get back to school." Becca was nervous regarding their relationship heading into this break, and it seemed she had good reason.

Xander took a few turns, and we found ourselves on a quaint downtown street.

"Oh my God, your town is so cute. All the decorations make it seem like a Norman Rockwell painting." The store windows all had holiday displays, and there were lights and wreaths on all the lampposts. It seemed right out of a movie scene. We pulled into a very full lot but luckily found a spot.

"How will we find them? It's crowded."

"Don't worry, Bryce makes himself very easy to find. You'll see." He laughed as we got out of the car. As we walked, I was pulling my mittens on when suddenly I was swinging in the air by a pair of arms that weren't Xander's. I frantically looked for Xander and found him smiling from ear to ear.

"Is this the gorgeous Lanie I've heard so much about? I feel like I already know you, kid!" He finally put me down, spun me around, and gave me a huge hug. Their mom was behind him with a smile to rival Xander's. "It's great you're here with us."

"Thanks, Bryce. It's nice to meet you, too." I tried to match his enthusiasm but feared I fell short. He was a bit shorter than Xander but not by much, and not nearly as broad. His hair was buzzed short, typical police cut, and not as dark as his brother's. But their eyes, an almost identical navy blue on the both of them, matched their mom's.

Together, I was sure they'd broken many hearts. The two brothers took off, punching and pushing each other as their greeting, but it was obviously one of love. Mrs. James, who had asked me to call her Jane, came up and put her arm through mine.

"I'm sure Alex, or Xander, has told you at least some of our story." She looked at me expectantly, wanting affirmation of me knowing anything of her husband. I gave a small nod. "The boys are inexplicably close, I think because of what they endured together so young. Even though we went through such horrors, some good really did come out of it. There is always a silver lining, right, sweetheart?"

I felt like she was talking about more than just her boys, trying to reach me in a personal way. I wasn't sure how much, if any, she knew of my story, but she seemed very wise, and I thought I should pay attention.

"You might think the bad things in life will always overpower the good, but they don't. Good always seems to prevail as long as you have faith and trust in the ones you love. So trust him, because I see it in his eyes, honey, and I know he loves you already." She held my cheek before moving on to find her sons.

I needed a moment after that. My eyes were misty, but I held it together. Did Xander love me? I didn't think I knew what love was yet, but could I love him? Could I be *in love* with him? Is that what this was, what I felt when I was with him, when he touched me? I knew I only wanted to spend time with him. When something good happened, he was the first person I wanted to tell. When I was sad or scared, I needed to reach for him and his strong arms to hold and protect me.

I walked up on the three of them, who were choosing

between two trees, and saw a family I thought I could see myself being a part of. Theywere laughing together but arguing about the trees at the same time. It was obvious the arguments were for the sake of their mom—she would be the decision-maker when it came to the tree they chose. Xander looked over and found me. A huge grin spread across his face, and the genuine emotion I felt from it was heart-stopping. He beckoned me to come to him with his wagging fingers.

"You OK, babe?" He looked at me with concern.

"Yeah, I'm good. This is good." He leaned in and placed a gentle kiss on my lips that made me soar.

"Xander, I can't have any more hot chocolate. I'm going to bust!" I yelled at him as I pushed his hand away with the kettle. He was trying to refill my cup.

We had spent hours decorating the house and tree. It was fun, but at the same time it made me nostalgic for my childhood, the years when Christmas was good back home in Texas. I couldn't help missing my parents on our first Christmas apart. I looked around at the three of them. Bryce had his arms around his mom on their own couch as they gazed at the tree. Xander and I were cozied up together on a chair. I felt a twinge of guilt for feeling happy with them.

"Well, children, I think I'm done for the night," Jane said as she stood. "I still have to get up for work in the morning. I think the tree and house look wonderful. Good night, kiddos." She came around with hugs and kisses for all of us.

Bryce was the next to stand. "I need to head out too,

bro. I have an early day tomorrow. But I put in to take some time off while you're home. Maybe come by the station next week to see some of the guys. They want to bust your balls. It's been a while." He leaned in and they did the bro hug thing. Bryce turned toward me as he was walking away from us.

"Lanie, I really don't get why you're with him, but I totally get why he's with you. If he pisses you off, I'm available to console you in any way."

Xander got up and gave him a punch to the arm. "Dude, get the fuck out of here, seriously, before I really hurt you. You forgettin' I'm bigger than you?" The two of them walked together, laughing, to the door.

And then it was just us.

Xander took me by the hand and led me to the couch. We settled in, cuddling, admiring our work around the room and on the tree.

"I like Bryce. You are a lot alike, and I love seeing the two of you together. You guys have a special bond." I snuggled into the crook of his shoulder and pulled the blanket higher up. The fire was dying down, and it was getting colder in the room.

"I really don't want to talk about my brother. I was counting the minutes for them to leave us alone." He maneuvered himself so our chests were aligned, and I looked up at him.

"Listen," he said, "I know last night didn't end well for us, but I'd like to try something to help you move beyond what you went through in your past. I'll go slow, but you only need to say the word and I'll stop. Would that be OK?"

I nodded.

"Lanie, talk to me. Tell me you understand. I really

need to know that this is OK, that you want me to try this, that you want this." His blue eyes looked almost black in the fire light, dark and stormy with both passion and worry.

"I understand." But I was a bit nervous. And way too shy to talk about it. But I somehow got the words out, knowing my consent was important to him. "I want to try this with you."

"OK, we're going to take this slow. I want to make you feel good. That's my goal tonight: to make you feel good." His hands were trailing their way down my arms to my hips, around to my ass. I involuntarily pushed up against him, his hardness up against me.

"Not yet, babe."

He got up and turned off all the lights except for the Christmas tree. Between those and the light of the fire, it was magical.

He came back to the couch and sat in front of me. "Do you trust me?"

"Yes."

"Then trust me to worship you and your body. I will never hurt you or do anything you don't want me to do. Only say the word and I'll stop, OK?"

All I did was nod. He rendered me speechless. My breaths were ragged as my heart beat wildly in my chest.

His hands inched forward and grasped the hem of my shirt, lifting it up slowly. "Remember, I'm yours, and you're mine. I'll never hurt you." His eyes were intent on mine, making sure I was ready for what we were doing, clearly afraid my past experiences with *him* would come back to haunt me.

But not tonight, not now. This was only Xander and me. No one else was here with us for this.

He lifted the shirt up and over my head, then ran his fingertips down my outstretched arms, making the hairs rise up all over my body. His fingers continued down the sides of my torso to the top of my jeans. He wrapped his arms around the back of me and found the clasp to my bra, and a small gasp escaped.

"Is this OK, Lanie? Do you want me to stop?"

"No, I . . . I'm good, I'm fine." I was so flustered I couldn't keep my eyes open, the lids fluttering closed.

"Stay with me, babe. I want you to stay with me." I opened my eyes to see him intently staring into my soul, seeing parts of me no one had ever seen before. It was almost too much. I felt like I had to look away. But I didn't. I held his stare, licking my lips.

"Do you know what you do to me, Lanie?" He swallowed hard after asking that. "I don't think you do. Just you licking your lips has me wanting to rip the rest of our clothes off right here, right now. But I made a promise to myself that tonight was going to be all about you. So, try not to make it too hard on me, OK?" he chuckled.

His smoldering eyes became hooded as he leaned in and our mouths merged as if one. His hand made quick work of the hooks behind me as his mouth pulled away.

I think I actually whimpered. But then my reflexes kicked in and I was covering myself up as my bra fell from my breasts. Being naked and exposed was never a comfort; rather, it always created terror and fear.

But looking upon Xander's eyes as they took in my body, I felt the devotion and respect emanating from him as his fingers gently trailed down my arms.

"Please don't. You're so beautiful, so perfect. Every part of you I feel has been made just for me. I want to kiss and touch every inch of your body tonight." His words evoked such emotion in me that all my walls came crashing down. I pulled my hands away from my body. And for the first time ever, I was partially naked and exposed in front of a man, and I felt free. I felt loved. "Thank you. Thank you for trusting me with your heart," he murmured as he stared lovingly at me.

Oh my God, this man. I knew I was falling in love with him at that exact moment, if I hadn't already been there.

"Xander . . . I . . ."

"Don't say anything right now. Sit back and let me look at you. Let me look at the most beautiful creature ever made. I can't believe I'm the lucky bastard who gets to call you mine."

He pulled me up to standing by my hands and moved to undo the button on my pants. He kept eye contact with me to ensure I'd be OK. I kept my eyes on his, making sure he knew I wanted him to continue with his exploration of my body. I reached out to caress his face, turned on by the light stubble lining his cheeks and jaw, wondering how it would feel if they rubbed against my thighs. He bent over to pull my jeans down and came back to standing.

"Jesus, woman, you are going to be the death of me. There's barely a strip of cloth going up your ass. Fuckin Christ, Lanie, that's hot." He quickly reached around, grabbing a hold of my ass and digging his fingers in while my mouth started ravaging his neck.

I don't know what came over me, where the impulse came from to be so bold, so brazen. But the warm feeling pooling in my core was spreading, my entire body overcome with the sensation. The need was strong. My fingers dug into him deeply, needing to hold on tight, feeling as though I were swaying from the sudden onslaught of heated passion. I jumped into his arms, wrapping my legs around his waist, my heated core resting on his hard length as he caught me.

"Fuck," he growled, "you feel amazing up against me."

I could tell he was trying to restrain himself from doing more.

He gently pushed me onto the couch. He joined me, our bodies chest to chest, as his hands continued to rove from the back of my knee, up to my hip, and around to my back.

"You're so fuckin' hot, Lanie. This is going to be harder than I thought." His mouth was leaving hot trails down my neck to the top of my breast.

"It doesn't have to be just about me tonight, Xander."

"Yes, it does." He looked at me with seriousness in his eyes. I wouldn't dare question his motives.

I knew he wanted to prove to me that he was the furthest thing from Max possible.

But I already knew that.

So quickly I didn't see it coming, Xander flipped us over on the couch and I was on top, my legs straddling him. Our bodies aligned perfectly, his desire very obvious, and hard, as it pushed up against me. It created a warmth that spread between us.

He reached up and pulled his shirt over his head, exposing the firm muscles of his abs leading below his pants. The moan that escaped my mouth elicited a sly grin on his lips, embarrassing me slightly. I quickly recovered as my hands were splayed across his stomach, the ridges below my fingertips hard as I made my way up to his chest. The flesh under my hands was hot and sweaty, solid as I kneaded. The tattoo teased my eyes in the dim light, his muscles flexing with every move he made.

I felt him move his hands below me, undoing his jeans, removing them underneath us. The feeling of him beneath me, with only his boxers and my thong between us, was intoxicating. His hands moved to my waist, around my back, holding me close to him, skin to skin.

What started as a warm simmer had built to a deep heat in my core. The urge to grind my legs together was suddenly strong as I struggled to close them, squirming in his lap. It was a pleasurable agony being on top of him, feeling him push against me.

He pulled back, a space between us as he held me by the hips. He dug his fingers in hard, gripping me, grinding against me as I felt the evident torture over his decision to be selfless tonight. His movements created a euphoria, my mind floating, my body drifting as it reached heights it had never felt.

"Xander." His name came out as a moan. "This feels . . . I can't even desc—" I couldn't form words, my mind and body on a journey where conversation was not welcome.

"I love watching you and how you move. I love knowing I make you feel good."

I arched my back as he spoke to me, his words evoking inner feelings of desire, ones I never knew I had. His hands reached up and found my breasts, thumbs caressing their peaks. I forced myself deeper into his lap, instinctively searching for a release I didn't know I needed.

Xander's hand clutched my waist, curving around to the flat of my stomach, leaving a trail of heat in its wake. The anticipation of where he may wind up grew deep in my belly. Our eyes connected the moment his fingers found the strip of cloth covering me and he deftly moved it aside.

My eyes went wide and my breath hitched as his fingers made quick work of finding my clit. He knew exactly what to do. As I ground my center into his hard length, his fingers rubbed and pulled. The combination sent tiny shocks coursing through me, and I needed to grab a hold of his forearms to steady myself. It was too much, the intensity of the feelings cresting inside of me.

I was flying, soaring, reaching new heights as he brought me places I never expected to go. The pinnacle was in sight. I felt it roll over me like a tide rushing the shores, rolling through my body in waves. I moved on top of him to a beat in my body, grinding as the pulsating explosions forced me to become still once I reached the top. I held on tight as I went over that edge, freefalling as I crashed to the bottom.

My body collapsed into a heap, drained of everything it had. My breaths were ragged and hard to come by. I realized my forehead was sweaty as it rested on Xander's shoulder, my hair stuck to the side of my face.

And then I was embarrassed.

Never before had I been the center of this type of attention. I didn't know how to act afterward. My head was still on his shoulder, but my eyes wandered. I tried to steal a glimpse of him without moving.

What was he doing? Were his eyes closed? Was he looking at me? I had no idea if I should say anything or be the first to move. Was I supposed to thank him for what he just did?

And then the panic set in. And then the panic about the panic. Because he was going to think I was panicking for all the wrong reasons. Because I wasn't.

He did it.

He got me to enjoy a sexual experience.

But I'm such an idiot because I was still panicking.

"Lanie," he said against my shoulder. "I can feel the wheels turning in your head. What's going on, babe?"

I didn't quite know how to answer his question. Rather, I didn't want to be having this conversation right then. I wished I was more normal. I wished I knew how to have a sexual encounter and how to act afterward, like other college-aged girls did.

"That was amazing." I pushed against his chest slightly, sitting up but still avoiding eye contact. "But I have no idea how to do this. I don't know what to do or say after something like that." My eyes bounced around the room, searching for something, anything, to focus on. I couldn't look at him. Suddenly, his warm hands found my cheeks and stilled my head, forcing our gazes to connect. My embarrassment skyrocketed as my eyes shifted to the ceiling.

"Hey, look at me." He paused, waiting patiently for me to find the courage. Once I did, he continued. "There are no expectations, no right or wrong here. We just do us. We do what feels right for us." His dimpled smile calmed me. "You don't understand how happy I am that I made you feel good, that I could do this for you."

I had to look away again. "That's what I can't do, Xander." I buried my face in his shoulder, eyes squeezed tight. "I can't talk about it. It makes me feel . . ."

He rubbed the back of my head as his arm wrapped around my waist. "Hey, it's OK. Then we won't talk about it." I felt his arm stretching behind us, then felt my shirt being pulled over my head. I raised my arms as he carefully put the shirt into place. He readjusted us on the couch so we were now lying chest to chest.

There were no more words that night.

But more was said in the way he held and caressed me than any words could have.

Chapter 16

There was sweat on my forehead when I woke up. My heavy lids were slow to open. It took a moment to realize there were multiple limbs intertwined with my own, which explained the extra body heat. Once my eyes focused, I saw his toned torso up against mine. It made me think of the activities from the night before. I had to chuckle, knowing they were what made me so tired.

I didn't want to leave Xander's side after our night, so we slept in his bed. There was no discussion about it as we walked up the stairs. We went straight to his room, both knowing we needed to stay together.

Consent and control. That was what he knew I needed for last night to work, and he allowed for both. You wouldn't think either of those things would be sexual turn-ons, but damn, it worked for me. I mean, he did plenty of other things that got the deed done. But if not for those two things, I would not have been able to open up to him at all.

Xander returned the most important first I'd had taken away from me.

And, actually, last night was a *real* first. I'd never climaxed from someone else before him.

I shifted and realized I was awake before he was, loving that I could steal some moments to stare and admire. I noticed how the straight line of his jaw, while relaxed in sleep, hid his deep dimple. And his full lips were slightly apart as his even breaths warmed me. We were so close. But then I felt a small shift in his body, his hips turning toward me.

"Good morning, beautiful." He hadn't even opened his eyes yet.

"Good morning, handsome." I leaned over and kissed his nose. One of his eyelids slowly lifted, a bright blue eye showing through an open slit.

"How is it that you're more beautiful when you first wake up? You amaze me." This man, he had my heart fluttering and butterflies in my stomach already.

"How is it that no one has stolen your heart before me? How am I the lucky one?" I shot back at him.

I turned over onto my back as he pushed up on his elbow and laid half his body on mine, looking down at me. That gave me a close-up look at the tat on his arm, making me want to see more.

"I knew I was waiting for you."

Yes, I was definitely falling in love with this man.

"And I could get used to waking up like this every day. I think we take my mom up on her offer, and when we get back to school, you're sleeping in my room every night. I'm not letting you go ever again." He relaxed his body on mine and held me, nuzzling his face in my hair. "What do you wanna do today?"

"For starters, I want to look at your tattoos. I've wanted to see them up close since you ran up on me at the pond months ago." Pulling the blanket down, I sat up a bit. I rubbed my hand along the muscles of his arm. Reaching down, I skimmed my fingertips along the hem of his shirt, teasing underneath.

The feel of his taut skin and ripples of muscles made my stomach flutter like it was full of butterflies.

"I can't see the one on your chest," I whined. "Take your shirt off." Quicker than I expected, he reached behind his head with one hand and grabbed the back of his shirt to lift it over his head.

Why was that so sexy?

Same way he took his shirt off last night—it seemed so much sexier than the traditional way to undress. I jumped on top and straddled him.

"Oh God, Lanie, that's not fair to do to a guy first thing in the morning. You feel amazing." He threw an arm over his face and groaned into his bent elbow.

"Kind of like last night, huh?"

He snuck a look at me from under his arm and smiled.

"Well, you've had the opportunity to explore my body already. I haven't had a chance yet," I said.

And what a sight it was. I regretted starting this on a Saturday morning, knowing his mother was likely downstairs starting breakfast for us. I used my fingertips on both hands to gently rub the outline of what appeared to be eagle or hawk wings spanning his broad, muscular chest. Every small move he made gave the appearance of the feathers on the wings dancing a bit. Xander's eyes remained closed, but I knew I affected him by the shivers and bumps I saw coming up on his skin. The detail was extraordinary, but I was most interested in the small numbers I found at the bottom of the tat near his rib cage, numbers that appeared to be a date. My fingers lingered on them; his eyes remained closed when he talked again.

"That's the date my dad was hauled away from this house, the day we were finally free of him. Hence, the eagle wings."

I nodded, understanding now the significance of this for him. He was free, free from the torment of his childhood abuser. And I felt that, truly felt that, in the core of my being. Xander must have seen something in my face, and he pushed himself to sit against the back of the bed.

"Hey, what's with that face?" he asked.

I didn't know if I should explain it to him. I didn't know if he should feel the pressure of knowing how important he had already become to my current state, my existence.

But I didn't want any more secrets, and neither did he.

"You've freed me."

And as we sat there, me straddling him on his bed, there was a significant shift for us. We both knew something was changing. The gravity of it hit me as the emotions dragged my eyes lower. His fingers grazed my jaw, stopping on my chin to lift it.

"You're a free bird, babe, just like me. My birdie. I'm glad I could do this for you."

Both of his hands reached out for my face, pulling it to him with intensity. His mouth went to mine with passion and warmth. The kiss was a message between us about what was to come. About how this was a start.

But then as I shifted my straddled legs over his hard

dick, we both froze. His eyes popped open, and he had a dangerous look in them as a sly smile came across his mouth.

"Are you sure you want to start something we may not finish?" he asked against my lips.

"Oh, I'm sure we won't be able to finish," I started as I pulled back. "I'm fully expecting to hear your mother call us to breakfast any second. But there's no way I can be expected to sit upon this beautiful specimen of a man, looking at these sexy tattoos, rubbing his bulging muscles, and not get turned on. You see my predicament, don't you?" I rubbed my hands along his chest, moving down along the ridges of his stomach, a true six-pack underneath my fingers. Hints of that deep muscled V dipped below his waist band and teased my eyes.

He stopped my hand from progressing any further, holding it in his own. He tossed his head back against the headboard, apparently frustrated.

"Oh, I understand your predicament all too well. I think all I can say is welcome to the club—the club of carnal anticipation. But with you, it's the best club to be in." He wrapped his arms around me and pulled me in even closer, both of us giggling. "Waiting for you is like waiting for Christmas. Leading up to it is almost as fun, if not as much fun, as the day itself. I'll wait for you as long as I need to."

"Last night was amazing, Xander." I said it almost as a whisper as I put my head on his shoulder.

"It was, my birdie." He pulled my chin up to look at him, such tenderness in his eyes. "And it's OK if you can't talk about that stuff. I mean it. I'm happy we could share that together." I could tell he still felt that way, still had a strong desire left over from last night. I could literally *feel* it beneath me, between my legs. "And I'm even more happy you're comfortable enough with me to do those things. Please, always tell me if it's too much." I looked down, getting shy once again, but his hand remained firm, pulling my face back up toward his. "I mean it, Lanie. You need to talk to me. Let me know if it gets to be too much or if I'm doing something that makes you feel uncomfortable."

I nodded while he pulled me closer, and our bodies were once again perfectly aligned with one another.

"Thank you for making me feel safe." I looked at him when I said this, really looked at him so he would know how important this was to me. And I could see the acknowledgment in his eyes, the reverent nod of his head.

He leaned in and kissed me gently, a contradiction to our current position. My urge to grind into him was great, but his restraint kept me from doing it. And as if on cue . . .

"Alexander . . . Lanie . . ."

Christmas Eve was when the James family hosted a buffet dinner for family and friends. Aunts, uncles, cousins, neighbors, and friends all gathered at their home, squeezed in tight. There were so many of them, talking and eating and drinking.

I was overwhelmed.

I only knew three people; the other fifty-seven or so were loaded with questions for me when we met.

"How did you and Xander meet?"

"'Are you and Xander dating?"

"Where are you from?"

"How long have you and Xander been together?"

They went on and on and on. I was doing my best to answer as many as I could. But some started getting too personal, and I got nervous. Thankfully, Xander rescued me and brought me into the kitchen.

"My mom told me you could help her in here, steer clear of everyone for a while. Sound good, birdie?" He kissed my forehead as he hurried back to his friends he hadn't seen since the summer.

I looked around and noticed Jane pulling dish after dish out of the oven.

"Tell me what to do. Let me help," I said to Jane.

"Oh, honey, I heard the hordes of guests weren't leaving you alone. I'm sorry. Here, start putting these on the buffet in the dining room for me." She handed me a hot dish with potholders underneath. I worked my way through the crowd to the room off the kitchen and looked for a spot on the sideboard. Dish upon dish of food were piled up on the space. Lasagna, charcuterie boards, dips, pasta dishes, casseroles, you name it, and it was on that table. I'd never seen so much food in one place before. But I guessed the enormous amount of food coincided with the guest list.

Once back in the kitchen, I realized Jane wasn't there. I grabbed a soda from the cooler and tucked myself away in a seat by the window where I could watch people coming and going. There was a dynamic between these people I wasn't used to—a closeness, whether family or friend.

Then I felt warm, muscular arms reach around from behind and elicit that familiar tingle through my entire body. I could have my eyes closed, ten guys could touch me, and I would know which was Xander. No one made my body respond the way his did.

"Hey, baby, you OK? Want me to stay here with you?"

He nuzzled his nose into the back of my neck, his warm breath making bumps rise on my skin.

"I'm OK. I was just hanging out here since I couldn't find your mom." And because I didn't want to be around all of these strangers. I felt him nod into my hair. "I'm enjoying watching you with your family. Go, keep hanging out with your cousins. It's only once a year. I'm fine, and I'll keep helping your mom with the food." He reached around and found my cheek with his mouth before I was cold from him letting go of me.

After dinner and dessert had been served, many of the older guests started heading out due to the late hour. I peered into the living room to see Xander and his brother still enjoying themselves with their friends and cousins. My insecurities about new people took over, and I decided to retreat to Xander's room to escape for a bit. Picking up my Kindle, I got lost in my book until I realized the hum of the voices quieted downstairs. I decided I should at least head down to see if Jane needed help cleaning up.

I passed Bryce on the stairs as he was heading up.

"Merry Christmas, kiddo."

"Merry Christmas, Bryce," I echoed as he fist-bumped me.

Once I made it to the main rooms, I realized all the guests were indeed gone.

Xander startled me as he grabbed me from behind while I was gazing at the tree. "Hey, birdie, I was just going to come find you. I hope tonight wasn't a complete fail for you. I know being with a crowd of strangers is probably not high on your list of favorite things to do."

I smiled at his new nickname for me. I hadn't been sure about it at first, but I liked it. The significance of it would never be understood by anyone else but us. And I loved that he only used it around us. He turned me to face him before he went toward the couch. I pulled toward the kitchen.

"I was coming down to help your mom clean up," I told him.

He kept pulling me toward the living room. "It's mostly done, and what isn't we'll worry about tomorrow."

He pulled some pillows and blankets to the floor, making a comfortable pallet to lie on beneath the lights. He pulled me by the hand to the ground, and we got comfortable. I lay against his side, my head on his shoulder.

"No, not my favorite, but believe it or not, I enjoyed myself. I loved watching you in your element, and seeing you with your extended family was great. You may not know this about me, but I love to watch people." I paused, getting shy, recalling the embarrassing moment I was about to disclose. "You may not remember this day—it was way back in the very beginning of the semester—but I was sitting on a bench by the student union. I was watching people that day, something I've done since Texas. It, um, it was a kind of escape for me. And, well, I wound up watching you that day. You with a girl. She obviously liked you, but you were trying, in a nice way it seemed, to dismiss her. And then you caught me looking at you. Oh my God, I was mortified."

With a nervous laugh, I looked at Xander, but he was quiet for a while. I wasn't sure if he was trying to remember that day or not. But he finally spoke.

"Lanie, that day is ingrained in my mind, and it will be forever." My quizzical look must have enticed him to continue. "That was the day I knew I had found the girl I would love."

"What?" I pushed up on his chest more, not understanding his words. "But how . . ."

"I don't know—I just knew. I knew there was something special about you, and I needed to find out what it was. By simply looking at you that day, I knew you were my future. I can't explain it, but here we are."

He rolled onto his side, facing me, and pulled me to face him. I could feel a significant shift in the mood, becoming serious, even life changing. He continued to stare into my eyes, not saying anything for quite a while.

"Lanie, I know you probably know this already, but you deserve to hear the words today, and every day from now on . . . I love you."

Those words, his words, reached every fiber of my body and soul. They warmed me from the inside out.

Never in my life did I think I would wind up in this position. He had shown up and saved me, rescued me from the despair and torture I'd endured for years. I was drowning, deep below the surface, ready to sink to the bottom. He had not only pulled me from the depths but carried me to shore and provided a safe haven.

He made me think everything was going to be alright.

The power of this feeling was overwhelming, all-consuming.

I looked into his eyes, straight into his soul, and I saw it. I saw his love for me.

"Xander, I love you, too. God, I love you so much."

He rolled me on top of him, and his mouth claimed mine with such vigor and intensity I felt as though I would melt in his arms. His hands were entwined in my hair as mine manically pulled up his shirt. He sat up a bit and did that sexy thing where he pulled it over his head with one hand, his torso muscles straining while he took it off.

I think I growled.

He looked at me with hooded eyes.

Then, I did something I never thought I could do.

I rolled us over.

Xander was on top of me.

Xander froze and stared down at me, pulling up slightly. "Are you sure, baby? Is this OK?"

"Yes, I trust you with all of me."

"Are we doing this, birdie? Are you OK with this moving on?" He lay back down on top of me with his arms framing my face, his eyes intent on me as he waited for my answer. I knew he wouldn't continue without permission.

"I want this," I said. "I need this. I want you. I love you." He leaned in for a more passionate kiss this time, slowing it down, trying to take control.

"You have no idea how happy I am to hear you say those words," he said as he stared down at me. "I feel like I need nothing else to be happy. I love you so much." His mouth found mine, our breaths fighting each other, and then he pulled away.

No more words were needed; the heat of the moment took over. He reached down to the hem of my shirt and pushed it up and over my head in one smooth motion, throwing it somewhere across the room. I reached for his belt buckle at the same time he reached for the button of my jeans. We both struggled to get them off each other in the position we were in. I finally took my own pants off, too impatient, needing this to happen quicker. He did the same and came back down, lowering himself over me, arms caging my face. His one hip was to my side, his hands finding the hooks of my bra.

Finally, there was nothing between us.

For the first time ever.

His solid body against me, skin to skin, for the first time, was unforgettable. The coolness of his touch on my scorching body was a perfect storm brewing. A collision, a driving force I didn't want to get out of the way of.

It felt as though we were meant to be.

His hands were all over, starting on my neck. He pulled me up so his mouth could devour me there, trailing kisses down toward my collarbone. His other hand reached for my breast, cradling, caressing, teasing. Its peak, at full attention, was hoping his mouth would reach it next. And he did not disappoint, taking my breast between his lips, my back arching to meet his desire.

His hand continued its downward exploration while his mouth remained attached to me. The lightest touch of his fingertips across my stomach sent me into a spiral already, making me moan loudly.

"Birdie, we're not alone. Your sounds are driving me insane, but . . ."

I couldn't control myself. His touch sent me into a euphoric state, causing moans and whimpers to slip from my mouth. But I bit my lip and kept them deep in my throat. That seemed to do something to him, his body responding with a firm grind up against my hip. An equally stifled moan rumbled deep inside of him.

At that point, things shifted.

His eager fingers began to explore the tender parts of my body, his eyes imploring for further permission. I granted that permission by separating my legs even further, allowing greater access. His every touch to my body created a warmth, a surging heat, all the way to my core. I shook with anticipation for what was to come next.

The undulating waves started before I even knew what

was happening. No one had ever focused on me; never before had I been intimately the center of attention, so loved and cared for until him. Right now, all Xander wanted was to make me feel good. Completely selfless.

I was always just a vehicle for someone else's pleasure, and it involved pain.

But this was completely different. The total opposite. I felt so cherished by Xander that it overwhelmed me. The tears started welling, uncontrollably, and I only hoped Xander didn't see them.

"Birdie, are you still with me, baby? Do you want me to stop?" Those words were whispered into my hair, my neck. His voice was full of concern, which broke my heart.

"No, don't. I'm OK," I whispered. "I've just never felt so loved."

His eyes moved to meet mine and conveyed the emotions I knew we both felt. "I do love you. Lanie, know that this is all out of love." He covered my mouth with his, pulled me close to him, rolled me on top of him, wiped away my tears, and put me in control.

I put my legs on either side of his hips, straddling his midsection, and we both moaned. His urgent need for me was now fully pressed up against me, and it hit me in a spot that made me see stars. I moved around, grinding into Xander in a way that started the waves again with a vengeance. His hands found my waist, grabbing my hip bones and digging in, holding on for the ride. I threw my head back, screaming out a bit, trying to stay as quiet as I could. I hit the peak of the wave and stilled, Xander holding on to me as it moved through me. I started feeling as though I were going to collapse, so I leaned forward onto Xander's chest, breathing hard, my cheek enjoying the hardness of his pectoral muscle underneath it. His hands came up behind and grabbed my backside, rubbing and kneading me.

"That was probably the sexiest thing I've ever seen."

I became bashful when he said that, again not used to talking. It never happened with *him*.

"Babe, look at me. It's me." He pulled my face up with his fingers, but I closed my eyes. "Please." I opened my eyes. "I know you don't like it, but talking during sex is normal, healthy. OK?"

"OK."

"Do you want to stop now? It's OK if you do."

"No, Xander. I'm ready for this, more than ready. I want this—now." I moved onto my side and pulled him close so we were looking into each other's faces, eye to eye. I reached behind and grabbed a hold of his firm ass, letting him know I needed this to continue.

And he took the cue.

He lifted my one leg over his, and I became completely exposed to him. He shifted himself on top of me. And when I looked up, I knew the darkness was not taking over, even with him over me. His one hand found my breasts, caressing them. At the same time, his fingertips on the other hand trailed down my stomach. They made a stop at my navel, circling it, teasing it. His tongue joined in the game, starting at my neck and leaving a trail of fire between my breasts. Both hands then worked their way down my thighs.

But then the fire was gone, and I was cold while he was reaching for his jeans, his back pocket, where he found his wallet. Out came the square foil packet.

Once he was covered, he centered his cock between my legs. His eyes found mine and were asking for permission.

"I love you, Xander."

That was all it took. His eyes never left mine, his arms bent at the elbow, surrounding me, hands cradling my head so he could hold my face all while supporting his weight above me. His mouth centimeters from mine, our breath mingling as one. He lowered his body against me, my anticipation growing, my desire spilling over. We were forehead to forehead, and his lips were crushing my mouth, stealing my breath, the intensity unmistakable.

One arm remained around my face, the other slightly lifted my lower body, opening me up for him.

Finally, I felt his fullness settle between my legs.

Finally, his fullness was begging at my entrance, breaking through, easing our agony.

And it was my first time.

My first time making love.

Chapter 17

"*O*h my gosh, boys, this is absolutely beautiful!" Jane had tears running down her face after opening her gift from Xander and Bryce. It was a stunning silver charm bracelet, the charms depicting the significant events of their lives. The room was littered with torn gift wrap and empty boxes. She indulged her boys with gifts at Christmas, even as adults.

I was showered with unexpected gifts from Jane and Bryce as well. A beautiful wristlet and a new cover for my e-reader were just a couple. As we continued opening our gifts, Jane moved into the kitchen. It sounded like she was pretty busy in there.

"Kids, come on in!" she yelled. "Breakfast is ready." Each of the guys jumped from their seat faster than the other. I was the last to make it into the room, and my eyes were met with yet another feast she'd prepared. I had no idea how she did it.

"Mom, you outdid yourself. This looks amazing! Thanks!" Xander gave her a huge hug while Bryce waited in the wings to give her one as well.

The spread of food on the table looked like it was right out of a Martha Stewart magazine. Aromas of pancakes and bacon hit my nose as I scanned the table, seeing mounds of muffins and stacks waffles on plates. As the four of us took our seats, we worked on filling our plates. The casual conversation came to a lull as our mouths filled with food.

And as we continued eating, Bryce had become noticeably antsy in his seat.

"So, Mom, I've been thinking about looking into the detective program at the department. Chief said even though I've only been there under two years, he'd recommend me. It's not common for someone this early on to get that recommendation, so, uhm, it's a pretty big deal." Bryce was trying to be humble, but you could tell he was bursting at the seams with this news.

"Oh, Bryce, that's exciting, sweetie. I'm so proud of you!" Jane's face lit up with pride for her son. Xander stood and went to his brother to give him a hug.

"That's great news, bro. If anyone can do it, you can." Xander finished off the hug with a slap to Bryce's back before coming back to the chair next to me. He caught me watching all of them, admiring them and their love for one another, and smiled down at me as he took his seat.

"Yeah, Bryce," I chimed in, "that's great news. Good luck."

He looked my way with a gentle smile, acknowledging my congratulations. Then he turned his attention back to Xander. "Yeah, dude, I'll make the arrests, and you can prosecute them!" Bryce laughed.

Jane smiled upon both of her boys with pride, her eyes watery. "I can't believe I'll have two sons working with the law."

Xander chuckled as he refilled his coffee. He turned around, leaning against the counter before responding. "Yeah, but it'll be at least another five years before I'll step foot in a courtroom. Let's hope I make it through." That hint of self-doubt was a surprise coming from him. The ever-confident Xander was showing a new side to himself, and it made me love him even more.

"Oh, honey," started Jane, "don't give me that. You'll not only finish, you'll be the best prosecuting attorney out there!" Her smile was wide as she spoke.

"Lanie," Bryce said as he spooned a huge pile of scrambled eggs onto his plate, "what are you studying at school?"

Xander beat me to the answer. "She's fucking brilliant. Smarter than all of us put together." He was beaming.

"Alex, language," Jane reprimanded.

"Sorry, Mom, but you don't understand. She's going to be a doctor!"

All three heads turned in my direction, I didn't know if in disbelief or not. "Well, that's not completely right, Xander. I'm planning on being a psychologist. So, I'm currently in the psychology program, but like you, I'll need many years of school to finish up and get the accreditations I need."

Xander walked the couple steps from the counter to my chair and wrapped his arms around me. "That still makes you a doctor, babe. Don't be shy about it." He kissed my cheek as he sat down to his food.

When I was picking my major, all that resonated with me was being able to help others in situations like my own. It made perfect sense to go into a career where I could give people the strength and guidance to navigate through the difficult times in their lives. However, I learned that I wasn't quite finished with my own journey. The twists and turns that kept jumping up on my path made me second-guess if I'd be capable of helping anyone.

"All that really sounds like to me is a shit ton of homework for you two and a lot of tuition bills," Bryce taunted as he pulled me from my thoughts. And he wasn't wrong. "Me, I'll be making money all those years you'll be doing your work." I wasn't sure how we made out the words he spoke, since his mouth was full of bacon and he was commencing eating a blueberry muffin.

"Well, I'm pretty happy at BRU, and I wouldn't change a thing." Xander was only looking at me when he answered Bryce. A look that had the flush rising from my chest to my cheeks.

"Christ, would you two take it upstairs please?" Bryce yelled at us, crumbs literally spewing from his mouth.

My eyes focused on a small piece of bread on the side of my plate. I was mortified by his words. I wasn't comfortable talking about sex with Xander, let alone his brother and mom. Thankfully, Jane rescued me.

"When are the two of you heading back to school? I hope not too soon. I'm loving having you here. You still have a couple weeks, right?" The sly smile she gave me as she stood up from the table was hidden from the boys. She moved toward the sink with some dishes, and they couldn't see her as she so eloquently changed the subject.

And that was worse.

I couldn't talk anymore. My embarrassment had stolen my voice, my words. I sat at the table, looking at my breakfast like it was the best thing since . . . well, since sliced bread.

"Yeah, Mom. We have about two weeks before classes start up again, so you're stuck with us." He had worked his way to her, his arms around her. The embrace made her beam as I stole a quick glance, a bit of a shimmer in her eyes. The love between these three was an enviable bond.

"Good, I'm glad." She patted Xander's arm, which was around her shoulders. "And remember, I'm going to Aunt Jill's today. Is anyone coming?" She looked around expectantly.

"Sorry, Mom," Bryce answered as he started standing from the table. "I actually have to head into work in a few hours. So, no, I won't be able to partake in Aunt Jill's feast." The chuckle that escaped his lips didn't go unnoticed. "I'll catch up with you guys in a couple days. I'm on duty for a bit."

Bryce was out the door before I realized there was a bit of an uncomfortable silence at the table. I looked back and forth between Xander and his mom, unsure how I should proceed. I decided to stay out of it.

"Xander?" Jane questioned. "Is her food that bad?"

A sigh escaped Xander's lips before he answered. "Yeah, Mom, it is. It's fucking terrible."

The silence remained after his remark, Xander seeming to wait for his mom's angry response. He sat back against his chair, awaiting the assault he knew would be coming. I couldn't believe he had said that, such an insult to his aunt. I only met her the night before when she was with them for Christmas Eve. She was the nicest of the bunch to me, not asking too many questions, giving me some space. *I* was even mad at Xander.

But then Jane spoke up and took us both by surprise. "It is, isn't it? It's fucking terrible!" The cackle that followed had us all laughing.

"Every time we sat at that table, the only thing I could picture in my mind was the scene from that movie—what was it? The Christmas one with Chevy Chase?" Xander looked at both of us for help, and I knew it immediately. It was my family's favorite movie, and we watched it together every year.

"*Christmas Vacation!*" I yelled. "And I know exactly the scene you're talking about!" I laughed along with him.

"Yes!" Xander exclaimed, pointing his finger at me in acknowledgment. "I mean, Mom, her turkey doesn't explode like that, but c'mon, you can't deny that unless it's in a bath of gravy, it's not even edible."

Jane nodded along with Xander, their laughter contagious. "Not even that," Jane contributed, "but every one of her vegetables is boiled to the point of mush. It's terrible, Xander, you're right."

Everyone's cackling had settled, the mood at the table relaxed. I felt bad that we'd enjoyed a moment at the expense of Jane's sister, but it did sound as though cooking was not her forte.

"Besides," Xander continued, "Lanie and I haven't exchanged our presents yet. We thought we'd do that once you left for Aunt Jill's." His eyes locked on mine as he said this, the message clear. And it stole my breath for a moment. The heat in his look was intense.

We would be unwrapping more than our wrapped gifts.

Jane got up from the table and started clearing the dishes and food.

"Mom, go ahead and get ready for Aunt Jill's. We've got this." Xander got up from his chair, taking the plates from his mother's hands. I joined by gathering up some things from the table as she scurried up the stairs.

As we cleaned the kitchen, we fell into a rhythm. We seemed to read what the other was going to do next. We did a little choreographed dance through the room as we completed our duties without bumping into one another. Such domestic tasks as loading the dishwasher and packing up leftovers were a big deal to me. I never thought I would be at this stage of a relationship with anyone ever.

My tortured past still trickled into my mind, trying to ruin the good I'd come to find. But it was happening less and less. Even a few weeks earlier, these thoughts pervading my head would've had me crashing to the floor, afraid to carry on, thinking this type of life wasn't possible for me. Or that I didn't deserve it. But Xander had changed all of that for me. He proved to me I was worth something and capable of being normal. He gave me confidence in myself, making me feel as though I could one day have a life without checking around every corner.

I felt his arms snake around my midsection as I dried the last glass that didn't fit in the dishwasher. His chin rested on my head as I leaned against his chest. I closed my eyes as I relished the warmth and comfort I felt in his arms. He gently turned me toward the window by their table and whispered in my ear. "Look outside, birdie."

I slowly opened my eyes to see small white dots drifting from the sky. They looked like tiny puffs of cotton floating to the ground as the wind swirled them around the trees.

"Oh my God . . ." I said in whispered awe. I ran to the window, needing a closer look. The glass was frigid to the touch as my eyes scanned the yard. "Xander, it's beautiful." He came up next to me, looking out as well.

"It is pretty. I always love the first snowfall of the year."

He leaned against the sill and turned toward me. "I don't think it'll be much more than a dusting, though, so no fun and games in the snow. But I'm glad you got to see it."

We heard his mom charging down the stairs and went to see her off in the hall.

"OK, you two, I'll see you in a few hours," Jane said as she bundled up for the snowy day. *"Enjoy yourselves!"* She sang and chuckled as she headed out the door.

"Oh my God, Xander, she knows, doesn't she?"

He laughed. "Knows what?"

"You know what!" I swatted him on the arm, which felt like a tree trunk.

"I don't know that she 'knows,' but I guess she thinks she knows. I don't care, though; I'll shout it on the rooftops. That's what's supposed to happen between two people who love each other, Lanie." He leaned over and captured my mouth in his, and I forgot all about any embarrassment I might have felt about anything to do with Xander touching me. There could be nothing wrong about that—he was right. "And thank God she's finally gone!"

He grabbed my hand and started leading me to the stairs, but stopped suddenly and pulled me close against him.

"Now I get to open the best gift yet. And as much as I would like to have a repeat of last night by the tree, I think we should take it upstairs. This next time deserves a bed." At that, he swung his arm behind my knees and scooped me up in his arms.

"Xander, put me down. I can walk!" I was screaming as he ran with me up the stairs. We got to his room and he plopped us on his bed, it bouncing from our weight. Our laughter seemed to echo in the now empty house and made it hard for us to catch our breath. But we did catch our breath as we lay next to each other. And the mood shifted the longer we lay quietly, looking at one another.

"Birdie," Xander whispered from above, my heart melting at his name for me.

I loved the name, the meaning he took from it. Because he had freed me. I felt like a free bird, ready to face the challenges that I knew were still ahead, because of him.

His mouth captured mine as we aligned our bodies. "Every time I look at you, I want you in my bed. I want to slowly peel your clothes off and take hours ravaging every inch of your body." His tongue delved into my mouth again before uttering his next words. "Last night was just the beginning."

The growl that came from deep in his chest started a hum inside me that had my body moving in ways I didn't think it could. My hips jutted forward as my hands reached for his head, pulling him in for another kiss.

This man was my undoing.

He didn't seem to mind. The growl deepened. He pushed himself up and looked down at me.

I was struck with the beauty of the man above me. The way his hair framed his face, falling around his jawline, a bit long and in need of a cut. His stubble was longer, not shaven in days while on vacation, but I didn't mind. It was sexy as hell. His arms were flexed as he held his weight off of me, his arms looking their biggest and showing off his tattoo. I reached up to run my finger along the lines of it and loved that it sent shivers through his body.

He started to take his shirt off in that way I loved as he lowered himself onto me, but I stopped him.

"Not yet," I said. "I'm still enjoying the view." Eventually, I reached down for the hem of his shirt, pulling it up and over his head. My hands wandered from his face down to the taut pectoral muscles covered in the wings of his eagle. I pushed myself up a bit so I could place kisses across his chest, causing an audible moan to escape from him.

"Lanie, you're killing me." His head was thrown back, his eyes closed. I continued admiring his muscular abs by running my fingers over the bulging planes of each one of them.

"Did you know you have eight of these, not six? Is that normal?" Giggling when he moaned again, I knew he wasn't happy with my line of questioning. I finally made it down to my favorite part, that sexy V. I'd admired this part of him for so long, dreaming of seeing it up close, feeling it. My fingers ran along each side of the tight muscles to the band of boxer briefs peeking out of his jeans, my finger dipping below for an extra touch. My mouth inched forward, aching to taste him. The softness of my lips against the flexed muscles of his abs caused a throbbing sensation between my legs. I rubbed my thighs together, seeking relief, as my tongue darted out to taste his skin. The saltiness of him combined with his heat made me want to devour every inch of his body. And he enjoyed that, moaning again.

This time, his moan was guttural, carnal.

Splaying my palms on his lower abdomen, I rubbed the entire area. I pushed my hands around to his backside, feeling his tight ass through his jeans, now wishing they were off. I quickly reached around for his button. He made quick work of that by standing up and taking them and his shirt off in a matter of seconds. My hands immediately went around him, finding his taut ass as he climbed on top of me, naked.

"I think it would only be fair for you to take your clothes off, too." His forehead was on mine, his eyes closed, and his voice was strained, as if in pain.

I knew I was doing this to him, and it actually made me feel good, kind of powerful.

"Can I take your clothes off, Lanie?"

I loved that he still asked my permission every time.

I loved him.

"Please do. Now."

He made quick work of that as well, nothing romantic like the other times. This time was different—it was need. Once we were both back on the bed, him on top, he looked in my eyes. His arms cradled my head, his knee separating my legs, our mouths only centimeters apart.

"I need you; I need to be inside you." His hair fell over his eyes as he spoke. I reached to push it away as he said, "I love you."

I nodded. My permission was granted, and he pushed his body into mine.

"I will always love you, birdie."

Our bodies found a rhythm.

"I will never hurt you," he promised.

That rhythm became stronger, faster.

"You will always be mine, and I will always be yours," he proclaimed.

He never once took his eyes off mine.

"God, I love you," he declared.

Our bodies slowed, and Xander lowered his head next to mine, kissing my cheek, my ear. He held me tight, as if he thought he was going to lose me.

"Xander, I love you, too."

Chapter 18

It was weird to hear the landline ring as Xander and I were getting our coats on. We were heading out to the station to meet up with Bryce and some of his coworkers for lunch.

"It's probably just a robo call," I told him as he looked toward the kitchen, listening to the phone ring and ring. He looked torn about what to do.

"You're probably right, but we don't really get those anymore. What if it's someone who really needs to get in touch with us?" He'd already started taking a few steps toward the kitchen when it stopped ringing, stopping him in his tracks. "Well, whatever. If they really need us, they'll call back."

And it started ringing again.

He bolted to the kitchen, leaving me by the front door, and was at the phone in a matter of seconds, clearly thinking it must be an emergency. Then I thought maybe it could have something to do with his dad and the jail. I didn't want to eavesdrop, but I wanted to make sure he was OK with the call. Tiptoeing down the hall, I tried being as quiet as I could. When I peeked around the corner, I saw him sitting at the island, phone in hand. A mask of rage was covering his face.

His words were mumbled, and he was obviously trying to keep the content of the call private. All I could make out were "How did you get this number?" and "Who the fuck do you think you are?" My mind stayed on the idea of his father, immediately thinking it was someone harassing him about their past. I started toward him to comfort him, and he heard me.

Xander's head jolted up in panic at the sight of me in the room. The rage that had been covering his face melted into sympathy, then morphed into hatred.

And that's when I knew.

He found us.

Max found me, Xander, and his family.

"I don't give a fuck what you say, dickhead. You can threaten us all you want, whatever. You will not get close to her again. Do. You. Hear. Me? Never again."

As he slammed the phone on the table, I jumped, startled, but completely understanding of it. I, myself, was unwilling to believe the truth of what was playing out right before my eyes.

How did Max do it? How did he find me? First, he had Karl following me, and then this. These weren't normal tasks that an everyday person was capable of doing. I always felt there was more to the Marcello family than what met the eye, but this was proof. I was dealing with the devil.

I looked over at Xander, his head in his hands. The

anger rolled off him in waves. This was all my fault; every-thing happening was because of me. The guilt filled every cell in my body.

I was frozen in place, not knowing what to do or what to say. I stood feet away from him, wanting to reach out but not finding the strength to do it. Looking around the room, I realized that everything looked the same yet felt as though everything had changed. In a matter of minutes, it felt as if our world, this perfect little world we had created for ourselves while here, was crumbling around us.

And then a thought struck me. What if he was *mad* at me? What if he blamed me for Max finding us, finding his family? I'd understand. Anyone would. And then I knew what I needed to do. I spun on my heel, about to make my retreat, when Xander looked up. The look on his face did nothing to help me understand what could be going on inside his head. The rage in his eyes was contradicted by the tears spilling onto his cheeks.

"Lanie . . ." He started to stand up from the chair, but I put my hands up to stop him. I didn't want him coming close to me, potentially changing my decision. He looked hurt, dejected as he stopped where he was standing.

"Xander, I'm, uh, I'm going to head back to school alone. I think Max is more dangerous than we ever realized, so you should stay here to keep an eye on your mom. I don't want any of you in danger because of me." He once again started toward me, looking distraught, the anger completely gone. "No, please don't." I shook my head as my voice cracked, my newfound strength threatening to dwindle. "I couldn't live with myself if something happened to any of you. I'm sick about this, and I can't take this anymore. He's ruining every part of my life and yours. Every good thing in my life will be gone because of him." I was pacing. I was shaking. The fear of losing Xander, losing everything, was crippling me. Whatever control I thought I had over this situation or my emotions was gone. I was furious—furious that I had to once again change my life because of Max.

But Xander simply stood there, stoic, still.

And that enraged me even more.

I didn't want him to be OK with this. I wanted him to blame me, to be so mad at me for bringing this into his world that he would walk away. Because that would be better. Anything would be better than him being dragged down by Max with me. I wanted him to tell me to get out, that he didn't want to ever see me again because of the shit I had brought upon his family. Because I didn't deserve him and he didn't deserve what I had done to his life.

I ran up the stairs, knowing that if I didn't get myself out of there as quickly as possible, I would lose my courage. Through my tears, it was near impossible to find my bag. I wasn't even sure if they were my clothes I was tossing inside.

I heard the stomping of his boots on the stairs, surprised he hadn't followed me immediately.

"Jesus Christ, Lanie, what are you doing?" he asked as he entered the room. He attempted to pull the clothes from my hands, but I resisted, yanking them back and shoving them inside. I was aimlessly searching for my things around the room, back and forth to the bathroom. All the while, he was leaning against his dresser, arms and ankles crossed.

His calmness put me more on edge.

My bag was overflowing as I tried to close the zipper. I gave up and threw the strap over my shoulder, ready to make my exit.

"Are you done? Are you ready to stop and talk to me,

or at least listen?" Xander's tone wasn't as calm as his body language let on, his frustration coming through. I turned to look at him, and he assumed this was me giving him permission to go on.

"Lanie, I've known pretty much from the start this is what we were going to be dealing with, but you're worth it. Why don't you understand that? I'm not going anywhere. We'll always have issues to deal with in a relationship, babe. We can't walk away every time things get a little tough." He stood there staring at me, almost looking defeated. "You haven't had people stick around to help you; you're not used to it. But that's not how it works around here, not how it's going to work with us."

He pushed away from the chest of drawers and approached me, footsteps slow, eyes on mine. He reached out, removing the bag from my shoulder, letting it hit the ground with a thud. I didn't put up a fight. He grabbed my hands, entwining our fingers, and pulled me closer.

"Let me be here for you, birdie. I'm not perfect. I get mad, but I'm working on it. I'll always be the best version of me that I can be for you." His words struck a chord. I needed to stop pushing him away. He tilted his head while waiting on my response.

I nodded, finally understanding I would have support. This time, I wouldn't be alone.

I would never be alone again.

The tears were escaping quicker than I could wipe them away, my cheeks damp. "But Xander, your mom, your brother, it's killing me."

"I know, baby, but they love you, too."

Our lunch with Bryce and his cop buddies turned into a meeting at the station. Xander thought it was a good idea to tell Bryce everything even though he was a local cop and couldn't do much out of his jurisdiction. But he could keep an eye on their mom.

I wasn't on board with the idea at first. I mean, knowing someone else would have to be told about my past and my secrets made me want to vomit. But I quickly realized I needed to think not only of myself. Getting help from law enforcement was a step in the right direction.

Bryce was professional as Xander and I recounted the facts from the past months. From hearing about Max's visit to campus to him having someone follow me, Bryce kept a cool demeanor while taking notes on his tablet. I limited how much I told him about my life back in Texas as well. We described it as a relationship gone bad. For now, Xander agreed that was sufficient.

As we sat in the room that looked eerily like the ones from crime shows on TV, the three of us decided it was best if Xander and I went back to school early. It was the only plan we could come up with to keep Jane completely safe.

"It'll be OK, guys. I'll have a car watching the house." Bryce's words did little to make me feel better. But it was all we had at the moment, so it would have to do. Xander and I jumped back into his Jeep, trying to figure out our next step.

"When we get home, why don't you finish packing up our stuff? I guess we need to head back to school." His hands were clenching the steering wheel, though he was trying to keep his words light. "He asked for your phone number. I wouldn't give it to him." Xander looked my way, clearly to gauge my reaction. "But I did give him mine."

"What! Why would you do that, Xander?" The fear came through in my question.

"Hey, it's OK. Bryce agreed it was OK. I figured it was a way to keep tabs on him too." He reached over and grabbed a hold of my hand, rubbing circles on the palm. I laid my head back for the rest of the ride, too tired to think about anymore of this.

And thankfully when we pulled in the driveway, we were alone. Jane was still at work. I had no interest in talking to anyone else about what was going on. But then that idea was shattered as we got ourselves inside.

"I think we should call your father," Xander said.

No, I couldn't have him talk to my dad again. I was lucky that he didn't get more out of my father last time.

"He could have some other information that might help." I was trying really hard to keep it together, but these new developments were about to put me over the edge. I really didn't need Xander talking to my father again. There was too much at risk. "I'll ask Bryce what he thinks. I have your dad's number. Bryce and I can call him if we need to."

"Do you really think that's necessary, calling my dad? I'm sure there isn't much else he can tell you." The concern in my voice came through more than I wanted, causing Xander to snap his head my way.

"He told me to call him if we needed to, Lanie. I think this is a time that it's needed. How do you know he can't help? Maybe there's something small he can tell Bryce. Ya never know." He put his keys and wallet on the counter, standing against the kitchen island, studying my expression, looking for answers I didn't want to give him. He walked up to me, close enough to kiss me, and asked, "Birdie, what are you not telling me? Is there something else about your parents we should know?" I shook my head instantly. "Listen, with everything going on, if there's anything that can help with this guy, ya gotta tell me." He was growing impatient with me, I could tell.

"I, um, it's just that, he might, um, have some . . . shit!" I was pacing in the kitchen and stopped by the back window, staring out at some snowflakes drifting from the sky. "Hmm, it's snowing again." I turned to look at him, knowing my eyes would convey what was coming. "It doesn't seem as pretty as yesterday's. Max really does ruin everything." I stalled, not wanting to continue but knowing the time had come.

Xander had to know it all.

And it had to come from me.

I found a chair at the table and slumped into it, my defeat evident. He understood the gravity of what was coming and silently sat in the chair next to me, waiting. I had several failed attempts at starting, my words getting clogged in my throat.

"So, you, uh, know there's more to my story." I looked up at him. The only acknowledgment I received was a small nod. "So, um, Max and me, we . . . I didn't meet him in the traditional way. We met at a dinner with our parents. His dad works for a big oil company, and apparently our dads were working together on a lot of things." My hands were on the table, and I was nervously wringing them together.

"Okaaay." Xander's indifference to the start of my story frustrated me, but I knew it wasn't his fault. He had no idea what he was about to learn.

"Lanie, please make sure you try hard to make this work tonight. It means a lot to your father. He needs this connection for his career."

"Mom, do you know what you're asking of me? Really? This is so weird. I can't believe you're trying to set me up with this guy's son. I can't believe you're going along with this. What if he's an ugly dork? And he doesn't even go to my school. This is ridiculous. You know that, right?"

"Lanie, when your father decided to go into politics, we all knew there were going to be sacrifices that needed to be made, things we were going to have to do that we weren't used to doing. This is one of those things. I'm sorry, but yes, I need you to do this. Go on a few dates—I'm sure he's a nice boy. They have a lot of money. I'm sure he'll buy you some nice things. And he's a bit older, actually already graduated high school. I'm sure he will know how to treat a young lady. So here, wear this, and let's get you all pretty for him. His name is Max."

The first sign I had of things to come that night was right after dinner. All of us were in the den. And I was about to experience my first kiss. Yep, my very first kiss in my life happened in front of my parents. They actually were the ones that told us to do it. It was the most awkward moment of my life, and it should have been foreshadowing of what was to come. Because darkness came after that, lots and lots of darkness. But that's the problem with abuse. It sneaks up on you. If you saw it coming, everyone would get out of its way. But it doesn't work like that.

And then there's the dress she put me in that fateful

night three years ago. It played a dual role as Max and I left our parents later in the evening. When he asked me to go for a walk around our property, I was more than willing, hoping we could have a redo of that ill-timed first kiss in front of everyone. At that point, I kind of had a crush on him. He was cute, older, all the things a girl my age would want. He grabbed my hand, and we headed out the back door for a tour of the grounds. My parents' house was nice enough. My dad was a lawyer before becoming a congressman in the state, so we had a decent piece of property with some wooded area in addition to a pool and a pool house. Everything seemed OK at first as we walked hand in hand, looking around as I gave the two-cent tour. He wasn't saying much, an occasional grunt here or there. Once he saw the pool house, his interest perked up and he started dragging me toward it.

"Is it unlocked? Can we get in?"

Those were the first full sentences he had uttered to me since meeting, and I didn't like the menacing look on his face as he asked the questions. I simply nodded in response as he opened the door and we slipped inside.

And immediately I was uncomfortable with the isolation. Max had dropped my hand and was walking around the space. He looked to be inspecting it. He walked over to the door, locked it, then came back to me, grabbed my hand, and pushed me onto the couch.

"Lanie, our parents have decided we're going to be together, and I've been with worse girls." As he said this, his eyes leered at my chest and he stood over me. Then, all of a sudden, he reached down with both of his hands, roughly grabbing both my breasts. I started to pull away out of instinct. No one had ever touched me there, ever, and

he was actually hurting me.

"Uh-uh, nope, you're not going anywhere, Lanie. Didn't you hear our parents? This is a done deal between us. This is permanent. We're together. It's you and me. We're together until we get married."

I wasn't comprehending what he was saying, but I also didn't have time to. He started restraining me by holding down my arms. He had pushed himself on top of me by this point and was talking into my ear, his mouth making my hair move with his breath, so close to my face I could smell the gum in his mouth. I will forever hate the smell of peppermint because of that moment.

"I thought I'd get a taste of the goods I'll be privy to for the rest of my life while I was here tonight, ya know, before I leave. Give you something to remember me by." I struggled under his hold, but it was futile. I couldn't move.

"Max, I don't want to do this right now. I've never done any of this with anyone. Please stop." I was crying at this point, pleading with him, but this seemed to incite him, actually excite him more. I tried to calm myself, but I was having a hard time, his heavy body making it even harder to catch my breath.

"I don't think our parents know what they've done for me. They've sacrificed a virgin. How will I ever thank them? Don't worry, Lanie. We won't go all the way tonight. I'll save that for another day. I only want a small sample of what I have to look forward to. This dress has been turning me on all night. Ever since you walked downstairs, I've been thinking about how I want to run my hands up it, get inside your underwear. It would be even better if you weren't wearing any. Are you naked under that dress, Lanie?"

My eyes were wide with horror as he waited for an

answer from me. My head slowly moved from side to side in response. It wasn't the answer he wanted.

He slapped me.

I paused in my story as Xander's chair scratched at the floor and fell behind him. He had catapulted himself clear across the room, arms against the wall, in search of something to hold him back.

"Xander, I have to finish this. I need to. Please."

He still hadn't moved. I could hear his ragged breathing from across the room.

"FUCK!" His hand hit the wall and my chair bounced back against the window ledge, my heart pounding. I watched as he straightened his body to standing, appearing to physically shake his anger from his body.

No words were said. He simply lifted his chair from the floor and came back to his seat. I wasn't sure what to do, but I needed to get this out while I had the nerve to do it.

When someone gets hit in anger for the first time in their life, many things happen simultaneously. First, I was stunned. I couldn't believe what happened—complete disbelief. Then the anger set in. I felt my fists roll up into balls reflexively, but Max was a big guy. I was in a prone position with him on top of me. I'd never taken any self-defense classes, and I knew I had no way of getting out of that situation. The

anger rolled into fear, and I comprehended the severity of the situation I found myself in. Finally, resolve set in. I decided I would do whatever it took to survive that moment.

All of that occurred within seconds, because moments after the slap, Max painfully ripped my underwear off. It shredded in his hands, and my legs burned from the force. He held me down with one hand on my neck, and I gasped for air when suddenly I felt him push his hand inside my body. He did this with such force that I let out a howl, forcing his hand from my neck to my mouth. His eyes conveyed a warning that if I didn't quiet down, there would be worse things done to me. He took his hand out of my body and started to undo his pants.

"You weren't lying about being a virgin, Lanie. I'm glad to see that. Know this: your life will be a lot easier as long as you do what I say and what I want. We can have a good life if you listen. This is only the beginning."

I turned my head and looked away; I couldn't look at him anymore. Focusing on one spot in the room, I was hoping I could forget, escape. Closing my eyes, I knew I was shutting down. That was when the first tears fell.

I felt him change position, struggling to do something, yet I didn't want to look at him. I heard his zipper go down and could feel him fumbling with his free hand, and he was sure to never let the hand that was securely over my mouth move. I felt him trying to hold himself over me, even shift a bit to the side, all while I was struggling for each breath through my nose. I could feel a change in his movements. There was now a rhythmic movement.

I refused to look, but I knew what he was doing. More and more tears streamed down my face at the knowledge he was using me like this. He stopped for a moment and used that hand to pull down the top of my dress and my bra to expose my breasts. I was disgusted and felt vomit rise in my throat, but I was terrified of what he would do to me if I allowed it to come out. I knew I had to swallow it. As his hand went to my breasts, he pulled them, hurting me. When he felt me starting to cry in pain behind his hand, he pushed on my face harder.

"Shut up, Lanie."

I didn't dare move or make a sound, too afraid of what else he might do to me. I felt him get off of me but wouldn't turn my head toward him. He stood up and found the bathroom. All I did was cover myself with my dress and curl up in a ball.

"Get up, and go clean yourself up in the bathroom. You're a mess." He yanked me from the floor and shoved me toward the bathroom. "Our parents will be wondering where we are. Make yourself presentable."

Once inside, I locked the door and slid down the back to the floor. The devastation I felt was palpable, pumping through my veins. I sat there, silent, not knowing my next move. There was no going back from what just happened. I would never be the same Lanie ever again. I was damaged. I held back the floodgate of tears that wanted to escape because I was afraid of his reaction.

I slowly got up from the floor and made my way over to the mirror, afraid to look at the reflection, afraid to see a different person. But it was still me. I didn't look much different on the outside, just some smeared mascara and the hint of a bruise on my neck. All the damage was on the inside, in places no one can see it, in places I will be able to hide it, because I was obviously going to have to. I jumped at the knock on the door.

"Lanie." His voice sounded softer now, as if he was trying to have a conscience after what happened. "Are you OK? Can you open the door?"

I quickly splashed some cold water on my face and tried to get the makeup out from under my eyes. My hands shook uncontrollably as I reached for the lock on the door.

"Yeah, I'm good." As I walked hurriedly out the pool house door in my attempt to distance myself from him, he raced toward me. He caught up and grabbed my arm, but not as hard as before. With my arm in his grasp, he turned me to look at him.

"Lanie, I'm sorry about this. I like it rough. I was turned on by you when I first saw you. I couldn't wait to get you alone somewhere. I promise next time it'll be all about you." As he said this, he put his fingers under my chin and lifted my face up toward his, actually trying to be, what, romantic?

The irony was not lost on me in that moment as he bent down and kissed me softly on the lips. I might have only been sixteen, but I wasn't naive. I knew this was a vicious cycle that was probably starting, and I was going to get caught up in it all because of politics, money, and a sundress. Needless to say, yeah, that was why I was never going to wear a dress again. And his apologies were always empty. His anger always won out the next time around, and then he apologized again, and it happened over and over. Until I left for school.

No eye contact was made during all of that. I stared down at my twisted fingers the entire time. But when I finished,

I peered up in hopes of finding a version of Xander I would recognize.

He sat in his chair, motionless. He was silent as the tears rolled down his cheeks, off his chin. A round, wet stain had appeared on his shirt. He slowly stood up and approached me, looking almost scared. His hands reached for my face; his lips came in for a simple kiss.

"It's probably the absolute worst thing I could be doing for you right now, but I need to walk away. I'm sorry. I'll be back, but I'm sorry."

And he walked out of the kitchen and left me alone.

Chapter 19

"Xander, is that you?" I ran down the stairs, hopeful, when I heard the front door.

"No, Lanie, it's me. Where is he, honey?" It was Jane. "What's wrong? You look upset. Is everything OK?"

I didn't have a good poker face, so I wasn't going to be able to keep this from her for very long. I'd hoped Xander would be back already.

"Um, well. Xander stepped out. Not sure where he went." I was trying to avoid eye contact, and I thought going back upstairs would be my best option. I began my retreat to the stairs.

"Lanie, what's going on?" Jane's tone was one of grave concern. She looked at me and saw the look on my face, the tears in my eyes, and came toward me. "Lanie, are you OK?" I shook my head no, and then the tears started cascading down my cheeks. "Come sit down, honey. Tell me what's going on."

About thirty minutes later, we heard the front door open.

Xander came walking into the kitchen and saw the two of us sitting at the kitchen table, Jane holding my hands, both of us crying. It was obvious what I had told her.

He walked directly to me, stood me up, hugged me, and whispered in my ear, "I'm sorry. I shouldn't have walked out. We need to talk." He turned toward Jane. "I don't know how much she told you, Mom, but we have a lotta shit going on. I need to talk to her, but then we'll fill you in. OK?"

Jane simply cupped his cheek as she walked away and up the stairs. Xander pulled me in for a tighter hug this time. I knew his embrace was a message.

"I'm sorry." The apology was muffled in my hair, his voice strained. "I'm so sorry. I'm sorry for everything you've had to endure. I'm sorry for your asshole parents. I'm sorry for you having to deal with all of that alone for so long. But most of all, I'm sorry I had to walk away." He pulled away and firmly grabbed my face, forcing me to keep eye contact as he continued. "I shouldn't have, but I needed to. I couldn't let you see that side of me, Lanie. Not when you needed a very different part of me."

It was then I noticed the chewed-up knuckles on both his hands, bloodied and swollen. He pulled them away from my face, instead wrapping his arms around my waist, pulling me in. His chin rested on the top of my head as he let out a deep sigh.

"It's OK, Xander. That was a lot. I get it. But I had to tell you, I had to tell you everything. I needed you to know." I felt the nod of his head above me.

"I haven't even met your parents, but I kind of hate

them right now. Who would willingly . . . who would allow . . .?" He couldn't complete his thoughts, but there wasn't a need.

We wandered into the living room, sat on the couch for a while in a comfortable silence. Eventually Jane made her way back downstairs, I'm sure more than ready to find out more of our tale.

"You two OK now?"

"Yeah, Mom, but we have some other stuff to fill you in on. While I was out, I saw Bryce."

He then proceeded to fill us both in on what transpired with Bryce over the past couple of hours. Apparently there was so much I was unaware of when it came to the Marcello family. Xander and Bryce did put a call into my father, which proved to be very helpful.

With his information and the digging some of the detectives were able to do, it had been determined the Marcello family was deep in the mafia.

The mafia.

And somehow, that news didn't surprise me.

The control they wound up having over my father led to the arrangement between me and Max. That was supposed to guarantee certain legislative wins with Congress through my dad, who they apparently blackmailed with information from his lawyer days. My dad was the perfect candidate for their needs: a lawyer with knowledge and the current connections that came with holding a political office. Merging the families was a top priority for them. As Xander predicted, this was much bigger than we could have imagined.

"Bryce and his detectives don't think they can really do anything, Lanie." He looked at me when he said this, knowing I would be crushed by his statement. "Don't worry, they're not abandoning us. They can't do anything because of the level this has reached. It needs to go higher. They're calling the FBI."

My eyes bulged. "What!"

"I know. Sounds crazy, right?" Xander continued. "But anything related to organized crime is automatically at the federal level. Bryce will be involved as our liaison to the FBI. He'll be our contact. It's already been initiated, and they've been contacted. You'll have to be interviewed. The, um, things he did to you, the, uh, abuse and stuff, it will have to go on record so he can be charged when they bring him in." He paused and stared at me after saying this, his eyes intent on mine. "Lanie, they will bring him in. This will end. But will you be able to do this? To tell other people everything he did to you?" He came closer to me, putting my hand in his, understanding what he was asking me to do.

Even weeks earlier, my immediate answer would have been *no*. But there had been so many changes in my life that my knee-jerk reaction couldn't be the fallback anymore. Not only was the safety of people I cared about in my hands, but I also had their support as I went through this.

"I can do it, Xander." My answer came out in a whisper, but the words came out.

His smile was huge. He was shaking with excitement at the thought that this could have closure.

But then Jane brought us back to reality a bit.

"Alex, keep in mind that these cases with the FBI can go on for years. You guys might be in this for the long haul. Don't get your hopes up that this will be over any time soon. But I agree, it's great news the proper authorities will be taking this over. It is awful what you've been through, Lanie, and it's awful that he continues to put both of you through it still. I'm not going to lie, I'm very scared, though, that he can still harm you both while this investigation is going on. You need to be careful."

Right then, Bryce busted through the front door, looking preoccupied and stressed.

"Hey guys, thought I'd stop by and go over some details with everyone. Xander, can I see you in the kitchen?" His steps were quick as he passed us all down the hall and out of sight. Jane and I remained on the couch, our silence now a bit awkward.

"They'll both take care of you, of us, I have no doubt."

All I could do was nod, my guilt building. I heard some raised voices in the other room, and suddenly Bryce was at our side.

"Lanie." Bryce's tone was serious. "There's something you should know about Xander that he hasn't told you." He looked nervous to talk to me, and now I was even more scared. "There's a part of Xander's past that's going to come up in the investigation. I think he should tell you about it now."

"Bryce, what the fuck are you doing?" Xander yelled.

Xander was standing in the doorway from the kitchen, swollen hands in fists at his side, breathing heavily, looking ready to pounce. I'd never seen him look this ferocious. Seconds later, Jane had her hands on Xander's arm, trying to pull him back into the kitchen, but he pushed her away, yelling obscenities at her.

This was a Xander I'd never seen before.

The one he'd tried to hide.

"Dude," Bryce said with an edge to his voice, "if you want any involvement in this at all, they will need to know this. Full disclosure, which means she will find out."

"Xander, she deserves to know. She needs to know. There's too much she's involved in right now, and if she isn't told by you, she's going to find out anyway." Jane's voice held sympathy as she spoke to him.

The look on his face transformed from anger to acknowledgment to shame in a matter of seconds. Yet he stormed away up the stairs and his door slammed, causing the house to shake.

Bryce and Jane must have realized they were going to be the ones to have to tell me, and they embarked on a story from Xander's past that stunned me into silence. My heart broke for Xander, while at the same time I felt as though I may not know the real him anymore.

I found him lying in his bed. I climbed in behind him and wrapped my arm around his middle. He reached up and grabbed a hold of my hand, which was across his chest, entwining my fingers with his. I felt the tension in his body ease a bit. We stayed like that for a while, silent, holding on to each other.

"I love you." And I did, but I felt this had changed things. I suddenly felt I may not know Xander as well as I'd thought I did. But I couldn't abandon him or walk away. He'd already been by me through much worse. I couldn't very well take off simply because of one secret he kept.

But I was shaken by his story.

And then his cries came. And they broke me. I swiftly turned him to face me.

"I will always love you, Xander. Just like you love me through all the crap I go through. This doesn't change anything. I'm catching you this time."

He grabbed me tightly and held on, crying into my shoulder, releasing so much pain. "But, Lanie, I was the one who hurt someone. I was the monster. I put that kid in the hospital. I hurt him, almost killed him. He'll never be the same. I was arrested, and I have a permanent record. I'm no better than Max."

He howled when he said this, the tears pouring from both of us.

"Stop saying that, Xander. You're nothing like Max! Jane and Bryce told me everything. You were so sad, and those kids were mean. They were making fun of you for having a dad in jail. It's not your fault. Please, Xander, you have to understand the difference! Please!" I was sitting up by now, trying to get through to him.

"How do you know Max doesn't have a fucked up past that made him who he is? I'm no different than he is." The emotion rolling off him was palpable.

"Don't ever compare yourself to him, ever. You're the kindest soul I've ever encountered, Xander. You made one error in judgment. People make mistakes, and you're not expected to pay for it the rest of your life. Max, he chooses, in every moment of his life, to render hatred and pain toward people, especially me. There is absolutely no comparison between the two of you, so don't even go there." I had him by the face, gripping him firmly, staring into his eyes, hoping to convey this message.

His gaze remained on mine, his body calming under my grip. But he didn't say anything.

We sat there, holding each other. I hoped my words were sinking in, making an impact.

Eventually, he moved away, stood up. His sigh was deep before his words came.

"I guess I knew you would eventually have to find out, but I didn't know how you would react. I didn't want you to have to come to terms with something like this about me right now. And today of all days, we've had a rough one."

It was a rough day.

And this was a side of Xander I wasn't expecting.

He was still the same Xander. The same guy who taught me how to trust myself again in so many ways. I stared at him while he looked out his bedroom window, leaning against the windowsill. His bedroom still held hints of his childhood. Trophies, plaques, and awards for his years playing football lined the walls and shelves. Then I noticed a gaming system gathering dust under the TV cabinet, which took me by surprise. That was a side of him I never saw. A gamer?

I walked to it and examined the array of games stacked on the shelf, long abandoned. They were games from a while ago, nothing from recent years, so he must have played as a younger child. I felt him come up next me, also looking, but not touching them.

"Bryce and I used to hide out in our rooms and play a lot when things got bad downstairs." He got quiet again, contemplative, thinking. "The loud sounds on the games helped." All I found myself capable of doing was nodding.

I really didn't know the man I was in love with.

And I knew I should be angry about the secret he kept from me, but that would make me a hypocrite. I did the same thing numerous times. I knew better than most how hard it was to share a dark past. I didn't blame him for not telling me. But the news was . . . unsettling. His anger issues were a bit more than I had thought. Going to jail for beating someone up so bad they were hospitalized for a week was no joke.

But maybe the scarier part was that I understood that as well.

He had returned to looking out the window, the snow maybe giving him some peace. I came up behind him and wrapped my arms around his waist, my head resting on his back. I felt him relax into me immediately, gripping my hands with his. He slowly spun himself around, sitting himself on the window's edge, both at eye level now. He pulled me closer, in between his widened legs.

"Why do you still have those games here?" I questioned. Xander was quiet for a bit, his hands wandering along the backs of my legs while he thought.

"I think," Xander started, then paused. "I think I keep them as a reminder. Kinda like a 'where there's a will, there's a way' reminder. For a while, Bryce and I had no idea what our lives would be like."

His voice cracked as he said that, showing yet another side of him, a sensitive side he never allowed anyone else to see. At school, he was always the tough frat guy others were a bit intimidated by, mostly due to his size. He played it up, although it wasn't all for show. He *was* tough, toughened by everything he had been through as a kid. But he was also vulnerable from those same experiences.

And now he'd shown that side of himself to me twice.

"I get that," I replied, "but look at the two of you now." He nodded but was still quiet. "Ya know, I don't like that I had to tell you about being forced to be with Max. But I do feel better now that you know. I feel freer, like I can breathe," I confessed as I smiled up at him.

I was graced with a dimpled smile. "Yeah, it feels better now that you know. It's been hanging over me this whole time. But I wish it had been on my terms," Xander said, anger still tinging his voice.

I was going to move on from this today. All of us had

pasts, secrets we would rather not divulge. But ours were coming out because they had to, not because we wanted them to. I would try to see beyond the secrets, the anger. He deserved that.

"I get it, but Max has a way of screwing everything up, so welcome to my world."

And there we were, full circle. Right back to the real problem at hand.

Chapter 20

We were heading back to school early. All the information had been given to the detectives and agents, and nothing more could be done. They interviewed me twice about the three years Max and I spent together in Texas, almost a total of fourteen hours of interrogation. It was exhausting, but I knew how necessary it was to take down the Marcellos.

I texted Becca, telling her we were heading back. She was full of questions I didn't want to answer. Her texts wouldn't stop coming in, incessantly begging for something. Finally caving, I told her that there was a big problem with Max. I explained it was better to deal with it at school rather than at Xander's home so that it wouldn't involve his mom. That seemed to satisfy her, maybe because of the issues she was having with Ty herself.

"Do you have my number, Lanie?" Bryce asked as we packed up the Jeep. "You need to call me if there's anything suspicious or if you two have any issues when you get back to school." Bryce was being as supportive as Jane, even though I still felt unworthy of it.

"I do. Thanks, Bryce, for everything." Reaching up, I gave him a hug. I'd given up on trying to not have them help—it was futile. "I'm lucky to have you and Jane helping us through this crazy shit I've caused. I hope you realize how grateful I truly am for both of you."

"Lanie, I don't think you realize how quickly you've become a part of this family. I see the way Xander looks at you. You're it for him, and that means you're family, kiddo. I'll do anything to keep you safe. Hey, I need to keep my brother happy." He moved his mouth close to my ear before saying, "Don't tell him, but, yeah, he can kick my ass."

Bryce still had his arm around my shoulder, mouth by my ear, when . . . our special "brother/sister" bonding moment got interrupted.

"What the hell am I interrupting? Dude, you seriously look like you're about to fucking kiss her!"

"Well, bro, make sure you're keeping her satisfied and I won't have to step in." Bryce cackled. He knew he needed to take off running after that comment. And he did, heading inside his apartment. Xander was barely one step behind him the whole way, cursing under his breath.

I heard Xander catch him, and it sounded like a few brotherly punches were thrown. From the laughter combined with their shouts, it sounded like it was more of a goodbye for them than anything else. They eventually came out, arm in arm, a small tear in Bryce's shirt the only sign of their scuffle. The smiles on their faces were contradictory to the noises that came from inside, but I was getting used to what being around brothers was all about.

"Remember, Lanie. I'm your backup when this douche doesn't treat you right." Xander's arm around Bryce's neck squeezed harder as they laughed.

"Well, I guess you're SOL then, because I'll never not treat her right, dude, so be on the lookout for your own perfect woman." They hugged it out, and Bryce came and hugged me goodbye as well, whispering in my ear so Xander couldn't hear him.

"Take care of him. He may not seem it, but he's scared, scared of you getting hurt. Call me if you need anything." He gave me one last squeeze and let me go.

We piled into Xander's Jeep, said our goodbyes to northern Virginia, and started our trek back to school.

"Lanie, oh my God, come over here. I missed you, goddammit!" Becca dropped her bags in the middle of the floor, swooped in, and picked me up in her arms. "We cannot go a full month without seeing each other ever again. That was awful. I needed you for many reasons, and texting did not make the cut. We'll need to make other arrangements over the summer, you hear me?"

She was her typical whirlwind self, and I couldn't be happier to be back in her presence. Amazing that I fought befriending this extraordinary person in the beginning. She'd become a lifeline for me.

"I missed you, too, Becca. So much. And I have a lot to tell you. Like, a lot, and not just about Max."

She stopped, frozen mid-step, and stared at me. The look in her eyes was full of curiosity and hope, and I knew she was wondering about Xander and me. All I did was give her a small nod, and it answered most of her questions.

"I knew it! No more friend zone! Finally, he sealed the deal. Like, did he really seal the deal though?" She then gave me the "other" look, with a raising of the eyebrows as she dug her elbow into my side. All I could do was blush.

"I knew it! That's awesome, Lanie. I'm happy for you guys. Like, really happy." At this point, my face was buried in her hair as she hugged me again, but I loved it. "I can't wait to see you two as a couple. You'll be so cute together. He's hot—like, super hot. And you're going to make so many girls on this campus jelly as hell! Do you realize that? Xander James is off the market!" She was bouncing around the room at this point, seemingly more excited about my relationship than I was.

"How are you and Ty doing? I know you weren't too happy in your text. Did you see him after that at all?" I wanted to shift her attention from me to her. There was still so much to tell her, and unfortunately, she knew all the good already, but none of the bad.

"Oh, you know, same old, same old. We saw each other some. But he isn't the same guy at home that he is here, and I can't figure out why yet. He really doesn't want me to see him at his house much. He'd rather come to my house, which is fine, but it's harder at my house with all of my brothers and sisters. We don't have much room. His house is better—he only has his one brother, and he's not there much, so I don't understand what's going on. I guess it's that his parents don't really like me?"

Her eyes conveyed her true emotions. She was more

upset about this than she was letting on.

"Well, I'm glad you're back, too. I missed you a ton. Are the guys back also? Xander and I wanted to talk to all of you about the shit that's going on with Max."

Becca looked over and knew immediately something was off. "What did the asshole do this time? Christ, you have to get him out of your life for good. He's ridiculous." Her exasperation did little to make me feel like sharing what was really going on. But she was right about all of it.

"Well, I'm ready to tell you guys everything about him. Xander's going to help me, but I only want to do it once, so I wanna wait 'til Ty and Logan get here too, if that's OK."

She came up to my side, smile wide, full of encouragement. A far cry from the Becca of just a moment ago, as she'd realized the gravity of what I said. "Of course, Lane. I've waited this long, so I can wait a little longer. Are you sure you want to do this? I mean, I don't want you to feel like you have to tell us something you don't want to."

I hated that the mood shifted so severely, of course always because of me.

"I want this to be over. We were happy a few minutes ago, and I want more of that. I need the darkness from my past to go away, and I think I need to admit it's happening to let it go. Maybe I should do that with professionals, but for now my friends will have to do."

Xander had suggested that I seek a counselor. Considering it was what I had chosen as a career path, I agreed it was a good idea. Once the semester got underway, I was going to the mental health center on campus to set up an appointment for a consultation. It was a big step for me.

"OK, then. That's what we'll do. We will be here for you, we will hear you, we will listen, and we will help you heal." She grabbed my hands and squeezed. She pulled away, then and reached for her phone. "Ty says they both should be here by five. It's already almost five, so let's go keep an eye out for them. Where's Xander?"

"He was at the gym. I'll go see if he's back, and we can meet up with the guys when they get here." I was getting nervous again. Telling Becca that me and Xander were now a couple was the easy part.

Xander gripped my hand as we walked toward Ty and Logan's room. We could hear Becca's screeching down the hall, so we knew the guys had arrived. I knocked on the open door as we walked in, and the three of them turned and looked immediately at our interlocked fingers.

Becca smiled warmly.

Ty responded with a look that suggested he had won a bet.

Logan's eyes darted away, but then they returned to me. He seemed to be trying to stay neutral, trying hard for my sake to not show his true reaction. He smiled, but it was forced, not real.

"Hi guys, I missed you so much!" I ran up to each of them, giving them tight hugs. Logan clearly wasn't sure how to respond with Xander watching. His hands were high up on my shoulders as I hugged him. The room got awkward after that, a few moments of silence following the hugs.

"OK, this is exactly what I don't want," I said. "I need us to be friends still. So, the real reason me and Xander are here is because I've decided it's time to tell the three of you a lot more about my past. I have some demons, one in particular, that are continuing to create havoc in my life. You all escaped his wrath the weekend you went home."

At this, all eyes landed on Logan, and he became even more uncomfortable, which I was not intending.

"He's not a nice guy, and unfortunately, he was my boyfriend back home. He, um, him and me, we were, um . . ."

I froze.

I started wringing my hands together and sat down on one of their beds, feeling like my legs were going to give out.

I lost the ability to breathe.

Did I really want to do this? There was no going back once they knew. And what I had to tell them was ugly.

So dark and ugly.

Becca came over and sat next to me, wrapping her arm around me for support. Ty and Logan both had looks of concern on their faces, eyes bouncing back and forth between me and Xander.

Xander cleared his throat in preparation to talk. I knew he was going to do this—it was the plan all along for him to take over if I couldn't go through with it—but I just didn't know if I was truly ready.

He first looked at me, and my slight nod gave him the permission he was looking for.

He started by taking a very defensive stance, his arms across his chest, his legs spread. It seemed having to tell this story put him in a very protective mode.

"OK, guys, listen. This guy at home, Max, well, she was actually set up with him by her parents. It's a fucked-up situation, right? He repeatedly abused her. He beat her, molested her."

Xander had to pause.

He ran his hands through his hair, making him

look crazed.

"He raped her. All under the watch of her parents. She had no one to turn to, no one to trust—no one, that is, until us. She has nowhere to live anymore but her dorm room, but I'll be working on that. I'm not entirely sure of the plan yet, but I'll figure something out. He knows about me, and he knew she was with me over break, so he has connections. So if you care about her at all, you'll help her in any way you can. And you'll help me carry out whatever plan I come up with to help her against this guy. And yes, she and I are together, Logan. Not you and her—her and I. Very together."

I was stunned into silence by Xander's speech, as was the rest of the group. I wouldn't have been able to say it any better than he did. He walked over, grabbed a hold of me, pulled me against his chest, and kissed me gently on the lips. The group was still grappling with what they just learned as I silently thanked Xander with my eyes for doing what I couldn't.

"I know, babe," he whispered in my ear.

I looked around the room briefly but couldn't hold eye contact with anyone. I knew they were going to think differently of me now.

I was afraid they'd all change the way they saw me now, as a broken person, someone who needed to be taken care of and coddled. That had always been part of why I never wanted to share.

Becca had tears in her eyes. I looked at her and shook my head, begging her with my eyes to please not make me cry.

"Hey, Lane, I'm going to shed a tear or two for my friend who has been to hell and back. But you're so strong, girl. Come here." She wrapped her arms around me in a tight hug and held on, her tears flowing. This was a lot of information for them to process at once, I understood that. "It all makes sense now, Lanie, everything. I'm sorry. So sorry for pushing you."

"Please don't be," I pleaded in her ear, my tears barely holding back. "If not for you pushing me, I don't think I'd be where I am right now. I need to thank you." I pulled away and kissed her on the cheek. Ty grabbed me by the hands next. He pulled me into a hug. He didn't seem to be able to say anything as a small sob escaped from his chest and he clung to me. He pulled away, then looked at Xander.

"Dude, I'll do anything you need. Anytime, anywhere—against that asshole, just say the word." They fist-bumped, and that was it.

I then looked at Logan, who was fiddling with a loose thread on his comforter while sitting on his bed. We all sat in an awkward silence for a few moments while we waited to see his reaction to the news he seemed to still be processing. I looked at Xander, hoping he wasn't getting angry while we waited for Logan's response, but he seemed relaxed.

Finally, Logan stood up and walked toward me. He was so tall I needed to crane my neck to look in his eyes. They were full of remorse and what appeared to be anger, though his movements were slow and deliberate. His one hand gently came up to my face and cradled my cheek, and I froze, hoping this would end well. One lone tear escaped each of his eyes, cascading down his cheeks. He opened his mouth to speak but clamped it back closed.

He looked to the ceiling, as if trying to summon the right words to say.

When he opened his mouth to speak again, all that

came out was, "I'm sorry, Lanie, for everything." He leaned in and kissed me on the forehead. He walked over to Xander, shook his hand, and walked silently out of the room. Once in the hall, we all heard a loud thud, which I think was him punching the wall. Then we heard the ping of the elevator.

Ty moved toward the door.

"I'm going to catch up with him, make sure he's OK." He left the room, giving Becca an apologetic look. She tried to return the focus to what Xander had said to the group.

"Xander, you have to know we would do anything to help Lanie against that douchebag." She turned her attention toward me. "Honey, I'm so sorry you've had to live the last few years dealing with the likes of that guy. You won't ever have to deal with any of this alone ever again."

Xander came to me, sensing I needed him. He had an uncanny ability to know exactly what was bothering me. Either that or I was more of an open book than I knew. But I could tell he was a bit upset himself.

"Lanie, you know my priority is you and only you. Logan is going to have to figure his own shit out. I'm sorry if he still has feelings for you, but I don't have time for his pansy-ass outbursts because he doesn't get what he wants. I did my best to let him do his thing."

I understood Xander being upset. But was it fair? This was such an unusual situation. Anyone in it would act like Logan was; at least, that was what I told myself.

"Xander, you handled that with dignity, and thank you for that. But I think his response goes beyond how he feels for me. I think he's struggling with our whole semester together and a lot of moments that finally made sense to him. Everyone handles things in their own way, and he has to find his right now."

He calmed a bit and accepted that from me, acting more like himself.

Becca was still sitting quietly. I moved to stand by her. "I know you probably want to go find Ty and Logan, and it's OK if you do. I understand."

She shook her head slowly. "Not yet. I think Ty needs some time with him alone. Ty knows better than me how to help Logan, and I'm not sure even Ty can do it. Logan's not doing great, and it may seem like it's all because of you, but it's not. I think you were the final straw. He's got some crap from home too, but he won't talk about it. Sound familiar?" She chuckled softly and looked at me with sad eyes. "I'll go find them in a bit. Right now, I want to be here with you."

"Well, aren't we a sorry bunch? What's that saying—'Misery loves company'? We've given it new meaning, I think," I chuckled, trying to lighten the mood. I sat next to Becca on the bed, and her head landed on my shoulder.

"How about the three of us go get some food? Becca, you text Ty. Let him know that's where we'll be." Xander was still all business, the adrenaline of the moment not out of his system. "They can meet us there. If not, we can meet up later and all talk again if they want to. How does that sound?"

Xander forced his hands into the pockets of his jeans, his forearms bulging under his pushed-up sleeves. Whenever he did that, his chest muscles flexed—involuntarily, but it happened.

And it was sexy.

He was so damn sexy, and he was standing here, trying hard to make this all work out for me. And that made him even sexier. Becca saw the way I was looking at him, and she cleared her throat.

"Maybe food is not what's on Lanie's mind at the moment," Becca said with a sly grin.

"Oh my God, Becca, stop." I was beet red and mortified that she'd caught me eyeing up my own boyfriend.

"Shit, don't be embarrassed. He's hot. He's some major man candy on a stick, Lanie. If you aren't eyeing him up, someone else would be, so you better be doing it, and a lot."

Xander started laughing as he shuffled us out the door and toward the elevators, obviously wanting to stop Becca and her comments. He started walking ahead of us, and she continued her line of questioning.

"So, are big muscles any indication of a big, you know, stick?"

"Becca, you know I can hear you, right?" Xander called from down the hall.

"Of course I do. Either one of you can answer my question. Curious minds wanna know." Becca wrapped her arm around my neck as we bounced down the hall behind Xander, my smile wider since she had returned. I was feeling more and more confident we could do this—together.

Chapter 21

"How's he doing?" I asked Becca as she walked into our room, Ty right behind her. I had hoped a night of sleep would help Logan handle everything he heard about me, coupled with what he was dealing with personally.

"He's a little better today, but still not talking much. I think he's struggling with it all, ya know, because of what happened with the two of you," Ty responded. "I think he'll be OK, Lanie. We just need to keep an eye on him the next couple of days, maybe distract him a bit, go out." Ty was being hopeful. But I think we all felt the potential for Logan to make another scene. My phone pinged, and I couldn't hide my smile at seeing who it was from.

"Gotta go. Xander needs to talk to me." I was concerned about Logan, hoping this wasn't going to put him over the edge. But I was thankful for the diversion. I wasn't comfortable talking about him anymore. Maybe it was self-ish, but I felt like I had enough on my plate. I didn't want to add his problems to my list of concerns. But my heart rate was rising as I approached Xander's door, unsure of what he needed to tell me. The door flew open as I got to it.

"What's wrong? Is it Max again?" I asked.

He grabbed me before answering, pulling me into his room. "Actually, the only emergency is I missed you." His mouth was on my mine before my next breath, but then he pulled back. "There's nothing out of the ordinary from the asshole, nothing you need to worry about. Still him asking where you are, why he can't reach you, why he has to deal with me and not you, yada yada yada. Threatening to come here again to 'set me straight' and 'set you straight,' and I tell him to do it. But so far it seems like empty threats. Bryce seems to have a track on him with the locals in San Antonio, and we should know ahead of time if he's on his way. They also don't think there's anyone here watching you, so we're good."

"Bryce could do that? Oh my God, that's amazing! I'll have to shoot him a text to thank him." I wasn't used to good news or the way it made me feel.

"Yeah, he would appreciate it."

I grabbed a hold of Xander's belt loops and pulled him closer, grinding my hips into his. "So, you missed me? Didn't we just see each other when we woke up this morning?"

"It's four in the afternoon. How long do you expect me to go without missing you?"

His hands worked their way around to my backside, easily lifting me up as I wrapped my legs around his waist, my arms grabbing hold of his neck. He walked us over to his bed and laid me down. He stood up, and I watched him in awe as he reached behind his back with a hand to pull his shirt over his head, his stomach muscles tightening while doing so. His almost black hair was longer now, hitting his shoulders; he had to push it out of his eyes as he leaned down, his arm muscles tightening as he held his weight above me. I rubbed my hands along the corded muscles in his arms as he lay suspended above me, his intense blue eyes looking deep inside.

"I love you, birdie. I will forever be falling in love with you."

The words came easily now but didn't mean any less because of it. My hands worked their way up his arms, over his tight shoulders, through his hair, finally to his face. My thumb rubbed along his bottom lip, and his eyes fluttered closed for a moment. I pulled his face down toward mine, bringing his mouth to me.

"I love you, too." I closed the distance between our mouths, our tongues mingling. The softness of his lips such a contradiction to the hardness of his body, the hardness of his need. I felt that as he gently laid his body on mine.

But the moment our bodies touched, intense desire took over, no space between us. Our limbs immediately entangled, our arms and legs entwined as if in a web, seeking as much of the other's skin as possible. Pieces of clothing were tossed across the room at record pace until both of us were finally at peace, warmed by one another in our embrace. The cool sheets on his bed soothed the scorching heat building between us as we settled next to one another, face to face.

Being bold in bed, with sex, was never something I would have considered myself to be. However, at that moment, I craved having the control.

My hand reached down and found his engorged shaft,

his hard cock twitching between my fingers. The smooth skin pulled tight as my fingers explored the full length of his dick, from the silky tip to the veined skin at the base. I had never taken the time to enjoy touching him, and the feel of him was creating a pool of wetness between my legs.

Maybe it was being back at school, with no parents to walk in on us.

Or maybe it was that Xander had made me comfortable with sex, comfortable with wanting to feel good with my body.

But all my inhibitions were lifted. I felt completely free.

And really horny.

"Christ, Xander," I mumbled as my finger swiped the warm liquid from the tip of his dick. I sucked it off my finger as he watched, his hooded eyes closing as he arched his back. His dick lifted toward me as an offering, and my head lowered as my mouth covered its swollen head. My lips felt stretched trying to accommodate his girth, taking him in slowly. His hands came to my head, lifting my hair so he could watch my mouth take him fully.

I struggled at first, gagging as I pushed him deeper into my throat.

"Babe, it's OK . . ." Xander said, attempting to stop me and pull away.

But I shook my head, sliding my lips further down his shaft. Eventually a rhythm took over and my throat allowed him in, hitting parts of me that had never been touched. One hand stroked him while my mouth pumped up and down, the taste of him all over my lips. Xander dug his fingers into my scalp, the moans escaping from him evidence I was doing things right. The muscles throughout his body were tensing. But then he pulled me from him, my mouth leaving him with a pop.

I stared up at him, wondering if I had done something wrong, not wanting to stop.

"Ugh, babe," he said with heavy breaths, "I don't want to come yet." He pulled me up and flipped us over, the flimsy college mattress squeaking under our weight. As he positioned himself over me, his knee spread my thighs. "That was amazing," he muttered into my neck. "You're amazing, but I wanna make you feel good now." His hand started on my breast, kneading and squeezing, pinching the nipple, which elicited a moan from me. As his mouth devoured mine, his fingers trailed down my stomach, slowly, until they were between my legs. They rubbed the length of me, my wetness coating his fingers.

"You're ready for me, birdie. I like that." As his hand rubbed me rougher, priming me, I prepared myself, knowing what was coming. Needing what was coming.

My hands gripped the sheets and my head flew back as he entered me.

One finger, two fingers, sliding deep inside.

"Fuck, you're so wet, birdie."

"Oh my God . . . Xander . . ." I moaned, able to form no other words on my lips.

His mouth latched onto my nipple, sucking hard and deep. I felt myself reaching for my other breast, kneading it and pinching its peaked tip. He peeked over and saw my hand at work on myself and turned his eyes up to me. "That's so fucking hot, Lanie." His tongue flicked at the nipple in his mouth, a new aggression in him as his hand came around and grabbed that same breast and pushed it against the other. His teeth grazed me, causing an electric current to go straight from my tits to my clit.

And as good as his fingers felt inside of me, what I really

wanted was for him to touch me there: my clit.

"Xander . . ." I started, then stopped. But he took it the wrong way.

"Babe, it's OK—you're OK," he whispered, thinking I was in my own head, going dark. But I shook my head and moaned at the same time.

"No, babe . . . I want you to . . . move your hand higher . . ." My words came out breathy, but he got the message. Without hesitation, his fingers found that bundle of nerves, which was swollen already.

The growl in my ear hummed with his satisfaction, no doubt pleased with me finally expressing my desires. His mouth lowered from my ear, down my jaw, to my breast again, and finally to my belly, licking a heated trail on the way. All while his fingers were pinching and pulling on my clit in a way that had me seeing stars. His tongue was getting closer and closer to the apex of my legs, my anticipation growing in bounds.

"Birdie." His husky voice broke through the fog in my brain. "I want to taste you. Can I taste you?" I looked down to find his eyes seeking mine for something, a nod of the head, anything. All I could do was moan and lift my hips as an offering to him. The small smile on his lips confirmed he understood the meaning.

And he began to devour me.

I felt as if I were floating, my body being worshipped by a god as his hands lovingly stroked my legs, my stomach, up to my breasts. At the same time, his tongue explored and dipped into parts of me never before touched like that by anyone. His fingers expertly worked in tandem with his mouth, alternating plunging inside me. The wave of orgasm was rising in me, my body tensing under him. He read the signs and moved his mouth to cover my clit, lips circling and sucking. His fingers reached up and found my nipples, pinching at just the right time, the surge hitting its summit. He had to keep me down on the bed with his hands, my body lifting, the ecstasy almost too much. With my head pushing into the pillows, my orgasm ripped through my body, top to bottom, pulsating against his mouth as he hummed with sated pleasure.

His urgency took over, ripping open the drawer of his desk as he frantically looked for the square foil pouch. I watched him roll the condom over his dick, which was hard and thick in his hands, and I was ready for him to be inside me. I reached up and grabbed a hold of his ass, pulling him back down. He fell onto me, cradling my head with his bent arms, body suspended. He nudged my legs apart with his knee while his tongue begged entrance to my mouth, the taste of me still there. I felt the fullness of him resting against my entrance, and I curved my body to meet his, forcing the connection.

Xander moved up onto his knees, which startled me. I wasn't expecting him to move away from us laying on the bed, against each other. He put both his hands under my ass, pulling me up and off the bed, opening my legs, and me, wide. I let out a grunt.

"Is this OK, Lanie?" He froze. I knew he was thinking he had pushed me too far. But for once, this was all OK. I was OK.

"It's more than OK, yes. Please!"

He held me by my hips and pulled me closer. My body slid easily along the sheets as he glided me onto his length, driving into me. The angle I was at gave him access to push deep inside me. He started slow, his fingers digging into my skin as he held on, my lower body suspended in his hands. His eyes locked on mine as his thrusts sped up, a wicked smile taking over his face. He started pumping harder, our skin smacking together, the bed crashing against the wall. I felt myself contracting around him as he pulled out, slowly. Only for him to ram back into me harder than before, the bed scraping across the tile floor.

"Oh God, Xander!" I shrieked, grabbing for something to hold on to, feeling as if I was falling, falling off the bed, off the earth.

The rhythm continued, steady and powerful. A sheen of sweat glowed on his chest as I peered up at him; his face twisted with exertion. I could feel it building again inside of me, inside both of us. His movements were jerky, and he was losing control as it all came to a head between us. He lowered me to the bed, our bodies close as he crashed on top of me with one final thrust, a cry emitting from his throat.

Our breathing was erratic, neither of us able to catch our breath or talk right away. Eventually, Xander's head fell against my shoulder; he was completely spent. He slid to his side, an arm draped across my torso. And we lay there, in each other's arms, quiet, for some time. His breaths calmed enough that I thought he may have even fallen asleep.

"Birdie?" His voice startled me. He picked his head up, hair disheveled and stuck to his sweaty brow. He rested his chin on the top of my breast. His navy blue eyes looked up at me before he spoke again. "You amaze me." A smile showing his dimple graced his face, making me smile back at him. "I'm amazed by you, how strong and resilient you are." A finger made a path from my belly button, up between my breasts, to my chin, finally resting on my lower lip. He pulled his body up as his mouth captured mine, the kiss slow and deep. "I know that you've struggled with, you know, talking about that kind of stuff. But you took charge, and fuck . . ." He ran his fingers through his hair, struggling with what to say next. "I don't want to just focus on the sex part of it, but, fuck, it was hot as hell what you did, what we did."

He reached underneath me and grabbed a hold of my ass, squeezing it hard.

"Ow!" I yelped as I grabbed a hold of him around his neck, our faces close once again.

"But, man, birdie, you blow me away with how far you've come, your confidence with all of this. I'm just, I don't know. I guess I'm proud of you, that's all." He looked shy, almost embarrassed to be saying that to me, but I understood what he meant.

"Thank you," I said in response, once again too shy to talk. But he was right. I was a different me. I had come such a long way. "It's all because of you. You've gotten me here."

But he was immediately shaking his head in complete disagreement.

"Nah, I might have helped with some things along the way, but birdie, this was all you." He leaned up and kissed me on the nose.

And I was pretty sure he was right. I had made the changes in me. He helped, but I did it.

I was healing.

I was moving on.

No one was perfect. I knew I sure as hell wasn't. I came into this with enough baggage to send him packing, but here he was. He had his share of issues as well. But the whole point of a relationship was give-and-take, compromise, working together to make it work. And all that other crap that goes along with it. We were still young and we had a lot to learn, but I knew with him was where I wanted to be.

"What are you thinking right now?" Xander asked me, obviously seeing something in my look.

I knew I'd been having some doubts about us, but at that moment, it clicked. He was it for me. I reached for his face, holding it, looking at him.

Finally, I said, "I never want this to end."

He stroked my cheek, his thumb grazing my lip as he stared deeply into my eyes.

"That makes me the happiest man alive to hear that, birdie," he whispered, leaning in and placing a soft kiss on my mouth. "Because I never want us to end either."

I would forever be his birdie.

Chapter 22

All those books I read on my e-reader should have prepared me for this. The normal we were living, the traditional lifestyle of college kids we were thriving with, was the foreshadowing I should have recognized.

The amazing night we had.

It was all foreshadowing.

The proverbial other shoe had dropped, but not in the way I expected.

I would have lost my life savings thinking Max would be the one to come in and destroy my life once again, but no.

No, it wasn't Max this time.

This time it was Xander.

Xander broke me.

Chapter 23

Xander and I were supposed to meet for lunch at noon. His text telling me to meet him had come in while I was finishing up some work at the library. I went to the cafe, got my food, and went to our normal table to wait for him.

And waited.

For an hour.

He never showed.

He never texted again.

Never responded to my texts.

That wasn't like him.

When I'd gotten to our floor, the first place I checked was the study lounge, thinking he'd gotten caught tutoring. Learning the tutoring he did was community service due to his arrest hurt my heart for him. It took up so much of his time, and he never complained about it. Unfortunately, the lounge was empty.

I then went to his room and knocked, but again, empty. Walking a few more steps to my room, I was happy to find Becca there. She was cozied up on her bed, watching something on her laptop.

"Hey, have you seen Xander?" I asked as I stepped over a mountain of her shoes that had invaded my side of the room. Becca was not the neatest of roommates. "He was supposed to meet me for lunch, but he bailed and I can't reach him." I wasn't necessarily panicked, but I was starting to get concerned. This was so out of character for him. Especially with everything going on with Max. Xander checked in on *me* nonstop to make sure *I* was OK.

"Oh no, is there trouble in paradise?" Becca joked as she closed her screen. "No, I haven't seen him. Did you guys have a fight or something? Maybe he went to the gym to sweat it out." She wasn't concerned at all about my situation, which did make me feel better.

"No fight, but maybe he just forgot. Maybe he is working out." I plopped on my bed, deciding to wait it out here for a while. I pulled out my e-reader and opened the latest book I was reading.

She got up from her bed and started gathering some things at her desk. "Well, the four of us are supposed to go to the movies tonight, so I'm sure we'll see him soon for that. Cheer up, buttercup." She threw her backpack on her shoulder and turned toward me. "I have class. I'll see you later." She waved and was off.

Time passed slowly the next few hours alone in the room as I continually checked my phone to no avail—nothing from Xander. Even my book couldn't hold my attention. I considered skipping my afternoon class so I wouldn't miss him when he returned to his room but thought better of it.

I'd gotten nothing from him since ten thirty that morning reminding me to meet him for lunch.

Six hours later, his room was still empty.

I may have checked on the hour.

Becca finally came back in her typical fashion, like a hurricane, barreling into the room.

"Hey, Lanie, let's head down and meet the guys for dinner so we can get going to the movie on time. I'm excited they agreed to see the chick flick for us!" She took one look at my face and stopped dead in her tracks. "What's wrong? Is it Max?"

"No, Becca, it's Xander. Still nothing from him. He's not here, and I still can't reach him. I'm getting really concerned, like, scared. Should I call the police?" I started pacing the room. I hadn't really thought that this could involve Max until Becca mentioned his name. The nervous energy coursing through my veins had me on high alert. "What if this is Max? What if he has something to do with this? Maybe I should call Bryce. He might be able to help."

Becca put her things on that ever-growing pile on her side of the room before joining me on my bed. I had resorted to curling up into a ball, trying to ignore the pit in my stomach.

"Are you ever going to put those clothes away?" I asked her as my eyes lingered on the mountain of clean and dirty mixed together.

"That's not important right now. Do you want me to try to reach Xander? Do you think he would talk to me?"

I looked at her incredulously. "Why would he text you and not me?"

"I don't know, but shouldn't we try that before we

jump to conclusions that something bad happened to him? I mean, it's worth a try, don't you think?"

I was angry at her, thinking he would answer her and not me, but then realized I was really just scared.

"Ugh, I don't know what to think. That's the problem. We haven't even had a fight yet. But sure, text him. See if he answers you."

I watched her type out her message, and we both waited. As the minutes ticked by, I actually found myself becoming happy he didn't respond to her, which was stupid. We still didn't know where he was.

"OK, so I guess he's not answering you either, which isn't good. More of a reason to think something's happened." Just as I finished saying that, Becca's phone pinged, and my heart sank. She looked down, then back up, her sad eyes finding mine. Her hands shook as she held her phone.

"Do you want to read it, or should I read it out loud?" she asked. Her voice was soft, quiet. So unlike the Becca I knew. It made me nervous because I knew what was in that text wasn't good.

"Um, I don't know. Let me see the phone, um . . . no, never mind. You read it."

I sank onto my bed, my legs about to buckle. Becca hesitated a moment, but then started reading.

Xander:

Hey Becca, yeah, I needed some time away from school for a bit headed home, need a break from Lanie for now, everything moving too fast I'll be doing classes online for a few days I'll be in touch.

This could not be happening.

This was not happening.

How could he do this?

Why was he doing this? He loved me.

I loved him.

"Lanie, say something. You're scaring me."

I didn't have any words for what I just heard. There was no reason for him to leave. We haven't even had a real fight yet.

"I don't believe him, Becca. Something isn't right here. We were together last night, like *together*, together, and everything was perfect. We were even starting to talk about our future. *He* was talking about our future together." I looked up at her, desperation in my voice.

"Well, that kind of makes sense with what he wrote. Maybe he got spooked. Even though he was saying it, maybe he got nervous. Guys are weird that way. He might have gotten caught up in the moment. Sex will do that to men. And maybe after he said those things, he got scared and ran. I'm not saying it's right. It sucks, and he sucks for doing it, but that may be why." She was sitting next to me now, rubbing my arms, trying to prevent a major breakdown. "I know he's one of the good ones, Lanie, but no one is perfect. Maybe give him this time. It doesn't mean you guys are over. It's a break."

When she said it that way, it kind of made sense, but it still hurt. A lot. This was a pain I had never experienced before, true and utter heartbreak. Every cell in my body felt like it was being pulled apart from the others. I couldn't hold back the tears that started flowing from my eyes.

"You'll be OK; you'll both be OK. This happens in almost all relationships. You'll see. He'll come groveling back to you, apologizing for acting the way he did. He's definitely handling it wrong, but what guy doesn't? Guys suck, but they're good in bed, so we put up with their shit." She stood up from my bed and found me a box of tissues. But her next step was to flit about the room as if nothing was wrong. She didn't think this was a big deal. "Trust me, Lanie. And if you want him back even sooner, start talking to some other guys. Make him jealous. That will get the ball rolling on his end."

I wasn't about to start playing games with Xander and our emotions. Only one part of what Becca said made sense to me. I would give him some time. I would give him time in the hopes he would come to terms with whatever unnerved him.

"I'm going to see if Logan wants to go to the movies with us. Do you still want to come?" Becca asked.

The last thing I wanted to do was go anywhere outside of this room. All I wanted to do was crawl into bed, curl into a ball, and disappear. Old habits were hard to break.

"Uh, no, I'm gonna stay in. I won't be good company right now."

Becca didn't come back, so my assumption was the movies worked out for the three of them, which was fine. I needed to be alone. But sitting here, wallowing in my despair and all the unknown, was doing me no good. It was driving me crazy.

Instead, I fought the darkness trying to keep me down and grabbed my sneakers and went for a run. It helped for a while.

But, of course, I found myself on the bench by the pond. I sat and thought for what seemed like minutes but wound up being an hour. The sky was dark by the time I realized how long I'd been sitting there alone. I pulled out my phone, deciding I would send one final message to him before giving him a full-on break from me.

Me:

> Xander, I'm not sure what I said or did, but I'm sorry. Take however long you need to work through this, I'll be here I love you I always will Xander you're my everything and I'm not giving up on us, not this easily and I don't really believe you are either

He didn't respond, but I knew he read it. He still had that setting on. At least I knew he got it. It hurt that he couldn't say anything back, but I felt better knowing he was aware of how I felt. I'd been through worse. I could handle a break.

At least I thought I could.

The next day, Becca tried to act like everything was normal.

"Lanie, Ty and I are going to the library after lunch. Why don't you meet us after your class?" She was flitting around her room, not even waiting on my answer. I was curled up in my bed still, pondering staying there indefinitely.

"Maybe."

"Lanie, don't do this. You can't let him get to you like this. Be strong. Get yourself up, get dressed, go to class, and meet us for lunch. Trust me, I've been dumped by enough guys to know the best medicine is to not let them think they won." She looked over and saw my big eyes. "And no, I don't mean you've been dumped, but I have been plenty of times, and I wanted to do exactly what you're doing now.

But you can't. So get up." She came over and ripped my comforter off of me.

"Uuugghhh! I'm not ready, Becca! What if he comes back today? I don't want to see him." I tried pulling the covers back on, but she wouldn't let me.

"That's the exact reason *why* you get your ass up and out." She stood, holding my comforter, her other hand on her hip, unwavering. I pulled my legs over the side of the bed, feeling like death warmed over. "Good, that's a start," Becca encouraged. "Now get up and get dressed. We're walking to class together. And then you're coming to lunch."

She continued getting herself ready while I pulled on whatever clothes I could grab out of the bottom of my closet. I might head out with her, but I wasn't going to care about what I looked like.

And I may have made it to class and gotten credit for my attendance, but my body was the only thing there; my mind was elsewhere. I comprehended nothing. With my hood pulled up and over, I don't think anyone even knew who I was, so no other students talked to me, which was the point.

I walked zombie-like to the cafeteria after class, people steering clear of me on the paths. My aura definitely gave off "stay away" vibes. When I found Becca and Ty, they were at a table right in the middle of the action. I contemplated not staying, but Becca saw me and waved me over before I could escape.

"Good, you made it, and here's a sandwich. Make sure you eat it. You look horrible, by the way." Becca was not holding back.

"Well, I look horrible because someone forced me out of bed today when I didn't want to get out of bed today." I pouted and pushed the food away from me in anger. "And thanks for the food, but I'm not hungry." Her eyes went to Ty, and they shared a sympathetic look for me.

"Lanie, I know it doesn't feel like it now, but this will all work out. The best thing you can do is try to take care of yourself. Eat a couple bites, even if it's just for me," Becca pleaded.

I succumbed and took the sandwich back. Forcing a few bites down, I realized I actually was hungry. As I ate the rest of it, I hoped she didn't acknowledge she'd been right. The two of them seemed consumed with each other at the moment, so I could resume my sulking in peace.

I sat back and looked around the cafe, immediately noticing Xander's frat brothers at a nearby table. They were sending glances my way, and a couple were having private conversations that appeared to be geared toward me. I could have been imagining it, but I instantly felt the need to leave.

"Thanks, guys, but I'm gonna head back to the dorm." I guessed they were satisfied with my performance for the day, because they didn't balk at me leaving as I stood up. "I'll see you later."

"See ya later, Lanes." As I was walking away from the table, I tried my damnedest to not look at the frat-filled table, but I heard the whispers and I couldn't resist. I stole a peek. Thankfully, they seemed sympathetic as well. They mostly had small smiles on their faces when I looked over. Some offered small waves. But I held eye contact for too long. I guess giving permission for one of them to come to me.

"Hey, Lanie, how ya doing?" he asked. I think his name was Zane.

"Hey, hi, I'm good." I didn't quite know how to answer that, unsure of why he would ask me in the first place.

"Well, we just wanted to check on you, make sure

you were doing OK with, you know . . ." he continued, his hands gesturing to the rest of the guys at the table, and then he looked back at me.

"Um, yeah, I'm fine," I continued, confused.

"OK, good. We told Xander we would, uh, keep an eye on you while he was gone. So if you need anything, let us know." He gave me a small smile and walked back to his table.

I spun on my heel and tore out of there as fast as I could, mortified that everyone knew.

They all knew!

They all knew he left and that we weren't talking. Xander told them he was leaving, but not me.

Another reason I really wanted to stay curled up in my bed.

Curling up in my bed seemed like what I wanted to do until I was doing it.

Alone.

Completely alone in my bed.

Thinking only of him.

And crying.

And then it didn't seem like such a great idea anymore. I had become used to spending my nights next to Xander, warmed by his body, held in his arms. I was missing the feel of his lips on mine, the heat of his breath as he slept with his face close to mine.

The solitude I now felt in this bed was agonizing.

I tossed and turned most of the night, seeing every hour

on the clock. By 5 a.m., it was useless to try any longer, so I got up, got dressed for a run, and headed out.

Walking past Xander's door had been one of the more difficult things to do the past couple of days. The pull I had toward his room was magnetic; the memories made inside filled my mind and tormented me. I walked by and had to force myself to not look at the number 504 as I passed it.

But I couldn't help it as I stopped right outside his door. I put my hands up on it, hoping to feel some remnant of that hum I felt in my bones when he touched me. But there was nothing but the coldness of metal. Checking the knob, I knew full well it would be locked. When it was, though, it still crushed me. My legs wouldn't continue on my journey outside. They were frozen in place. At least here I felt somewhat close to him. It was quiet in the hall. No one would see me for a while. So, I sat down, up against his door, and dreamt of the days when we were happy on its other side. I could almost hear our laughter as I thought of the times we were in there binge-watching Netflix while making out, and more, under his blankets. My head was on my folded knees as I reminisced about our last few months together.

The next thing I knew, Becca was shaking me awake.

"Lanie, come on, honey, wake up. You can't stay out here."

"Oh shit, I can't believe I fell asleep." I quickly grabbed her outstretched hand and walked with her to our room. I had no idea if anyone saw me, but the chances were good considering it was after eight already. "Well, that's embarrassing." I plopped on my bed once we were in our room.

"Don't sweat it. I'm sure if anyone saw you, they thought you were drunk. I've seen people passed out by doors like that before. People don't really care too much." I guess she didn't see the scene with Xander's frat yesterday, but it wasn't worth bringing up. "You look like crap. Not a good night?"

"The only sleep I got was right there by his door. I was going out for a run and stopped there for a minute, and then you found me. So, no, not a good night."

"It'll get better, I promise." She looked at me with compassionate eyes.

I wanted to believe her, but I wasn't so sure.

Chapter 24

Knowing Xander read the text I sent the other day did something to me, soothed me in a way nothing else could. My words were still being heard, seen. That made me feel . . . better. I decided I was going to continue to text him, to talk to him, even though it would be one-sided.

I pulled out my phone.

I didn't care that it was three in the morning.

Me:

> So, I've decided I'm going to keep texting you, I need to, I can't sleep I can't stop missing you I miss your bed, my bed doesn't feel the same anymore - I hope you're doing whatever you need to be doing, fixing what you need to fix, so you can come back to me - I can't do this without u I love u Xander and I need u here, with me, tell your mom and Bryce hi for me come back soon, please You're my everything xoxo

As soon as I sent it, it said it was read.

Immediately.

I didn't know what that meant, but it had to mean something. It did tell me I was going to keep sending them. Maybe they would bring him back to me. For some reason, knowing he was on the other end of the message, reading it, gave me a sense of peace.

Me:

> Morning, I was actually able to fall asleep last night, I think because I sent that text to you - I'm sitting here wondering what you're doing at home - are you laying in your bed, thinking about me the way I'm thinking about you? I don't like this missing you thing that goes along with loving some-one - it hurts - but you're worth it I'm not giving up on us not yet anyway. I have to start getting ready for class, Becca is making me go, even though I don't want to - she's making me do lots of things I don't want to do right now - anyway -
>
> Love u Xander, Always xoxo

And right on cue, he read it immediately.

I popped out of bed, a bit more spring in my step, and got dressed for class. No hoodie—I put on a sweater and jeans and dressed like a real human. As I headed to the elevator, Logan met up with me in the lobby.

"Hey, Lanie, how ya doing?" I wasn't sure how much he was aware of. I hadn't seen him since this whole thing started with Xander a couple days ago. But by the tone in his voice, I could tell he knew. Everyone apparently knew.

"I'm good, thanks." And I even smiled.

Logan still wasn't doing his best either, but he smiled

back. We got on the elevator together once the doors opened, a few other people already in it. We didn't talk for the remainder of the five-floor ride to the bottom, but he stayed close protectively.

The sun was shining, adding to my improved mood, even though the temperature was chilly. We were bundled up against the February wind as we headed to our respective buildings, obviously in the same direction. Logan was still by my side.

"So . . . you seem to be better than Becca was describing," Logan said, being careful with his words. The air was so cold, white puffs came from his mouth as he spoke. This was definitely not weather my Texas blood was used to, and my face was wrapped behind a scarf. He didn't even have a hat on, though his puffer coat looked warm.

"Yeah, I'm doing a bit better." My words were a bit garbled, but he seemed to understand me as he nodded. I didn't feel like expanding on it. We kept walking down the stone path, a quick pace due to the climate. He slowed when we came to what must have been his building.

"Wanna meet us for lunch later? I'm meeting up with them." He looked hopeful, his eyes tearing from the wind as he waited for my response.

"Sure, I'll see you guys in a couple hours," I replied. I waved as he headed up the stairs to his class, me on my way to mine.

"To what do we owe the honor of your presence?" Becca was thankful I had shown up.

"You're right. I need to keep living, so here I am," I answered as I shrugged my shoulders. "Besides, I promised Logan I'd come." I looked around but didn't see him yet, which explained why she didn't expect me.

"Well, good girl. Glad to see the little shit isn't getting the best of you. We're probably going to a party tonight. Wanna come?" She immediately got excited. Thankfully, Logan showed up to save me.

"Hey, Lanie, you made it!" he said. The smile was wide on his face as he sat with a tray mounded with food. It would never cease to amaze me he could fit all of that in his body.

"Yeah, here I am," I said awkwardly. Logan's smile didn't waver.

"Good," he said. "I'm glad." He dove into his food as Becca resumed her begging about later that night.

"Logan, get Lanie to come with us tonight!" she shrieked, his head turning toward her. His eyes latched on mine next, seeking a clue as to what I wanted to do. My pleading eyes gave him the answer he was looking for.

"I don't think I'm even going. Maybe Lanie and me will stay in and watch a movie or something. You and Ty can have a date night." His sly smile told me he knew what he was doing, as did I.

And it worked.

"What a great idea! Ty, it's just you and me tonight, baby, and I have lots of ideas for what we can do!" The two of them resumed their private conversation on their side of the table as Logan leaned in closer to me.

"We don't have to watch the movie, Lanie. I just knew going to that party wasn't on your radar for tonight." I simply nodded, my thoughts moving elsewhere as he got back to his food once again.

But then I looked around at the table at the four of us here in the cafeteria, and I lost my appetite. My once elevated mood I'd worked so hard on plummeted to the ground. All I could think about was Xander. He would normally be here with us, eating. He would have kissed me when he sat down, probably hooked my leg over his under the table. The need to be with him was strong, urgent. All my progress of the day was washed away in mere moments.

I needed to text him again. That tether connecting us became the only thing my mind would focus on, the only thing I wanted to focus on. I pulled my phone out as discreetly as possible.

Me:

> I'm at lunch with Becca and the guys and it doesn't seem right for you to not be here with us - I still don't understand what's going on I'm trying to give you the space I think you need, is that all you need, space? What if that's not what this is about? What if it's more than that?

"Who are you texting, Lanie?" Becca had been talking to me, but I had no idea. I was so engrossed in my phone.

"Umm, a friend from class. They need the notes from today." I was pretty sure she wouldn't approve of me texting Xander all day long. I even knew I shouldn't be doing it. It was as if I'd become an addict, addicted to the person who had abandoned me.

And it was true that he'd abandoned me, wasn't it? Xander was gone. And not even talking to me. Reading my texts and choosing not to answer.

And that sucked.

But it was also wrong. Wrong for someone who supposedly loved me to respond that way. And I shouldn't be accepting it. I should not be tolerating it. I'd taken enough shit in my short life already—I didn't need to take more. Maybe I needed to act a little bit more like Becca than I thought. Get a bit tougher rather than sitting back and waiting for him to just come back to me.

Because he may not.

"Hey guys, I'm gonna head back." I started getting up, gathering my things, and went to pick up my tray. Logan put his hand on it, holding it down to the table.

"I've got it, Lanie. Don't worry about it." He knew I was struggling, I could tell by the way he looked at me. My façade was breaking. I needed to get out of there.

As I walked back to my room, my once great idea of texting as a connection to him felt like the worst idea I could have come up with. It made me feel weak and insecure, as if I needed him in order to go on living. And even though I felt an inkling of those things most of the time at my lowest moments, I knew I had gotten beyond that.

If Xander had taught me one thing, it was that I was worth more than any guy not treating me right, even if it was him. He always prided himself on showing me how a "real guy" should treat me. Well, this wasn't it, at least not anymore.

It was time—time for the last text.

Me:

So here's the thing, I thought I knew you Xander, but this isn't something I expected you to do You've deserted me, and I don't think I deserve that. I can't allow myself to be treated like this, not again, not by you. I've finally found an inner strength, and even though you helped me with that, I can't sit around waiting for you to figure this out while destroying me in the process

And it was read.

Dealing with a "break" from Xander while he wasn't at school was tough, but somehow I made it through two weeks without him. The last text I sent him helped strengthen my resolve to stick to my guns; I wouldn't reach out to him again. If he wanted a break, he was getting a break.

But then it got worse.

The next morning, I walked out of my room and felt that familiar hum in my bones I would feel when he was near. I immediately lifted my eyes to see him struggling to fit his key in the lock of his door.

He paused; he felt me, too.

He didn't look my way, though, and continued to turn his key, open his door, and go into his room.

He may as well have punched me in the gut. That would have hurt less.

I'd finally gotten used to the idea of not having him around, and that was still miserable. But once he returned, I knew it was going to be impossible.

I spun around and went right back into my room, slamming the door. Leaning up against it with my eyes closed, I tried to make what just happened go away, to will it away in my mind.

"Lanie, what's wrong? You look like you've seen a ghost." My head shot toward her voice, not expecting to hear her. I forgot Becca was still in the room.

"Um," I stalled, "I guess that's one way to put it."

She opened her mouth to say something, then snapped it closed, a knowing look on her face.

"No, he's not. Are you kidding me?" She ran to the door and pulled it open wide before I could stop her, looking down the hall. At what, I don't know. The hallway was empty. "I'm going to go have a talk with him, set him straight. He needs to be put in his place, Lanie, and I'm the perfect one to do it." I ran to her, dragging her by the arm into our room, closing and locking the door securely.

"Becca, please don't. He saw me and ignored me, completely ignored me, and went straight into his room."

"More of a reason to tell him off." She was seething, flipping her curls over her shoulder as she paced the room. "Why would he not talk to you, Lanie? This makes no sense. He said he would be back when he worked his shit out. He's back, so he should be ready to talk."

"Can we give it some time, see how it plays out? He just got here, still had his bags with him." I didn't need her making this worse between him and me. To be honest, I think I would be more upset and jealous if he talked to her simply because he wouldn't even look at me.

"Fine, but let it be known I'm not happy about it." She kind of stomped away from me, gathering her coat and hat. "Come eat with me and the guys. You're wasting away to nothing. You barely eat one meal a day." She was right, but I didn't have an appetite. "Don't let him do this to you. He's not worth it."

I climbed into my bed, the covers securely up to my chin as she watched me from the doorway. She wasn't surprised by my decision or my actions, I could tell.

"I can't. I don't want to see him. What if he goes for food? I can't do it right now, Becca. I'm not ready." She walked to my bedside and leaned in to give me a quick hug.

"I won't be long," she said before heading out to meet the guys.

They'd all been trying to keep me distracted, and it had been working a little. Becca would watch a show with me; Ty would study with me at the library; Logan was always around to walk with me to class. But naturally, the moment I was alone, my thoughts took over and always gravitated to Xander.

And now he was here, a few doors down. I wasn't sure how I was going to handle this.

I'd put a call into my parents the other day. I hadn't spoken to them since before Christmas, so the conversation was a bit awkward at first. But my dad soon had us talking as if we hadn't had years of estrangement between us. I didn't tell them exactly what was going on in my world, only that I might want to leave school early this semester. With the way our life had been, they didn't question it. Rather, my dad sounded a bit relieved, thinking I might come stay with them for a while. So, if things didn't improve, the plan was I'd be taking a leave from school to meet them in Italy for the rest of the spring and summer.

Xander's return may have jump-started those plans. I didn't think I could be there, on the same campus, the same floor as him, and survive. Not with him not talking to me, not even looking at me.

No, I definitely couldn't do it.

Chapter 25

The text came in while Becca and I were in our room. My finger slid over my phone, and my whole world came crashing in on me:

Max:

> Lanie, I know you're here, and I know Alexander is here too so pay attention

> I'm outside your building and if you don't want anything to happen to him you will come downstairs now. ALONE

The room started to spin.

The black consumed me, gathering in every corner of the room and swirling around its edges, filling up its entirety. It pressed on my chest, stealing my breath.

How was I going to do this? How could I go to him?

How could I willingly go to the one person I'd been working hard to escape from for months?

If I went to him, I knew I wouldn't come back. This was it; he was going to take me back to Texas, and all my efforts would be null and void.

But he wasn't only threatening me anymore.

I knew I had to, for Xander.

I got up from my bed and tried to make it look like I was going for a run, hoping Becca wouldn't ask too many questions.

But no, then I couldn't grab anything but my earbuds, and I wanted to take more of my things with me if I was leaving. Then I thought I could say I was going to the library to study. That way I could at least bring a backpack full of my belongings.

It was then I realized I'd been aimlessly walking around the room with no real purpose, and Becca took notice.

"Lanie, you OK? What are you doing?" She didn't give me much of a different look now than any other she had in recent days. Grave concern was always across her face lately.

"Umm, I don't know. I feel like I need to get out of here. I was either going to go for a run or maybe the library, not sure." I was stalling, still trying to figure it all out, when another text came through.

"It's too dark for a run, Lanie." Becca was going to make this hard for me.

Max:

> The clock is ticking, I wouldn't take much longer Lanie you don't want me or any of my guys coming up there for you because there will be a scene with you and him

I needed to respond; I needed more time.

Me:

> I'm coming, I need a minute, please don't come up, trying to get away from my roommate

"Who are you texting?"

I jumped, not expecting Becca to be right over my shoulder. "Oh, it's no one, just someone from class. That's who I might meet at the library to study with. I need to get out of here, ya know?" I was filling my backpack, trying to decide what to grab, when she reached for my hands.

"How about *we* go get some food first? You haven't eaten in a long time. Then you can meet your friend. Have them give you an hour." Her eyes were pleading with me.

"Um, I'll grab something to munch on while I'm there. I still don't really have an appetite, ya know, with everything going on. How about a late dinner when I get back? You, me, and the guys?"

Thankfully, she backed away. "Sure," Becca said, sounding hurt.

If it helped keep her safe, it was worth it, but I hated hurting her.

But then my phone pinged again.

Bryce:

> LATE INTEL!!! MAX IS ON HIS WAY – COULD ALREADY BE THERE!

Well, the FBI blew this one; they were a little too late. But it gave me some hope knowing that Bryce and help were on their way. Hopefully I wouldn't have to face Max alone down there. I just needed them to make it on time.

But in case they didn't, I grabbed my laptop and stuffed it, and some essentials, into my backpack. I made my way to the door but then stopped.

Suddenly, the thought of maybe never seeing her again was heart-wrenching. So quickly she had woven herself into the fabric of my life, becoming important to my daily existence.

I couldn't make this awkward by saying a goodbye. She would know something was up. Turning to take one last look at her, I memorized the image of her on her bed, earbuds in, listening to music while on her computer.

I wanted to run and give her a hug.

I wanted to tell her no one else could have done for me what she'd done.

I wanted to tell her I would never forget her.

I stood there too long. She looked up from her screen and pulled out one bud.

"What's up, Lanie? What's wrong?"

I must have looked odd, standing there by the door, hand on the knob, staring at her.

"Nothing. I'll see you tonight, Becca. Love you." I didn't wait to hear her response. I tore open the door and escaped out the side stairs so I wouldn't have to go past Xander's room. I'd already taken too much time getting downstairs, and I needed to send another text to Max.

Me:

I'm coming now

I had no idea where to go once outside. When I reached the bottom, I opened the door slowly and peeked around its protective barrier. Expecting to see multiple of his and his employees' cars taking up the parking lot waiting for me, I was shocked to see nothing out of the ordinary.

But it was dark, so dark.

And eerily quiet.

I hadn't stepped outside yet, and I was waiting to see what was out there when I heard footsteps coming down the stairs from up above. This door and these stairs were rarely used, so it unnerved me to hear someone else here with me.

But I felt him before I heard him, the hum in my bones, the shot of electricity that went straight to my heart. And my heart swelled at the thought of him coming to get me, to stop me from leaving.

"Lanie!" a loud whisper came from above, Xander running down the stairs two and three at a time to get to me. "You can't go out there. Please don't go out there!" He was jumping down the stairs, trying to get to me as fast as he could.

I stood, frozen with my hand on the knob, the door slightly ajar as he rounded the last step. He wouldn't come any closer, though, keeping his distance as his pleas continued.

"Lanie, please, go back upstairs. Do not go out there. Whatever he's told you, don't listen."

My breaths faltered when he said that, my body tensing up at the sheer notion he was aware of what was happening.

"What are you saying, Xander? I don't understand. How could you possibly . . ."

When I finally looked at him, I saw the torment in his eyes, in his stance. His hands were in balled fists, the anger rolling off of him in waves. His breaths deep and loud, measured but sporadic, as if he were preparing himself for a fight.

I was torn. It would be easy to go to him, seeking that refuge I always had in his arms.

Just let go of the knob and run to Xander! my mind yelled at me.

"Xander, are we . . ."

His face answered me before I even finished my question. His hardened eyes staring at me while he gave a tiny shake of his head.

There was no change between us. We were over.

My eyes found the floor, unable to continue looking at him, seeing what I wanted but was no longer mine to have. I tried so hard to keep the tears at bay. I wanted to appear strong, unaffected by his decision about us.

Instead, while I tried to keep the tears stifled, bottled up in my throat as they burned and threatened to come out, they exploded in a sob, echoing in the hollow of the stairwell. I refused to look at him. Refused to see if my devastation affected him or not. Instead, I turned my attention back to the door, the knob in my hand. Knowing what was waiting for me on the other side of that door made it near impossible for me to finish pushing it all the way open.

But my pain and heartache didn't warrant what that monster could have in store for Xander if I didn't.

Without warning, I pushed the door open and ran outside at full speed.

At the same time, I felt the text hitting my phone and was confident it was Max demanding my presence. The moment I looked up while running, I saw him and Karl exiting a car up ahead.

The months that had passed since being in Max's presence had allowed my mind to heal, to forget the torturous pain he had put me through for years; the healing process was crazy like that. Yet, at first sight of him, it all came crashing back. The nausea rolled up from my stomach as I moved my feet forward. Fear of the first thing he would do to me once I was in his grip took hold, and I almost stopped and turned around. Somehow, I kept moving, my determination coming from somewhere deep inside.

But as I got closer, I made out his features, his expression. It made me falter for a split second, seeing the sick, smug smile on his face under the glow of the streetlight.

It was the face of someone who felt he had won.

I stopped my advance as Max made his way closer to me. Karl remained close to the black sedan, covered by the darkness of the night, refusing to look at me. I'd hoped he would be a confidante of mine still, but it looked as though Max won him over.

I frantically looked around the lot, hoping to see a sign of Bryce or someone else here with us. But there was nothing. The frigid temperatures kept students in at this time of night as well, so we were completely alone and isolated.

My attention went back to the man from my horrific past. I never thought I would have to see Max again, yet here he was. And I was going to him, willingly.

"Lanie," he said my name with a sneer, his voice making the bile rise into my mouth. Him saying my name like that usually meant one thing back at home.

Come give me what I want, what I need.

And it usually involved pain.

My physical reaction to seeing him, hearing him, was visceral; my body shook, uncontrollably, and I had trouble staying upright. My instincts yelled at me to run in the opposite direction.

But I needed to forge ahead.

I was almost within reach of Max, his outstretched hand getting closer, my brain expecting the pain of it on my wrist already.

"Lanie, stop! Please don't go with him!"

I froze at Xander's voice, my heart melting and hurting. At the same time, Max looked over my shoulder at the approaching force.

"What do we have here? Looks like someone has decided to bend the rules and come out for some play time." Max wasn't making any sense as he continued his advance toward me.

I was between the two, closer to Max than Xander, not sure which way to turn at that point. As Max continued toward me, I noticed him waving his hand in the air, a signal to Karl, I believed.

"Xander, go back inside. It's better this way, please. You don't know what you're dealing with when it comes to Max," I begged him. He looked at me with pleading eyes as I spoke, apparently trying to tell me something, but the message wasn't clear.

"Listen to Lanie, Alexander. She knows what she's talking about. She knows all too well what happens when someone doesn't listen to me. And she's about to find out again."

As soon as he said that, he lunged for me, wrapping his arms around my waist and dragging me toward their waiting car. Karl popped up, and Max handed me off as he turned his attention toward Xander.

That was when I saw the gun he had in his hand, at the side of his body.

"No, Max, no! I listened to you, Max! I'm here! Leave him alone and take me!" I was screaming, kicking at Karl as he dragged me toward the imposing vehicle with blacked-out windows. It was then I realized there was another person in that car, a driver waiting to take me away.

"Karl, what are you doing? Don't do this! Let me go, please!" I begged Karl as he dragged me toward the car.

I clawed at him, digging my heels into the ground as much as I could. I got a hold of the handle of a parked car, but my grip wasn't strong enough, my nails breaking off as he pulled me away. His hands slipped for a moment as I flailed, and I almost got away, but I crashed against the door of the car, my head cracking into the side view mirror.

"Fuck, Lanie," he whispered in my ear as he pulled me tighter to his body. "Please stop fighting me. Are you OK?" He pulled me closer to him, his voice pleading with me. "I'm trying to make sure nothing happens to you, but you have to stop fighting me. And now you're fucking bleeding." He reached up to my forehead, where I felt a big knot forming. I froze and looked over at Karl, his serious eyes connecting with mine. "Listen to me: I can't get you and your boyfriend out of here. You're my priority. I have to think about you, only you." His solemn face told a story of pain; he didn't want to be here, with Max, any more than I did. He was stuck in this mess just as much as I was. We looked toward Max and Xander, who were still yelling, the gun still pointed at Xander.

"I have to get back to him, Karl. Max is going to kill him!" I struggled against his hold, but he wouldn't budge.

"Lanie, you're not understanding me. You can't go near Max. I have to get you out of here." He tried to move me toward the black car again, but I couldn't leave, not without Xander.

"Karl, the FBI is coming. They can help you. Let me

go and they'll help you!" I knew I could get Bryce to help Karl, and I could stay here until they got on site. I would tell them about the time he helped me in Texas as well. But Karl only shook his head.

"Lanie, you don't get it. I have no way out of this." He was a handsome guy—brown hair, shaven on the sides and a bit longer on the top. His dark eyes looked darker in the dim light of the lot. But he looked older than his years, the work he did aging him faster, I was sure. "My priority right now is to get you out of here, even if it kills me. I don't care anymore. He can't do this to you. I won't let him." He started looking around, a bit of panic on his face. "But it's not good that the feds are coming. That's going to mess things up. My plan . . ."

The next moments must have happened quickly, but they felt like slow motion.

"What the fuck did you say, Karl?" The voice of a monster was over us, looming over us as we crouched next to the car. "What did you fucking say to her, you motherfucker? Did you double cross *me*? After all these years? For *her*?"

Max raised his gun as Karl slid along the pavement, pulling me with him. The small space between the cars made it hard for the both of us to advance quick enough. Karl tried to put his body in front of mine as a barrier, as the barrel was pointed right at us. Max's finger was moving; the trigger was being pulled. I turned my head to protect my face, knowing the worst was coming.

Max was aiming for me, I knew it.

That was when arms came from behind him, wrapping around in the perfect football tackle. Max wasn't expecting it as his body jerked forward, his torso wrapped tight by Xander's arms, both of them falling forward.

"Freeze! FBI!"

The parking lot was surrounded by a thicket of trees and bushes. I wasn't sure what I saw as the lights moved through the bare branches. But then bodies emerged from the edges, surrounding the lot, huge spotlights illuminating the space and forcing me to close my eyes.

But then I saw the spark from the gun in Max's hand before I heard it. The one shot Max got off before Xander got him to the ground, before any FBI agents made their advance. Xander's hands immediately pummeled him once they were down.

The screams of my name, screams telling me to stay down, didn't register.

All the men in black jackets running around in the parking lot around me didn't register.

My vision was blurry as I attempted to make sense of the spectacle unfolding around me.

Then I looked down and realized Karl's body was slumped in my arms.

"Karl!" My screams were masked by the chaos, but my hands held his head as the puddle started to trickle under the car. The dark red liquid looked black, the streetlamp from above reflected in the quickly transforming shape on the pavement. I seemed to be lost in thought, the blood a welcome distraction from the pandemonium around me.

"Lanie! Lanie!" The panicked voice was close but sounded like whispers. It felt as if my ears were stuffed full of cotton. Then I looked up and saw a friendly face.

"Bryce?" I wasn't sure my words even came out. My breaths were hard to come by suddenly, and I felt myself gasping.

"Lanie, come on. Let's get you out of here." He

tried to lift me up, but I refused to let go of Karl. Bryce looked confused.

"I can't leave him. I don't know if he's still alive or not. He needs help, Bryce." I was crying, my words garbled. I knew it didn't make sense to him.

"I'll get him help, Lanie, but I have to get you out of here. We need to get you somewhere safe." He scooped me up, completely disregarding Karl, whose body slumped to the ground.

Once I was in his arms, my eyes stayed focused on Karl's body, which lay on the cold ground, alone. Bryce hauled me away so quickly from the lot I didn't have time to realize we were leaving the scene. I turned my head away from Karl to see where we were going, noticing the dorm was behind us; we were heading around to the front of the building.

"Bryce!" I struggled to get out of his arms. "Xander is still there! Max had a gun!" It was all a jumbled mess in my brain, but it was coming back to me. I knew Xander had Max on the ground, and I had no idea what had happened to either of them.

"Lanie, they're getting it under control. That's no place for me to even be right now. Xander'll be fine. I need to get you looked at. You're covered in blood." I looked down at my coat, which was soaked through with a black stickiness. But I didn't hurt anywhere, so I knew I was fine.

"It's Karl's blood, Bryce. I'm fine." He was continuing around the building as I was struggling to get out of his hold.

"Lanie, you have blood dripping down your face. You're not fine."

The stickiness on my fingers after touching my forehead surprised me. I'd forgotten I hit my head on the mirror.

But I didn't care; all I wanted to do was go back and find Xander. I needed to make sure he was safe.

I continued to struggle in Bryce's hold as we approached a waiting ambulance. But it was to no avail—a medic got a hold of me as soon as Bryce put me down, and they dragged me inside the open doors.

"Lanie," Bryce called out to me as the medics guided me into the ambulance. "Don't worry, I'll take care of things. Once I know what's going on, I'll be in touch." And then he closed the doors.

Two medics met my stunned gaze once I looked up. Everything was happening so quickly, I had no words. The girl, who appeared to be in her mid-twenties, speedily buckled me onto the gurney. The guy, older by about ten years, slapped his hand on the window separating us from the cabin with the driver. We lurched forward seconds later, I can only assume on our way to the hospital.

Neither of them spoke to me directly right away. Instead, they began speaking in medical jargon to one another. Soon enough, they started giving me brief directions on what they needed me to do. They were gentle, the girl being the one to remove my coat and lift my shirt to check for any damage under the carnage of the bloodied clothes. Once they realized I wasn't shot, they covered me with a blanket, encouraging me to lie back on the gurney. The other technician worked on inserting an IV into my arm once I was flat, the needle barely registering as my mind still strayed to the events that had just happened. I may not have been badly injured, but I heard the word "shock" being whispered between them a few times.

"You're definitely going to need to some stitches when you get to the hospital," the guy said as he came to my side. "You'll only need a few. The gash isn't that big." He applied gauze to my forehead with some pressure, securing it tightly with tape. "This will slow the bleeding until we get you there." He moved aside, his attention now on his tablet.

The young girl sat on the gurney with me. "Can you look at me, Lanie?" She had a tiny light shining in my eyes, which she flicked back and forth. She then started rattling off a list of questions.

"Are you dizzy?" I nodded because I was, slightly.

"Do you have a headache?" she asked. She pulled out a laptop to record my answers.

"A little," I replied. "Mostly where the bump is." But I guess it wasn't a bump if I needed stitches.

"Are you nauseous, or do you feel like you need to vomit?"

I shook my head. I didn't want to answer any more questions. But they kept coming. Questions or not, I think it was pretty obvious I had a concussion.

Eventually, the questions ended. "Just sit back and relax," the tech said. "We'll be at the hospital soon." They both resumed filling out whatever forms they needed to on their respective devices, leaving me to myself.

But I couldn't relax. Not knowing what was going on back at school was driving me crazy. I peered out the small window, trying to see if anyone was following us, hoping to get a glimpse of Bryce in a cop car maybe. But I saw nothing but the passing trees along the highway.

I had never felt more alone.

I looked around the ER bay they put me in, realizing my bag had gotten lost in the craziness, which meant my phone was misplaced as well. I was completely cut off from everyone, and I didn't like it. I still felt like a prisoner, even if I wasn't with Max.

Suddenly, the curtain tore open and a man I'd never seen before charged into the tiny area I was being housed in. He took up a lot of the remaining space with his wide frame. His suit was rumpled, as if he'd been at work for many days.

"Elaina Montgomery?" he asked in my direction, holding an official-looking folder in his hands, and he had a badge on his belt.

I nodded. "Yes," I answered feebly.

At that moment, a nurse entered our space, completely ignoring the apparent "official" stranger that had joined me. She grabbed my wrist and scanned the bracelet they had placed there. "The doctor will be in shortly to stitch you up, sweetie. How's your head feeling?" Her calm demeanor was welcome after the chaos of the night. I didn't want her to leave my side. I almost latched onto her hand to keep her with me.

"It's better." My meek response as I peeked at the looming figure behind her didn't go unnoticed.

"Well, good. I'm glad to hear it. You let me know if you need anything else for the pain." She patted my hand before spinning on her heels to face the now impatient visitor. "And you," she said sternly, almost pressing her pointer finger into his chest. "I know you need to talk to her, but go easy on her. She's had a rough night." She turned and gave me a small smile before walking out and pulling the curtain closed.

"Yes, ma'am," the stranger responded, yet she had

already left.

He was a burly guy. My assumption was he was from the FBI. He looked around the tight space we were in and huffed in frustration.

"Elaina," he started.

"Lanie. Please call me Lanie," I corrected him.

"Lanie." His voice softened a bit. He looked around the space again, but I couldn't decipher what he was looking for. "Don't they have chairs in this godforsaken place?" he exclaimed. Then his gaze landed on me. "Any chance I can sit here on the cot with you? It's been a long night, and I'm fucking exhausted."

Agent Simcox didn't have much to say to me. He asked very basic questions. "How did Max get you to come outside? Where is your phone? Who is Karl?" That was kind of it. He wouldn't give me any information about Xander or Max, but he was nice at least.

My stitches were done, and the doctor told me he didn't think I was suffering from shock. The only thing they were waiting for was the bag of fluids to finish in the IV, and for my ride to arrive. Considering I didn't have my phone, I had no idea who I was waiting for.

I tried to calm my mind as I lay in the bed. But it was near impossible. The events of the night kept circling through my head when I closed my eyes. The blood, the gun, the FBI. That coupled with a headache was why I couldn't get comfortable.

"Where can I find Lanie Montgomery?" I heard a

familiar voice off in the distance.

"Bay four," someone had offered in response.

The curtain tore back.

"There you are, kiddo." Bryce looked a bit frazzled, but happy to see me. He smiled, but not completely. And he looked distracted. So I knew things still weren't completely settled yet back at the scene. But he did plop my bag on the bed next to me.

"Hey, Bryce. And thanks for this. I thought it was gone." I hoped he wasn't upset by the disappointment in my face and voice, but I think he understood. Agent Simcox told me they had Max in custody, so I thought it would be Xander coming to pick me up.

Bryce eyed up the needle in my arm and the wires still attached to me. "I guess you're not quite ready to go yet?" he asked. He pulled the curtain completely open, looking for someone to help, it seemed. "Let's try to get you out of here. I need to get back."

"Bryce," I cried, my weak voice squeaking out through some tears. He froze, halfway in the hall of the ER, and turned my way. The broken look on his face as he raced to my bedside made me cry harder.

"Shit, Lanie." He reached down as he sat on the narrow cot and held me. "I'm sorry. I'm such an ass." I held on to him, the need to let the pent-up emotion out strong. "I should've realized you'd be upset, need answers. I'm not so good at the sensitive side of being a cop yet." He rubbed the back of my head, but I wasn't calming down. My breathing was still erratic when I tried to talk.

"Where . . . is he . . . Bryce?" I hiccupped.

"Who, Lanie? Who do you want to know about?" He pulled away to look at me as he spoke. "They have Max in custody. Karl, he's here, he's in surgery. They think he'll live." He forced eye contact with me, holding my face. "Xander is fine, Lanie. He's completely fine. Not a hair harmed on his body."

All I could do in response to him was nod vigorously as more tears poured from my eyes and fell down my cheeks.

"They have him somewhere safe while they talk to him, OK? No need to worry. So, let's get you out of here." Bryce pulled away and stood, resuming his search for a nurse in the hallway. I did my best to calm myself, wiping my tears with my hands. "Hi," Bryce said to someone off to the side that I couldn't see. "I'm here to take Lanie Montgomery home. Any chance you could get her ready to go?"

"Of course I can," I heard the same nurse say as she appeared through the curtain. "Lanie, what's wrong? What did he do?" Her accusatory look aimed at Bryce could bring any man to his knees. Bryce put his hands up in complete defeat as she looked back at me.

"Nothing, he did nothing." I shook my head. "It's just everything from the night coming out. He's my boyfriend's brother, and . . ." I took a sharp intake of breath. Because I realized that statement may not even be true anymore. I looked over at Bryce as my eyes filled with tears once again.

"I'm kind of family but also involved in the case, so we were talking about the events, and she got upset. Sorry, ma'am." The nurse looked at the badge Bryce showed her as she nodded her head.

"OK, let me get the IV out and get you on your way. I'll be back with your discharge papers."

We were both quiet when she left. Bryce paced in the small space, seemingly nervous. I didn't know what my next question should be. But there was only one thing I really needed to know. And I think I knew the answer.

"So, I'm not going to see Xander when I get back, am I?"

All Bryce did was stare at me.

"I need to sit out here and wait for him, please." I must have looked pathetic, begging to get a glimpse of him when he returned. "Please," I begged again, my voice cracking.

There were still two cars out back, and the scene was taped off. That was the only evidence of the events of the night before. But Xander still hadn't come back to his room by the next morning.

Since I got home from the hospital, Becca and I had been sitting in the hall, waiting for him to return. My feet were tapping on the floor in nervous anticipation of how the meeting would go. We both took turns dozing on each other's shoulders as the hours passed. She didn't want to leave me alone; I refused to go anywhere else.

"Honey, I'm so sorry all this is happening to you." She seemed nervous to say her next words. "Yesterday was a lot for both of you. Maybe seeing him right now isn't the best thing. I mean, you were almost kidnapped by that asshole. The FBI—I mean, shit, it was like a movie was filmed out there. Your head, that has to hurt. And I mean, it's *your life*."

I didn't think I'd registered what happened.

I had seen the monster that raped me repeatedly for two years of my life standing in front of me for the first time in almost seven months.

Maybe it would hit me later, but maybe it wouldn't. Maybe I was over what he had done to me. I knew my heart was more crushed by what Xander had done to it.

"Seeing Xander has been so much harder."

And then I heard the elevator doors open. I stood up immediately, as did Becca. Xander was walking down the hall, alone, with his head down.

As he approached his room, I started toward him, and I knew he felt me; he stopped but didn't look up. His whole body tensed, sensing my approach. I continued to him and heard Becca retreat into our room, giving us privacy.

"Xander." I spoke his name tentatively as I approached him, afraid he would disappear into thin air. "Is Bryce gone? All the cops, are they gone?" He nodded, not even willing to talk to me. His hands were fisted at his sides, as if he was still trying to avoid a fight.

"Do you hate me so much that you can't even look at me, that you have to restrain yourself from what looks like wanting to hit something when you're near me?" My voice cracked with the emotion spilling out with my words, my cries. "I mean, Christ, we were both almost just killed out there and you still can't even look at me. I would have thought this would be enough to bring us back together." I paused, not sure if I should go on. "What did I do, Xander? Whatever it is, I'll fix it."

I didn't want to cry, but it was futile. I thought that I could move on from him, that I could move on from us. But this was my life; he was my life. And it was crashing and burning right before my eyes. He still wouldn't even look at me, his jaw muscles ticking in what appeared to be anger. His one hand rubbed the back of his neck in what seemed to be frustration.

"I'm sorry for whatever I did, whatever I may have said to make you feel this way, Xander." I was pleading at this point, my desperation evident in my voice. "I still love you, Xander. I always will."

The tears were flowing, my voice cracking through the sobs. He finally lifted his head slightly and peered at me with a sideways glance, a pained look on his face. I couldn't make sense of any of this. I took another step toward him, but he put his hand out to stop me.

"Nothing has changed between us, Lanie." His voice was strained, like he was forcing his words through his teeth. "But just because we aren't together doesn't mean I would want you to be with that asshole. Ever."

He started toward his door, and I reached out and grabbed his arm, that familiar tingle still there with every touch we shared. I started to crumble, my legs giving out. But then something snapped inside of me. How could he do this? How could he do this to us? How could I let him do this to me?

"Ya know what, Xander? Fuck you!" I was sobbing even harder, unable to breathe, but furious. "You haven't even given us a chance to talk this out. I'm over letting guys walk all over me. I can't live like this anymore. So, fuck you." Becca must have heard my screams; suddenly she was at my side, trying to pull me away from him.

"Lanie, I'm sorry." Xander stood there, stoic and still, as Becca dragged me away. I swear I saw a tear slide down his cheek. Did I imagine it? Why? Why was he doing this?

Eventually, I allowed Becca to lead me back to our room. The pain and fury inside needed to come out, the tears prolific.

But I was still without Xander.

Becca and I were cozy on my bed watching a show later that night when I told her of my plans to leave school. She was devastated but understood. All it took was one look at me to see I was broken. Completely and utterly destroyed. And that devastation was caused by the man I loved, who was down the hall. So I couldn't stay here, not this close to him.

"What if you put in for a transfer of rooms? You could live somewhere else for the rest of the semester and at least finish the spring term." I appreciated the ideas she was coming up with, but it wasn't possible.

"Becca, I won't perform well the rest of the semester at this point. I'm better off withdrawing now and coming back in the fall to start again. You and I still have our apartment for August, so we'll still be together. That hasn't changed. I just can't do this right now, that's all."

"I know, but I'm going to miss you so much. I mean, one week? You'll be leaving in less than a week? Dontcha think . . .?"

"Spit it out." I looked at her, waiting patiently to hear what she needed to say.

"Well, I think you should let Xander know you're leaving. I know you're not talking to him. But if he knows you're leaving the country, that may be a game changer. Maybe that's the kick in the pants he needs. Why don't you send him a text?"

I was shocked she had suggested that, what with how mad she was at him. But after thinking it through, I knew she was right. As mad as I was at him, I still loved him. I didn't want to be like him. I would let him know I was leaving.

"How do I tell the person I love that I'm leaving, that I'm giving up?" I looked at her with my sad eyes but picked up my phone.

Me:

> Hey wanted to give you a heads up I'll be leaving school at the end of the week I'm heading to Italy to spend some time with my parents I thought it would be better for both of us if I wasn't here, on the same floor, I can't do it, not sure how you can I'll be back in the fall I still love you Xander, always will

I showed it to Becca for approval before I sent it. Of course, it showed up as read with no response. It continued to break my heart every time. It confounded me how he could move on after what we had together, the non-emotion coming from him bewildering. It was further justification I needed to leave.

I couldn't survive here. I was drowning.

"Well, let's make the best of your last few days. Can we go out one night, you, me, and the guys? One last time? Pretty please?"

I owed this to her. She was the one responsible for me having a somewhat normal life this year. "Yeah, of course we can. Anything you want. You guys pick, and we can do it tomorrow night. Nothing too crazy, though. My head still hurts. Sound good?"

She wasn't jumping for joy, but it made her happier as she walked out of the room to tell Ty.

I started packing to keep my mind off things. I grabbed a case from under the bed, and with it came a pile of pictures I meant to put in an album. They were pictures of all of us from the past few months, but most of them were of Xander and me. I sank to the floor as I looked at selfies of us by the pond, in the library when we should have been studying, in the cafeteria. All the memories came crashing back, one after the other. The tears were starting spill over my eyes as I looked at the photos, my heart hurting with each new one. The images became blurry, some drops landing on the images. I hurried to wipe them dry, not wanting to lose what little I had left of us.

I threw my head back against the bed, done with these raging reminders showing me what we once had, my heart heaving from the pain.

The sobs were now coming out uncontrollably, my body racked by waves of emotion.

I needed to get away from him, but the idea of leaving was now scaring me to death. The pull he had on me was so strong that I still felt him in everything I did. I felt him now and I knew he was here, on this floor. I felt him near, the thrumming in my body constant from his closeness.

I pushed the photos back under the bed, needing them out of my sight. I stared at the ceiling, hoping the distance coming soon would help heal this ache, this unrelenting pain that had taken over my heart and my soul.

Then I heard the skim of paper on the floor.

I looked to the door and noticed that a note had come underneath.

I scrambled to see who it was from, opening it with shaky hands.

Give me one more day birdie
Please, X

Now what would I do?

Chapter 26

It was a good thing Becca slept in Ty's room.

I never fell asleep.

At all.

The note hadn't left my hand, which I still clutched like a lifeline.

I didn't know what to do, what to expect to happen next. All it said was to give him one more day. It was torture staying here in my room, knowing he was down the hall in his, having this new information. I had conjured up so many possible scenarios over the past twelve hours while sitting here in what felt like a cell. But not one of them seemed a likely explanation.

Nothing would have kept me away from him.

Do I go to him? Will he come to me? I needed a sign, something to keep me going. I kept rereading the note to remind myself it was not a dream, not an illusion I created in my mind.

Cleaning the refrigerator was a good distraction for me. As I wiped the sponge along the back shelf, the door to our room banged open, startling me. My head banged on the ceiling in the fridge, hard.

"Ugh, that freakin' hurt! Geez, you scared me, Becca!"

"Oh my God, your head! And why are you cleaning? Something is usually wrong if you are. What happened?" Pulling myself out of the refrigerator, I saw her standing with her hands on her hips, staring down at me. I sat back on my butt and slumped against the side of my bed, blowing my hair from my face. I gestured to my desk with the sponge in my hand so she'd look at the note.

I saw her eyes go wide as she read it. "What the hell does this mean? What's *'birdie'*? Is this really from him?" Her look screamed "skepticism."

"It has to be. That's his nickname for me, and no one else knows about it. It's from him, but I don't understand. I've been up all night, waiting. Waiting for another sign from him. I don't know what to do." That was all it took. The whole night of pent-up emotion came spilling out. Becca fell to her knees next to me and held me while I let it out.

"Lanie, oh my God, it's OK. This is a good thing. He's here, and he hasn't abandoned you. Relax, honey." Her arms around me were the only thing keeping me from fully collapsing. I should have felt more relief at that point, knowing he still cared, but the anxiety of the long hours of the night had taken their toll. I couldn't come down from this roller coaster, stuck on the top, hanging over the edge. My words came out stuttered in between my cries.

"The whole night . . . I just wanted to . . . go knock on

his door . . . Becca. Do you know how . . . hard . . . it was to stay here . . . in this room . . . with him . . . so close? I'm going crazy, Becca . . . I can't do this anymore. I need . . . to talk to him. I need . . . to know what's going on. What . . . should I do?" She was working hard to calm me down, rubbing my head, stroking my face. My breaths were hard to come by; I couldn't catch them.

We sat like that for a while, me trying to calm down, her stroking my head.

"Lanie, where's your phone?" she screamed.

"I don't . . . know . . . why?"

"Lanie, where is it? I just heard it!" She raced around the room trying to find it for me as I tried to find my legs. She uncovered it mixed up in my blankets.

"Lanie, read this." She held it out for me.

I did. And then I looked up at her, still hiccupping from trying to catch my breath, tears streaming down my face.

"What are you waiting for, silly? Go to him!"

My feet moved me toward Xander's door on their own accord. I didn't remember getting there. I stood outside his door for a moment, nervous about what I would find on the other side. I raised my hand to knock, but it was yanked open before I could.

Standing in front of me was a version of Xander, my Xander, I'd never seen before.

His eyes were swollen and red, possibly as bad as mine.

The scruff on his chin looked days old.

His defeated stance didn't give me any confidence at all about the potential outcome of this reunion.

I started breaking all over again. I couldn't do this.

"Lanie." His voice came out strained and tense, and his hands reached out to hold my face. "I'm so sorry. But it's . . ." He sighed. "It's over."

I started collapsing, his hands holding me up.

My grieved face looked upon his, his eyes full of confusion. "Xander . . . why . . . why are you doing this . . . it's been over . . . I can't . . ."

My words were barely whispers, coming out as gasps through the tears, his fingers working hard to push them away as they fell. He then pulled me into a full embrace, his strong arms enveloping me. A feeling I had been longing for swept through my body, my heart now defying my brain, allowing me this brief moment before I knew it would be stolen from me again. I wrapped my arms around him, knowing this would probably be the last time I would feel his body with my own.

As he held on tight, he shook his head, and his entire body began trembling in my arms. His hand came up to cradle the back of my head as his own sobs were about to take him to the floor.

"Lanie, what have I done? What have I done to you, to us? I love you, baby." His words were broken between his cries, sounding as broken as I felt. "We're not over. We were never over." He was sobbing into my hair, his fingers digging in tight, holding on as if afraid I would be the one to leave. "I'm so sorry. Please forgive me. You have to forgive me. I can't live without you. This was all to make him go away, for you, for us."

I pulled back, my eyes opening wide as I looked up at him. It wasn't registering.

"Xander . . . what are you saying?"

At that moment, his mouth crashed into mine with such fierceness that my body was thrown back. He held on to me so I wouldn't fall to the ground, keeping me tight in his arms, his lips mangling mine, claiming me before letting me go. The saltiness of our tears mixed on our tongues, a reminder of what this moment was truly about: a final goodbye for us. My mind refused to allow the clarity of the situation to settle in. I finally tried to pull away.

"Xander . . . I . . ." I was crying again, trying to get my words out but failing. "I can't . . . do this . . . if we're over, I need to go . . . this hurts too much."

He froze, grabbed my face, and looked into my eyes intensely with such passion.

"Lanie, stop and listen to me. You're not hearing me. We. Are. Not. Over. I. Love. You. This whole damn thing was a ruse, a damn setup, and I'm sorry, but I had to do it. I'll explain it all to you later, but I'm so sorry, baby. I never wanted to hurt you." He was sobbing again as he fell to his knees, pulling me with him into his arms.

It seemed as if our tears had transitioned from tragic to joyous in a matter of seconds.

And it clicked.

I finally got it.

We were good.

And Max was gone.

Chapter 27

"You have got to be kidding me." Becca was in total disbelief at most of the story Xander was telling her, Ty, and Logan. "So, they were going to have your father released from jail if you didn't break up with Lanie? How in the hell were they going to do that? And how did they know if you broke up with her? Were they literally watching us? They were actually a mob family? What the fuckity fuck?"

Her steady stream of questions continued, never giving Xander the chance to even answer most of them. As the five of us sat in the student union, trying to make sense of the past few weeks, I looked over at Xander. I took in his handsome features, his sexy hair, his incredibly muscular body. But none of that was the real reason I loved him. He was my best friend; he was the most sincere, selfless person I had ever encountered.

He caught me looking at him and reached under the table, grabbed my hand, and squeezed it closer to him. My leg was already wrapped over his. Ever since this all came to an end, we weirdly always needed to be touching in one form or another when we were with each other, as if we both required reassurance that we were still together, not leaving. We were definitely both traumatized by these events, no doubt, and would need to heal. But it appeared we would be stronger because of it.

"Yeah, Becca, they were watching, but we had people watching, too, so you were always safe."

Becca's eyes lit up. "What do you mean you had people watching too? Who was watching? The FBI was watching? Where were they? Oh my God! This was going on right under our noses and we had no idea? This is some crazy shit. Imagine how often this happens and we don't know. Where were they watching us from? Were they college students? Were they dressed like Men in Black? Come on, Xander. Give us something!" Becca was unforgiving. I didn't think she was ever going to give this up. Ty was trying to get her to stop badgering Xander, but he didn't mind. He was happy as long as we were together.

"My brother, Bryce, had some guys from his team here, plus there were some FBI guys stationed around. The only reason I came back to campus was because I heard from Bryce that they thought there might be movement from Max. I, uh, wasn't supposed to know that, or be here, for that matter. But, well, things worked out." He leaned over and kissed me deeply. He pulled away and kept talking. "I wasn't supposed to come back here at all until it was over. The Marcellos, Max specifically, told me to stay away from Lanie. They had connections at the jail, and if I came near Lanie or talked to her, they were going to get my dad released. Even after they had Max in custody, they weren't sure if they had it all figured out. It took a few hours for them to learn who the officer working at the jail on the Marcellos' payroll was."

His eyes softened when he said this, and this time he had a hard time looking at me, though all had been forgiven by now. "But when I heard he might be coming here, my decision was made. I had to come back. They had no idea what his intentions were, and I had to keep her safe."

Becca looked as if she were about to swoon after hearing that story. "It's like a modern-day fairy tale. He's your knight in fucking shining armor! Oh God, Lanie, he's a keeper for sure. Don't let him go, but if you do, I'm scooping him up! Sorry, Ty!" Ty gave her a playful shove, and my slap came in a close second. Logan laughed out loud. She fended off the assault through all the laughter.

"Yeah, well, she actually had another knight help her, too. Karl is the one that really saved her." Xander seemed a bit upset when he mentioned Karl's name. Not in a jealous way, more that he wished he could have done more to keep me safe during it all.

Turns out Karl survived his surgery but was taken into custody along with Max. I tried to explain the help he provided to Xander, but he didn't seem too interested in learning much about him or his help.

"Well, it's not completely over yet," Xander continued. "There still has to be a trial, but Max, his father, and a lot of the soldiers in the family business are in federal custody until that happens. So for now, anyway, we're safe and know where they are. And my father is still safely in prison." We all looked at Xander, acknowledging the gravity of the situation after he'd said all of that. It silenced the group for a moment.

Becca and the guys eventually stood up from the table, obviously taking off.

"Will we see you guys later?" Becca was still working hard for the five of us to hang out.

"Sure, we can hang out later," I answered for both of us, knowing he would be fine with it.

Xander settled back in his chair and mindlessly started rubbing my thigh as we sat quietly once we were alone. His contemplative look had me concerned.

"What's wrong?"

He took a moment to look up at me, his eyes relaying the guilt that still plagued him. He reached out and touched my forehead stitches. "Talking about it again with them brings it all back. I hate what I put you through. It tears me up every time I even think about it."

"Xander." His name was a whisper through my lips. I couldn't imagine how he felt, knowing what he did during all of this, not being able to tell me any of it. "But we're OK now. That's all that matters." I reached out for his face, caressing his cheek. His head was down, still refusing to look back up at me. I forced his face up, making direct eye contact. "I. Love. You. I completely understand everything you had to do. How could I not, in hindsight? I know what Max is capable of, and it doesn't surprise me one bit that he could pull any of this off, at least almost."

A deep sigh released from him, the weight of the world still appearing to be on his shoulders. "Lanie." His voice cracked with emotion. "My heart broke with every text you sent me. My mom was with me most of the time, helping me not respond. It broke me, completely broke me." The tears that had built up were now spilling over.

And that was breaking me.

I wiped his tears away for him and smiled gently.

I stood up and grabbed him by the arm. "Let's get out of here. We don't need to do this here." He followed me out of the student union without a fight. I started heading back toward the dorm, but he changed our direction.

"I have somewhere else in mind."

We found ourselves at the bench where it all began, the bench from the fall where I was sitting when I first laid eyes on him.

"Have a seat, birdie. I need to get this off my chest." I felt his urgent need to tell me what he wanted to say. We sat on the bench, though, and he remained silent for a long time.

"I love this bench. I actually come and sit here quite a bit. Usually once I'm done at the gym." The revelation took me by surprise—I had no idea. But it completely warmed my heart knowing he felt strongly about the first place we saw each other. "I think back to that day when you were watching me, often. I'm thankful for that day, but on the flip side, I know you sat here because of the demons you were dealing with. And that makes me feel guilty." He finally looked at me, the pain evident in his eyes. "I am where I am with you because of what that asshole put you through. Do you know how much that kills me? Knowing we wouldn't be together if you hadn't gone through what you did?"

I reached out to grab his hand, holding it and rubbing it. "Xander, I . . ."

"No, Lanie, let me get this out." He pulled his hand from mine and stood up, pacing back and forth. And then just as suddenly, he was on his knees in front of me, a pleading look on him. "I'm sorry, birdie. I don't want you to feel like anything I'm about to say is your fault. That's the farthest thing from what this is. It's all just . . ." He faltered, struggling with what to say.

"It's all just fucked up," I finished for him. And he looked at me, sadness still in his eyes, but also appreciation that I understood.

"Yeah, it's fucked up. Everything that's happened to us, I feel like there's a movie out there already made that mimics our life these past six months. I mean, I don't think anyone who hasn't lived it with us would ever believe it." We both chuckled at that, knowing full well he was right. "But that's the thing—you've come through such a difficult thing, survived such adversity, and I'm benefiting from it." He looked away from me, almost ashamed to be admitting this to me, and himself.

"Xander, I know where you're going, and you need to stop. None of this is your fault, not one bit of it. The time you stayed away from me, I completely, one hundred percent understand it. Did I like it? Of course not, but if you had done it any other way, I'd be mad at you. You did what you had to do to keep everyone in your life safe, and I'd expect nothing less from you. That's the Xander we all know, and that's what makes you, well, you." I pulled his face closer to me, gently finding his lips with mine. But he was in no mood for my kisses. "You need to let go of this."

"That's just it, Lanie. I'm trying, but knowing I have you only because of what you went through . . ." Again, he paused, seeming to find the right words. "I hate that you needed to go through what you did in order for us to be happy."

"Isn't that life though, Xander? If I hadn't gone through it, I may not be the person you fell in love with, either. Did you ever think of it that way?"

But I understood what he was saying. If the roles had been reversed and his pain brought us together, I knew how I would feel.

"Listen, I get it. I do. Overall, it sucks how this all happened. But I wouldn't change it for the world, because it brought me you. And that's all I care about right now. Everything I've been through, well, it's changed me, but it made me *me*."

He looked at me, a slight change in his demeanor. "You never cease to amaze me, Lanie. You're so strong." He stood up, bringing me with him. I found myself in his arms, his face nuzzled into my hair. "I love the person you are and the strong woman you've become." He spun us around, and I found myself sitting on his lap while on the bench, his arms wrapped tight around my middle. I leaned my head on his shoulder and we stayed like that, appreciating the privacy we luckily still had in our special spot. "All those texts you sent me while I was home, and when I came back, they showed a different you."

I pushed myself away from him to see his face. "What are you talking about?"

"Those texts showed me how strong you'd gotten during all of this. I knew by what you were saying that you weren't curled up in a ball, letting this completely destroy you. I was waiting for the one where you'd tell me to go to hell, saying you were leaving me. I deserved it." He reached out, knuckles grazing my jaw, his thumbs lazily rubbing my cheek. "And then, in the hall, well, you kind of did tell me to go to hell, in your own way." We both laughed, remembering my outburst, thankful we could laugh about it. "You're even stronger now than before. I saw it in you when you were dealing with Max in the parking lot." His hands stilled, holding my face. "I hate that I have to be thankful to him for bringing me you. That's really the part in all of this that pisses me off the most. But I'll come to terms with it. I guess I already have. Because I can't live without you."

The raw emotion emanating from him was gut-wrenching. This man, in such a short time, had been through so much for me already. "Well, that's something we both agree on. Xander." I turned again, making sure I had eye contact with him. "I can say, with complete certainty, that you saved my life. From him and from myself." The reality of that hit me, and it seemed to resonate with him. He nodded and grabbed a hold of me again. We sat in silence for a bit as I settled back into his embrace.

"You need to know how truly sorry I am for putting you through that while I was home. I had vowed to you and myself to never hurt you, and I broke that vow. I felt helpless, knowing the agony I was putting you through, because I felt it, too." The soft shaking of his body vibrated against my body as I heard the quiet sobs he was trying to hold in. "I'm happy to be on the other side of it. I wasn't sure we would ever get here again. It felt, at times, like it would never end. And . . ."

I turned abruptly and forced him to stop talking by claiming his mouth with mine. The forceful kiss took him by surprise, but the response was immediate. He answered my kiss with such force, such conviction. Our tongues lashed against one another's, searching with such urgent need. The need to convince ourselves it was over. His hands reached around, pulling me to straddle him, neither of us caring who could see us. This was our way of letting the other know we would be OK.

I pulled away, only momentarily, to utter my pleas. "Xander," I said as I continued to kiss him between words, hoping to reassure him. "I'm here, in your arms." Another onslaught of his tongue searching for mine, his need obvious underneath me. "I will never not be here in your arms ever again." My tears now mingled with our mouths, the saltiness mixing in. "I can't live without you, never again. You're my everything. I love you so damn much it hurts."

At this, his cries became so overwhelming he had to pull away and bury his face in my chest. My tears trailed down my cheeks, landing on the top of his head as I held on, trying to help him through this.

"I fall in love with you more every day, birdie. You're such a gift. Each one of your touches, kisses, makes me melt. I will always be falling in love with you."

I woke up before he did. I loved those few extra moments I could steal to gaze at him without him knowing. He was a beautiful man, his long bangs hanging over his one eye that was facing me. He was lying on his stomach, his arms folded under his pillow. The muscles in his arm were tight and strong against my gentle touch. Even in sleep, his skin reacted to me, the bumps leaving a trail behind my fingertips. His long, dark eyelashes were against his cheek. I knew I shouldn't be touching him, risking waking him. He'd had such an emotional day yesterday. But I couldn't stop myself; his magnetic pull on me had yet to weaken. I let my hand wander down his shoulder and onto his back, reveling in the feel of him, but he moved a bit, so I refrained and went back to gazing.

"Don't stop. That felt amazing." His lips curled up in a knowing smirk. "You can rub me in other places, if you want." I took him up on his offer and allowed my hand to wander even lower, the roundness of his ass under the blanket begging to be caressed. "Oh, fuck, Lanie, that feels even better. I could get used to waking up like this." My eyes were still trained on his face, and eventually his lashes lifted and a midnight-blue eye stared back at me.

He still took my breath away.

He reached out with the arm closest to me and scooped me up and under him in a move that startled me. But the feel of him now on top of me was intoxicating, his mouth close to mine. He was looking deep into my eyes as I tried to convey my need and want for him in my look.

"Lanie, we've talked about all of these 'firsts' I've wanted to give you. I've been honored to give them to you, and I want to continue to, if you'll let me?" He paused, looking at me, anxiously. Then he sat up abruptly. He continued talking nervously. "Will you? Will you let me continue giving you all the other 'firsts' there are to be had in this lifetime?"

He leaned down then and pulled my face toward his with his finger on my chin, our eyes connecting.

I stared deep into his eyes, deep into his soul. "Of course, Xander. There's no one else for me." I leaned in and kissed him gently. The kiss was short, though. He pulled away, and I whined when he did. He sat up and reached over to the side of his bed, revealing a small, black velvet box. My eyes got wide.

"It's not what you think. Well, not exactly. I hope you don't think this is corny." He proceeded to open the box and present it to me. "This is a ring of promise—and it's yours, if you'll wear it."

My breathing hitched as I looked in the box. Inside I saw a ring, a silver heart with a diamond in one curve. I peered up at him with tears in my eyes as he continued.

"I am incomplete without you, birdie. You need to understand this is a lifetime commitment for me, if you'll have me." Tears welled up in his eyes as he spoke. "I know we're young, and this is quick. Kinda why it's not a bigger diamond." His shy chuckle conveyed just how nervous he was. And I was waiting too long to respond.

I wasn't sure he was ready to catch me when I leapt into his arms, straddling him on the bed.

But he caught me.

Like he always said he would.

Chapter 1
BECCA

I was done taking his shit, so we broke up. Let me rephrase that: *I* broke up with *him*. Saying "we" broke up makes it sound consensual, like we both wanted it or that we decided it was the right thing to do. It was neither of those things. I was just sick of his shit, so it had to end.

But with school starting up, I faced having to see him again.

For the first time.

And I decided I was going to make an impression.

"Oh darlin', this is going to look gorgeous. All your friends are going to be so jealous! Now you send them all my way when they are, sweetie, ya hear?"

What I really needed her to do was shut up and finish the dye job so I could get the hell out of here. I was second-guessing doing this more the longer I sat in this godforsaken chair. I loved my long, dark hair, and so did Ty. But wasn't that why I was doing it?

"These caramel highlights really make your green eyes pop, and with that tan you have, my God, you are one hot potato! Lula, come look at her!"

Oh, Jesus Christ, I was never getting out of there!

"Thanks so much, Ellen Jean, but I really need to get going. Big party to get to, and so many people will have time to see the new me! Thanks so much!" Turning around, I looked in the mirror, and immediately tears sprung into my eyes. Ellen Jean came right to my side, her bony arms going around my shoulders.

"Oh, honey, what's wrong? Dontcha like it?"

That wasn't the problem. I actually loved it. What I didn't like was the feeling that I needed to change myself to get Ty's attention. And why did I want his attention, anyway? I broke up with him.

"I actually love it, Ellen Jean. Thank you so much!" I turned and hugged her. She hugged me back with a fierceness I didn't expect from those stick arms. "I'm sure all my friends will line up by next week."

"Now, remember," she said as she held me by my arms, "you'll need some maintenance on those roots in about five weeks or so, so I'll see you soon, sweetie." The bills barely made it in her hands before I ran out the door.

I raced to my car so I could make it back to our townhouse before Lanie, my roommate, got there. We were living together again this year, and I was hopeful our second year here at college would go better than our first. Xander and her were driving down from NOVA together. She stayed with him all summer, since her parents moved overseas last spring. Lanie and Xander went through so much last semester because of her sick ex-boyfriend back in Texas, who was now thankfully in jail. His family was mob related, and he was such a douchebag. He abused Lanie, like, really badly, sexually, mentally, in ways I didn't even like to think about. It took most of last year for her to open up to us about it. And thank God she found Xander. He was her saving grace. He saved her, literally and figuratively, I guess. But I played a big role, too. I stuck by her all year. I'm good like that. A good friend. That's me.

So I was racing to our new home together to be a good friend.

But I felt like a terrible friend.

The worst.

It would be the first time I was seeing her since last semester.

And that made me a terrible friend.

I raced into the apartment but came to a screeching halt when there were two other bodies inside I didn't recognize.

"Hey, you must be Becca," the one with long, dark brown hair and almost the same color skin said. "I'm Macie, and this is Ava." She pointed at the one with a black pixie cut and a few piercings. Christ, they were both beautiful. That sucked. And since they were also my roommates, I would probably need to be friends with them. And they would meet Ty as well. Fuckity fuck! Why has he made me so fucking insecure?

"Hey guys, yeah, I'm Becca. Lanie should be here any minute, so you'll get to meet her, too. It's nice to put a face to all the texts we've been exchanging."

Ava turned to me, and I was stunned by her eyes. It was as if emeralds were popped into her head, literally. I mean,

I had green eyes, but hers were outrageous. They had to be contacts. Combined with her hair, she was fucking hot. "Well, we'll have to wait to meet her later. We were just heading out. See ya." And she had a freaking deep, sultry voice to go along with it all, too. Shit.

And then they were gone. And I was alone. Nothing good came of me being alone lately. Me alone with my thoughts usually meant scrolling through social media or old pictures and getting myself more and more upset with each passing day. But the odd thing was that Ty had no new posts on any of his accounts this entire summer, not a single one. I mean, he was a guy, so he didn't post much, but he posted. But nothing. Nada. Nilch.

While I was upstairs putting some clothes in my closet, I heard the front door and I went running.

"Lanie, is that you?!" I screamed from the top of the stairs. As I turned the corner, I saw her and her oh-so-hot boyfriend standing in the hallway. Running full speed across the room, I wrapped her in a bear hug and squeezed tight.

"Oh my God, girl, I missed you so much. We can't go that long not seeing each other. Like, never again. I thought we made a promise last Christmas break to never do that, and this time it was even longer!" I screamed. She pulled away from me to look at me, I knew to look at one thing.

"Becca, oh my God, you look amazing! When did you do this?" Her face filled with amazement as she took my appearance in, holding my shoulders and keeping me in place. "And yes, I missed you too!" She hugged me again, and it felt so good. I don't think Lanie really understood how much I relied on her. Last year, she needed me so much, but I needed her too and she didn't even know it.

"The hair? Oh, it's no biggie, I actually just did it today.

Just felt like I needed a change, ya know? Start sophomore year off with a bang." Pulling away, I looked away quickly, not wanting her to see the lie in my eyes. Unfortunately, that put me in the direct gaze of Xander. And that one, he wasn't like most guys, in a lot of ways.

"And look at you. I think you've gotten hotter! Lanie, hold on to him. I'm going to steal him this year for sure if you don't." Her eyes were rolling, knowing full well I was joking. But Xander knew better, and he knew something was up with me; he kept staring at me with a look in his eye that said, "Get your act together, Becca." I went straight to him and gave him a hug next, just to make him even more uncomfortable. My arms went around his body, and I ran my hands up and down his back. I felt his body stiffen. "Oh, Xander, lighten up. I'm allowed to appreciate a fine specimen of a man." He pulled back and looked me straight in the eye, almost sad for me, and that made me feel pathetic. What was I doing, hitting on my best friend's boyfriend right in front of her the moment they got there? Shit, I was a real mess.

"OK, you two, break it up. I know we all haven't seen each other in a while, but come on now." Lanie was fine with me being a bitch, thank God. I needed to pull myself together. Xander was right. I pulled back and looked over at Xander, trying to convey my apology with my eyes.

"I missed you, too, Becca." He chuckled, and it lightened the mood. "Hey, birdie, I'm going to head over to my place." I loved the nickname he had for Lanie, though neither of them would tell me what it really meant. "Why don't you girls join us once you've caught up and unpacked? The guys are hanging out, I'm sure drinking already. I'm sure Ty told you to stop by, right, Becca?"

He looked at me, waiting for my answer, but I couldn't give him one. At least not right away. Had Ty not told anyone that we broke up? Ty was rushing Xander's frat, and they would spend a lot of time together now that we were back at school, but I guess he hadn't seen him yet either. And I did my share of secret keeping this summer as well.

My gaze shifted to Lanie. Hers was more knowing. She could read me and knew there was something going on, but she couldn't quite figure out exactly what.

The two of them stood there, waiting.

"Uhm, we kind of ... broke up."

If either of them was surprised, they held it in. Xander stood stoic, being the serious type, and looked ready to go beat him up if I needed him to. Lanie walked to me and wrapped me in a hug, knowing that was exactly what I needed.

"Oh Bec, are you OK? When did it happen?" Being around the two of them made me feel safe enough to drop the shields and *feel*. I hadn't let myself feel anything about it all summer long, not a tear dropped. Not until that very moment, with Lanie's arms around me.

"Oh fuck, Lanie, now you've got me crying!" With my safety net with me, I let it out, and she held me as I did. Xander wandered away to give us some time alone. Her arms didn't leave me until she felt the shakes and sobs subside. But then I knew the dreaded questions would be starting.

Lanie, of all people, was well aware of the problems Ty and I had. Freshman year, I confided how Ty treated me when I would go home with him. How the couple times we made the visit to his house, he acted like we were nothing more than friends. He wouldn't kiss me, hug me, not even hold my hand. It was as if he was embarrassed of me in front of his parents. Utterly and completely embarrassed. It was heart wrenching to realize the man I had fallen in love with was ashamed of me.

I was enjoying the comfort of Lanie's arms still around me when we were interrupted by a soft throat clearing from across the room as Xander's long strides brought him closer to us.

"I'm gonna leave you girls to it," Xander said to us both. "But Bec, if you need me to take care of anything, just let me know. I'll be at the house. You guys head over when you're ready." He kissed Lanie and walked out the back door.

Lanie and I went to sit on the pleather couch that came with the apartment, which was full of furniture safe enough for college parties, our legs squeaking against the material as we tried to get comfortable.

"Oh my God, we will need to put some blankets on this thing." Lanie's eyebrows shot up; she knew I was trying to change the subject. "OK, fine, what do you want to know? But, FYI, there isn't much to tell." I fell back against the couch in defeat, wiping the remaining tears from my cheeks.

"Well, I guess I'd like to know who broke it off? And why?"

Well, those were easy.

"Me, and it was just the same ol' shit. The summer started, and he said I couldn't come to his house. I was done. Don't need that shit. So I ended it." More tears welled up in my eyes. "The worst part is that he didn't really fight me on it, and we haven't spoken all summer." And now those tears spilled over again, and the lump in my throat was growing as the emotions were getting harder to keep tamped down.

"Bec, why didn't you tell me? Why didn't you call or text over the summer to talk about this? I could've made my way to you somehow if you needed me." There was a reason, but it wasn't a good one. There's never a good reason for a girl to not reach out to her bestie in a time of need.

"I didn't want to make it real. If I told you, it would have made it so ... real, like I actually did it. I just wanted to go about my summer in blissful ignorance as if nothing was wrong. But here we are, and now I have to see him for the first time since I told him I was done with his shit."

She didn't offer any magic bullet fixes, only sat there with me, letting me know she would always be there.

"Ugh, why do I even care? Why don't I just let him go?"

"Well, a little birdie once told me we put up with their shit because they are good in bed. I'm sure that has something to do with it." Her small laugh told me she knew there was more to Ty and me than just sex.

But was there?

We both laid our heads back against the couch and stared up at the ceiling. "So listen," she started, her voice serious. "First, before you see him, you need to decide if what you really want is to still be broken up with him. Seeing him for the first time will most likely make you feel things, things that could confuse you." I knew she was talking from experience. Lanie's ex forced her and Xander to spend time apart last semester, and it did things to her. And when she first saw him, let's just say she didn't handle it well.

"What's the second thing?" I asked her. She stared at me for a moment, her face unreadable, before answering.

"Well." And then another pause.

"Lanie, what is it?" My voice almost screaming, I sat up straight on the couch, getting nervous. She finally conceded.

"You look amazing, Becca. If you wanted to fade into the woodwork when heading over there, it ain't happening.

But something tells me that wasn't the plan." Her eyebrows tilted in a knowing way. "I think you want to get his attention, and maybe the attention of others? But be careful if your plan is to get him jealous. I'm afraid that could backfire."

Shit, was I that transparent? I plopped against the back of the couch in defeat again.

"I'll be there with you. We can make it through today together. I can finally be there for you the way you were there for me." She grabbed both my hands in hers and squeezed them tight. We shared a knowing nod. We had been through a lot together last year.

We both stood up, and she headed toward the front door. "I'm going to get changed so we can head over there," I told her. I strode toward the stairs, knowing I would have to change the outfit I had picked out, maybe multiple times. "Come up and get ready with me!"

"No, I'm good. You know I don't really care what I'm wearing, Bec. I have a few more things in the car to bring in, and I'll be right back."

I went straight to my bed to look at the sexy green halter top I had picked out to wear—braless, of course. It would have played off my new hair color so damn well. But it also barely keeps my tits contained, so I was wearing it with an agenda. Lanie was right.

A whole new outfit was in order, and that could take hours. Plus, I still had to do my makeup. This day was not going the way I had envisioned.

"Becca, you almost ready?"

"No, I need a bit more time. But go ahead, you can head on over. I'll meet you there. You know which one it is, right? Go out the back door, look to the right, and you'll probably see some guys setting up in the yard."

"OK, I'll see you there. Hurry!"

I plopped on my bed in frustration and looked around the room. It was an amazing room. Pretty big for a sophomore in college, with a walk-in closet. So I had most of my clothes with me, which was part of the problem: I had too many choices. Lanie saw right through my intentions, which made me think I needed to switch things up. I needed a new plan.

I pulled out my best push-up bra; I would never forego using my best asset. But instead of the typical outfit, I reached for my prettiest little white sundress. It had eyelets and tiny spaghetti straps on the shoulders but was kind of low cut in the front, allowing my bra to do its job. It was short, but not too short, and the color really showed off my tan and my new hair color.

I threw on a pair of flip-flops, some mascara and lip gloss.

The complete opposite of the Becca Reynolds everyone knew from last year.

I looked in the mirror and wasn't completely unhappy with what the reflection showed me. The tan definitely helped, but my winter look would have to be reconsidered. Before I changed my mind, I grabbed my phone and ran down the stairs.

As I walked over, my resolve weakened the closer I got. I realized that all the sexy clothes and makeup I wore were my security.

But in this, I felt naked.

Nothing to rely on to help with the facade.

I wanted to see Ty; I was desperate to see him. But what would I do if his response to seeing me wasn't what I wanted it to be? I mean, even though I broke up with him,

I still wanted him to look at me like he wanted to take me upstairs and do the nasty. The closer I got to the house, the more nervous I was getting, close to hyperventilating.

Yeah, of course it bothered me he didn't even try to contact me over the summer once I broke it off. But I broke it off. It might have destroyed him for all I knew. I never gave him the chance to talk it over; I just ended it.

"Hey, Becca! How was your summer?"

"Hi, Becca! You look fucking hot! Are you still seeing Ty? Let me know if you're not."

"Hi, Becca, where's Lanie? Are you guys living together?"

"Hey, Becca, where's Ty?"

I was bombarded by people as I approached the party. Friends, other fraternity brothers, even people I didn't recognize. It was overwhelming. It would've been a nice welcome if I'd been in a better headspace, but all I could think about was seeing Ty. I nodded at everyone, smiled, but they must have thought I was a total bitch. I didn't stop to talk to anyone, just kept walking. My eyes scanned everyone as I did, and there was no sign of him.

He must have been inside.

I pushed the slider open and was met with a wall of heat, the A/C not keeping up because of the number of people. I stood there for a minute, my eyes trying to adjust to the darker room once inside.

The kitchen was immediately to my left, with tons of booze bottles on the island. Behind that was a living room, and that was where they had a keg set up. It looked like that was where most of the pledges were, tapping and pouring from the keg by a bar.

That's where I found him. He was by the keg. He'd

been watching me since I'd come in. I couldn't read his look at all, which scared me a bit. Our eyes locked on each other, neither breaking the stare.

He looked mostly the same since the few months I'd seen him last. His golden locks were a bit more golden, the tips lightened by the summer sun, it appeared. His tanned skin made his light whiskey eyes pop even more from across the room. He looked like he'd been hitting the gym more than usual. Still not the total gym rat body, which I was happy about. But his muscles looked a bit thicker.

He looked more like a man. Less like a boy.

As he looked at me, refusing to take his eyes off of me, he leaned down and started talking into someone's ear. Only then did I realize he was talking to Xander, who immediately found me in the crowd. He nodded at whatever Ty said, then said something back. Ty nodded to Xander, never taking his eyes off mine.

I still hadn't moved.

I stood even more frozen as Ty walked toward me, guiding himself through the crowd effortlessly.

I stood, almost in fear of what this meant as he approached, afraid of what could and would happen once we talked.

What did this mean?

Chapter 2
Ty

"Christ, Ty, move your ass, dude." I couldn't remember the name of the frat brother yelling at me, which was a problem. Rushing required me to know all of them and how they wiped their asses, too. But there were so many of them and I didn't spend enough time this summer learning them like I needed to.

This summer.

This summer sucked. For so many reasons, but mostly because of Becca. I didn't blame her for breaking up with me. I was an asshole. Still was. But there were some things that needed to be the way they were, and I didn't have a choice.

I wasn't supposed to meet someone like Becca, someone who would make me want to fall in love. But she was right there, almost from the first day of freshman year. And it was super easy while we were at school to pretend that everything was OK.

But it wasn't OK. It never was, but she didn't know that. She only got an inkling there was a problem when we would go to my hometown for the weekend, to my house. But I was too much of a chickenshit to fess up and tell her what was going on in my life back at home. The real reason my parents treated her the way they did. Like she wasn't my girlfriend.

Because they couldn't think she was.

"Hey, man, how ya doing?" I felt his hand on my back, and it startled me out of my dazed thoughts. I turned to see Xander, his hand held out.

"Hey," I greeted him with equal enthusiasm, grabbing his hand firmly. "Dude, how was your summer?" Xander was one of the future guys in the frat I was most looking forward to calling "brother." I stood by and watched how he handled everything he and Lanie went through last year. It made me feel like a bigger piece of shit for how I handled things with Becca. But I could only hope I could learn a thing or two from him over time.

"Well, from the sounds of it, my summer was better than yours." He motioned his head toward the back of the house, which only meant one thing.

He had already seen Becca.

"Um, yeah, so I'm guessing Becca got here?" I asked.

His eyebrows lifted high and his eyes widened before a tilt to his head told me that things did not go well in the other apartment. "You could say that," Xander replied, his tone holding a warning. "Man, I don't know what fuckin' happened between you two, and I don't want to know, but she's in a bad way. Can't say I've ever seen Becca Reynolds quite like that." And then he started walking away, working on getting some cases of beer ready for the party.

"Xander, dude, wait!" I whisper yelled. "You can't leave me hanging like that." I ran to him behind the makeshift bar. We, the pledges, pushed the dining-room table close to the wall and put side tables next to it to protect the booze. The place was already filling up, students more than ready to party after a long summer away from their friends. Soon enough it would be standing room only and the newcomers would have to move it to the yard. It was the responsibility of us pledges to keep an eye on the booze during the party, serving the guests but making sure it didn't go missing as well.

And then, when the party was over, it was our responsibility to clean the entire house. This pledging shit kinda sucked.

Xander was already with some frat brothers by the time I caught up to him, so I couldn't fucking talk to him. I made eye contact with him before I walked away, hoping he would know I needed to talk.

Seeing Xander made me realize how much I was missing my best friend. He was supposed to be here, by my side, doing all this stupid shit with me. We were supposed to have each other's backs. But he didn't return to school this fall.

Last year was rough for him. He brought some problems with him from home that resulted in him drinking too much. Most kids at college drink too much, but most kids when they drank didn't get overly handsy with the girl they claimed to be in love with. That was Logan—with Lanie. Unfortunately, it happened before any of us knew the extent of Lanie's abusive past, so it really hit her hard. But they worked it out, were even friends again by the end of freshman year. He turned it around a bit after that. Spring semester, he stayed dry and made it through. But apparently this summer did a lot of us in, him included. So, he's taking this semester off.

"Hey, Ty," Xander said as he appeared behind me. "Listen, don't worry too much about what I said about Becca. You know her. She can be, um ..." He stumbled on his words, not wanting to offend me.

"Dramatic," I offered.

Our joint laugh lightened the mood.

"Yeah, dramatic," Xander concurred. "I'm sure Lanie is calming her down as we speak." As he said those words, his head snapped up as if attached to an invisible tether. His eyes widened as they zoned in on something across the room as his mouth turned up in a small smile. I watched him drop everything he was doing and move effortlessly toward Lanie, reaching her before she even closed the back door. They weren't one of those couples that disgusted me; he didn't start making out with her right there in the middle of the room. No, they were more subtle than that.

But everyone knew Xander loved Lanie.

And I wish everyone knew I loved Becca. Because I did. But timing was everything in life.

"Ty!" Lanie screamed as she approached us, almost jumping into my arms giving me her hug.

"Hey, Lane, how are you?" I asked into her hair since she was refusing to give up on the hug.

Her mouth found my ear, and her words were soft. "I think I'm doing better than you are. You OK?" She pulled back, making eye contact. The sadness in her eyes, combined with a hint of accusation, told me everything I needed to know. As happy as I was to see her, I wasn't ready for the inquisition. I started pulling back, but she held on. "Ty, I won't pry. But you've been a significant support for me. Last year, I couldn't have gotten through without all of you being there for me." I looked away, my eyes trying to find something else to focus on, knowing where this was going and wanting no part of it. "I'm here for you, Ty. I mean, with Logan not here, and now this with Becca, this is a lot for you. Talk to me if it will help. OK?"

I nodded, my eyes still nowhere near hers, and pulled out of her grasp. "Yeah, I'm fine, really."

Xander graciously interrupted a tense moment of silence. "Ty, can you work the bar? It's getting crowded and we need a few guys over there manning the keg."

I nodded—seemed it was all I could do at the moment—and started in that direction. But then I felt a small hand on my arm, holding me back.

"She's excited to see you."

I didn't look at Lanie but didn't walk away either, waiting to see if she had more to say.

She noticed my piqued interest and continued. "She's back there still, trying to pick the best outfit to wear, knowing she'll be seeing you."

I turned to her. Her wide eyes held concern and told me I needed to be ready, ready for the tornado known as Becca Reynolds when she fucking came through that door.

"That bad?" I asked.

"Well, I've seen her worse, let's put it that way. She's not mad, if that's what you're wondering. She's—" Lanie paused as she thought about what Becca was, making me even more concerned. "Becca is nervous."

Shit, that was worse than mad. That meant today could involve tears and talking. And I didn't have time for either. And she was going to read that completely the wrong way.

I would have to figure out some way to make some time to talk to her.

"Thanks, Lanie," I offered with a small smile. She nodded and headed to the bar to get a drink. I followed to the keg as Xander asked, the crowd already getting rowdy.

Today was setting up to be a full-on rager. Someone had said there were possibly over two hundred people already, and it was only three in the afternoon. If we weren't careful, it could easily get shut down by the cops. First weekend back, though, the cops were usually pretty chill about parties, as long as we kept it under control.

"Hey, man, you good?" Jake asked. He was one of my roommates this year, and a great guy. I met him last year when Logan and I went to the rush event for the fraternity. Once I knew Logan wouldn't be here, he and I hooked up with a few other guys we knew would be interested in rushing the frat.

"Yeah, I'm good." My voice didn't match my words.

"Ya sure, dude? You look like fucking shit. What's up? Today'll be fun. Look around at all the fine ass we have to pick from." His arms spread wide as his gaze scanned the girls he felt were at his disposal. He was a good-looking guy, and he usually had girls lining up to hook up with him at every party we were at. "I know we have to work a shit ton today, but there is no way I'm not getting my dick sucked by one of these hotties. I mean, look at them. Each one is hotter than the next." He sidled up to a gorgeous blonde with huge tits as he was talking, his arm hooking around her neck as she walked by. Her wide smile as she looked up at him told us both he was right; they would be upstairs in a matter of minutes.

"Where the fuck does Jake think he's going?" Xander's

voice boomed in my ear. I turned his way and shrugged my shoulders. "Maybe later tonight you guys might have some time to hang out, but today is all about getting shit done as a team."

"You don't have to tell me." We both moved toward the keg, hearing one guy having trouble with it. As we were working on it, bent over, I felt the oddest sensation run up my spine. It was as if tiny explosions of electricity blasted each vertebra, making me bolt upright. It ran to my neck, spreading across my chest, constricting my breathing.

I froze. But only for a moment before I felt compelled to look up.

And that was when I saw her.

Standing by the back door, looking around the room, I think for me. She hadn't found me yet. The first thing I noticed about her was what she wore. The white dress was not as innocent as it first appeared. It was tight and low cut, pushing up her ample chest, making it about to spill out of the damn top. Up against her tanned skin, the dress looked damn sexy. And her hair. Fuck, it had some, like, reddish color to it that made her eyes pop even in the dim light of the room. Already some heads were turning, and that was pissing me off.

And then she found me. Our eyes connected. I had been standing still for what felt like hours but had to be only seconds. And Xander noticed.

"Hey man, I guess you're going to want to talk to her, huh?" he asked. I turned to him and bent low to ask him my question.

"Is there somewhere upstairs I can have a few minutes alone with her? I won't be long, I promise. But I need a few minutes, man." I looked up and knew he got me.

"Yeah, second room on the left should be open, but don't be too long. I'll get some shit for letting you off." I nodded before turning toward Becca.

And I started making my way toward her. I wasn't exactly sure what I was going to say, or do, once I got her upstairs. All I knew was that I needed to be close to her. And get her away from these guys who were staring at her. At least if they saw me take her upstairs, they might think she was still mine, even if she wasn't. There was no way of knowing if she was going to kiss me or punch me.

But that was a chance I would take.

Newsletter Signup

Would you like to receive monthly updates? Would you like sneak peeks on the next book on the series? For that and more, sign up for my monthly newsletter at:

kristaswansonauthor.com/newsletter

Acknowledgments

First and foremost, I need to thank the main man in my life. Scott, you are the reason this is happening at all! You encouraged me a few years ago to make sure I was doing what was making me happy in life. Well, I found it. So, thanks, babe. If you had not pushed me to go outside my wheelhouse or fully supported me along the way, this book would not be written. The mounds of undone laundry and piles of dishes that remained in the sink as we both sat at our respective desks working are a testament to our dedication to getting this book out there. Your hours paid for our food, our home. Mine, well, that remains to be seen. But we have high hopes!

Molly, Danny, and Maddie would always check on me. I would never say my children do not support me—they 100% do. Always checking on me at my desk, making sure I'm still breathing, seeing if I need anything. It's the content that does it to them. Let's just say, if my TikToks embarrass them, they probably shouldn't read my books!

My parents are a constant support and of course need my thanks. My mom has been my loudest cheerleader from day one of her learning about my book. I think every checkout clerk, fast food worker, and receptionist at her doctor's visits knows about it thanks to her. From the time I won a writing contest in third grade, she knew this day would come. Thanks, Mom. And Dad, it's OK if you don't read it!

The first person I reached out to in my journey was a friend, Anthony. He is in the publishing industry and helped guide me in the right directions when I was floundering. I had no idea what I was doing in those early days, and he took the time to answer all my ridiculous questions and give me some well-needed encouragement. I'm not sure I would have persevered and finished my book if I didn't have his guidance.

Melissa and Claudia—you are the two who read my earliest version of Lanie and Xander, my alphas. You both gave me invaluable feedback and, though it may not be noticeable in the final cut, your ideas are embedded in the final story. (But Xander is still Xander :))

My beta readers: Heather, Alex, Lauren, and Larissa. What can I say? These books don't happen without people like you. Sometimes the feedback is hard to hear, and sometimes it makes you feel good. But it always helps. And I appreciate you—from the bottom of my heart, I appreciate you! I look forward to working with you on my future projects, and yours as well.

I need to acknowledge a very special person. ALL MY FIRSTS is in book form as early as it is due to one person, and one person only: Jamie. Without the time you put into your 'Operation Author' initiative on TikTok, I wouldn't be where I am. The countless hours you spent putting together publishing packages for indie authors is admirable. I was a lucky recipient of one of those packages, bringing me where I am today. So thank you, Jamie, so much, for simply being you. The world needs more Jamies to make it a better place.

My cover designer, who I was connected with through the Operation Author initiative, deserves a vacation after working with me. Niki, I promise I will become more decisive as this process continues! Your patience with me along the way helped make our time working together a true pleasure.

I was also linked with my editor, Chloe, through the Operation Author initiative, and I couldn't have picked a better editor myself. We connected immediately, and she was exactly what my newbie brain needed. Being halfway across the world and a day ahead didn't stop us from making this work, and I look forward to making more magic with you.

Author Bio

Credit: Jillian DeVoti

Krista Swanson lives in New Jersey with her husband. They have three children, but only one is left to get out of the nest. Once that last kid is off to college, traveling across the US and Europe with her husband is in Krista's plans. She loves the beach, mainly the Jersey beaches, which she feels don't get the love they deserve.

When she's not writing, she is most definitely reading. Her lifelong love of reading romances gave her all of the ideas busting to get out of her brain. While doing either, though, the mug in hand will not have coffee in it. The blasphemy—it will be tea!

She's newish at the social media thing, but working hard at it. You can find her on TikTok and Instagram at *kristareadsandwrites*. Also hop on over and join her Facebook reader's group, *Krista Swanson's Booklover's Besties*. You can also sign up for her newsletter on any of those platforms.